Wreckin' AMETHYST

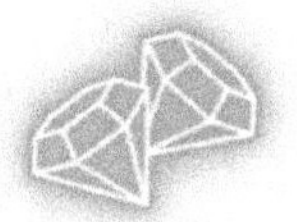

Money doesn't buy happiness.
Payback does.

Dirty Talk

PUBLISHING

To my Elites.

Those who beta, alpha and brainstorm with me all hours of the night.

Those who provide continuous love and support whenever I need it.

Kayla, Joy, Lou and Kristina.

This one is for you <3

Foreword

You are about to venture into Book One of the Billionaire Badboys series. Within these pages, you will find a fiery, quick-witted con woman and the murder mystery which unfolds from the secrets she keeps. Being a why choose romance, each book in the trilogy will feature a different man from a tight-knit group of billionaires. Only one male POV will occur in each book, building the harem steadily. Book One, in particular, contains explicit description of male-male love scenes, and if this is not to your liking, make a note to skip over chapters 22 and 35.

If you're still here and gagging for more, then it is time to dive straight in!

This book inappropriate for under 18's. Themes such as sexual addiction are featured. This series is a Why Choose romance with a Happily Ever After at the end.

Contents

Prologue

Fourteen Years Ago...

B *eep. Beep.*

My brow furrows, the thinly veiled reprieve of sleep evading me once more. Squeezing the cover closer to my chest from my mattress on the floor, I blink through the early morning sun spearing the ragged curtains. Our house is nothing like the inviting space it once was. Not now my mom's shining light has been dimmed, reduced to a motionless figure spread across the adjacent bed. Pushing myself to my feet, I brush her hair free of her forehead and place a featherlight kiss there.

"Morning Mom," I force a smile. My gaze snags on the scribbled post-it note I stuck to the headboard before passing out last night, and that smile slips. It's dialysis day.

Stalling by checking the heart monitor, making notes and adjusting the tube in her nose, I tap her IV bag. It needs changing; I can't hold off any longer. Even if that means I'll have to use our last one and brave the outside world to fetch replacements. Something I used to avoid, until the phone company cut our line. Now it's all on me.

Turning the IV bag upside down, I pinch the tube before carefully twisting the spike free and inserting it into a new one. I learned by watching, my knack for observation coming in handy. Next, I give mom her morning sponge bath, hunting for veins which aren't too bruised in her forearm to accept a needle.

It didn't used to be like this. Before dad died and mom fell sick, there wasn't a pile of overdue bills and last notices on the kitchen counter. There wasn't a weekly pounding on the door from the truancy officer or social services. I hadn't maxed out all of her credit cards to pay for nurse visits, and the medical supply company wasn't threatening to take back their equipment if I couldn't pay the debt.

My only saving grace is my appearance. As the mirror-image of my aunt, I swiped her ID last time she came to visit. That was over a year ago, and before mom's condition plummeted. Being the tallest girl in my grade and well developed, I can apply enough make-up to put me well in my twenties and convince mostly anyone to believe I'm who the ID says I am. To keep the welfare officers at bay, I even filed a missing child report on myself just so they'll leave us alone. As far as the world is concerned, I'm a ghost.

Once I've started mom's dialysis cycle, I head downstairs in hunt for some breakfast. What furniture I haven't sold on Craigslist is coated in dust, unused and forgotten. Opening the refrigerator, a foul smell bursts *free and forces me to gag. My stomach clenches, hunger consuming me from the inside. Slamming the door shut, I opt for a bowl of dry cereal instead, the flakes long since stale as I pick at them, sinking down against the washing machine. I'd forgotten about the load inside, sitting in its own water for longer than I care to remember.*

Days bleed into each other. Hours slip by without realizing I'm still here. A yawn pulls at my lips, my head slumping back as the walls close in on me. I read once that sleep deprivation is used as a form of torture in rural prisons. Consider me tortured, but I have no choice. The doctors tried to convince me mom wouldn't improve, but I can't accept that. Then I would have no one, and on the odd occasion, mom rouses enough to clear the haze from her blue eyes. To mumble sweet sentiments through her cracked lips. Tell me how proud she is before sleep claims her once more. Those are the moments I live for.

Leaving my bowl on the ground, I drag myself upright. I need to get to the hospital early, pick up the IV bags and leave before too many people leak through the doors. The more people I fool into thinking I am my aunt, the more confident I become. But baby steps. After a brisk, cold shower, I dress in my mom's yellow dress with cork wedges. No one would suspect me of being sixteen by the ample cleavage on show, or the self-assurance to my strut. To be believable, I must embody the character I'm creating. Coating my face in a layer of make-up, I tell mom I'll be back as soon as I can and find myself in the entrance hallway. Bracing myself behind the front door of our town house, I exhale deeply.

Just get it over with.

A shadow appears on the other side of the glass, making me jump backwards as a thick bundle of mail is pushed through the letterbox. I wait for the mailman to retreat before retrieving the stack, dumping it on the table with the rest. A leaflet slips free, tumbling to the ground.

Crest Financial Holdings. The bold print catches my attention, giving me a long enough pause to pick it up and look inside.

Struggling to keep track of your expenses? Yep. Need to settle past loans to ensure a better future? Yep. Consolidate the payments into one, simple monthly sum.

My eyes race over the text before I force myself to go back and absorb every word. Is this the answer I've been looking for? There's nothing stopping me from taking my aunt's ID straight to the bank, acquiring the loan which could save us from sinking. As soon as the idea takes root, my mind starts spinning. I could offer the house as collateral, pay all the backdated bills, buy the medical equipment for good. With a little more time, mom will start to get better. I'll find a way to pay off the loan and we'll be free. Leaflet in hand, I leave the house and lock up, a real smile taking root this time. Visions of moving out of the city, a life by the beach, sunsets framed by laughter, fill my mind as my wedges eat up the pavement all the way to the bank.

This is the answer I need.

Chapter 1

Present Day

"Oh yes, baby, just like that," the elderly man sitting beneath me croons. Withered hands grip my thighs through the netted material, earning a cautionary slap on the wrist.

"No touching, mon chèri," I lay on a delicate French accent. "Or I may have to restrain you." I smile easily. All part of the effortless mask I wear.

"I think I'd like that," he chokes on a laugh. I'm inclined to agree, but being a dancer for the Thirsty Kirsty isn't my main vocation. It's merely a talent which can aid my true intentions. Maintaining the move your inheritance quick; he's not going to last much longer in there." Moving to leave, Bill Stanford Jr grabs my arm and roughly pulls me to a halt.

"We've been back and forth with this for weeks, and suddenly you were able to get all that information so fast? You were barely in there for fifteen minutes." *Tell me about it – fifteen long excruciating minutes of blackening my soul.* "Whore or not, no one's that good." I jerk my arm free. Of course this asshole thinks all dancers are complete sluts too. I am, but it's a choice.

"If you must know," I stomp my heel into his dress shoe and shove him back into the wall, holding him there by my forearm across his chest. He's a fair amount taller than me, but I'm not easily intimidated. "The phone is his birth year backwards, because I knew he'd be a cantankerous old bastard. The tablet is his favorite cigar, number five with the dial code for Costa Rica and the pin...well he told me that one for free." Blue eyes similar to his father glare back until he shoves me away and straightens his jacket.

"No way," he chuckles, ducking his head when a few more of the dancers walk by. Witnesses aren't good for the future congressman who is swindling his father out of millions. "There's no way in hell you're that smart." Bill huffs, trying the codes I gave him on each device. I fold my arms, waiting for the astonished look he gives when everything works exactly as it should. Clenching his jaw, he doesn't mutter any compliments, pushing a pre-signed cheque and pen into my hand. He watches me add two more zeros to the figure in the box, before writing the name of a local orphanage on the line.

"You don't seem like the charitable type," Bill grunts over my shoulder. My eyes roll of their own accord, landing on his sharp jaw. It really is a shame to waste such a good pussy eater on someone so clueless.

"I don't want your money, or anyone's for that matter. I had a personal vendetta to settle here," I sigh, pushing the pen into his jacket pocket for him. Folding the cheque, I push it between my cleavage for safe keeping.

"See, not smart after all," he grins, daring to touch a rogue strand of my violet hair. Just like I have it on good authority he does to the girls who clean his house. That's the only reason I accepted his job offer, sensing I could kill two birds with one stone – so to speak. "At least you're hot." Pushing away from the wall, Bill leaves in one direction and I take the other, his wallet twirling between my fingers. *That's right – all I am is a hot, dumb stripper. Not the cunning, undercover con-woman who just robbed your slimy pocket.*

Heading through a red velvet curtain, the bar and club beyond fall into view. Tacky gold adornments on crimson walls, sticky patches on the sparkly black floor. A stage split into three catwalks with poles on each end, all highlighted by churning strobe lights and hosting tonight's entertainers. Tuesday's theme is burlesque, meaning there's the extra foreplay of shedding many, *many* ruffled and feathery layers.

Navigating the low-slung armchairs and booths, I round the end of the bar where my Charley is waiting, as instructed. She says we're besties, although the concept of friends is a strange notion to me. More like bitches who are tolerable enough to keep around for an extended amount of time. But Charley has wormed her way into my soul, remained loyal to me for years and has yet to give me a reason not to trust her. That's a strong case towards a best friend if there ever was one.

The rough scratch of a tongue licks at my ankles, so I kneel, stroking the overly large head of my two-year-old pup hidden in a hatch amongst the beer cases. As beautiful as the day I rescued her, Pig - the blue and white English bulldog - is my one true love. Six months we've been undercover at the Thirsty Kirsty, and the owner is still yet to realize I've broken his no pet policy. Art is non-existent these days anyways, barely a glimpse of his white cowboy hat and protruding belly and that suits me fine.

Pig jumps up at me in excitement, eager to leave the confines of the crate. Nudging back thick folds of skin that hang over her eyes, I press kisses to her forehead whilst ruffling the loose wrinkles at her neck. She nuzzles into me with slobbery licks, a series of grunts rumbling from her stunted nose. That's my sweet girl.

Tucking Pig back into her hidey hole, I grab my laptop from the shelf and place it onto the bar. The handful of clients we do have in are regulars, all facing the girls on stage lazily spinning around their poles. Midweek shifts are the worst. No hype, no energy. But that's what Charley and I signed up for when we decided to lay low here for a while. Including the free room and board.

"So, did you get all the details you needed?" Charley whispers, leaning in to avoid the nearby matron from overhearing. Being an ex-dancer herself, Shelia tends to busy herself in the sewing room or behind the bar when one of us isn't having a dilemma. I merely side-grin at Charley, shedding my bunny head piece and before long, my fingers are flying across the keyboard.

"Watch," is my only instruction. Pulling up a series of windows, I display the bank account of Bill Stanford Jr beside the clone copy I made. All we need to do is wait for him to start the transfer and watch my offshore account soar. Simple flicks of numbers which mean oh so much more. His balance doesn't shift a cent. Charley gasps, suddenly realizing what I've done.

"Wait," her chocolate brown eyes widen in shock. "Did you just con the con?!" My arm drops around her shoulder as I push the cheque into her hand.

"Who, me?" I flutter my lashes innocently. "Why, I'm just the performing circus monkey. A bimbo such as myself could never pull off something so complex," a smile stretches across my painted lips as Charley starts to giggle. Like my appearance, beauty is a weapon, and knowledge is my blade of choice.

"Oh Ami, this is everything," Charley gushes at the words on the cheque. I was never inclined to stay at an orphanage after my mom passed, but when I found Charley sleeping on the streets to avoid going home, I convinced her to stay at this particular one. It's where she developed a thirst for playing a character, living life as whoever she wanted to be that day. Gave the owner absolute hell, and now she can consider her debt repaid.

With Charley tugging on my arm and Pig getting overexcited, I turn away before letting my smile fall. I've perfected this mask a little too well. I had almost convinced myself this is what happiness feels like, but there's something missing. Watching the sickening amount of dollars being transferred gives me no satisfaction. It's all for a purpose, but still. Knowing I've just made myself technically richer than eighty percent of the state makes my skin crawl. With money comes greed. A never-ending cycle of wanting more, bigger, better. Of taking what isn't yours and losing your humanity in the process.

I reckon I'll never know happiness like when I lived on the streets; just me, Charley and Pig sneaking into the botanic gardens project to sleep under the stars. No debts, no connections, no pressure to conform to society's rules. But it's naïve to think those times could last. Not when I have a score to settle, and a mysterious bastard to find and punish. All of this, it's practice. Foreplay, if you like.

Bill Stanford and his father are just the beginning. The very first to feel the retribution from years of seething rage. But it's not enough. Robbing them of their undeserved riches hasn't made one drop in the vast ocean of retribution in the pit of my soul. Even as a stunned roar reverberates through the club, Bill storming back inside, there's no hint of delight to be felt. It's time to admit, I'm dead inside.

"You fucking bitch!" Bill screams and I snap back into reality. Grabbing my laptop, Charley's wrist and Pig, we drop down behind the bar. Shelia doesn't hesitate, lifting the floor hatch to the basement while reaching for a concealed shotgun. Now there's a woman who would defend her girls to the death. My heels hit the stone floor at the base of a rickety ladder, an icy chill claiming my netted legs and bare arms. There's a network of walkways down here, leading to our dank dressing rooms and the emergency fire exit beyond, ensuring a quick getaway. But I can't force my feet to move.

"Ami," Charley hisses my nickname, taking Pig from my arms. "We have to go!" Thumping sounds overhead as the music cuts out, Shelia screaming for the bouncers posted out front. There's a commotion, bottles smashing against the ground, a whole host of grunts before Bill's voice breaks through.

"I'll find you, you little slut! You're going to be sorry you ever messed with me!" A shot splits the air in two.

Thu-thump.

And there it is. A trickle of excitement causing my heart to flutter. I hold my breath, frozen still until I hear his voice once more. *Oh thank fuck.* I briefly thought the chance of an elaborate retaliation had been stolen from me. Bill's threats grace my ears like a smooth caress, a flirty stimulating stroke. Butterflies ignite in my stomach, the same kind I used to rely on to see me from one day into the next. I made myself a promise once to rid the world of the type of bastards who use their status as a weapon. At least until I can locate whoever did just that to me.

Dress shoes kick out and skid across the floor above our heads, as I track Bill all the way to the front door. He's still hollering, making sweet promises he doesn't have the balls to see through. I do though.

Charley is already shaking her head, reading my intentions all over my face. Pig, however, is grinning wide, her tongue hanging free and dripping saliva. I nod along with my pup, a smile also growing on my face. The cops laughed me out of the station all those years ago, and from that instant, I knew I would be my own savior. That the girl I reinvented myself into would be their ultimate downfall.

"I agree, Miss Piggy. Robbing these assholes isn't enough. I'm going to have to get a little more creative."

Chapter 2

"Well," Charley sighs, "there's no going back now." She tosses the newspaper she's been pouring over onto my extra-thin mattress and returns to fixing her make-up in the dresser mirror. I barely glance at the headline.

STANFORD & SON SLAUGHTERED IN STATELY HOME.

Below, a photograph of the assholes and their brain-dead wives standing in front of a mansion I would only believe existed in fairy-tales, if I hadn't been there two nights ago. Turrets, gargoyles, hedges trimmed into archways and Greek sculptures as if the roses were competing against the hydrangeas for blossom bust of the year. That signed the Stanford's death warrants long before I saw their crimes against art déco.

"Are you sure you didn't leave a trace of DNA behind? What about your hair, one strand falling loose and we're fucked," Charley whines. I kick her stool, jogging her eyebrow pencil halfway up her forehead.

"I have a hard enough time with the rest of the world underestimating me," I growled. A soft whimper comes from beneath the bedframe as Pig senses my souring mood. "I don't need it at home too." Home being wherever I kick off my shoes that day.

"I'm sorry, okay," Charley pouts, scrubbing her head with a baby wipe. She has the wounded-puppy look mastered, her chocolate brown eyes filling with tears. But I won't let her pull on my congealed heartstrings this time.

I'm many things - none of them being an amateur. It may have been my first intentional kill, but I made my peace with death long ago. The smell, the life draining from their eyes, the blood. None of it bothers me. If anything, the thrill of slicing a blade across Bill Stanford Sr's throat while his wife slept pressed into his side...I can't even think about how good it felt. How natural. Or how my fingers have been itching to grab the knife beneath my pillow and score my own finger to relive the high.

"It's just..." Charley huffs, and my eyes snap upwards. Guided by my own desires, my hand was halfway across the bed without even realizing I was reaching. Craving.

"Just what?" I ask breathily. Heart pounding, my mind whirls with bad decisions.

"We can't all be the crowning jewel that is Amethyst Boudreaux," a grin breaks across her full lips as she waves a hand in my direction. "Being calm in the face of danger doesn't come as easily to all of us." I return her smirk, replacing the nonchalant mask in an instant as she references my stage name. Six months ago, I was Ange Bennett, and before that, someone else completely. The beauty of pulling a long con; this little nobody can dye her hair, roll her hips and be whoever she wants.

"That's it. We're going shopping," I suddenly announce, jumping up off the bed. Charley hardly has time to argue before Pig has wriggled her way from beneath the bed and is jumping up at my calves.

"But...our shifts start in an hour. Art would lose his shit, and we have a no-drama policy. Do you really think it's time to be–"

"I said, we're going shopping," I halt Charley's rambling with a rough shake of her shoulders, kiss on her cheek and smack on her ass. It was that or throttle her just to get the words to stop. I realized fairly young that I have a knack for thinking several steps ahead of the average person. If Charley is just considering something, I've already got three alibis and an escape route all mapped out. Although, it is cute she still tries to use our two-year age gap against me.

Spinning towards our shared wardrobe, I start tugging out clothes until a pile has accumulated on my floor. When the perfect outfit presents itself, I grab it with greedy hands and change quickly. Unhooking the diamond-studded leash from the back panel of the wardrobe, I bend to link it to Pig's matching collar.

"Get your ass moving or we're leaving without you." I straighten, brushing the short white hairs from my PVC leggings. A soft gray sweater I stole from Charley's side hangs from one of my shoulders, stopping short of the tattooed sleeve spanning from my upper arm to wrist. Twisting my vibrant purple hair into a fishtail braid, the one I usually reserve for bondage night, I watch Charley scramble to shrug a denim jacket over her sunflower summer dress, brushing the length of her brunette waves out of the collar with a bitchy swoop.

"Did you not want to take some money?" She gestures to the base of the wardrobe. I roll my eyes to the loose panel hiding our duffle bag stash. Sure, I could grab a few rolls of hundreds, but nah. It's more fun this way. I grab Charley's wrist and tug her out of the dressing room we share, with Pig waddling by my ankle combat boots.

"You don't need money when you look like us. Just a distracting pair of tits and the false promise of a good time," I wink.

Walking the corridor, I frown. It wasn't so long ago I was a novice in heels, but now, strutting in boots with a distinct lack of added platform height, feels akin to breaking the law. The obvious loss of the unheated air licking at my exposed skin, the approach of a darkened staircase without strobe lights or a backing track. All of it makes me squirm uncomfortably in the sweater. My body is my power and to hide it from the world is like admitting I have something to be ashamed of.

"Fuck it, hold this." I push Pig's leash into Charley's hand. Ripping the sweater off, I dump it into the gigantic handbag Charley grabbed on the way out and sigh in relief. Boning lines the corset either side of my torso, hooked together with silver clasps at the front and disappears into the high-waist leggings. The lace over my breasts heightens the icy chill in the air, toying with my nipples deliciously. Every step is like foreplay, the life I've forged for myself being the ongoing climax I've yet to come down from.

"Do you wear that under all your clothes?" Charley narrows her dark eyes, heading up the stairs to be my look-out.

"No," my voice calls out after her. Hoisting Pig up under my arm, because the stairs are too much for her stubby little legs, I wait for the signal to ascend and re-join her side. "Usually I wear less."

Luckily, the club hasn't opened yet, so it's a ghost town. The only light source is dotted above the bar, highlighting an unpolished and sticky surface. Glints from the stripper poles call to me, the tackiness of the stage beneath my soles gripping for me to stay. *Not this time, my loyal friend.* Just like Santa, this bitch is coming to town.

"So, where to?" Charley opens the back door for us and I set Pig back on her feet. The sun is in our favor today, gracing us with an usual glow for the end of autumn. My favorite time of year, if only for the pumpkin-spiced lattes that should be a regular on all cafe menus. To be fair, a cheeky wink at the local barista gets me pretty much what I want, and I'm not above trading bj's for pastries. I've done far worse to ensure Charley hasn't gone hungry these past few years.

A skip in my step, I relish the goosebumps lining my exposed skin, moaning at the shudder racing down my spine. Not even the thickly rancid stench of the dumpsters or eroded batches of puke along the alleyway can dampen my spirit, as I briskly walk into the street at a pace Pig struggles to keep up with.

"Upper East Side," I smirk. Hailing a yellow cab, I get lucky on the first try, my PVC-coated ass sliding into the back seat. Charley pauses long enough to hoist Pig onto my lap, dive in and slam the door closed as the cabbie is still moaning about some 'no animal' rule.

Regardless, we're catapulted from the slums and into city traffic, where the buildings stretch higher and the price tags grow longer. The anxious young girl I once was buries her face into Pig's scruff, using my canine's strength to boost her own. We don't belong here, that much is clear. But life has a way of teaching the lessons that are most important, and mine was to fake it 'til I make it.

Twisting her head, Pig licks at my cheek, itchy tickles bringing a relaxed smile back to my face. I scratch her belly, thankful for the millionth time for the little pup I found just when I needed her. Clutched beneath the arm of a crackhead looking for her next hit, I traded her for the shoes off my very feet. They were stolen anyway, and as I trudged smooth roll of my hips over his non-existent crotch, I reach around the back of his neck, lowering my barely contained breasts towards his face.

"I bet you were quite the stallion back in your day." I give them a jiggle. His raspy breath fans my skin and if my attention wasn't diverted, I'd shudder with all the disgust I'm suppressing. Surely there's an age men get to and decide to hang up their shriveled dick to spare the world moments like these.

"I'm eighty-seven years young, and reckon I could show you a thing or two," he croaks. I lean back, puckering the purple lipstick that matches my hair and colored contact lenses. Even with the bunny mask and make-up concealing my tattoos, there's no denying I'm not who he chose for his private entertainment. Only his looming dementia prevents him from realizing we've met before. In fact, I've been dancing for him three weeks straight, waiting for the fog in his mind to clear enough for a slip of clarity to leak through.

"Can't wait," I lie. Aged blue eyes sparkle with excitement as I swing my leg free of his waist. These six-inch, spiked heels allowed me to hover over him just enough to not snap his hips beneath my full weight. I had cheesecake for breakfast...three days running and will continue to do so, because that's living my best life.

Spinning between his open legs, I bend in half, pushing my ass into his face. Beneath the netted tights, a thin thong - also in black - neatly covers my goodies from his prying eyes. His gasp is followed by another smoker's cough, a shaky hand gripping his heart when I peer back.

"You seem like a cigar man to me. What's your poison?" I bat my eyelashes. The coughing seizes into a heavy wheeze as he struggles to reply.

"Never leave home without a Gran Habano number five in my pocket," he lifts the cigar from inside his jacket. A paper seal around the middle holds the Costa Rican flag. Returning to my full height, I stretch my arms above my head. A soothing beat trickles from hidden speakers which I slowly wind my hips to. I know what's coming before he smacks my ass, having mastered his inner workings. Taking two measured steps away, I slowly turn on my heels, fold my arms and pout.

"Strike two. You know the deal, mi amore. Physical contact costs extra." He doesn't hesitate, scrambling in his pocket to produce a wallet. Plucking out a gold credit card and shaking it at me, I lean all the way forward, holding my tits high. "Swipe right here and enter the pin." His smile is nothing less than sinister, a flashback to our first meeting threatening to rise. He was feeling extra promiscuous that day, not half as forthcoming as he is currently proving to be.

"Six-four-two-zero," he willingly plays along. Squeezing my breasts together mid-swipe, I extract the card from his fragile grip.

"Transaction approved," I bop him on the nose. "You've been credited for the VIP treatment." A few strides back put me beside the exit, and upon rasping my knuckles on the door, it promptly opens. The pair of gorgeous blonde twins I had waiting outside stride in and with the flurry of excitement, I duck out into the hallway. What the old man is desperate for, those girls will provide on my behalf. In return, I'm fronting their entire bachelor degrees to get them the fuck out of here by morning. One last job and they're free. Mine, however, is ongoing, and I wouldn't have it any other way.

"You get it?" a younger version of the man I've just scammed grunts. Six foot with slicked back hair, suited, booted and glowering at me. I pick the credit card from my cleavage, the tablet from beneath my corset, the phone out from the netted tights waistband and hand them all over.

"Pin number is six-four-two-zero, passcode to his tablet is five-five-zero-six and his phone's is seven-three-nine-one. You'd better through the needle-ridden streets, blue flashing lights flared behind. A place to stay and free rehab - you're fucking welcome Crack Lady, but I got the better end of this deal. My pretty Miss Piggington.

The cab pulls to a swift halt, almost slamming me into the back of the driver's seat. He mutters about the traffic and in true city fashion, I find us gridlocked by fancy vehicles I couldn't even afford to clean. A digital clock on the dashboard mocks me, the one and only day of freedom I'll have this year dwindling down minute by minute. *Fuck that.*

Popping the door open, ignoring those rushing by to aid the fallout of a crash on the crossing, the three of us slip out of the backseat as the cabbie screams words I'm sure he means to offend me with. Unluckily for him, I'm completely comfortable with being a thieving whore bag. Gotta love myself for who I am, right?

Weaving through parked cars, receiving a mix of angered horns and wolf whistles, we disappear into the streets of high-end fashion stores, Pig trotting just behind.

"I don't know about you," Charley slips her arm into the crook of mine, "but I'm feeling like a splash of Kouture." My lips slant as I peer at the glass front at the other end of the street. It's not so hard to remember Charley for the anorexic girl I found eating out of the trash. We've both changed for the better.

Approaching the store, mannequins line the window display, fitted with blonde wigs and adorned in black leather. Scooping up Pig along the way, I place the pup in Charley's gigantic handbag just before we enter the store with a nod to the security guard. That's when you know shit is too expensive.

Fluorescent lights beam down on a sea of shining leather. Not the PVC stuff like the leggings clinging to my shapely legs, but legit studded pelts. A whole rack of jackets embellished with skulls and buckles, a backwall of boots I'd give my left foot for and hobble around in. More mannequins are dotted throughout the medium-sized store, one in a catsuit drawing me closer. A tear drop in the cleavage is wasted on the plastic humps, a loose belt around the middle sparkling with diamantes.

"Can I help you, ladies?" a shop clerk asks, swiftly rounding to halt us from entering any further. I raise a brow, sizing up the woman in red heels that put her a few inches above me. She's stick thin and pale, a full lack of nutrition causing her lips to shrivel like a prune. At least, that's what it had better be because I don't let anyone look down on me anymore.

"Oh, no," Charley intervenes when the tension radiating from me thickens. "We're just browsing."

"Perhaps," the clerk lowers her heavily painted lashes down to our tennis shoes, "you would be more comfortable in a store more...attainable for your means. There's a Target not more than a mile from here." My lips curve up in a wide smile. Oh, this bitch went there.

"You must be Denise," I take a stab in the dark. Seems like a typical, stuck-up, try-hard name. The clerk's eyes rise and narrow as she smooths a hand over her perfectly slicked-back ponytail.

"It's Debbie, actually." I take it back – Debbie suits her even better. Side stepping to the rail, I tuck in a price tag and smarten the jackets collar.

"Well, Debbie, it's with regret that I must inform you–you're fired." A half-snort, half-shocked laugh bursts from behind me, until I turn my head. No humor resides on my face, the confidence of my stance causing Debbie to falter. I sigh dramatically and fold my arms.

"Charlotte and I are the leading directors at HR. We've been visiting stores to understand customer relations. Here, at Kouture, we pride ourselves on providing quality service to *all* customers, hence the disguises. You have failed on the spot. Please go pack up your belongings and exit via the back. We wouldn't want to cause a scene now, would we?"

"Wait, please, I–I," Debbie flounders, holding up her hands. She looks for assistance in a young girl at the counter, who instantly shrinks down behind it. Panic filters through her eyes, fake tears pooling in their murky depths. "I'm so sorry. Kouture is my life. Can we just, I don't know, start over? Lesson learned, I swear it." She crosses her heart and hopes to die, causing my smile to resurface.

"Perhaps," Charley leans her chin on her hand and mimics how the clerk dismissed us a moment ago, "we've fired enough people for this morning. If *Debbie* would be so kind as to fetch us the newest arrivals, we could overlook this indiscretion?"

"You're too soft," I spare Charley a side glance and swish my hand in the air. "But fine. Debbie, my dear, put together an outfit for each of us from the latest collection, complete with footwear. Think biker chic." I shimmer my fingers in the air, looking to the ceiling as I quickly scope out the security cameras.

"Is–is this a test?" Debbie appears physically jittery. I nod. "Of course, right away." She turns to leave.

"One more thing," I raise my finger. "We will need to inspect the type of wigs you're using, to check they are indeed humanely synthetic." Debbie nods her head as if it's ready to fall off, slinking away with a trail of mumbled 'thank you's', she disappears from view.

"Humanely synthetic?" Charley whispers in a laugh. I half shrug, taking her arm in mine. Pig pops her head up from the bag to lick my elbow and I nudge her back down. We maintain our authoritative act, roaming the rails and scoffing every so often.

A group of teenagers flood the store, the blonde in the center accompanied by a bodyguard, daddy's credit card in hand. She barely looks at the garments, throwing hangers over her bodyguard's arm as they steam roll inside. He catches my eye, then checks out my tits in the corset and for one moment, doesn't look like he's considering jumping off the nearest building.

"Ugh, I hate rich people," I moan, holding a sequin dress up to my body in a mirror. Charley winds her arms around my sides to pull it tighter, showing off my curves. The cleavage dips scandalously low, a slit from the floor to hip meaning I couldn't wear underwear. I love it.

"You have enough stashed away by now to be considered 'rich' yourself," Charley gives me a lingering look in the reflection. I scowl right back.

"Okay, firstly, don't try to offend me with that word again. And secondly, once my scores are settled, I will only keep what I need." To prove a point, I roll up the dress, step into a blind spot from the security guard and cameras and dump it into Charley's bag.

"Is that so, Robin Hood of the hood?" she laughs, rearranging the dress so it's not covering Pig. "Tell me then, what's the next charity case you're going to take sympathy on?" I roll my eyes, strolling back into full view of the store. The shoes along the back wall are to die for. All black and steel, studded or buckled, dangerously high heels or chunky soled. Charley steps into my way, pursing her lips to wait for an answer.

"When's the last time you got a call from your stepdad?" I hit her back with another question. Her face falls into shock.

"Wait...seriously?" Her gasp is lost to the teens squealing and taking selfies. Charley grabs my arms and shakes vigorously. "You've paid him off?" Keeping the simple smile on my face, I quirk a brow and give Charley the answer she needs. Or the one she prefers, because the truth is that asshole is dead. I hired a hit on him after I caught a PI sniffing around our dressing room last month. Charley's stepfather received custody of her after her mom went off the rails, and took it upon himself to be fully invested in how her body was developing.

"Why didn't you say something?!" Charley is still shaking me with giddiness. Sweet, mostly innocent Charley. She balances me out and reminds me I'm at least doing something right in the world by keeping her safe. "We need to celebrate! Dinner at Al Fresco's?"

"You know it," I wink. Al Fresco's is a new joint across town, fully booked months in advance with a high-list clientele. All the more reason for us to find an 'in', and once I set my sights on something, nothing stops me from seeing it through.

"Here you are ladies," Debbie appears at our backs, a pair of gigantic white bags clutched in her hands. The Kouture logo glints on the side in gold, matching the rope handles she passes to us. "I believe you'll find everything to your sizes and tastes. I pride myself on my observation skills,." Debbie juts her chin and I retain my laugh. Yes, her *observation* skills are second to none. Smiling sweetly, I give a slight bow. A performance well done, on my part.

"I'll be sure to put in a good word for you, Debbie. With a talent like yours, you'll be regional manager in no time." I lay it on thick, her face lighting up with joy. It's all about knowing your mark's desires and playing into them. "Ring this through as a company expense, and have yourself a lovely day."

Walking past the security guard on the way out, a slither of the rush of adrenaline I live for pulses through my veins. Pulling off a con is like riding life's dick; the bigger the risk, the more fulfilling that veiny shaft is. Right now, my core is clenched and I'm chuckling inside. But it's nothing compared to when my limbs are languid with after-climactic bliss from punishing those who don't deserve what they have. That's my personal mission. The stealing, the clothes, the stripping – they're all just a bonus.

We duck into an alleyway to change, quickly stripping from my leggings and pulling the glittery dress over my corset. Jazzing it up with a leather jacket like the one Debbie saw me fondling and a pair of studded boots, Charley and I take turns fitting the wigs. Once she's also dressed like we're about to party into tomorrow, we leave the alleyway arm in arm, our discarded clothes left behind.

The dress sparkles endlessly, highlighting my tattoos in the sunshine. From wrists to biceps, I'm inked with wispy black and white flowers. They fade into the random other objects I've collected along the way on various drunken nights. A stopwatch on my wrist, pterodactyls on one elbow and spiral clock on the other. A steampunk contraption sits on my upper left arm, causing me to chuckle each time I look at it. Funny where the mind goes when I'm intoxicated.

"Okay, I'm starving. Let's go eat." I pull Charley from the alley, diving my arm into her bag to stroke Pig. A slobbery tongue greets my hand, the bag grunting and shaking with delight. Al Fresco's is across the city, about a forty-minute walk using back streets, but we don't make it that far. A few blocks over, my feet come to a sudden halt, my eyes lighting up. At the end of the junction, the sun glints like a shining beacon.

Diamonds sparkle from the glass front of a jewelry store. A ceiling, easily two levels high, is visible through the huge double doors with gold handles, matching the glimmering of the chandelier hanging in the center. A U-bend of transparent cabinets sits against the inner walls, leaving the front windows as an alluring display for the rich passer-by. Diamonds sparkle, the shine reaching out and beckoning me to 'come hither'.

And I obey. Drawn forward by my heart's desire. The anticipation of my best and most rewarding heist yet.

Better than that, a guy I could break like a toothpick is being trained by some tight-ass clerk. The bun on her head is tight enough to give her a free facelift, her aged features stretched and pinched in all the wrong places. The skirt clamped around her waist is too tight to bend over as she retrieves a tray of gleaming jewels from the counter and places them on the glass surface. Looking for something in her strained chest pocket as I cross the road, she holds up a finger to the trainee and disappears out back. *I'm doing this.*

"Oh, good gracious!" I sweep inside, taking Charley with me. "That's the one! The necklace my future husband asked me to approve of. He's right, it truly is stunning. May I?"

Blinking up at the trainee from behind a fan of tinted lashes, the thin guy stutters, the collar buttoned above his navy tie tight enough to choke. His attention drops to my cleavage as I lift the heavy necklace to my chest. Charley is quick to fasten the hook and secure it in place while I fix the matching bracelet on my wrist. "Oh yes, this is perfect for my big day. Don't you think Charlena?"

"So perfect," Charley falls into character quickly. The girl has promise. "But poor Miss Piggy needs accessorizing too. What kind of ring bearer would she be without a ring?" Dragging Pig's wrinkled weight from her bag, producing her pink belly free of the blue patches on her snow-white fur, a glint of mischief glistens in both of their onyx eyes and I smirk in approval. I knew Charley had it in her.

"Oh, my darling, you're absolutely right! Here you go gorgeous," I hook three diamond stunners onto Pig's collar and drum my fingers through them. "Perfect. Daddy needs to see this at once!" Pig's tongue hangs out the way it always does when we're having fun, still clutched in Charley's arms when we begin to walk away. I can't believe we make it all the way to the doorway before the trainee finally finds his voice.

"E-excuse me ma'am." I stop and snigger under my breath. He thinks I'm a ma'am. "I need to return those back to the cabinet."

"Oh, don't stress, darling," I flick my hand with a perfect British accent. It's better to be British when shoplifting, right? "My fiancé is just outside in…that limo," I point at the sleek black vehicle parked by the sidewalk. "I'll be right back with his credit card."

Passing back a reassuring wink, Charley rushes me out with my trusty companion snorting all the while. A shrill from the stuck-up assistant, returning to find her tray bare, splits through my ears at a heightened decibel and I wince. Calm down Anal Annie, it's only a couple hundred-grand clinging to my throat. Rushed footsteps click against the polished marble, a pair of dress shoes and heels taking chase.

"Stop right there! Return those diamonds at once!" she calls. Without the need for a discussion, Charley turns left and I take the right, to split up and regroup later. But who else should I see than a pair of policemen strolling my way down the crowded street? *Fucking perfect.* So I do the only logical thing. I pop that limo door and scoot my ass inside.

Four pairs of eyes along the two benches adjacent swivel my way, glaring out from the most chiseled, model-worthy faces I've ever laid eyes on. So perfect in fact, they make the diamonds at my neck seem dimmer as I keep budging my butt along the seats. Voices shout through the darkened window, the police now accompanying the clerk and stuck-up boss bitch. She scowls as if she can actually see me, although her eyes seem to be roaming over the reflection of her own popped hip and crossed arms.

"Excuse me fellas, just passing through." I draw the blonde wig over my face like a curtain, dismissing myself. Reaching for the opposite door handle, the lock drops with an audible click. I try it anyway, swallowing thickly when forced to face the band of suited wolves scowling my way.

Only one of them moves, drawing my attention to the sharp jaw speckled in shadow as he rasps his tattooed knuckles across the closed screen dividing us from the driver without ever taking his stark amber eyes from me. The limo pulls forward sharply, driving me back into the leather on a gasp.

"Hey, wait a darn tooting minute," I start, keeping up my British accent. Zooming towards an intersection at full speed, I spot Charley hiding on a street corner with Pig wriggling in her arms. Twisting back and pressing my hand to the rear window, I mentally shout for her to get back to the Thirsty Kirsty, and for the love of all shit, hide those damn diamond rings. I'll make it back soon enough and then I believe it's time to move on. Get the fuck out of dodge and start clean under a new guise.

"Pull this thing over right now. I'm a busy lady; I've got places to be!" I turn back and shoot a glare at the faces I can barely comprehend right now. Too much brutal beauty for such a tight space. Or at least, the limo seems small, with the bulk of their muscle expanding from suit jackets. Amber eyes chuckles, a deep throaty sound that coils around my clit and tugs.

"You mean, you have more of our stores to rob?" My throat bobs beneath the necklace. My chest rises and falls harder in the glittery dress. Sinking back into the seat, once more caught in the headlights of their hardened, unwavering stares, I chew on my bottom lip and press my hands into the leather either side of my butt.

This is fine. Totally fine. There's never been a con I couldn't talk my way out of before.

Chapter 3

"Myles." Carter elbows me. "Myles!" His whispered shout leaks with desperation. But the fog has taken root in my mind, and I'm no longer listening. Someone tries to lean across me, intent on pressing the speaker comms to the driver. I swiftly punch him in the face, not caring which of my best friends it was. They want me to pull over this car. They want me to stop looking at her. Neither of which are happening.

A pair of the most intriguing eyes I've ever seen hold my stare. Deep purple, alluring, captivating. Rarer than any diamond we stock in our co-owned jewelers. Just a side project really, when Owen decided his Rolex collection needed company. Yet if we managed to obtain anything as beautiful as the jewels currently in my eyeline, I'd visit daily. Purchase an armchair just to sit and stare from the corner, but even the brief few moments she's been in the limo have me edging forward. I need a better look. I need to grace my fingertips with the smoothness of her skin and savor every inch of her curvaceous body.

"No," Carter nudges me back in my seat and pinches the bridge of his nose, reading my thoughts. It's fine, even from here I can feel the pull of our attraction. She inhales deeply, lifting her large breasts sandwiched together by a hint of black lace beneath the dress. My hands fist. I could go full King Kong at this moment, carrying her up the side of a building just to keep her all to myself, but that would undo everything my friends have spent the past fifteen years trying to implement.

But something's not quite right. There's an artificial edge to her that doesn't quite fit. The longer I look, the more evident it becomes.

"Take. It. Off," I growl. A thin brow raises, slender shoulders shrug. Beginning at the slitted side of the fabric, she starts peeling the garment off, revealing long, smooth legs and my dick jumps to attention. It strains behind my zipper and pulsates with the instant need to be inside her. "No, not your dress. Your wig," I barely rasp out. She smiles then, full lips forming into an 'O'. The throbbing of my cock intensifies and I groan.

"We're not doing this," Carter announces, twisting, so he blocks my view of the alluring female in our vehicle and only his stern face fills my vision. "We have a business meeting uptown, then a photo shoot for Vogue. Of all the days to fuck our plans away, so to speak, this is not the one."

"Maybe Carter is right," Sebby's nasally voice comes from the seat opposite. He's holding his nose, which I evidently tried to break, yet shifts until his knees are touching either side of mine. "Today, we're busy - but there's always tomorrow. We could get her phone number?"

"Or we could just get our diamonds back and leave her on the side of the road," Owen pitches in. The limo pulls to a stop as Owen jerks his thumb at the blacked-out window. A bunch of hookers on a street corner peer over, whistling and waving their fingers in a bid to gain our attention.

"No." My stern voice growls amongst the four of us until I shove Carter aside. Preparing myself to glance upon the most perfect set of eyes to be seared on the inside of my brain, empty leather meets my gaze. *What*?! The tiptoe of a boot disappearing through the open sunroof proceeds a glittery dress sliding past the rear window.

"Motherfucker! Stop the limo!" I bang my fist on the divider when Shane, our driver, tries to pull away. He skids to a sudden stop and I barrel through the arms trying to hold me back.

"Myles, man, just let the police catch up with her," Owen whines.

"We have an extremely tight schedule," Carter grinds out. Neither I pay attention to, and I shrug my hand out of Sebby's when he softly tries to grab for mine. Not wasting my time on the locked doors, I shoot myself through the sunroof, wriggling as my hips get stuck. Carter will be having a heart attack about me creasing the Saville Row suit, but I finally manage to drag myself from the hands trying to yank me down and throw myself over the side of the limo.

The midday sun sparkles from her dress like a beacon. A lighthouse threatening to blind me, but nothing will stop the pursuit of my latest craving. The faster she runs, the tighter the tug on my chest pulls. Dress shoes eat up the pavement, those in my way not occurring to me as actual people. Simply objects I need to shove aside. When the glittery dress disappears around a corner, my breathing stalls. I've craved sex every day of my life since puberty, but the object of my desire has never been so defined.

Pushing beyond the limitations my lungs try to impose, I fly around the corner and stumble into oncoming traffic, at a loss of the vixen I'm hunting. Horns blare, my friends scream out as they also take chase, yet it's the fog in my mind that's all consuming. I make it across the street, hunting for a glimpse. One tiny clue of which way she'd go. Stumbling into a hot dog vendor, a splash of condiment flicks onto my suit just as Carter catches up to me.

"No, no, no! Fuck's sake, Huds, not today please," green eyes beg of me. Grabbing a napkin, he foolishly tries to salvage the powered blue jacket until I grab his wrists.

"I have to find her," I tell him. Demand of him. Carter is a stern bastard, but everything he does is for my best interest. He won't deny me now. Tossing aside the napkin, Carter's shoulders sag in defeat.

"Tomorrow, I promise," he nods. I suppose that's as good as I can ask for. Nodding, I begin to trail behind him, ignoring the cell phones that follow my every move. Footage for TMZ, no doubt. Owen and Sebby catch up to us, agreeing with Carter's short, clipped commands. A call to our PA to have a replacement suit at the office prior to our meeting. Delay said meeting by thirty minutes. Have Shane bring the limo around.

All three of them fall into hushed discussions while I investigate the sidewalks branching off in all directions. Even in the city, she can't have disappeared. I look up to the sky, willing the cloud threatening to eclipse the sun to hold off just a few moments longer. Just until that telltale sparkle catches my eye, causing my head to whip sideways.

There! Slinking down a street lined with town houses and fences. Falling three steps behind my friends, I turn and run for it. Lost to the crowd, pushing myself to full speed this time. I won't let her escape again. Darting across a busy road, my mind is crystal clear this time. Attune to the sway of her hips, the shifting of her blonde wig. Beginning to climb a set of stone steps, I shoot behind her, whipping her backwards by the waist. Her surprised scream is cut short when she tumbles into my arms and stares up into my eyes. But those which greet me are not the violet I was hoping for.

"Well hello there, handsome," a woman leers up at me, grinning a toothless smile. Grime coats her cheeks, the wiry hair beneath her wig writhe with small bugs. I almost drop her, until I remember people film me everywhere I go. Every second of my damn life outside the businesses we own is caught on camera, someone waiting to blackmail or sell me out to the press. Myles Hudson, the reformed sex addict who will no doubt strike again.

Clearing my throat, trying to not show how strongly her stench is affecting me, I place the woman back on her bare feet.

"Excuse me. I didn't intend to frighten you. Can you tell me where you got that dress, I'll pay you for it," I reach into my jacket and start to pull out my wallet. Wait, I can't be seen fondling this homeless woman and then handing her money. The tabloids would have a field day with that one. The imposter brushes the wig over her shoulder, drawing my attention to the thick diamond bracelet on her wrist. I smirk to myself. This woman has already been bought off, and it seems I've underestimated my prey. "Never mind," I shake my head and take my leave.

Carter is waiting for me at the end of the street, his shoe tapping and face contorted with anger. The limo is parked up behind, forcing me to make the walk of shame all the way back to them. As I merge from the side street, a group of teenage girls with a bodyguard barge into me, taking a selfie and not watching where they're going. One on the outside, with purple hair that mocks me, stomps her studded boot onto my foot.

"Watch it, asshole!" she scoffs, scowling at me from behind a pair of sunglasses. I frown, watching her saunter by in a corset and tatty old skirt, before shaking myself back to reality. My mind's tripping, causing me to question everything. Once the coast is clear, I finally make it to Carter and he pops the limo door, ordering me to get in.

It was fun while it lasted, but I fail to convince myself. Sebby shimmies up the seat to my side while Owen leans forward and pats my knee. At least something came out of today. I *felt*. For the man who can and does have it all–women, booze, sex–I'd become lost in the motions. Dulled to routine. But not anymore. She's the vixen I didn't realize I was missing. Like a blood hound, I have her marked, and nothing will deter me from finding her.

Chapter 4

I watch the limo drive away before diverting from the main street, where I can finally compute what the hell just happened. I could have left when I traded my stunning gown and wig for that tramp's soiled skirt, but curiosity prevailed. I needed a closer look. One last glimpse, I scold myself.

Forcing one boot in front of the other, the city falls into the shadow of dense cloud as a faint pitter patter of rain speckles the stolen sunglasses. Light at first, until the heavens open, intent on washing away our sins with a sudden downpour. I'd need an entire tsunami to tackle mine.

Tossing the sunglasses in the nearest trash can and hitching up the patchwork skirt, I make a run for it. From the city's mass of umbrellas to the drenched souls in the slums. Never once stopping, I'm on the verge of cardiac arrest by the time I clamber into the Thirsty Kirsty. Hair stuck to my face, eyelashes dripping.

Several of the girls are lounging in plush armchairs, the stench of weed drifting towards those helping themselves to the bar's inventory. Still no sign of the owner then. I don't pay any notice, heading directly backstage and down the stairs. The sodden skirt hinders every step, weighing heavily on my waist. If it weren't for the sturdy boots I refused to give up, I'd have been shivering long before now. Pushing open my bedroom door, a body slams into me.

"Oh my fuckity dickballs," Charley gasps, shaking more than me. "I was so worried. I didn't know what to do." Leaning on her until I find the strength to straighten, I plaster an easy smile on my damp face and usher us into the safety of our room.

"I've told you, if anything happens to me, take the duffel and move Pig to Hawaii. She deserves a life of luxury." Dropping to the ground, Pig crawls from her hiding space beneath my bed. She knows to stay out of sight when I'm not around, but one sharp whistle has her shuffling and grunting out to greet me. Scratchy licks coat my hand until she wriggles up my thighs and I lift her into the cradle of my arms.

"So, what happened?" Charley shifts from foot to foot. "I saw you enter the limo and not leave. How did you manage to get away?" I continue to give Pig's spotted belly a good rub before settling her on my bed. Rolling onto her back, Pig's tongue hangs out, her pointed teeth on full show as she almost instantly falls asleep. It's been a long day all round.

"Shower first, then we'll gossip. Stash these with the rest." I shove my hand into my cleavage and draw out the length of a diamond necklace. Charley gasps, easing it from my pruned hands.

"You...you got it. When it wasn't on your neck...I figured–"

"You should know me well enough by now. I don't lose easily or gracefully."

Once in her possession, Charley opens the wardrobe and uses the shoehorn we keep tucked just inside to pry open a plank in the base. The duffel below is loaded with jewels and money, and that's exactly how I know I can trust Charley. She could have taken the cash and ran at any point in these past six months, especially since she knows I have no attachment to it, but it's still right there. Loyalty like that can't be faked.

***

True to my word, I told Charley everything the other night. It's the least she deserved, after having the genius idea to order in a pizza while I was using up every last drop of hot water. Usually, a set of satin pajamas and a belly full of comfort food would have been enough to put the strange encounters of that day to rest. If not that, laughing with the only friend I've managed to obtain for myself and Pig licking my face should have done it. But no. I layed on my thin mattress all night, lost in my thoughts.

Or rather, trapped by the stone-cold face imprinted behind my eyelids. Bright amber eyes. Sandy blond hair, tousled and lazily lying on his shoulders. Tattooed hands and neck, muscles straining against the powered blue fabric. Everything about him seemed at odds with the sharp suit he was squeezed into. But it's the way he looked at me I can't forget. Hungry. Practically famished.

"Amethyst!" a shout right beside my ear jerks me back to the present. Music pounds through the fraying red curtains lining the backstage area. The buzz of excitement emanates from the full house beyond, wolf whistling and cheering the two dancers on stage. However, the vibe out back isn't as pleasant. A short, rounded man with a bright red face is glaring up at the side of my face, close enough for the smell of his whiskey breath to wash over my nostrils. I shove him back a step, not hiding my grimace. I don't care if Art is the club's owner, or if he thinks his white suit and cowboy hat gives him some type of influence, no one has authority over me.

"You rang?" I raise a brow. My heels put me a few inches above him, my breasts practically in his face. Charley, being the doll she is, kept my Koulture bag safe until I was able to retrieve the leather jacket I've thrown over a sparkled bikini. I've decided to incorporate the garment into my act, roughing up my purple hair with some back combing and a whole can of hairstyle. Even in my make-up, I've gone punk rock with thick liner and black painted lips. Art's nostrils flare, his cowboy boot tapping.

"You missed your cue! Get your head straight and get out there on that pole!" I scoff, rolling my eyes to regain a hint of composure.

"Excuse me, little man," I leer over him, using my body to push him another step back into the corner behind the curtain. "Don't forget, for one second, I'm not one of your hopeless girls with no sense of self-worth. You don't intimidate or scare me. I am here, because it's exactly where I choose to be. The second I'm over the hype of dancing, I'm gone, and there's nothing you can do to stop me."

A challenge ignites between us, much like the one I started during my 'audition'. Art wanted me to perform for him *personally*. I told him to buy a ticket like everyone else and show me to my dressing room. The current song draws to a close, flawlessly bleeding into the next and Art's eye twitches. Breaking away from our standoff, he shoves past me, striding away and grumbling about getting my ass on stage. My feet falter, because I am itching to do just that, but also stubbornly hate doing as I'm told. Screw it.

The second my shoes grace the marbled stage, a purple hue descends. My name is announced by the in-house DJ, a round of enthusiastic cheering following. But none of that rivals the physical rush that bursts from my chest, filling every fiber of my being. It was like this the first time, and has yet to dim. It will–because nothing lasts forever–but as my long legs carry me to the pole at the end of the catwalk, my heart begins to race. Wrapping my hand around the cool metal, my eyes close and I just *feel*.

No routine. No rehearsals. My body floats to the rhythm of whatever music plays, accepting the beat as my very lifeline. Smooth R&B floods my veins, directing my limbs. If I were on a heart rate monitor at this present moment, that bitch would churn out the tune to any Beyonce song like nobody's business. Coiling the back of my knee around the pole, I hang to the side, pushing my hands through my wild hair. Another round of cheers come across the club, but I don't look for who's responsible.

Instead, I climb the pole like a monkey, hanging upside down. Unraveling the jacket along the length of my arms, I toss it further back across the stage. The bikini bottoms stretch high on my waist, creating a V that wraps around and disappears into my ass crack. Rolling my body, my arms stretch, even my finger dancing to play an invisible piano. Lost. Adrift. Found.

This is the only place I've felt true freedom. My scars may be internal, but I refuse to allow my wings to be clipped. Spiraling around the pole, swirling through the air. Here, I can fly. In front of an anonymous crowd, my true self is revealed. Bold, daring, memorable.

A version of me which the world will one day receive, and they'd soon wish they hadn't. Shrouded in blood shed, coated in revenge, they will know my face and fear my name. As I keep telling Pig, the best con is yet to come.

Righting myself, I spin with my legs extended, slowly lowering to the stage. The marble flooring rises to meet me and once fully seated, I lower onto my back. My legs rest against the pole until I spread them wide, planting my heels either side to grind my sparkle-covered pussy on the metal. The hollers around me turn into roars, my head rolling aside with a lazy smile. Validation is a warm caress, and my body is enveloped in its snug embrace.

Songs roll from one to the next, molding together as flawlessly as the show I provide. Each roll of my body smoothly transitions into a new position. Each slow spin plays to the entirety of the club. Releasing my breasts from the confines of the tiny bikini, I throw it into the audience somewhere. My body is all me, completely natural and a damn sight to be proud of. Not to share it would be a crime. A thud pounds beneath my heels but I'm already on the path to becoming air born, throwing myself around the pole with vigor. Climbing higher, I hold on with one hand, twisting in full circles with my head rolling back to view the scene spinning past.

Following another announcement, the central strobe light shifts to shine on Charley taking center stage, catching on a head of sandy blond hair in the front row. I only catch a glimpse, yet it's all I needed. Inked fingers pressed over his stomach, a darkness emanating from his watchful eyes. The ones that have refused to let me sleep, and now cause me to falter. My hand slips for only a second, but it's enough for my hip to slam into the pole before I can catch myself. Dropping to the stage, my ankle gives out, the high heel twisting beneath me and I topple onto my ass. Hard.

I grimace against the pain, turning my back on the crowd to pull the wall back over my emotions. I'll ice later. For now, I desperately cling to the adrenaline rush. The one I won't feel until I dance again tomorrow evening. But it's gone, and Art, hiding beside the curtain and gesturing me to get off the stage, thoroughly kills the mood. Sparing a look back to the crowd, not seeing any trace of shoulder-length blond hair, I drag myself up with the pole's assistance, grab my jacket and hobble out of view.

"Want to tell me what the fuck that was about?" Art growls, shoving his chest into me as I tug on the leather jacket and bat him away.

"Not particularly," I groan, intent on leaving. Tail between my legs, let me crawl back to my room and wallow in self-pity peacefully. But Art doesn't get the memo, tugging on my arm, forcing me to stop.

"I knew taking you on was a risk. You're the oldest dancer here, if you're going to start slipping up–" Grabbing the label of my jacket, he raises a hand and slaps my breast sharply. I gasp at the stinging shock, wasting no time to rear back and punch him directly in the face. Bones crunch beneath my knuckles, the splatter of blood spewing in all directions.

"I'm twenty-nine, asshole." The fat wanna-be cowboy gangster stumbles back, clenching his busted nose and widens his eyes. I stare right back, daring him to throw a punch my way. I'd actually pay to see it. I haven't been training to fight since I was fifteen for no reason. In fact, the violent beast within has awoken, whispering in my ears to finish the job. *Do everyone a favor, don't stop until he's no longer breathing.* Peering at my bloodied fist, I wipe the crimson over my breasts while smirking.

"Count this as my official resignation. The only traces of you ever touching me, will be this smear of blood. Next time, it'll be your head mounted on my wall."

"You...fucking bitch! You're done! Pack your shit, be gone by morning!" Art splutters. Giving him a two fingered salute, I slink towards the stairs when I'm sure a muffled scream sounds beneath the beat of music. I peer back, seeing no one nearby, but a white cowboy hat discarded on the ground. Art must have sulked back to his office, leaving only the shadows to watch me descend the stairs.

Entering my room, I kick these damn heels off and slump on the bed. Pig shuffles beneath the metal frame to lick my bruising ankle and I absentmindedly reach down to stroke her. The rush in my chest, which has woken for a whole different reason, has well and truly soured. Killing Art serves me no purpose. He's not even a bug on my windscreen, and trust me, this bitch has a massive pest problem to take care of before the likes of Art rattles me into a murdering spree. I know better than to be controlled by emotion. Now, at least.

At some point, I doze, only realizing when Charley returns. A wet cloth is slapped on my face, clearing away the make-up and then works on the blood between my cleavage. Rolling me over, the jacket and thong are removed and I'm covered with a blanket. Muttering a thanks, the lights go out, putting an end to a horrid evening. Or so I'd hoped.

Just like the past few nights, sleep comes in fits of passionate dreams and sordid nightmares. Shadows chase me from one fantasy to the next; from Sandyman's steel jaw propping me up to his hands wrapping around my throat. In every instance my mind can conjure, his crisp amber eyes never leave mine. Just like in the limo, sexual tension swirls within their splendor, barely-contained power radiating from his toned body.

He's exactly the type of man I've spent most of my life avoiding at all costs. Because, just like in my fleeting dreams, he wouldn't be satisfied with a basic fuck; he'd devour my soul. Strip me bare of everything that is Amethyst Boudreaux and take me back to a place I left far behind. A darkened corner where fear reigns and submission thrives. Nope. Never again.

Chapter 5

There are many ways I've described my soul in the past. At peace, is not one of them. Yet I can't deny, watching the purple haired minx dance on stage, utterly lost to the sensations of her own movements, there's an unusual silence within my being. A recognition of hunger, yet an unnerving patience to watch. Normally, I take whatever I need and don't waste time on names. But I won't rush with her. I will savor every second of foreplay she's already providing me, as I stroke my hard cock through my jeans.

My boys and I fill the front row surrounding her portion of the stage, blocking anyone else from getting too close. Owen drums his fingers to the beat on his armrest, Sebby's attention is divided between the stage and me. Carter forces himself to look away from the leather clad, bikini wearing goddess, and fails. There's no denying her appeal. The air of danger and desire is too much for any of us to deny.

Popping my button and tugging down my zipper, I take myself in hand. I'm painfully hard, each touch of my calloused hand like sandpaper to a firework. I could blow my load by merely watching her, but it's her touch I crave. Soft, small hands to stroke me into oblivion. My balls are already hating me for it but my decision is made – I'm not going to come again until it's in her tight cunt. My sweet obsession. My perfect fascination.

In quite possibly the worst strip club I've ever visited, she's a shining jewel amongst the scum-filled clientele. Tacky gold fixtures on the walls, fraying curtains lining the edge of the stage. When the private investigator I'd hired presented me with images of this establishment, I can't pretend I wasn't surprised. Seems I've been looking for some-one to capture my attention the way she did in all the wrong places. 'Amethyst', as she was introduced, works the pole, using her body as an instrument of lust.

"Myles, not here," Carter growls, nudging my arm. I ignore him. I'm not a fucking child shaking my winky about. I'm a grown ass man, pumping his cock over the woman he's craving. There's nothing more natural than that. Owen doesn't spare a look my way, pulling a pack of tissues from his back pocket and tosses them at me. Trust him to be prepared. He may be more discreet about it, but Owen's sexual prowess is as writhe as mine.

Another dancer is introduced, her name lost to the roars of cheer-ing. A clear favorite, which is fine by me. They can keep their eyes off the one I've decided to claim. The strobe light shifts in time with the music blending into a new song, and for one split second, Amethyst's eyes catch mine. Dazzling violet orbs, which have been imprinted inside my mind since the moment we met. My hand clenches around my shaft, lighting the fuse to blow. Her hand slips on the pole. She falls. My heart lurches. Shooting up from my seat, several hands grab for my t-shirt, yanking me back from climbing the stage.

"At least put your cock away first," Carter shoves me back into my seat. My friends purposely get in the way of my view, only allowing me small glimpses of Amethyst picking herself up and hobbling off stage. I grumble, slapping Sebby's hands away when he offers to assist, shoving my dick behind my zipper, doing up my pants once and for all. After that, there's no stopping me from jumping onto the stage without the use of my hands and entering the backstage area. Amethyst has her back to me, walking away as some short guy in a white suit grabs her arm. I step behind a dusty curtain, molding myself into the shadows to watch their argument.

I listen to him insult her. I watch as his hand slaps her breast in the most degrading show of authority I've ever seen. Clenching my fists, I'm about to step out of my hiding place when Amethyst punches him directly in the face. And just like that, my dick is throbbing once more. I'm left with a full view of the most incredible sight. Fierce violet eyes assess her prey, then the back of her hand before smearing the blood between her breasts. I'm certain she doesn't even know when she did it – but I do.

Amethyst, or whoever the tenacious woman hiding behind her stage name is, is a survivor. She's seen death. She knows the bitter taste of violence. Possibly walked the tightrope of depression more times than she can count. But she's here. Alive, and more resilient than ever. I watch her retreat, all fine legs and swishing purple hair. That's when I see my chance.

Lurching forward, my hand closes around the short man's mouth. I take great satisfaction in knowing this same palm was so recently on my dick, and probably a little salty from my precum. I smear it back and forth, just in case, as I drag him out of view, knocking his cowboy hat onto the ground. He bucks, making a useless attempt to be freed which I permit, once Amethyst is fully out of sight.

"Who the fuck," the short, red-faced man starts. Until I step into the light. Until the three men I consider kin enter the backstage area from all sides, caging him in.

"I'm going to take a stab in the dark here," I choose my words carefully, "and presume you own this club?" The man trembles, his eyes darting to the hat he doesn't dare reach for. I imagine it provides him with a sense of authority, which I'm happy to strip back and expose the coward underneath. After a shaky nod, I step into his personal space. "Then it's only polite to show us to your office, don't you think? I have a business proposal for you."

None of us budge, forcing him to barge through Owen and Sebby in an effort to scurry away. Carter holds me back as the others follow, leaning into my ear with the words I already know he's going to say.

"Lead with your brains, Myles. Not your balls." Patting my chest, he remains by my side as we navigate the backstage hallways to a small stack of stairs, 'Art's Office' hand painted on the door above in black, swirling lettering. Carter is a particular kind of personality, one most would find tricky to understand. He lives by his self-made rules like it's fucking law, and we're all damned if caught committing treason in his eyes. But once you scrape away at his untrusting, almost impenetrable exterior, once he's accepted you in, his loyalty is unlike any other.

Entering the tiny office, Art makes his way around the desk while we file in and fill the space. Shoulder to shoulder, there isn't an inch to move between exposed wooden paneling and a desk in the center about to give way to termites. It's all good, since I didn't plan on remaining on this side of the room anyway. Carter closes the door and positions himself in front of it, Owen and Sebby taking my lead to stand either side of the desk. Rounding the back of Art's leather chair, I slam my hands down on his shoulders.

"I've been looking for a certain purple-haired performer for a few days now," I tense my fingers into his collar bone.

"Amethyst?" the slimy little weasel chokes out. I want to rid him of his tongue just for uttering her name, but I need to hear what he has to say first. "What's she done this time? That girl is nothing but trouble, I swear." My grip tightens.

"Hmmm. Surprisingly, I couldn't find a slither of information on her, but I found out quite a bit about you. Or rather, the financial strains you've put your club under." Oh yes, once Carter had scratched the surface, the extent of Art's debts started spewing all over the computer screen. A few calls later and I'd managed to uncover a rather aggravated crime family who Art had paid a visit to, the exact same day Amethyst found herself in my limo. It's what he offered in return for writing off his debts that made me sick to my stomach. I'm supposed to be the deprived addict here, but sex trafficking has never been my forte.

"Wh-what is it you want?" Art begins to panic and I realize my hands have traveled upward to clamp around his neck. "Amethyst? Take her, it'll be one less bitch to deal with in my eyes. I'll provide the alibi, whatever you need. Nothing will be traced back to you, I swear." Owen chuckles first, his blue eyes glinting with mischief.

"See, the thing is," I release Art's neck and take his wrist in my hand instead. Pinning it to the desk, Sebby copies without needing to be told, tightening his grip on Art's arm. Owen takes over from me, freeing my hands up. "That 'bitch' has caught my attention, and once such an occurrence happens, I don't let anyone else touch what is mine," I catch Owen's hitched eyebrow, "without permission." His smirk is mirrored by Sebby, the impending bloodlust affecting the three of us. Once upon a time, I could have encouraged Carter to join too, but he's long since lost his sense of fun. It's all meetings and security reviews now.

"Okay, fine, I see what this is about. You want me to apologize to her, is that it?" Art really begins to stammer now. I round the desk once more, stroking a path between Sebby's shoulders as I pass. He shudders, responding to me the way a submissive would. Forever loyal, easily pleased.

"We're a little past apologies," I sigh, finding a nutcracker on the table amongst discarded walnut shells. "Your fingers have not only touched, but assaulted the one I've decided to claim for myself. And for such a crime, there simply are no words." Guiding the nutcracker down the length of Art's index finger, he suddenly realizes just how deep in shit he really is. Bucking against Sebby's hold, his finger shakes and I decide to do him the courtesy of not being kept in suspense.

Crunch.

"This little piggy touched what isn't yours, this little piggy decided to roam. This little piggy will resemble chopped beef, and this little piggy should have stayed home."

Each bone crimps at an unnatural angle. High-pitched screams become muffled and I look up from my trance of blood splatter to see Carter has appeared at Art's back. Having loosened the tie at Art's neck, Carter raises and slots the fabric into Art's mouth, wrapping it around his hand to hold the asshole's head still. See—undying loyalty. With Carter joining the fold, now the beating of my heart slots into place. I feel whole. Complete. My men at my side, our victim screaming between us.

At some point between his ring finger and pinkie, Art passed out. It gave ample time to raid his office, access his cell via thumbprint recognition and similarly retrieve his laptop password. His inkjet printer whirring causes him to stir, just in time.

"Ahh, there you are," I smirk as Carter removes the tie from between Art's lips. Pulling up a stool, my men gather at my back, acting the role of security rather than best buds. "Now, for that business proposal."

"Wha...what?" Art blubbers, tears streaming down his cheeks. Owen passes me the page from the printer and I slam it down on the desk, now cleared of blood. "I'm offering you a one-time deal. Sign this club over to me, and I'll pay off your debts." If the situation wasn't dire before, Art's eyes widen and his face pales impossibly more.

"I can't–not my club. This is my legacy," he sniffles. Checking my watch, I note the second hand ticking down on my patience.

"And what a sad legacy it is. Sign." I tap the dotted line. I may be impulsive, reckless and all the other things the tabloids call me on a daily basis, but I'm also smart. My father ingrained the use of a binding contract into me since I could read. I can pay off the judge in reference to Art's broken fingers, but no one can dispute the agreement currently sitting on the table. "The terms are clear and absolute, printed with your own header and prefilled with details of both parties. All you need to do is sign the damn thing."

"But...but, my hands," Art holds up the horror show that are his digits. Crimson coated, mangled and crooked in all different directions. I smirk. Even if he manages to call an ambulance, they'll never be set in time for the chance at full movement again. Instant karma for slapping and humiliating Amethyst the way he did. Leaning across the desk, I remove a pen from a holder and shove it between Art's teeth.

"Trust me, we're doing the world a favor," I pat him on the head as he ducks low to add the scrawilest mess of a signature to the contract. Once done and has spat the pen away, I grab a fistful of Art's thinning hair, dragging his head up to meet mine. "And if you even think about laying your hands on a woman again, I will hunt you down. You will beg for mercy and find none. Do I make myself clear?"

He nods rapidly and against my better judgment, I shove him back in his seat, take the contract and stalk away. Carter wouldn't let me go through with murder under such sloppy, unplanned circumstances, but Art has been warned. I'll have him followed, waiting for him to slip up. It won't take long, then he'll know what it truly means to disobey Myles Hudson. For now though, I have a club to claim and a walking heartbreaker to win over. Let the games begin.

Chapter 6

"Ami, wake up! Something's happening!" hands shake me and I startle. Pig yaps, her best attempt at defending me lost as she topples from the mattress. Luckily, it's close to the ground and I'm fairly certain she's made of pure marshmallow. Charley's dark eyes are wide, her hair spilling around my face to block out the artificial light.

"What...what fucking time is it?" I nudge her aside and sit upright. I feel worse than if I hadn't slept at all, my eyes stinging and head throbbing.

"Barely eight in the morning. Come on, we need to leave." Leave? My brow pinches as I stumble out of bed, finding myself completely naked. Clothes are thrown at me from the wardrobe as Charley pries open the bottom panel. Shit, this is serious.

"Is it Art? Because I broke his nose?" I ask whilst pulling on a white vest that comes to my navel and a pair of white panties. Brown ankle boots are tossed by my feet before Charley stills.

"Wait, you broke Art's nose?!" We stare at each other as Pig continues to yap, scratching at my calf to pick her up. I obey, hoisting her chubby body into my arms before snapping my fingers for Charley to un-pause. "Oh, um," she blinks several times, pulling out the sacred duffel. "No, not Art. No one has seen him since you fell last night. This is something else." At that moment, a pounding sounds a few doors down.

"Get your asses out, ladies, last warning," a gruff voice sounds. Another comes from the opposite end of the hall, repeating the same. I rush to grab Charley's huge handbag, nestling Pig inside. Winding my arm into hers, we exhale in time behind the closed door.

"Remember. No matter what–duffel, Pig, Hawaii." In one swift movement, we barge into the hallway and walk arm in arm, chins held high. Considering her occupation, I would have considered Charley as rather meek six months ago. But now, she understands the lessons I've been eager to teach–to tackle life the way you want to be remembered. With confidence and just enough bitchiness for everyone nearby to want to either fuck you or be you.

An outbreak of chaos ensues from the cramped hallway. Whoever is forcing us from the only home we know, is lost in the flurry of fellow dancers who are scrambling around, half-dressed and in a panic. Charley and I carve our path through the center, up the stairs and out the open back door. A commotion sounds from the front of the building.

"Sir, we can't legally begin knowing there are still people inside," a nervous voice trembles. I pull Charley to a halt on the corner, listening in before we step into view.

"Five minutes and I'm giving you the green light," comes the reply. I vaguely recognize the voice and my heart clenches before I've fully grasped who it might be.

"But I–"

"Either you do the job I'm paying you for or I'll strap you to one of the poles on that stage and do it myself." There's a scuffle before heels scrape and the bully storms away. Peering around the corner, a man is crumpled on the ground, his back against the brick wall. Yellow hard hat and hi-vis vest on his body, I quickly scan the machinery across the parking lot. All the equipment needed for a shift demolition, and a team of burly men to operate them.

Amongst the huge machines, a suit leans against a Mercedes, the AMG version in a sleek coat of yellow, phone pressed to his ear. Dark hair, that shimmers brown in the rising sun, is cropped short at the sides and left longer on top. His face is the image of frustration, until Sandyman approaches. I watch their exchange, how Mr. Anal visibly relaxes and even cracks a smile for his companion. Speaking of which–holy hell.

No longer crammed into a suit, blond hair puddles over his broad shoulders in a white t-shirt. Dark tattoos leak through, covering every visible inch from his neck to low-hanging jeans. Cracking his knuckles, my eyes are drawn from the width of his bulging biceps to the arrows inked on fingers I could make good use of.

Two more men in casual wear appear from Thirsty Kirsty's main entrance, completing the four I had the displeasure of meeting in the limo. Equally tattooed, their muscles just as defined, with thick veins trailing the lengths of their arms. Pig wriggles in the bag on my shoulder, reminding me to pick up my jaw and do something.

Sliding the bag from my shoulder to Charley's, I give Pig a few slobbery kisses before making my way across the parking lot. Remaining out of view, the flat boots I'd usually loathe provide the perfect amount of sneak, all the way up to machine number one. It's a beast of yellow and green, with a giant claw attached to the front. A similar man to before is sitting in the driver's seat, hard hat in place and a coffee cup in hand as he reads an oversized newspaper. I use that paper to my advantage, climbing the side of the vehicle to pop up at his side, still shielded from the assholes by the Mercedes.

"Pssst," I grab his attention. He jerks, almost spilling his coffee. "What's going on here?" The man raises the paper to hide both of us while I relieve his coffee cup and drink it for him.

"Immediate demolition of this club, as per the new owners instruction. We were called in the early hours of this morning."

"New owners?" I frown and then scowl. Not just because this coffee tastes like it came from an oil can. It's no coincidence the very men who tried to kidnap me are now trying to destroy my place of work. For some reason, they have it out for me, and are about to get a dose of what screwing with Amethyst looks like.

"Accidents happen all the time in the workplace, right?" I ask my friend with a squishy dad bod I could cuddle into next week. I won't though, because he's wearing a wedding ring and I don't do long term ties. A man who's into commitment sends me running in the opposite direction.

"Um, I suppose so," he nods and I grin, handing him back his cup of shit. I mean, coffee. Leaning further over, pressing my boobs into his face whilst peering at the sports car, I push the machine's stick into reverse without him realizing. Call it my good deed for the day. No one likes being called out of a warm, cozy bed at stupid o'clock in the morning just to sit around waiting.

Slinking back to ground level, I pick my timing carefully to move between the machines without being seen. A gaggle of girls stumble from the front doors, glitzy dresses and heels bundled in their hands. They are quickly escorted out by a pair of bodyguards I haven't seen before, burly guys in suits who barely match Sandyman's size. Stopping by the nearest machine, I kick up my foot and check my nails until they walk by, passing me off as just another whore. Everyone in the vicinity should know, I'm the Queen of Badass Whore's.

Once the coast is clear, I roll my neck before climbing up the metal hunk of machinery. Thick rubber tread stretched over the tires, providing me with a level platform to scoot along. Unlike the other machines, the driver's seat of this one isn't open for creepy crawlers to gain access. It also means whoever is sitting inside the cab can merely watch through the windscreen as I round the front of his vehicle, use the bumper for a boost and throw myself onto the wrecking ball. One hand grips the chain, my pole dancing experience coming in super 'handy' and I drag myself up the rest of the way.

"The fuck?!"

"There she is!" Voices holler, muscled men run. It would seem someone has been looking for me. Hands make a grab for my boots, angry faces surrounding the ball. Before they can reach me, the chain is drawn higher and I catch sight of the person in the cab. Charley beams, Pig sitting on her lap with a long pink tongue hanging over the steering wheel. Lifting me higher, the ball swings and, never one to miss an opportunity, I plant my ass down, legs straightened with the chain practically inserted in my hoo-haa.

"I came in like a wrecking ball!" I sing, totally off tune and loving every minute of it. Other workers receive barked orders to block us in, and my good old dad bod friend is the closest between us and sweet freedom. Unfortunately for him, as he shoves his foot onto the pedal, his vehicle shoots backwards and proceeds to trample the Mercedes directly behind. The gigantic wheels crunch over the yellow metal with more efficiency than I envisioned, my cackle trailing behind as we drive from the parking lot. Sure, this hunk of a machine isn't fast, but it wasn't a speedy escape I was going for. It was a dramatic one.

Turning out on the main road, it becomes quickly evident Charley has no idea how to drive this thing. Props to her for trying. The ball jerks, cutting off my singing as I cling on for dear life. The metal slams into the crane holding it suspended, jerking my grip looser. I wrap my arms around the chain, squeezing my eyes tight. The ball gives way beneath me and suddenly I'm freefalling, leaving my stomach several feet above me. Jolting to a sudden halt just before I meet the ground and my maker, I'm fully dislodged this time and none of my flailing for the chain can save me. Hair rushes past my ears, my back slamming into a solid weight.

Arms band around me, squeezing the remaining air from my lungs. Long, sandy blond hair tickles my face and the moment my feet are lowered to the ground, a cool ring of metal is slapped around my wrist. The other end is attached to Charley, securing us together via handcuffs. Pig dives into my free arm, nuzzling into my neck. I soothe her with sweet words, but it doesn't escape my attention how the firm chest doesn't shift from my back. Three others close in, circling us like prey. I ignore them however, because it's clear who is calling the shots. Not the guy avoiding all eye contact, not the one who eases Pig from my arms and definitely not Mr. Anal in his sharp suit, despite the aggression emanating from him.

"Do I at least get to know the name of my captor?" I turn to Sandyman. He raises a brow and scoffs, as if I should instantly recognize his face. Yep, rich and conceited. Called it.

"Myles Hudson. And captor is a strong word. I'll take 'your new boyfriend' instead." He winds his arm around my back. It's my turn to scoff.

"Boyfriends are for girls who, should they get hit by a bus tomorrow, need constant reassurance they won't die alone and unloved. I have neither of those worries, because I prefer to be alone and I love my damn self." A moment passes before he grins. A wide, easy smile amongst light stubble that would melt my icy walls if those bastards weren't cemented in iron cladding. The shine of a black limo pulls up from behind, the door popped and Charley is urged inside. I, however, am not so easily pushed around.

"You're the new owners of the Thirsty Kirsty, right?" I stare into the orbs of iridescent amber drinking me in like a refreshing sex on the beach. He inclines his strong jaw. "A little overkill to get my attention, don't you think?" My head signals towards the bulldozers.

"If you'd stayed in the limo long enough to give me your phone number, it wouldn't have been necessary."

"I don't use cell phones. They're too easy to track," I half-shrug. Looking around at the parking lot turned demolition project, a bunch of the girls have huddled to watch on in horror, not a possession left to their name. Typical – I would have one of those arrogant douches with more money than sense latch on to me. Reassessing the situation, I hunt for the power I still hold and decide to utilize that. "I want your word you won't bulldoze the club. There are young women here who rely on the money and have nowhere else to go." Strong brows pinch in confusion.

"This establishment is a shithole. We'll be doing them a service by scrapping it and starting fresh," Myles nods sharply, trying to nudge me into the limo again by my waist. I restrain, not letting his confidence overpower me.

"No."

"No?" he halts in surprise, as if that word is unusual to him. Maybe he's hard of hearing.

"No." I repeat back, just in case. "You can't steamroll in and decide what is and isn't worthy of fixing. Either you agree to redecorate while the girls are still able to dance, or I'm not stepping foot in your limo. Again." By his side, Mr. Anal tries to argue that I'm already hand-cuffed with no chance of escape, until I produce my freed wrist from behind my back. I've already passed Charley the pin I kept stored in Pig's collar to work on her own inside the limo while keeping the guys busy out here. Mr. Anal's green eyes narrow, his throat bobbing to shift the tie at the base of his neck. Another steps into Myles' back, his unusual gray eyes finally finding mine beneath a sweep of black hair.

"Surely it makes more sense–" he tries but Myles cuts him off with a swish of his hand.

"It's fine, Sebby. If that's what Amethyst wants, then so be it. We will renovate the club as it stands and see these women are properly cared for." The four of us enter a standoff, a silent fight for dominance taking place. Myles breaks first, brushing down his crease-free t-shirt and clearing his throat. "Now will you accompany us to our manor?"

"Oh, a formal invitation?" I act shocked, placing a hand on my chest. All eyes drop to my nipples through the white crop top. "Apparently stubborn dogs can grow new dicks."

"That's really not–"

"Keep up, Sebby," I refer to the nickname Myles used earlier and similarly swish my hand in the air before descending into the limo. "I dance to the beat of my own drum." And ain't that the truth.

Chapter 7

Our manor is what he said. As in, the four men crammed into the limo all jointly own and live in the approaching building. Permitted entry by a set of sturdy gates, the property is contained by a stone wall well over fourteen feet high. And yes, I am already looking for escape routes for when my welcome quickly wears out.

Rolling my neck, the prickle of awareness begins to rise again. My legs have long since cramped, cross-legged on the leather seat since my duffle is in the foot space, but at least Mr. Anal had the good sense to detour via a Starbucks drive-thru. His cup labels him as Carter, but

I'm not convinced it suits him any better. At the end of the lengthy driveway, the limo stops and a shudder rolls through my shoulders.

The entire structure beams pale gray in the sunlight. Either side of an upper level balcony, huge slabs of stone create twin extensions pulled forward from the main house, creating a U shape in perfect symmetry. Large windows framed in thick, black archways match the main entrance, concealed within a fully glass front. Four columns shoulder the porch before a set of stone steps. Manicured gardens spread as far as the eye can see, but I'm busy counting the chimneys. No less than five, and my gut flips with each one. How, of all places, have I ended up in the epitome of my burning hatred. A pit of wealth, concealed hours away from the nearest amenities.

"What are we doing here?" Charley whispers for the first time since ordering a double mocha Frappuccino, twisting her head into my ear. I unhook the chocolate waves from behind Charley's ear, allowing it to drape forward like a curtain and shielding us from the rest of the cab.

"Enjoying the ride. Trust me, it'll be fun." Moving back just enough, I catch her panicked expression and give a reassuring nod. Pig agrees, licking at both of our jaws until I scratch her hind leg and she collapses onto Charley's lap.

"And when it isn't?" Charley worries her lip. Pulling it free with my thumb, I cup her cheek, searching her brown eyes for the ballsy chick who was so recently shoplifting with me.

"As much as I'm enjoying this exchange," a voice I haven't heard from comments, "can we get the fuck out already?" A mass of floppy brown hair drops over piercing blue eyes, thick arms covered in colored ink resting on his knees. Straightening, I run my tongue along my top lip, testing how long it takes for his quirked brow to drop. Too easily, that's how.

"Manners, Owen. They're our guests," Myles kicks Owen's sneaker with his own custom painted Air Jordan. Sebby remains close to Myles' side, touching him wherever possible. An interesting exchange all around.

"For now," Carter huffs beneath his breath and leans across to pop the door. Owen shoots out first, stretching his long legs and cracking his back. Not one to sit around for long, I take his lead. Owen pauses, turns and leans halfway back inside to lift Pig from Charley's lap. She yaps, nipping at his jaw but is quickly subdued by a belly rub. Fickle bitch.

"Jesus, you girls pack heavy," Myles comments, taking the duffle and exiting next. Charley's eyes snap wide with worry again, while I keep a cool exterior and slide out before she starts hyperventilating.

"Perhaps if you earned your muscles through hard work as opposed to steroids, it wouldn't prove so challenging." I tug the duffle's strap from his shoulder, bearing the weight of a million dollars in cash, jewelry and drugs. Never know when and where I might need a quick getaway, and this stash ensures I'm covering all bases.

"Steroids?!" Myles chokes, scooping me up in his arms, bag and all. "Does this feel like a steroid-hype to you?" Hoisting me higher, my bare stomach is grazed by his blond stubble, scratching my skin with all the deliciousness I will refuse myself until death. He can go full necrophilia on me, no sweat. The front doors are opened from within, permitting smooth entry into a lavish entrance as I prepare to go full-Rambo and kick his ass. Unfortunately, Myles has the good sense to lower me onto the marbled flooring so I threaten him with my fist instead. I'll get him next time.

If outside was disgustingly impressive, inside is even worse. A chandelier glimmers overhead, a full penguin-suited butler at the door. I don't even look his way, staring directly into the amber eyes that are responsible for bringing me into my worst nightmare.

"Okay, you wanted me here. Now what?" Myles runs a hand through his shoulder-length hair, suddenly unsure of himself.

"We could start with a tour?" he offers and I roll my eyes.

"Hard pass. We can start with food and cocktails. Whatever you want me for, I intend to be shitfaced for it." Myles' small smile shows he knows I'm mostly full of shit. Yes, I know exactly why he was intent on bringing me here, and I do need to be drunk in order to calm the ball of anxiety batting around my chest. He wants me. Practically starving for me, of that I have no doubt. But there's also no version of this world where I'm giving some rich boy another amenity from his never-ending wish list. In fact, withholding it from him might just give me the most amount of satisfaction I've ever felt.

With Charley at my heels, we enter a large, open kitchen at the back of the manor. Black speckled marble lines the counters and middle island breakfast bar. The same one with a dozen chrome and black leather stools, hosting a spread of platters. Canapes and all the fancy shit I wholly expected, with four girls in tiny French maid outfits working on them. The rest of the guys enter from the opposite side of the room, apparently taking a longer route.

"Myles, a word?" Carter asks in a 'this is not a request' sort of way. Green eyes narrow on me and I give Carter the middle finger. Myles chuckles, appearing far more relaxed now we're in his domain.

"Make yourself at home," he brushes a hand across my lower back and takes his leave. Yeah, right. Owen is still nuzzling Pig, drowning in her traitorous kisses while Sebby attempts to sneak a canape. One of the maids slaps his hand away.

"Not a chance Sebastian," she giggles, showing her youth. "These are for the gala." Sliding into one of the stools, I take in the help with keener eyes. I'd put the four of them around their early twenties, tall and stick thin with long flowing ponytails of each color. Blonde, honey brown, red and sleek black. None of them seem to care for me, or Charley who remains at my back, until I reach out and take a canape, pushing it between my lips.

"Holy shit," I gag around a mouthful of something overpoweringly fishy, tart and laced with sriracha. "That's disgusting." Scraping the offensive taste off my tongue, I dump the chewed mess back on the edge of the platter. "Whoever you're serving, let's hope they don't have tastebuds."

"And let's hope you don't make it past the initial interview," the redhead glares at me. I frown but it's Charley who speaks up first.

"What interview?" The girls all begin to laugh so I stand, shielding Charley behind me.

"To be one of Hudson's Elites," the blonde rolls her eyes, drawling her words. "There's always five of us. Leslie resigned to go into pageants. Carter has been trying to replace her for months, but not everyone is a perfect fit for Hudson." The four of them rub shoulders and giggle, as if part of some secret club. You know what, I don't think it was the canape that made me feel nauseous after all.

"You mean Myles?" I query, and get the reaction as if I just individually slapped each one of them.

"You can't call him by his first name," the brunette gasps. It's all so theatrical. With their tits practically on display, skirts not covering their thongs and piping bags of salmon mousse in hands, I've just about reached my limit of wealthy privilege.

"Come on Charley, I need to find a bathroom before we start hitchhiking back to the city." I'm certain I hear one of the maids mutter 'good riddance' and 'did you see what she's wearing' from another, but leave them to their snickering. Surely I'll find a barbie pink convertible

I can key on my way out. Bypassing Owen, I remove Pig from the cradle in his arms.

"I'll talk to you later," I mutter into her treacherous ear, exiting into a spacious lounge. Oh, how the other half live. Flat tv mounted on a brick wall above an electric fireplace, plush cream sofas larger than the dressing room Charley and I shared.

When each door on the lower level remains firmly locked by a keypad, we're forced to head upstairs. This is where the real fun begins – snooping around bedrooms. First, I grab Charley's hand and tug her left. No one seems to be following as we step into what I can only hope is one of the maid's rooms. Baby pink, everywhere. The rug is fluffy, the pillows are glittery. I like a pop of color as much as the next girl, but it's the unicorn theme throughout that makes my head spin. No thank you.

The next one is more my style. Dark reds and black, accents of leather and suede, so I permit myself entry and head directly for the wardrobe. The bitches were right. My Miley Cyrus moment was perfectly acceptable in the hood, but we're not on the streets of depravity anymore. Taking an outfit from the rail, I pause in front of a mirror. Not the usual kind for a bedroom, more like that of an interrogation room. Spanning the entire wall above a dresser and leather chaise. Red lights blip in each corner of the ceiling, our movements being caught on camera. Oh well.

Dropping the duffle, I place Pig on top to guard it. Charley tries to hide me from view, but I couldn't give less of a shit. Peeling the crop top off and shedding the waist high panties, I opt to leave the brown ankle boots in place. The outfit I've opted for is a form fitting dress. The material is slitted from ribs to knees, giving the right amount of cleavage and heady dose of sensuality. Not my usual style, but as I fluff out my purple hair, even I can't help but check myself out in the mirror.

"Woah, Ami, look," Charley breathes from where she's drifted across the room. Beside an armchair, a magazine has been discarded on a small table only big enough for two wine glasses. An image of Myles stares up at me, all rugged blond hair and enticing chocolate eyes.

"Oh my god, how could I not recognize him?! I know who he is," Charley quickly flips to the double page spread of Myles. Scanning the article, her eyes fly a mile a minute until she finds what she's looking for and reads aloud.

"Myles Hudson, son of billionaire Charlton Hudson, has spoken about his sex addiction for the first time. In his teenage years, the business tycoon in his own right was charged and sentenced on two counts of sexual activity without consent. Hudson spent a total of seven years frequenting rehabs, until moving to a quiet residence in the country with his three best friends. Upon speaking with our interviewer, Hudson assures he is well, coping with his compulsions in a healthy manner and no longer a danger to society."

"A danger to society?" I scoff. Sure he's eccentric, but this is the reason I avoid the media at all costs. Everyone has a story to be taken out of context, even me. Especially me. But still, with two felonies, there must be some truth to the article. Studying the image of four young boys, all gangly limbs and baggy trousers, in front of a mansion, a snort erupts from my nose that over-excites Pig.

"Dude, check out Carter with those highlighted curtains," I laugh, tossing the magazine onto the armchair. "Could these guys be any more...asshole-ish?" Clicking my tongue, I make a move towards the exit when I realize Charley isn't behind me. Looking back, my easygoing smile slips. Only Charley can access the true me underneath all the bullshit, and her expression shows I'm not going to like what I'm about to hear.

"Um, Ami? I was thinking...I might interview, or audition, or whatever this bullshit thing is," Charley looks away, fiddling with a loose hem on her t-shirt.

"You want to be a fake drone, used for chores and sex at someone else's command? What about all these years we've laughed at women who fall over themselves to please a man? Especially after your stepfather." My tone drops, a thinly veiled warning hidden within. Charley winds her arms around herself, uncertainty in her gaze. Pig whines as if I should apologize, but we've come too far, learnt and seen too much to become puppets on someone else's string now.

"It might not be so bad," Charley argues. "Look around. There are worse places to shack up, carefree." I shudder. Shack up? As in, forget about everything I've been working so hard to achieve, all the rights I still need to wrong, and Charley chooses now to go cold on me. Shaking my head, I pace in a circle and sigh.

"The cons may be an adrenaline rush for you, but they're necessary to me." Sure, it started off small. A little robbery here and there, tricking semi-rich men and women alike of their undeserved fortunes. And don't get me wrong – I did my homework. Only taking from those who deserved it. But the bolder I grew, the more daring the heists became. The more privileged my targets were. Once I saw a renowned pedophile parading around on TV, wasting money quicker than his pitiful existence should allow, I knew I had to step up and take more. More they use to fuel their bad habits. More revenge to remind them they're not untouchable. I'm doing karma's dirty work here.

"And you still won't tell me why?" Charley implores. I stop, staring into her brown eyes. We've been here before, had this argument multiple times, but my past is my burden to bear. It's the one part of myself I keep under tight lock and key, and for good reason.

"Ami, I've followed you around for the past nine years, staying wherever you chose and living whatever life you decided is best. It's my turn to make a choice, and I want to stay here a while. If I'm chosen, at least. And then I'll demand you and Pig must remain here as my sturdy companions, although Myles doesn't seem to need much convincing." She smiles and winks, forcing me to rethink my entire strategy.

"Maybe for once, we don't need to survive. We can just...be," Charley continues, oblivious to the small voice in my mind telling me to jump out of the nearest window. I sigh, lick my lips and give a hollow nod.

"If you really want to be one of those stuck-up, snobby bitches, I will support you." I force a smile and stroke the lengths of her brown curls. Charley truly is a hidden beauty. Some of us are too comfortable hiding behind a smear of muck and resentful attitude, and I hadn't considered until now that Charley may want more.

"I promised to always keep you safe. Besides, I'm sensing there's still much havoc to be caused around here," I wink, dropping back onto the mattress. Charley dives on top of me a moment later, a mess of tickling, giggling and a round of slobbery licks from Pig ensues. Hugging my two girls into me, I sigh as that ball of anxiety starts to ebb.

I've always chosen rundown shitholes to lay low in. Using their cash-in-hand policies and codes to look the other way to our advantage. Perhaps mingling with the rich for a change will work in my favor. My skin will crawl every second of it, but that's a small price to pay to finally avenge my mother's death. She was stolen from me. Robbed of life in the same way my innocence was taken from me. Someone has to pay in order for me to move on. And who knows, once Charley is an Elite and I'm fulfilled, Pig and I could hang up our vendettas for an easy life on our stolen riches.

A pretty fantasy, to be sure. I only wish I could indulge in it.

Chapter 8

"There's a process for a reason!" Carter shouts for the thirtieth time. I peer up from my book, sensing he's not going to stop until I give him the fight he's after. Dog-earring the page, I toss the paperback onto the sofa beside me.

"Fuck the process. I know what I want." Threading my fingers together and resting my elbows on my knees, I watch Carter pace around the library. Usually a place of solace, when I'm not being scolded like a child. A thirty-four-year-old, heavily muscled and tattooed child.

"Sure you do. You want to land right back in rehab, bringing more shame to your family. Hasn't your father suffered enough? You know what this month is," Carter huffs, kicking the edge of a bookshelf.

"Oh you must have read my diary, I've actually scheduled my own mental breakdown for next Tuesday," I drawl, rolling my eyes. It takes more effort than it should to keep my voice level. Irritation grates at the edge of my patience, scratching to be let in. This is probably my fault, allowing Carter to take charge of my entire life. Laziness was a key part of it - when someone is offering to handle every decision and I simply get to enjoy the easy life. Sex on demand, whenever and however I want it. No repercussions. But along the way, I've become a spoiled asshole. Exactly what Amethyst's eyes told me she thought the second she first saw me. Exactly what I've been fighting against ever since.

"I promised I would look out for you," Carter half-shouts, flying into rant mode. I heard the same lecture the day I first saw Amethyst, and he only let me pursue her if I promised just looking would be enough. Watch her dance, throw a few hundred dollars her way and retreat home with my fantasies to keep me warm at night. But I was never going to be content watching. There was never an option where she wasn't coming home with me, and it's safe to say things escalated from there.

"I'm a fully grown man Carter," I push to stand. "At some point, you're going to have to let me make my own choices."

"Make your own mistakes you mean," Carter approaches and spears my chest with his finger. "Forgive me if I don't want to see you in the back of a police car again."

"Oh well, thank fuck for Reggie Carter, the savior. Your charity knows no bounds." I smack his hand aside. Carter shoves at my shoulders, his fists clenching.

"Don't you dare start this shit with me. You were complacent until that whore put stupid notions in your head." My patience snaps. Punching Carter in the gut, he doesn't even falter in reciprocating. Taking me down with his shoulder, we hit the sofa and roll onto the floor, a mess of grunts and fists.

"You're not well, Huds. You're never going to be well, and I'm never not going to be here to keep you safe." Carter shouts, shoving my head aside. There's no real goal here, just a point to prove.

"Naturally. It's what you're being paid for anyway." I buck him from my hips and knee his ribs, rolling on top. Swinging my fist, I stop just short of his eye. No noticeable marks is the one rule I do abide by and we spar often enough to ingrain it into me. Switching direction, I throat punch him instead and shift so Carter can roll aside whilst choking.

"Sorry to break up your little bitch fit," a female voice echoes from invisible speakers. I still, gazing at the large, mirrored wall. Amethyst has found the secret room behind, and is currently using the comms system to her advantage. "But this *whore* heard a rumor about a gala? Maybe I should wait for the formal invite, but Miss Piggington will need a full pamper session. Anti-wrinkle massage, nails trimmed – the whole shebang."

"No," Carter shakes his head, his voice barely a rasp. "Not a chance." Forcing himself to sit upright, I hold out a hand to drag him to his feet. Green eyes meet mine, the stern glare within melting away at my puppy dog expression. Carter's a harsh bastard, his entire world is black and white, neatly categorized into lists, but he has a weakness. Me.

"I've never felt such an instant attraction," I whisper into Carter's ear. "And I'm not being blindsided by my dick. I genuinely want her. Her body, her quick wit and smart mouth. It's different this time."

Carter sighs, even before I've pulled back, grinning at him knowingly. At the heart of everything he does, my happiness is Carter's only goal.

"She has to adapt to how we do things around here," he sighs and I know I've got him.

"She will," I reassure him.

"She will not," a hushed whisper comes from the speakers. I chuckle, patting Carter's shoulder as I make my way to the door. A huge, metal structure, barring me from the outside world. The library is one of a few rooms, including the games room, gym and my bedroom, which have a keypad to gain entry. Only the men of this manor have keycards, but the code to the keypad next door is unknown to me. Before Carter has a chance to call Owen or Sebby, the door releases. Amethyst must have found the button within the control room.

Stepping into the hallway, she meets me there in a sleek black dress. I've seen it before, but holy hell. Not as comfortably and confidently worn as this. Slits in the fabric start at her ribs, leading all the way down her hourglass figure to the knees. The gaps are risqué, and easy to see she's not wearing any panties underneath. Tall, studded heels put her at my chin height, her violet hair ruffled into an after-sex look. My mouth has gone dry, but there's a compliment on my tongue until Carter barges past.

"How did you manage to get in there?" he growls, quickly slamming the control room door closed. As if I care to sneak in and watch back the footage of myself screwing the help on every surface imaginable. I take no satisfaction in my depravity.

"Um, easily? The code is the license plate to the limo," Amethyst purses her lips. Carter groans about needing to call the security company, storming away with his cell pressed to his ear. That leaves me alone with Amethyst for the first time. A dangerous notion indeed. Dragging her gaze over the length of me, Amethyst's purple eyes shift to the keycard lock on the library door. "So, what's with the security?" I take her hand in mine and for once, she doesn't fight me.

"Sometimes I need a safe space to...vent or escape. A sanctuary, if you like, to keep me out of trouble and away from the Elites when I'm in a certain mood. I can only leave when one of the guys buzzes me out."

"So it's a prison," Amethyst nods in understanding. I can't help but smile at the nonchalance of her tone.

"A very lavish prison," I agree. I don't expect Amethyst to understand how my life has come to this. In fact, no one really understands, not even Carter, how it feels to have your own mind constantly sabotaging you. For your body to take charge, flooding you with fuel-filled testosterone that needs expelling if you are to survive the next breath. And once you've had that taste, fulfilled that need, the next begins bubbling beneath the surface. No high is big enough, no pleasure lasts long enough.

"Come," I lead her along the hallway. "Let me give you that tour. You might be pleasantly surprised." For the next hour, Amethyst allows me to show her my home. Starting with explaining what she thought were the Elites bedrooms, are in fact sex rooms. Five in total, each decorated for whatever fantasy I wish to indulge. Dominatrix, barbie girl, doctor's office, classroom and prison cell. Each specially designed with built-in bathrooms.

The Elites actually live in a self-contained apartment block in the gardens. Carter thought they should have a safe place, off limits from sex in the same way they are banned from entering our bedrooms in the manor's west wing. The lower level is for recreation; every guy's wet dream complete with a gaming room and theater. A home to be damn proud of. Yet, each door I open, Amethyst peeks inside, hums in neither appreciation or disappointment and then we move on.

"You know, usually by now, women would be stuffing their panties in my mouth," I joke, knowing I'm coming off like a complete dick. To be honest, that is my reality and I don't know how else to act around her lingering silence. Amethyst scoffs, pausing by the French doors looking out to the pool.

"Seems like you've got everything you could possibly want," she sighs. Breathing heavily to create a fog on the glass, she draws two eyes and a slanted mouth that indicates one emotion only. Boredom. "Seriously Myles. What the fuck am I doing here?" My name on her tongue is a sin. A shudder teases my shoulders, ending in the base of my spine. Leaning my forearm on the glass, I lean into Amethyst's body. Stealing her breath, absorbing her aura. Curling a stand of violet hair around my finger, I murmur into her ear.

"This can be yours too, if you'll stay a while." Another scoff, her toughened shell harder to break than I'd originally anticipated.

"I also have everything I could possibly need. My pup, that one ride or die best friend, my sharp wit and a string of men at the ready for my *base needs*. There's nothing you can offer me." A growl rumbles from my chest at that last one. I'll make it my life mission to locate each of the men she has on standby and ensure they can never pleasure her again. It's me or nothing. Reining in the pulsing anger that would have her bent in half and my cock seethed to the hilt, I exhale a shaky breath.

"I beg to differ, Amethyst." Before she can catch me off guard with another quip, I grip her shoulders and shove her into the nearest room. A fucking broom closet no less. But it doesn't matter. The forced proximity is preferred actually.

"You're going to stay," I whisper huskily through the darkness. No more games. I'm locking her down as if my next breath depends on it. "And you're going to fucking enjoy it."

"Are you sure about that?" Amethyst challenges. Always challenging, even when her body is making no move to back away from the hard press of mine. The stubble I haven't been bothered to shave scrapes her cheek. Thoughts of her have consumed my every waking thought, only to be tortured by her in my dreams. I haven't fucked in days because nothing would compare. I want to savor her, devour her, and relish every second.

"Give me consent," I breathe, borderline begging. Through the crack of light seeping around the edge of the door, I see her interest is piqued. "I can't....do anything without consent." My knuckles trail up her arm, wrist to shoulder. I pluck at the thin strap barring me from her ample breasts. Those pert nipples I can feel scraping against my t-shirt.

"Can I be honest?" Amethyst tilts her head, her lips brushing my jaw.

"Please," I beg, stroking a finger beneath her chin. I lean in, about to close my mouth over hers as she suddenly grabs my dick through my jeans. A gasp quickly turns into a groan, my hips thrusting forward of their own accord. I've got her now.

"The longer I'm in your company," Amethyst replies amongst the darkness. "The more luxury I see," she squeezes my shaft harder. "The more I start to loathe myself." My hand gently laid against her throat freezes. She releases me with a shove, but I don't move. Can't fathom the meaning of her words. Fingers trembling, I struggle against the voice in my head.

She's so close. So ripe. I can fuck away her reservations and she'll see. I'm all she'll ever need, and no one else will compare.

"It's not a sin to have nice things," I manage to croak out. To convince myself I haven't invented this connection. Amethyst makes that non-descript humming noise again and lord help me, I almost squeeze my fingers at her throat shut. Cut off her oxygen supply and tell Carter it was a little asphyxiation play gone wrong. Two delicate hands wrap around my wrist, tugging my arm back down to my side.

"I'm not a nice thing, Myles," she says my name again. My cock jumps, throbbing to slide into her slick cunt and make her scream it. "And you will never have me."

Blinding light bursts through the haze of my reaction, several hands dragging me out of the closet when I shove her back into the wall. I struggle against their hold, my vision fading in and out to see the smirk cemented upon her pretty face. A mocking purse of her lips that sends me into a spiral of fists and strangled roars. A blow lands in my gut, giving enough leverage to wrench my arms behind my back.

"What the fuck did you do to him, Pauper?" Owen grunts from behind. The nickname he's chosen for Amethyst isn't lost on me, and my anger flares even further. "Get him in the gym!" Kicking my calves to move me along, I'm edged through the lower level of the manor to the nearest safe room and thrown inside. The metal door slams closed before I can run at it, smashing my fists until my knuckles are coated with blood. And all the while, her smirk is visible in my mind.

Amethyst thinks she's won. That, by being the first woman to reject me, she's somehow taught me a lesson. As I aggressively shed my jeans and drop onto the weight bench, adrenaline floods my veins. Exercise will give me clarity, and if not, the exertion should provide enough relief to get my head straight for our next encounter. The one where I convince Amethyst I'm not the spoiled asshole she believes me to be.

Today has not deterred me; it's only made me hungrier. A man ravenous for a taste only she can provide. The tightness in my chest thickens, stealing my breath as I drop the weighted bar onto my throat, trying to force a black out. Anything to put me out of my current misery. To speed forward to a time when she's wrapped in my arms, begging for more. Every throbbing inch. Every shared moment. She'll give her soul to connect with mine, taking more from me than I've ever been prepared to give.

Without a doubt, I already belong to Amethyst. She just doesn't know it yet.

Chapter 9

"Have you seen Pig anywhere?" I ask Charley, zipping the gown over my ass. The open back dips scandalously low, exposing the expanse of flawless skin which is begging to be tattooed.

"She's with Owen, lounging by the pool," Charley peers beyond the balcony on the other side of the large window. Despite Carter's arguments when he delivered the dress, I refused to be relocated to the Elites outbuilding. I don't mix well with gold diggers, so for everyone's safety, I'll be staying right here in the bondage sex room. It's where I'm most comfortable.

Rolling my eyes, making a mental note to have serious words with Pig, I turn to look at myself in the wide expanse of mirror covering the wall. I wonder if anyone is watching us, envisioning Carter with his cock in his hand. Dude needs a release before he busts a nut from stress.

Preferring to keep my contacts in, my deep purple eyes sparkle with an unknown emotion, my hair artistically pinned thanks to Charley. One single curl breaks free of the updo, rolling the length of my cheek to rest on my collar bone.

"Holy shit," I breathe, my cheeks pinkening through the make-up. In the front, spaghetti straps hold the slim triangles which strain against my breasts, connected by a teardrop cut out on my sternum. The glittery lace shifts from silver to the faintest blue at my hips, before the lengthy skirt with a high slit ombres into the deepest navy. Paired with gloriously sparkling heels, I stand six inches taller and cinched in all the right places.

"Yeah, you look amazing," Charley joins my side in a classic black gown. I purse my lips.

"No, not that. Holy shit, I'm my own worst nightmare." My hand subconsciously moves to stroke the inked sleeve of large flowers on the other arm. Between the clutches of branches, lilies and roses break free to bloom. My mother's favorite.

"Can I make an observation?" Charley tries to give me a set of elbow-length navy gloves. I bat them away. "You have no idea what you want out of life."

"Duh," I scoff. "I'm twenty-nine years old and have never had so much as the same man in my bed twice. The closest relative I have is 55 pounds of blubber and saliva, and currently betraying me with that prick out by the pool." Charley's eyes narrow on mine in the reflection as I wave my hand in the air and stride towards the bed. "Don't even get me started on you, selling out for an easy life. There's nothing easy about retribution."

"For one night," Charley pinches the bridge of her nose, "can you just...let it go? Whatever it is. Set it free and allow yourself to enjoy something real." A knock sounds at the door, saving me from answering. Instead, I fight against the urge to chew on my painted bottom lip, taking to picking at my nails instead. It must seem so simple to an outsider. That I should get over my past, ignoring my night terrors and move on. But Charley doesn't know what it's like to be on the receiving end of greed, and with my protection, she never will.

Leaving the door wide open, Charley steps aside for a suited Sebby and the smooth roll of an orchestra somewhere within the building to travel into the room. The jet-black sweep of his hair has been gelled back from his face, fully revealing the pewter grey eyes currently set on me.

"Myles requested you wear this." Opening a velvet box, an exquisite necklace lays upon a plum-colored cushion. Necklace may be an understatement, for the diamond-studded neck piece resembles more of a collar. Crystals band around the rim in a solid line, wrapping around the back to break into two tendrils. The first would curve my nape to stop at my collar bone while the other would dip into my cleavage. Charley excuses herself to the bathroom, grumbling that she doesn't want to witness me being an ungrateful whore. Blinking a few times to get the sheen of glinting diamond from my eyes, I plaster on an easy smile to approach Sebby.

"How does Myles know I won't steal it?" I ask, stroking the heart-shaped jewel hanging at the lowest point.

"I don't think he really cares. Said something about shining like the jewel you are," Sebby's cheeks flame as he ducks his head. There's a clench to his jaw, producing the feather of a tick. Accepting the necklace before he bites through his own cheek and spoils his crisp white shirt, he moves to leave until I clear my throat. Sebby begrudgingly fixes the collar around my neck, his fingers lingering against my skin.

"Don't hurt him," Sebby's breath fans my back. "He suffers enough. Forcing himself to crave the Elites, just to keep the peace. They're Carter's idea of perfect, not his." A hint of desperation and longing twinges Sebby's tone. As I turn, I slink my arm through the crook of his.

"It isn't my intention to do anything with Myles, especially being craved by him." Sebby visibly relaxes, his chest puffing out in a crisp, white shirt. Despite being the shortest of the guys, he still rivals my height in heels. His suit fits snuggly, tailored to sculpt his muscled body. Black tie knotted high into his collar, I'm briefly curious about the hint of ink pushing against the cotton on his arms.

Charley returns from the bathroom, having raided the duffle bag we've hidden in the hollow compartment beneath a bath panel and donned her own full set of diamonds. Clusters of gems hang from her ears on thin chains; her neck, wrist and fingers all shining like a beacon of wealth. Firmly nodding her head, I gesture for Sebby to lead us to the party, keeping my arm in his the entire way.

Stepping off the bottom stairs, onto the lower level of the manor, streams of guests enter through the double doors. A butler either side offers champagne flutes from silver trays. I divert, tugging Sebby along to grab a glass for Charley and then myself. She smiles, although I note the spike of jealousy in her rigid posture. Not for the handsome man on my arm, because anyone with eyes can see he's no threat, but for the fact I always seem to flourish without trying. No matter how many manifestation journals or podcasts she endures, I keep telling her – it's all in the confidence.

Following the crowd along a hallway I've only briefly explored with Myles hovering over my shoulder, we glide slowly towards the open ballroom entrance. I'm yet to see the main man since his outburst earlier this afternoon. Only to myself, I'll admit – I was impressed.

After what I'd read in the magazine about his convictions, I had to test Myles' restraint myself. Set a baseline for how far I could push him before he caved. He was able to take my taunting, even through a haze of sexual frustration. Guilty of previous crimes or not, he's doing well to control his urges now, and that puts a damper on my fun. Had I been in the company of a wealthy rapist, I would have taken pleasure in pulling out my dagger for another play. Instead, I'll have to settle for toying with his psyche.

The ballroom displayed before us is nothing short of castle worthy. Crystal chandeliers spiral downward from an arching sky-blue ceiling, illuminating the glimmering golden walls and a floor so polished, it should come with a 'slippery surface' sign. A full orchestra claims the gold steps on the far left behind red ropes, playing a delightful mix of pop songs in the gentle harmony of woodwind and brass. Guests are drawn towards the huge windows, displaying the expansive estate beneath an ombre sunset.

"I have a question," I spin on Sebby, downing the champagne and handing him the empty glass. "Does Myles know you're in love with him?" His arm tenses in mine, his whole body stiffening as I'm clicking my tongue around my mouth. The bubbles continue to fizzle, a crisp tingle fresh in my throat.

"What?! That's ridiculous," Sebby rushes out in one breath. Charley and I share a knowing look.

"So, the sexual tension between the two of you-" Sebby yanks me away from those piling through the entrance, his eyes darkening with malice.

"You have no idea what you're saying," he growls this time, caging me into an unnecessary velvet curtain which lines the wide doorway. I laugh, easing him back a step.

"Consider the topic dropped." Sebby watches me clearly, hunting for...something. Ridicule, perhaps? Easing the deep frown from his brows with my thumb, I brush a loose tendril of his hair into place and slide my arm back into his. I'm many things, but I only blackmail those who have wronged me. Not some guy who's in love with his best friend and is apparently still ashamed about it.

The outside of the dance floor is framed by rounded tables, eight chairs to each, dressed in white covers with gold sashes. Cutlery gleams, crystal flutes sparkle and the napkins resemble swans in the center of giant dinner plates. I only now notice the table plan at the top of the room, directs guests toward name plates dotting around abundant lily centerpieces.

A flash of brown hair announces Owen's arrival. Unlike the effort Sebby has made, Owen had no such inclination. Forgoing a tie, leaving the top button popped and rolling the shirt sleeves up to the elbow, he pulls off the classic badboy look with an air of ease. Tattoos travel from his jawline to collar bone, blending into the colorful artwork covering his shoulders and arms.

"Doesn't she look beautiful?" Owen thrusts Miss Piggy into my face. Her tongue hangs lazily from the wide smile on her wrinkled face. An oversized pink bow has been fixed between her ears, matching the pink dress with a tutu she has adorned. Owen couldn't look happier with himself, roughing up Pig's flank and placing kisses to her neck.

"Owen loves dogs," Sebby drawls.

"Like you love-" I begin, until he reaches behind and punches me in the kidney. A chuckle is drawn from my lips but I remain at his side, having far too much fun to distance myself just yet. Sebby may leak wealth like the others, but his absence of arrogance makes him my best bet for company around here. I'm going to need someone to talk to when Charley joins the Elite's, because you can bet your ass, whatever my girl wants – she gets. I'll see to that personally.

The current song comes to a gentle end as the lights brighten enough to make me squint. In the doorway, like a pair of suited soldiers entering a battlefield, Carter and Myles appear. No announcement required. The crowd beams fake smiles, a wave of applause echoing around the ballroom.

Carter pushes his hands into the pockets of his fine slacks, charcoal gray like the rest of the three-piece designer suit, quietly confident. Striking green eyes scan his adoring fans, the sharpness of his solid jaw at odds with the slackness of his slanted lips. I lose myself in the thought of what Carter's jaw is capable of, as Myles instantly seeks me out.

All-encompassing amber eyes spearing the space between us, un-caring of anyone else present. His golden waves have been tamed into a ponytail at his nape. Thick fingers twitch at his side, toying with the veins disappearing into his cuff. In a matching suit to his comrade, the sky-blue tie pushed high into his collar fails to hide the evidence of bruising lingering underneath. Upon receiving my attention, Myles' face relaxes into a smirk. Even as his gaze drops to the connection between mine and Sebby's arms, who I refuse to let retract, and his brow jerks in surprise, that smile doesn't falter. As practiced as my own mask, I see.

"Please, find your seats. Dinner shall be served shortly." The or-chestra begins to play again, softer this time as Carter spreads his arm in a wide arc and directs his guests to the seating plan. I move against the flock, allowing Charley, Pig and Owen to follow in the pathway I create, and head directly for the top table. One which is set apart from the rest with extra care being taken to ensure each large bow on the chairs are perfectly symmetrical. Instead of champagne flutes, a range of wine, whiskey and beer glasses surround the lilies, all in full bloom. The Elites took extra care of this table for a reason, which means it's exactly where I'm supposed to be.

Carter meets me there, a glare contorting his handsome face. Shuffling aside, I pick up the name card between Sebby and Owen's, admiring the hand drawn calligraphy. *Joy.* A wide flourish on the 'y' leaves enough room for a heart, and I stuff it into the central vase.

"Excuse me," a woman rushes up behind. I barely recognised her from the kitchen earlier, the redhead having swapped her maids outfit for an elegant green gown which allows her hair to pop. Vibrant red curls sit on her delicate shoulders, her band of bitches close behind. The Elite's eye twitches as she forces a sweet smile. Her tone betrays her though, laced with irritation. "Can you please put the card back where it was?" A frown pulls at my lips.

"Why? You spelt my name wrong." Pulling out the chair, I sit and tweak the cutlery. Carter's growl of annoyance is drowned out by Owen's laughter, as he grabs a heightened cushion from the abandoned orchestra area and uses it to prop Pig up on my neighboring chair. He sits on her other side, his hand never leaving her flank as he finds her special spot. Sebby takes the seat on my right, Charley joining next, while all of us keep our backs to the Elites quietly arguing with Carter.

"Just...keep the fucking peace, okay? Find somewhere else to sit," he mutters. The heat of his anger licks my exposed back like a caress, this game we've begun to play becoming quickly addictive.

"There is nowhere else," another Elite whines. I can practically taste Carter's fury, and I savor the victory dancing across my tongue.

"Then eat in the kitchen. Just stop causing a scene," he growls low. Another hushed round of arguing is quickly cut short and the Cling Quartet storm away on clicking heels.

"Wait," Myles barks. Many others nearby still, as well as the hopeful Elites. The redhead catches my eye, half smirking and snarling as she turns back to her master. Myles reaches over me, his warmth lingering long enough for his cologne to invade my senses, and removes the large vase from the table. "Take this." Shoving the flowers into Joy's hands with enough force for the water to slosh over the rim and mar her gown, Myles strides to sit opposite me. Directly in my uninterrupted eyeline, where I'm sure he'll place himself for the rest of the night.

At some point during our staring contest, drinks are supplied and the napkin swan is flicked free to be spread across my lap. Myles pushes his tongue into his cheek, bristling for every second the unimportant figure lingers over me. Carter paces a while longer, making small talk, ensuring the guests are happily seated before he finally takes his.

Pulling the lapels of his jacket sharply, he wears his suit like amour. As a reminder to all nearby that he is the most important person in the room. I mimic Pig's wide smile, sharing the same thought. The most important person in the room means the biggest target in our books. Roughing up Pig's neck, she grunts in response, her tongue hanging out to drip all over the tablecloth.

"Mutts are supposed to eat on the floor," Carter grumbles and I know he's not only speaking of Pig. Opening my mouth with a smartass response, Sebby squeezes my knee and leans into my ear.

"Tonight is important." His grey eyes hold a plea and I'm inclined to believe him. Strange, how quickly I have warmed to Sebby when many struggle to breach my barriers. Men especially, but Sebby has no problem confusing my eyes with my tits.

"AKA, don't fuck it up. Got it," I whisper back. "I can still screw with Carter though, right?" Sebby only smirks, a rarity for his wounded-puppy vibe and I take that as a solid yes. Removing his hand from my knee, he sits back and I'm left with the silent demand in Myles' expression. Jealousy radiates across the space between us as waiters appear with starters. Serving the top table first, each waiter stands to our right until a superior signals for them to lower the plates in perfect unison.

"Oh, how the other half live," I breathe, looking at the plate before me. Usually, the average consumer may expect only one type of seafood, but it would seem the Hudson crew go hard. Strips of salmon in the shape of a rose, pan-seared scallops, a crab claw and some kind of terrine. All artfully presented with a swirl of foam and sprinkling of herbs and caviar.

To think, I could have had a life like this had I made different choices, makes me more nauseous than the scent of seafood. For years, I've layed awake at night, picturing such a life in my mind. Only to come to the conclusion I would have been bored to the point of suicide. Nothing beats the rush of a con, knowing you have nothing to lose and everything to gain. The deception of slipping from character to character, becoming the epitome of your own fantasy overnight. And when that fantasy no longer serves, you move on. Search for the next high, a bigger fix.

"Ami," Charley whispers. I look up to see everyone is watching me, waiting. For what – I can only imagine is my refusal. Instead, I spear a scallop with one of the many forks provided while Myles rolls my nickname around on his tongue.

"So," I break the tension when those stares become too probing. "What's the special occasion?" Myles tips back a full glass of whiskey.

"On the surface, we hold a yearly gala to celebrate and raise funds for the rehabilitation program which saved me from myself. While most guests are A-list celebrities and investors, there are also therapists, nurses, admin staff from the recovery center I attended. Even a few other reformed patients I grew close to during my treatment."

I watch Myles closely, picking up on small details others may overlook. How his lip involuntary curls as he said *'treatment'*. How the fullness of his chest, supposed to resemble pride, is withholding a deflated sigh. Myles doesn't feel comfortable in these surroundings, with these people, because he doesn't believe he needed rehabilitating.

"And under the surface?" I ask, not missing how he gave me the rehearsed response. Clenching his jaw, Myles looks to Owen, passing a silent message to fill me in on whatever he doesn't want to admit.

"Table four are our business associates," Owen lowers his voice, leaning over Pig. "They're invited under the guise of supporting Myles' journey, but really, they are watching for a hint of a relapse. Any indication he is a flight risk which could result in damaging their company's reputation further down the line." I peer back, and true to Owen's word, eyes continually flick our way every few seconds. I give a small wave, causing the suited men and uptight women to swivel in their seats like anemones shrinking back into themselves. I scoff.

"What do they think is going to happen over dinner? That Myles will drag me over the table by my hair and fuck me senseless while you all hold me down?" A concoction of groans ignite around our table, Myles' eyes scrunching closed and his teeth sinking into his fist.

"Don't tease him like that," Carter spits. His green eyes burn with hatred, like I'm the very essence of what he's been protecting Myles from. Unfortunately for all, Myles has decided I'm exactly what he wants. I roll my eyes, filling my mouth with the largest scallop I've ever seen and pointing my fork in Carter's direction.

"You can't protect him from everything, especially *words*. Not when your pupils have dilated with lust as much as anyone else." A stale silence falls amongst the curious exchange of looks, except for Carter's. His stare is cemented on me while I continue to eat, that same tick beating in his jaw. He should really get that checked out, although I'm certain it has a direct link to the stick up his ass.

The remainder of the starters are devoured, mostly to keep mouths busy. Mine in particular is salivating for every salty, delicious bite and I hate myself for it. I'm not a classy bitch. I'll have to sneak away soon to order and binge on many greasy hamburgers with Pig to atone for my sins.

The waiters clear our plates, the orchestra carrying the evening seamlessly from one melody into the next. Although their instruments are kept at a gentle volume, it's enough cover for Carter to mutter into Myles' ear without me being able to eavesdrop. The clever twist of his head also means I can't lipread, so I turn my attention elsewhere. To making mischief, more or less.

"Swap seats with me," I mouth to Charley. She passes the quickest glance to Myles one seat over, purposely distanced, before standing. We cross at Sebby's back where Charley warns me to '*go easy on him*'. I smile sweetly, planning to do no such thing. Myles may be many things, but he doesn't believe a sex addict is one of them and I'm inclined to believe him. Catching snakes in the grass is my specialty, and Myles' resentment for his past may be the only thing we have in common.

The moment I lower into Charley's seat, Myles' attention swings to me. Attentive amber eyes, which could no doubt turn glacial if required, drink in my face. I give him a small smile, sitting back in the chair. Toying with the heart pendant at the top of my cleavage, he falls directly into my fickle trap, not even realizing the mains have been served. I barely look at the food myself, spotting a full-length carrot out the corner of my eye. Picking it up between thumb and forefinger, I slowly push the vegetable sideways into my mouth. It nudges against my inner cheek before I bite down hard with a wink. Myles shudders.

"You're embarrassing yourself," Carter sits forward, glaring daggers at me once more. I shrug one shoulder, laughing if Carter thinks this is anything. I'm fully in the mood to climb onto this table and really give him something to tense his jawline over. "Myles does not care for your display. He knows where and when it's appropriate to indulge himself."

"Does he sit and play dead too?" I muse. Sebby kicks me under the table. I kick him right back, keeping Carter in my eyeline. "I'm just saying, I thought you were his friend, not his owner. And since mutts are supposed to eat on the floor, perhaps you should tell Myles to slide on beneath this table and hunt for some dessert." Carter's hand slams down on Myles' forearm before he can act on the pained groan escaping his lips. And all the while, that same hint of lustful dominance swirls within Carter's green eyes. He wants to punish me, tame me, and I'm in half the mind to let him try.

"Dance with me," Sebby suddenly announces, pushing to his feet. When I don't immediately react, he wipes his mouth on the napkin and throws it onto my full plate, before dragging me up by the arm. We swirl into the center of an empty dancefloor, earning everyone's attention as Sebby whistles to the orchestra. Their soft tempo increases as one, blocking out the hushed whispers filtering around us.

"You don't know when to quit, do you?" Sebby murmurs, jerking me into his personal space. "For what I imagine is the first time, let me damn well lead."

Slipping a hand into mine and placing the other on the small of my bare back, Sebby whisks me into a waltz. Our surroundings blur, a self-induced breeze fanning out my skirt. The singular curl framing my face is batted around, constantly moving between our fixed eye contact. I keep pace with Sebby, much to his surprise. Each sweeping movement of his dress shoe is pre-empted by the shift of my heel. I've spent my entire adult life learning to adapt to any environment, especially those which will grant me access to my enemies.

"Answer me one last question and I will be on my best behavior for the rest of the evening," I mutter into Sebby's ear. He breaks away to spin me, his grey eyes holding disbelief as I resume my place pressed against his front. "Pinky promise." Sebby can't fight his smirk as I curl my little finger around his, leading me through the fluid footsteps of our dance.

"Ask it quickly. The song is almost over," he grunts on a nod. My skirt swishes about my legs, the sweet symphony cascading over my exposed skin. Every muscle in my body works to keep in time with Sebby, and every eye in the room is carefully watching each one.

"Why was Myles in rehab for sex addiction, if he clearly doesn't have it?"

Chapter 10

Teasing a small pebble between my fingers and thumb, I skim it across the water of a huge concrete fountain. The type you'd see in a town square, where those desperate for divine intervention might toss coins and hope gods exist. Above the shimmering moon's reflection, a woman stands twelve feet tall, her naked body sculpted from the marble waves consuming her. She struggles against their lasting grip, one lone hand stretching towards an endless and forgiving sky.

Dear fuckery, I've entered a stage of poetic fallacy. Delving this deep beneath the Amethyst persona is dangerous, and if I let emotion impact my judgment, we're all screwed. Yet, I can't stop replaying Sebby's words over and over in my mind. We'd skipped out after our dance, lingering near the balcony as I was given a brief rundown of Myles' past. My feet began moving afterwards, seemingly bringing me way out into the gardens, needing some space from the gala for a while. My knack for being perceptive told me Myles was innocent, and now I know the truth.

"We were in our second year of boarding school, young and stupid. Myles was a god among men, his family being one of the founders meaning he could do no wrong. When you're freely given attention like that, and classmates are throwing themselves at your feet, no one would have done any different. Our house parties were just as renowned as Myles' high sex drive, putting a target on his back.

But with popularity comes those seeking to steal it. A group of gold-diggers created a scheme to let him fuck them, be as rough as he likes and leave as many bruises as possible. In the morning, they all cried rape. Provided each other's alibi's, corroborated stories. To keep business intact, Myles' dad paid out huge settlements and committed Myles to a rehabilitation program. It seemed like the only way at the time, and Carter vowed that day to keep Myles safe at all costs."

I shudder, and not because of the chill creeping along my spine. In contrast, my blood boils, untamed fury leaking from my heavy breaths. The problem? Knowing Myles is as much a victim of wealth as I am puts a real dampener on my distaste for him. Where I was scorned for my poverty, and treated as though I was expendable to the families who killed my mother, Myles was trapped. Targeted for his money and forced into the staged life he leads. His every movement is under a microscope and all decisions are approved by Carter.

Picking up another pebble from the graveled pathway at my feet, my arm is half-raised when a rustle sounds in a nearby bush. Too big to be an animal, too careless to ignore. A shadow side steps out of sight too late, without the need to show themselves in the first place. Someone wants my attention. I can only imagine how long Myles has forced himself to hold off, and now he wants my attention. Alone and as seemingly vulnerable as I am, it was only a matter of time.

"I'm not currently in the mood for games," I sigh. Either side of the four pathways leading away from the fountain, neatly trimmed hedges stand tall. Every few yards, an archway is formed from the foliage, speared with small white flowers. The full moon casts an ethereal glow over the garden and woodlands beyond, the elevated manor glimmering in the distance. Music from the orchestra can just be heard if I strain my ears, between the hollers and splashes of those dive-bombing into the pool atop hundreds of stone steps. There's always someone who can't resist free alcohol and the call of a nightly swim.

More rustling. A soft 'pssst.'

"Seriously, get back to your party." I roll my eyes. "There's loads of other guests who'd prefer your company." Again, the shadow behind the hedge remains silent and somewhat hidden. Regardless of the revelations I've had about Myles, he's an idiot to think I'd be caught dead chasing him around the gardens. I'm not one of his groupies.

Instead, I spin my skirt and head back the way I came. Gravel crunches beneath my heels, all of my weight leaning on the balls of my feet. The path is long and trailed by a row of white roses on either side. At the far end, a pair of marble statues frame the stone steps surrendering to the shadows. One man and one woman, both captured by unyielding branches which coil around the bottom halves of their bodies. I'm starting to notice a theme here.

The diamonds on my neck weigh heavily, my breasts pushing against the gown with each exasperated rise and fall of my chest. I shouldn't have left Charley and Pig alone with those vultures.

Shouldn't have let my awareness drift so far, Myles was able to get this close.

For each step I take, a rustle creeps along the bush at my left. Dude is relentless. Swooping mid-step, I yank a metal spoke from between the roses, spotting a break in the hedge coming up. Another talent I forced myself to learn – fencing. Anything that would put me at an advantage should I find myself followed by a six-foot-plus brute who has issues hearing the word 'no'.

I swing around the hedge, the metal bar hidden behind my back. Raising a hand, I stop the shadow from progressing closer, pushing against his chest. A dress shoe slides backwards through the grass, a slender frame fighting against the force of my palm. Cheap cigarette coils through the air, setting in my nose.

"You're not Myles," I suddenly stand taller. Using the extra height of the heels to make myself seem more imposing, but the stale croak of laughter around his cigarette doesn't seem to get the hint.

"I can be whoever you want me to be." A hand brushes my cheek, fingers toying with the singular curl framing my face. I remain still, frozen in place. Through my hand, his heart picks up a beat, the excitement of having me so near thrumming through his entire being. He sees my lack of retreat as acceptance. All the while, I'm hunting for weak spots.

"Bold move of Myles' bloodhound, letting hookers attend his charity gala. Especially considering the guests." His hand drops to the diamonds at my neck, casting speckles of light across his face. With the moonlight spearing the top of the hedge, casting us in mostly darkness, I strain to pick up on my stalker's finer details.

Scruffy hair appears around his silhouette, his suit crumpled as if it's been in a protective bag for too long. Hired, more than likely. The most telling trait is how bunched his shoulders are, uncomfortable with his attire. Curving his spine, his head sunken into the collar suggests he's particularly used to curling up in a small, padded cell.

"You haven't completed the rehabilitation program," I state. The cherry at the end of his cigarette flares, illuminating the tick in his jaw and confirming my suspicions. Gliding my leg forward, my lace skirt separates at the leg split. Rough polyester from his slacks scrape my skin as I nestle myself between his thighs.

"Let me guess – day pass? Perhaps assigned to the care assistant you've ditched." My ankle knocks his, noting the bulky presence of a police tag. "Actually, make that a parole officer." A dry huff shoots from his nose, plumes of smoke billowing around my face.

"I'm getting the impression that's even more of a turn-on. Whores always love a bad boy." A part of me is fairly certain he meant that as a compliment to us both, yet here I am, calculating the ways to escape subtly. Running and screaming never work out, more energy used on fear than regulating key emotions. Power, cunning. I could keep him busy until his parole officer comes looking or lure him back to the house under the pretense of sex. Although, neither of those options are viable when he flicks his hand out of his pocket, the glint of a needle catching the light. "And here I was thinking I'd have to use this."

Fuck. That.

The spike clutched behind my back is whipped out before he even senses me move. Bringing the heavy weight down on his wrist, I throw it upwards to catch his chin. Not as hard as I'd like, but enough to shock him. Shoving him away, I roll the shortened pole around my hand, stepping back into the break between the hedges. Here he can see me in the full light of the moon. Here he will recognize a woman who doesn't flee, calling for a tough man to save her. I'm my own hero.

Scruff dives for me, his arms wide and careless. I twist out of reach, slamming the pole down on his back as he withdraws. The next time he strikes, he's prepared for my swing. Mimicking my sidestep, his shoulder rams into my middle, quickly succeeded by a punch to the gut. I grunt, elbowing the back of his head. Tugging on my middle, Scruff isn't prepared for the strength of my willpower, my legs refusing to buckle. The dress doesn't have such an inclination, shimmying downwards. Once past my breasts, revealing the nude bra cups concealing my nipples, I give a quick twist to free myself of the dress. Scruff tumbles to my feet as I step free, in only my heels, underwear and the diamond necklace.

"Stay down, asshole," I warn. He's up on his feet within seconds, all macho pride puffing out his chest as he raises his fists. Okay so we're doing this. Rolling the metal spoke, I widen my stance. He lunges first, jabbing towards my face. He's easy enough to dodge, his movements spurred on by bitter fury whereas I'm more skilled in finesse. Spinning this way and that, I enter into my second dance of the evening, landing blows between his sluggish attempts to tackle me. The expensive champagne will do that to someone who has been sober for a long time.

Grabbing his hair, a quick thrust drives his face down towards my knee, his nose crunching on impact. On a strangled roar, he spits a wad of blood across my bare stomach. Raw anger ripples through his hidden muscle, radiating from him in thick waves. I'm chuckling as his fist hits my ribs with surprising force, knocking the air from my lungs. In a moment of surprise, his hand closes around my throat.

"I'm going to have so much fun breaking you," his rancid breath coats my face. "And you're going to beg for more." The hand at my throat twitches, my vision becoming clouded. Through his grip and the tendrils of air my lungs will accept, my confidence takes a temporary sabbatical.

"I can already feel you submitting," Scruff huffs a laugh. Swallowing thickly, my head slowly leans forward until our foreheads are touching. The eyes peering up at mine are dark and creasing in the corners. This convict, and no doubt rapist, sought me out. Intended to drug me with fuck knows what. And if it wasn't me – he came to this gala with the intention to attack someone. Anyone. The Elites? Charley? My heart stutters at the thought of her coming to harm.

"In your dreams," I breathe, tightening my grip on the metal pole before ramming it up between us. Scruff gasps, his hand tightening before he goes slack, stumbling a step into me. I keep hold of the spoke, jamming it harder into his sternum. Heat pools around my hand, his weight lowering onto my arm. I had no idea if the pointed end was facing the right way, but if this was the flip of the coin, I've come up heads. My hand slips on the cool metal but with a sharp jerk, I manage to tug it free. Bracing my arms beneath his, I drag Scruff into the shadows once more, dropping him by the hedge.

"I'd like to see a hooker do that," I mutter. I should be frightened of the steely calmness washing over me. I should be running towards the gala, hunting for the nearest shrink. But I can't bring myself to move, or care. The sight of his limp body, the knowledge one more asshole has been removed from the world, does nothing but relieve a morsel of the guilt I'll never fully shake. For all those I wasn't able to save, this has to be their retribution. It's the best I can do.

"Amethyst?" a voice calls out from the other side of the hedge. "You out here?" I will myself to move, but I don't. Or rather, can't. Knees locked, my arms slouch lower to the ground and just as I drop the spoke, Sebby and Myles run through the partition. They stop, assessing what little they can see until Carter pushes through the center.

"What the fuck are you doing-" he grumbles, switching on a flashlight and coming to a swift halt. The brightness is blinding, yet my finger only manages a twitch as I attempt to cover my eyes. Beyond the light, I can't see anything. Crimson red catches my peripheral vision, my chest coated in blood. The night air prickles at my skin but I can't bring myself to feel cold.

"Did you..." I struggle to hold onto the thought. "Did you set this up...Carter...you Cockmunch?" My head lolls to the side, knocking into something between my neck and shoulder. I hadn't noticed the sharp sting before, but now, it's as if all of my nerve endings rush to that exact spot. Bitter cold invades my veins, stealing the use of my left side, flooding my system with a harsh chill. The world topples before I do, a pair of arms catching me before I hit the floor.

"Is tha you, Jack Ffffrost?" I slur. An unyielding heartbeat beats against my ear, the chest concealing it firm and smooth. In the glint of the moon, icy blue eyes delve through mine. Into my psyche, prying through every character I've layered onto myself to shield the fragile girl underneath it all. Intrusive, yet curious. Intense. My mind wonders, a soppy smile playing about my lips.

Damn, Jack Frost had one hell of a glow up, is all I can think as everything goes black.

Chapter 11

"Give her to Sebby," Carter orders quietly. I'm as aware as he is, there's a parole officer back in the manor hunting for his charge. I felt the same trepidation, after Charley couldn't find Ami in any of the bathrooms.

Plucking the syringe from her neck, Owen appears to take it from me, deftly unhooking the blood-stained diamond collar in one, smooth move. Reaching for the discarded ballgown, he then places both items and bloodied spoke inside, wrapping the lace into a bundle. The whole lot, body included, will be buried within the grounds tonight, until we're able to burn it all tomorrow. Just like the ease which Amethyst displayed lingering near a dead body, this isn't our first rodeo either.

"Myles. Pass her over to Sebby," Carter growls again. Sebby takes a tentative step forward, but we both know he won't be fighting me for her. Not when my arms tighten protectively, her gangly frame appearing so small in my hold. Amethyst would probably attempt to shaft me too for holding her like this, but nothing will force me to let her go. Making a move to leave, heading west towards a hidden entrance to the manor, Carter steps into my way.

"You can't be trusted."

"I may have done many things Carter, but I've never taken someone without their consent and I stand by that." My nostrils flare, daring him to argue. We both know I'm innocent of my accused crimes, and to suggest otherwise now would destroy whatever thread of self-esteem I have left. Sighing, Carter allows me to pass. I make sure to shoulder barge him anyway.

"Wait," Sebby whisper-shouts. My fists tighten, careful not to harm Amethyst, until Sebby helps me out of my jacket without needing to put her down. Placing the jacket over her almost naked body, I give him a nod of thanks. Crossing the grass on impatient strides, I near a darkened corner at the base of the hill. I know the blind spots, accustomed to needing a breather from the tightly structured life I must lead. Above, idle chatter floats from overhanging balconies. Carter's voice penetrates the air, announcing it's time for the auction. I huff. Typically, he's chosen not to get his hands dirty.

Following the steady incline of a path worn into the grassy bank, I round the manor, ducking back as headlights flash. Teens, dripping wet with pool water, are being bundled into a limo by security, the door slammed closed on their protests. Daughters of a main investor who sneak champagne when no one is looking. The same shit happens every year.

Holding back until the limo has veered through the driveway and disappeared through the gates, a soft click sounds above my head. Peering at the window, Carter regards me with the usual clench to his jaw. The one that says I'm disappointing him again, and I long since stopped caring.

His outline retreats, leaving me to push the window open and navigate climbing through whilst supporting Amethyst all by myself. I'm careful, taking more time than I should to brush the loosened tendrils of her hair back from her face. She'd never let me get this close whilst conscious. My hand cups her cheek, my thumb stroking a path at the corner of her mouth. So serene. So unaware of the emotion she stirs within. Blood splatter flecks her chest above the cover of my suit jacket, leaving me bereft with a mixture of anger and pride. I wholly believe I'd forgotten how to feel anything before she came along, a lifeless drone following orders.

Movement sounds beyond the door of the study. I stagger back into reality, dipping behind the door which Carter left slightly ajar. Bastard. Whoever it is moves on, and as I peer across the entrance lobby, there's no one in sight. Waiting another moment to make sure, I bundle Amethyst closer to my chest and make a run for it. Across the shining marble, up the staircase. Briefly pausing at the top of the stairs, I look left towards the sex rooms. Amethyst has claimed the bondage room as her own, but that's not the direction my feet travel in. Turning right, I make a beeline for my room at the end of the hall, but I don't make it there fast enough.

The handle to Owen's bedroom twists, his door beginning to open from the inside. Diving into the closest room available, I spin into the en-suite bathroom just as the light from the hallway fills Sebby's room. I don't know what caused me to hide, but I put it down to instinct. There's no way Owen could be back already, unless he needed something. Gloves, perhaps? Shaking my head to myself, I begin to move when a silhouette catches my eye.

Watching through the crack of the door, a woman steps inside. Her heels move silently, the outline of her dress clinging to her tall and slender frame. I strain to watch as she steps out of view, curiosity getting the better of me. It's an Elite. It has to be. No one else would manage to bypass the security guards, or know where to find our bedrooms. The manor is a maze to those who aren't familiar with it.

Ahh fuck, I think to myself. She's probably looking for me. It's not uncommon for me to ditch these parties and entertain myself by any other means possible. Anything to avoid being watched for when I inevitably slip up, and leave a mess Carter has to fix. He's ensured it's how our dynamic works best. The Elite moves further into the room, lingering. She must have seen me. I press my forehead against the tile, careful to not squash Amethyst. Not that it matters now – I'm screwed either way.

Whether the Elite signed an NDA or not, finding me hidden in the dark with the bloodied, unconscious body of a woman who turned me down mere hours ago would be too much of a headline to miss out on. I already know I wouldn't be able to buy her out, because the Elites aren't just here for the money or the sex. It's the fame. The association of being one of my top five, like Hugh Hefner's bunnies.

Becoming one of my Elites, after Carter declared I have the need for them, gains immediate spotlight. Entry to the classiest parties, the most exclusive clubs. The more I can be seen with consenting females, the more I'm able to prove I deserve to run my father's company. That I'm not the type of leering asshole who stalks women down in the gardens and drugs them. I hate being associated with such men. If I can even call him that. Yet the longer the Elite remains stationed outside the door, the more I can feel the life I've done everything to protect slipping through my fingers.

Somewhere through my barrage of bitterness, drawers open, papers ruffle. The hangers in the wardrobe scrape as they're shoved from side to side. A frown claims my features, my brows pinching. Using the darkness to my advantage, I step forward to peer around the door just as Amethyst murmurs in my arms. Freezing on the spot, I try to still her gentle squirming, a soft moan leaking from her lips. My heart judders, thoughts jumbling inside my mind. Without a better option, I do the one thing I swore to Carter I wouldn't. My mouth closes over Amethyst's, silencing her with a stolen kiss. The presence in Sebby's room is sent into a panic, a flurry of movement rushing towards the bathroom.

Fucked. We're so fucked. Yet as an alarm blares inside my mind, a click sounds. Ringing out, releasing the iron-tight grip on my heart. Releasing Amethyst's soft lips, I peer into Sebby's room, noting we are completely alone. Rushing to the door and throwing it open, there's no one to be seen. A ghost of the night, gone. But there's also no time to dwell on it now, as Amethyst squirms again and I don't stop moving until she's being lowered onto my bed.

"Shh," I soothe. "It's okay, I'm here." I'm not sure who my words are supposed to comfort, but it clearly wasn't Amethyst. She shudders further, her hands finding the sheet to clench them tight. Knowing there's nothing I can do for her until the drug-induced haze passes, I attend to her body.

Removing her heels and fetching a cloth, I wet it in my bathroom, ensuring the water is lukewarm. Grabbing a bar of soap and hand towel, I return to clean her. Inch by inch, until her creamy complexion is returned, albeit slightly reddened. I try to resist trailing my fingers, gently dragging my knuckles over the indent at her waist, and fail. Once I've done all I can, I settle on the edge of the bed, exhaling deeply. My eyes fall to her blood-stained bra and thong. They have to come off. They must join the bloodied hand towel and cloth in the nearby trashcan to go into tomorrow's burn pile.

My fingers flex against the edge of the mattress. And here is when I enter that gray zone. The torment between receiving everything, everyone I've ever wanted, and being denied the one I truly crave. I didn't know what yearning felt like until Amethyst denied my advances. Looked me in the eye and had no inclination of lust. My therapist is going to have a field day at our next appointment, but for now and for once, I'm all on my own.

Carter will bust my balls over this, but there's nothing else for it. Averting my gaze, I twist back and drag the thong down her long legs. Her bra consists of suction cups I need to pry from her breasts, ignoring the way they jiggle once freed. A groan locks in my throat. Heading for my dresser, I catch sight of my own bloodied suit in the mirror.

"Leave her alone," Amethyst twists, her face contorted with pain. I rush to grab us a matching set of white t-shirts and boxers, changing quickly to return to her side. "I'll do it...just...leave her." Each mumbled word clenches my gut tighter. Hovering over her body, I hesitate. Her movements become more erratic, and as I slide the boxers over her feet, she jerks and attempts to kick me in the face. Yet being caught with her stark naked in my bed and seemingly in distress would be so much worse, especially as she begins to cry out.

"No. No!" Fuck it. Pinning down her legs, I drag the boxers into place and fight Amethyst to get my t-shirt over her head. She has full use of her limbs again, but her eyes remain tightly closed. Scrunched shut. Shoving the shirt down over her flat stomach, I sigh and drop back into the mound of pillows, my weight dislodging hers. Now pressed against my side, Amethyst begins to weep. Her voice filters into a pained whisper.

"How could you?" My own heart shatters. I don't know what happened to Amethyst, why she's so tormented, but in this moment, the wash of pain is as real as if I'm the villain of her nightmares. I'm the cause of her heartache.

Careful not to move too quickly, I ease my arm beneath her head and pull her into my side. Drawing the cover over us cements my decision. She'll flip out when she wakes, but there's nowhere else I trust her to be safe tonight. Laying here, I will absorb every truth she unknowingly reveals, and tomorrow I'm going to hunt down every fucker who's ever hurt her. Not because I want her body, but because I want her soul freed of the weight it's burdened with.

"You'll wish you never met me," she promises. I nod, already knowing that will be the case. But damn me if I can't resist her.

"It's okay, baby. You're safe here. You're safe with me."

Chapter 12

Rousing from a fitful sleep, I become vaguely aware my head is moving. Rising and falling in time with the deep breaths rattling through a solid chest. Remaining in place, my thigh slung across a solid groin, I recount the events of last night. There was the gala, the waltz...oh fuck, surely not even I could have convinced Sebby to ride the other bus for a night? Blinking my eyes open, thick blackout blinds conceal the time of day. Light colored hair lays upon strong shoulders and instantly, I know I'm not draped across Sebby.

"Don't freak out," a deep baritone rolls through the chest beneath my ear. I stiffen further. "Nothing happened." Yet the memories of last night slam into me with the force of a freight train and I propel myself across to the other side of the bed.

"The guy...the, the convict," I stutter. My arm jerks, feeling the weight of him slumping onto the pole in my grasp. Lifting my hands, I expect to see blood. Thick, crusted layers of dark red, but there's nothing. My eyes drag across the fresh white t-shirt, inhaling the manly scent enveloping me. An expensive mix of vanilla and lemon, colliding in peaceful harmony. Myles slowly sits upright in a matching one, too alert to have just woken.

"Everything has been taken care of. You have nothing to worry about." Standing with the bed between us, his morning glory tents against black boxers, and he makes no move to conceal it. My throat bobs, drawing my attention to the dull ache in the side of my neck.

"You handled my shit?" I raise my voice, rubbing the tender spot. Myles gives a half-shrug.

"You're welcome," he replies nonchalantly but I can sense the smugness brimming just beneath the surface.

"No, no. I'm not thanking you. I don't need you to swoop in and handle my mess." It's as I continuously rub my neck, I remember the outline of the needle in my peripheral vision. A hint of disbelief leaks through Myles cocky smirk, as if to say 'yeah right'. Unfortunately for him, he's never met someone as tenacious as me. Not stubborn – just tenacious. "A quick nap and I would have been all over it. Now you've got the leverage to trap me here, to do your bidding and stay in your bed?!" I gesture to the bed with two hands of splayed fingers, my voice escalating in pitch. Myles gawks.

"What do you think I am, some fairytale villain?" An uncomfortable silence ensues, ended by my nodding.

"Yeah, pretty much. You're both the spoiled prince and unruly beast in this scenario." My mind drifts into the books I used to have stacked beside my bed as a young teen. Sebby is no doubt LeFou, the trusty and too eager sidekick, and Carter is Frollo, the scornful judge. I've yet to pin down Owen's distinctive traits.

When I return to the male across the room, Myles' arms have gone slack, his jaw loose. Shadows chase the movement of his eyes, as if reconsidering his entire persona based on my opinion. I don't see why it would matter to him so much.

"I apologize for going *slightly* caveman and forcing you here, but you are free to come and go at your leisure. I just hope you'll decide something here is worth sticking around for." Too much effort is put into controlling Myles' breathing, his chest rising and sagging with the deepness of his contemplation.

"Then...what's the whole point of using the Thirsty Kirsty as blackmail? Of all this?!" I wave my arms around like a lunatic. It's safe to say, I'm still drugged and slightly loopy.

"I just...I just wanted to spend some time with you, okay?!" Myles fists his hair, desperation leaking across the room to taint my nose. His amber eyes plead for...something. Misery swarms their speckled depths before he drops onto the edge of the mattress, back hunched. "I'm intrigued by you, and I thought with all your deceptiveness, you might just find something intriguing about me too." I drop my head back. This is too much tension first thing in the morning. Especially with the trickle of a headache seeping into the space behind my left eye.

"I'm putting a pin in your midlife crisis until at least after breakfast. People who can be rational before coffee terrify me."

"I don't drink coffee." Myles mutters and I throw a hand to my chest. Holy Satan. No wonder he's so confused by himself. It's likely Myles has never had a true moment of caffeinated clarity to look in the mirror and think, 'Well, I have all the money in the world at my disposal and I'm still miserable. Something isn't right here'.

I dive bomb across the bed, almost becoming tangled in the sheets as I skid off the other side and slip my arm into his.

"Come on big guy, we have a travesty to fix." It isn't until I'm heaving Myles upright, that I feel the slice of pain in my ribs. Hissing, I lurch forward, and find myself at the mercy of gentle yet prying hands.

"Fuck," Myles growls, easing the t-shirt up. I don't fight him, the air knocked from my lungs taking too long to replace. As the cotton skates over my side, I catch sight of my body in the huge two-way mirror spanning the nearest wall, and wince. Purple and black smudges are blossoming over my ribcage, deepening with the promise of a slow recovery. That convict landed more hits than I realized last night. More than I should have allowed.

Tender fingers lightly brush across my skin, as Myles tells me to take a deep breath. I aid his request, just as he pushes hard between each one of my ribs. To his credit, my sudden string of verbal abuse and the yank on his golden hair doesn't deter his examination, until the shirt is allowed to fall back into place.

"I don't think anything is broken. Will you let me call a doctor for you?" His amber eyes study my face, hands still lingering by the hem of the shirt. If I were to shift, even the smallest amount, his knuckles would drag across my hip bone and we'd both be treading dangerous waters.

"You're asking me?" I cock a brow. Myles steps half an inch closer, forcing me to tilt my head upwards to maintain his gaze. Yet he doesn't touch me any further.

"I'm not the unruly beast you think I am." We stand in the wake of a fresh understanding. Myles doesn't need my torment any further. Not when I suspect I'm only voicing the opinions he already has about himself. And in turn, he is reeling back his forceful nature, providing me the option to accept or decline his help. In this instance, it will firmly be the latter.

"No doctors necessary," I shake my head. Where there's medical forms, there's the need for identification and that's a deep dive I'm not willing to take. "You can call a barista though. Tell him to bring every syrup flavor and bean blend he has. We have a mission of a morning to get through before I can even contemplate asking about what happened after I passed out last night." With a shared, small smile, we mutually walk towards the door, Myles' phone already placed against his ear.

Chapter 13

S imon, the barista, is just packing up as the front door slams open. If I turn, bend back on the bar stool and angle my head right, I could see directly through the center of the manor. But with a stomach filled with more coffee than sustenance and the realm of hyperawareness I've entered, I can't be bothered. I just wait for Storm Carter to whip into the kitchen, his green eyes filled with outrage.

"If you want coffee, you're shit out of luck. We used the last of the milk," I eye his flustered cheeks. His gaze swings across the mess of discarded mugs and sugar packets across the breakfast bar, many full and untouched as Myles couldn't settle on a taste he liked. It's the sight of Myles himself, slumped over on his forearms and trying to come down from a caffeine spike which really sets Carter's temple throbbing.

"Myles! Your therapy session started forty minutes ago?!" Carter slams a leatherbound notepad down on the counter. Myles doesn't jolt, barely reacts as he withdraws from the stool and slinks away. Lifting an ice latte, the straw just touches my lips as Carter swipes his hand through the air. The plastic cup files across the kitchen, splattering against the oven. That'll be a bitch to clean.

"I don't like you," Carter seethes, bracing his fists on the bar to lean into me. Pressing a hand to my heart, I force my bottom lip to wobble.

"Oh, my fragile little heart. How can I go on?!" The back of my hand on my forehead seals my award-winning performance, just as Owen appears. Nuzzling Pig's scruff, he places kisses upon her head and regretfully passes her over to me.

"Take care of her for me, Pauper. I've got business to take care off," Owen talks to the pup rather than me. "Be good Princess Piggy. I'll be back soon. Oh yes I will." My brow raises the longer he consoles her droopy face. I was rather enjoying the show, but Carter grows impatient, dragging Owen up by the back of his t-shirt.

"You're going now?! We're already running late because I was caught up at the dealership," Carter throws another glare my way, as if him needing to replace his sports car was somehow my fault. Oh wait... Regardless, I've moved onto a cup of steaming mocha, sleep be dammed. Pinching the bridge of his nose, Carter's sharp features seem to age before my eyes. A sigh echoes around the empty space in his chest as he addresses Owen once more. "You know what day it is."

"Exactly. That's why I made sure I was busy." Owen winks while taking the mug from my hand and places a quick kiss on my forehead. Then he's gone, and Pig is left whining for him. Sebby bumps into

Owen halfway down the hall, being handed the now empty mug on his way towards us.

"Um, Carter? The applicants are all waiting in the lounge area. Should I call the first one through?"

"Applicants?" I sit up straighter. My nipples push against the t-shirt, still opting to laze around in Myles' boxers. If he wants me here, everyone needs to get used to me not wearing underwear a majority of the time. "For the fifth Elite? How exciting." Standing, Carter pushes my shoulder to knock me back onto the stool.

"Unless you're applying, you're not invited," he growls, his shining dress shoes already moving. Sebby tries to warn me to leave it be, but his warning has the opposite effect. Taking Pig with me, I follow Carter into the dining area, which has been set up as a formal interview space by the Elites hovering around. Today, they're dressed in smart pantsuits in a similar shade of navy blue to Carter's. The redhead rushes forward on skinny heels to help Carter remove his jacket and place it over the back of the chair he sits upon. I throw up in my mouth a little.

Peering at the top brown folder on a stack before him, Carter calls for 'Anita Dobson'. Two Elites by the doors blocking us from the lounge rush to pry them open, allowing a slip of a girl to enter before closing them on all other curious gazes peering in. I don't know what I expected, but the too-tight cocktail dress as black as her long, straight hair wasn't it. The most striking detail is the clunky flat shoes she's chosen to pair with her glamorous evening attire. I haven't seen buckles like that since learning about the Pilgrims.

"Hi, I'm Anita," she gives a small wave. "I'm very excited to meet you all." Lowering into the singular chair across the table, I find myself also sitting beside Carter. He mutters at me to fuck off but I'm too invested. Too intrigued. Sebby takes Carter's other side, while the

Elites curtsey and make their way into the kitchen. There's plenty of mess to keep them entertained while we conduct business in here.

"Thank you for coming," Carter smiles. The expression looks strange on his face. Downright creepy. "As you are aware and have already signed the NDA agreement to agree to, this position is for a coveted spot as one of Myles Hudson's Elites. The job is a full time role, working four-days a week on rota with the other girls. In addition to an unbeatable salary, you'll receive full coverage of healthcare expenses for the time you're with us, a private pension, and live on site. Not to mention, invites to some of the most exclusive events and parties, accompanying Mr. Hudson wherever he deems fit to have a date."

"Doesn't seem like he's deeming anything from this side of the table," I mutter beneath my breath. Carter's jaw ticks but he keeps face in front of the girl gaping at him like he shits glitter and owns the pot of gold at the end of every rainbow.

"I'll quickly run you through the process before we get started," Carter nods, kicking my ankle beneath the table. Crossing my legs beneath me, Pig curls up in my lap to fall asleep. Lucky bitch. "Today, we're conducting the formal interviews. Those shortlisted will be subject to a full credit and health check, including STD testing. Next will come a trial day here with the current Elites, ensuring you all get along well and are able to keep up with their workload. The decision on who reaches the final stage will be down to myself, Sebastian Lloyd," Carter gestures to Sebby, "Owen Grayson and the other Elites."

"Shouldn't Myles be present, considering his opinion is the only one that should matter?" I ask out loud. Anita's perfectly sculpted brows twitch, a general disdain emanating over this side of the table. The feeling is mutual.

"Only once we've vetted, tested and selected the best applicants for Mr. Hudson, does he choose who he's most attracted to," Carter replies to Anita as if she were the one to ask the question. "This prevents him from picking some insignificant whore off the streets." All eyes in the room quickly flash in my direction and I burst out laughing. Pig joins in, with a jolted howl. Sebby's face pleads with me to behave, yet by the way Carter is glaring daggers, it would seem I am rather significant after all.

When no one else speaks, I simmer down and gesture for the interview to continue. It starts out pretty basic, with Carter inquiring about Anita's employment history, her strengths and weaknesses. Aspirations, priorities. I grow so bored listening to the rehearsed dribble, I slide Anita's file across to read through her resumé.

Keen archer? Not with those nails.

Miss Teen South Carolina? Studying Anita's face, I note how, every so often, one of her eyes drifts a millimeter to the side before she blinks to correct it. With closer inspection, I reckon the artistry of her brows is to cover the mess a patch would leave for her lazy eye. Not a look Miss Teen USA would sport strolling down the runway, especially in flat shoes. I call bullshit.

"Can I ask a question of my own?" I butt in over something Carter was saying. Couldn't have been too important, since he's already jotted in his notepad she's an ideal candidate. Anita blinks, unsure of who to look at, but Carter grinds his jaw shut and allows me to ask it anyway.

"I'm curious, considering the lack of funds you must have had to come to a Billionaire's home dressed in an outfit from Target, why you chose to have your nose fixed instead of your lazy eye?" Anita's back bolts upright, her mouth popping open. "Because to me, I would have gone for the medical issue before the cosmetic." And there it is, the answer written all over her worried expression. "Ahh, it was a medical issue. Let me guess, deviated septum? Cocaine will do that too you. How long have you been clean?"

Anita slams both hands over her nose, a little too hard because her eyes start to water. Eyes which will no longer meet any of ours.

"Not clean then. I'm sorry, but I think one addict under this roof is enough, don't you?" I tilt my head, Anita drops her head into her hands and excuses herself, cutting a wonky line through the kitchen where the blonde Elite begins to console her. I should feel bad for her, but Myles doesn't need any more stains on his already ambiguous record. Best twist the blade and send a final message.

"Maybe try again when your dirty habit is under control!" I shout before she's walked out of view. Again, evil glares slam into me and roll off my back like droplets of water.

"That was quite invigorating actually," I beam. "Who's next?" Reaching over Carter, we enter into a game of slapsies which lands me back into my seat. Pig is jostled in all sorts of directions until she grows bored and belly flops onto the floor.

"Why are you even here?" Carter hisses. The bitterness of his tone is sharp enough to cut through the tension he radiates, like a viper about to strike. And the fact it does nothing to affect me riles him up even further.

"I'm looking out for Myles' best interest," I shrug.

"No, that's what I'm doing." Carter slams the next file on the table, scanning the contents. Placing my hand over the page, I force his venomous green eyes back up to mine.

"Manufacturing a life which is easy to oversee and control isn't for Myles' best interest. It's for yours."

"Maybe it's good to have her perceptiveness on hand," Sebby tries to muscle in on the icy moment of strong wills battering against one another. "Cause you know…it takes a con-artist to spot a con, right?" I smirk, unable to argue. Carter growls like an animal, shoving the file towards me.

"Fine." Crossing his suit arms, I tuck my smile behind my shoulder. Someone is used to throwing a tantrum and getting his own away. Watching him stress himself into a coma is going to be the highlight of my time here, however long I decide to stay.

Calling out the next name, Lily Blackmon, the same pair of Elites appear to open and close the sliding doors. Unlike the stick insect who just left, a real woman enters the dining room. Cute summer dress, mousey brown hair which needs a trim. She hasn't applied a face full of make-up as I imagine all the other barbie's have, and I instantly respect her for it.

"Oh honey," I frown at the reddened cuticles she tries to hide. Within an instant, her bottom lip is pulled between her teeth and those hands are back in front of her, picking and fidgeting before she's even sat down. I understand the stress of poverty. I've been there myself. "How bad is it?"

"They…they're about to repossess the house. I have a four-year-old daughter." Her eyes glaze with tears. Sympathizing, I reach across to pluck the pen from Carter's top pocket and flip her resumé over.

"Write down your bank details and I'll see to it personally you have nothing to worry about come tomorrow. You don't want to work here, trust me." She only hesitates for a moment, but let's face it. If I were looking for my next scam, it wouldn't be from someone who has nothing to offer. Scribbling down her details from memory, probably because she's had to stare at her bank statements, scanning each and every charge, she thanks me generously and leaves via the kitchen. Folding the page, I tuck it into my waistband, ignoring Carter and Sebby's curious looks.

"What was all that about?" Carter begins but I cut him off.

"Next!" The Elites have only just walked away and are forced to clip-clop back, opening the door to the next girl who shimmies her way through a riot starting to take place on the other side. Tall, slender, a hint of muscle. Good fashion sense, in a jumpsuit with sunglasses propped on her blonde messy-bun. I almost like her, until I see the thickly coated lipstick and match it with the leather fingerless gloves on her hands, no doubt hiding rashes.

"Hang on, what's the name?" Carter is sifting through the stack of files. I still his movements.

"Don't bother – exit is that way, thanks for coming." I smile sweetly. Blinking in confusion, the spunky blonde allows an Elite to lead her away before I turn to whisper to Sebby. "Syphilis lips," I circle my mouth with a finger and then shudder.

"This is turning into utter chaos," Carter groans. I sigh also, all energy I had from the coffee buffet quickly zapping from my bones.

"For once, I agree with you. Let's just speed it up, shall we?" Snatching a random file and taking the pen, I walk around the large table to the doors and slide them wide open. Then, I step into the lioness' den.

"Nope. No. No. Oh my god, who were you kidding?" I work my way through the women, picking off the gold diggers one by one. It's not that I condone the life Myles has, but since it's not of his creation, I can at least make sure the view from the top is a decent one. Call it a lapse in judgment, or repayment for getting rid of the evidence of what I did last night. Either way, by the time I've ensured only the genuine and free-of-butt-implants remain, I spin to find two girls sitting on the sofa beside Charley. A wide smile spreads across my face.

"Your turn," I jerk my head. Charley stands slowly, her leather mini skirt creased. Batting the material smooth, I readjust her netted top over the lacey black bra poking through. A quick ruffle of her chocolate brown hair and I deem her fit to enter, whilst quickly adjusting the info in the file. "Here you are, a decent candidate at last. Enjoy," I chuck Carter the file and make my leave. Charley doesn't need me hovering over her shoulder. She wants to be one of his prissy maid/fuck buddies, she can manage the interview on her own.

Carter mumbles behind me that I've ruined his system while I click the pen top and leave it on the now clean breakfast bar. Between running back and forth, the Elites have cleaned every trace of the fun-filled morning Myles and I managed to have. Seems like days ago already, and something I doubt Carter will let happen again. I hate to admit this, but it was sort of fun while it lasted, but watching Myles spray liquid everywhere and scrape his tongue free of the taste was like one of those recurring videos you can't help but leave on replay.

Meandering through the lower level, I drag my feet. Sunlight beams through the expansive windows, not leaving a trace of a chill on my bare legs. The swish of my purple hair against the back of my arms becomes a dance, a swaying drift until I pull my ribs too far and groan. Shuffling nearby draws me through into the west wing.

"What are you doing all the way back here, Miss Piggy?" I bent low, stroking her back. Pig's pink nose is too invested in a particular section of the baseboard to care who's trying to drag her away. Frowning, I lift her by the collar, scooping the wriggling puppy into my arms.

"Seriously girl, what is it?" Like an optical illusion, once I see it, it's so glaringly obvious. A gap between the floor and wall, less than a centimeter in diameter. Following the line along and upwards, a slip of a crack separates the wallpaper. Strategically dark, hosting a wood-like pattern, I could have walked past the wall a hundred times and never noticed anything different about it. I bet many have.

I release Pig back to her sniffing, rasping my knuckles a few times. Hollow. Then I hunt for an in. A push release, an object on the nearby table to trigger the lock. Anything cliché, but when all else fails, I go in hunt of a blunt object and return with six. Screwdriver, butter knife, spatula, crowbar, nail file, and if all else fails – a hammer. All of which is unnecessary. Pig snuffles and grunts, prying up a corner of the wallpaper to reveal a bolt underneath. Lifting it, the door swings inwards to a dark and eerie hallway. Cocking her head, she whines and runs away. Pussy.

Leaving the objects filling my arms on the table and permitting myself entry, I'm two steps inside the hallway when I hear muffled voices. Concealing myself inside, I walk on silent feet, ducking beneath low hanging rafters which hold up the manor itself. The hallway opens into a circular space around a central beam, various pathways spanning in all directions. I follow the low voice I can still hear, echoing around me like a softly spoken tease.

"What's wrong, Myles? You seem restless today." A male. Licking my lips, I approach the stark glare of light penetrating through yet another crack in the inner wall. Too strategically placed to be an accident. Lowering onto my knees, I peer through to see Myles sitting on the floor, his elbows leaning on his knees.

"It's her," he sighs and I still. He's facing my direction, his amber eyes lazily scanning the wall. Could he really see the presence of my shadow through such a tiny crack? Yet as Myles throws his head back on the classic, shrink chaise, the tightened band in my chest lessens. "I'm consumed with wanting to know where she is, what she's doing. It's driving me insane." The therapist sitting on an adjacent chair sits forward, placing his reading book down to pick up a notepad and pen.

Holy shit. I've found the master peep hole into Myles' life, and it turns out, there truly is no privacy where Carter is involved.

Chapter 14

S lotting a piece of jigsaw into another, I puff out my cheeks and push the table away from it. I've done this particular jigsaw a hundred times over, since Gillian became my therapist. I stopped trusting therapists after the last one took all of my inner thoughts to the press. Now the job entails sitting around in the study with me, lost in our own hobbies until Carter deems it time to release the door. Walking across the room, I drop down onto the floor with a huff, throwing my arms over my knees.

"What's wrong, Myles? You seem restless today," Gillian comments. He's nice enough, in his fifties with salt and pepper hair.

Lowering the glasses perched on his straight nose, he looks at me with genuine curiosity. In all these years, Gillian has never pushed me. Forced me to open up, pried in my thoughts. If there was ever a time to confide in someone, this would be it.

"It's her," I sigh, losing myself in the mural painted upon the opposite wall. Two ships sailing against choppy waters of the night, the sea a vicious collision of the deepest blues and white highlights beneath a full moon. Facing each other head on, sails billow from tall masts. The only visible crew members are captains, at the helm with deadly intent. I've often pondered upon the piece, wondering if the captains are unable to see each other, or if this is where they've come to battle under the guise of the night to decide their fates.

"Her, as in your mother?" Gillian asks. I know he's here to help, but my heckles rise even further. I know what month it is. Almost nineteen years since my mother's suicide and something Carter has been reminding me off incessantly. He thinks my fascination with Ami is a fleeting distraction. He couldn't be more wrong.

Throwing my head back on the cream chaise lounge, I decide I'll never know the answer, and I can no longer push aside the raging ships of my own thoughts for the siren who has captured my mind.

"I'm consumed with wanting to know where she is, what she's doing. If there's something I could help her with. A way to prove to her I'm worth spending time with. It's driving me insane." Gillian shifts, setting down his copy of War of the Worlds to pick up his notepad. *Finally*, he's probably thinking. Something worth listening to.

"I'm presuming this is the girl with purple hair I saw you with in the kitchen when I arrived?" Gillian asks. I nod.

"Amethyst." A protective streak presents itself in a low grumble. I've heard Carter refer to her enough as 'that girl'. It is important people know her name, and know that she's with me.

"Amethyst," Gillian nods, writing on his page. "Why don't you start from the beginning? Tell me how you met."

Pushing myself up to lay back on the chaise lounge, I relay the entire story to Gillian, not missing a single detail. Not about how I hunted for her on the streets, what I did to Art for touching her, how I convinced her to come here. Through it all, he's silent, making notes. I should be worried about any and all of this information leaving the room, but I'm genuinely in need of advice. Understanding, unbiased advice.

"So...what do you think?" I inquire when the silence after my story stretches too long. Risking a look at Gillian, his gentle eyes are watching me. Stoic, unjudging, as he sets his notepad aside.

"Let me ask you this - do you think the turmoil you're feeling is because of her specifically? Or could it be this is the first time you've been thrown a curveball outside of the carefully orchestrated life Carter has provided you, and the unknown is causing you discomfort?" I sit upright at this. Did I imagine the contempt at Carter's name, or is Gillian far more understanding of my situation than I've foolishly thought this whole time?

There's no easy answer. No real way of knowing, and it takes several minutes of pacing to put my thoughts in order.

"I've been ostracized my entire life for crimes I didn't commit. And I've never given a shit. No one's opinion of me has ever mattered, until I'm stripped bare by her stunning, violet eyes. None of the fame or money can shield me from her, and I'm convinced she doesn't like what she sees."

"In the same way you use the accusations against you as a protective shield, or allow your father to continue paying Carter to keep you sated," Gillian makes a small noise in the back of his throat. I still, looking at him quizzically. I'm sure he's saying more than he should, but I need to hear all of it. Gillian waves his hand through the air. "What I mean to say is, it's easier to be the man you're perceived as, even though innocent. You're hiding in plain sight, and I believe Amethyst is the reason you're only just realizing it."

Dropping back down on the chair, the weight of my confusion leaks out on my next exhale. Like a fog clearing, my mind is suddenly blank. Gillian has summed up my entire internal struggle in a few simple sentences. I should have confided in him years ago.

"Do you believe there is a right person for everyone?" I hang my head, elbows braced on my thighs. All I need is a simple 'yes', to validate my motives going forward. To convince me Amethyst is my person, and my gut instincts have been right from the start.

"I believe there are certain people for the versions of ourselves we allow to be known. Who could have been right for you ten years ago isn't necessarily right for you now, as we change and grow so much through the years. But if Amethyst is who you need now to be your best self, there's nothing holding you back from pursuing her."

"Perhaps. But she rejects my advances at every turn. No amount of charm can convince her otherwise." I push my hands through my long hair, fisting tightly at my scalp. These words, as reassuring as they are, don't change the fact Amethyst doesn't want me.

"And how does that make you feel?" Gillian pushes, delving deeper to the root of my anguish.

"Scared," I admit, my voice low.

"Why?" Gillian pushes again. I don't have to contemplate my answer, my head jerking upright to pierce him with a gaze so direct, there's no room for doubt.

"Because if she can look straight through all the bullshit, she'll realize there's nothing there to see at all."

A buzzer breaks through the tension in the air. The door pops as Carter releases it from the outside, permitting my escape. Usually, I'd be two steps out the door within seconds, looking for a quick fuck. A fast release for the pent-up frustration I will never hold Carter accountable for. He saved my life by taking the manacle of my future, but he's damned me all the same. Gillian reaches for his satchel, packing away his notepad and book. Rising panic congeals in my throat. Unanswered questions all melding into a rush within my ears.

"So, what would you suggest I do?" I shoot upright to stop Gillian from leaving, grasping onto our session like I never have before. Gillian pauses before me, smiling kindly and pats my chest.

"Not as your therapist, but as your friend, I advise you to give yourself some grace. Rushed, forced connections are your go-to. Give Amethyst the chance to fall for the man behind the money. It's going to take a little more time. Requires a little more work, but the reward will be worth it."

Chapter 15

At some point during the afternoon, I decided to put some real clothes on. Fitted jeans with enough stretch in them to squat, a black tank top and a pair of converse. More material than I've worn since becoming the embodiment of 'Amethyst'. The persona before, a shy girl called Fiona who was a girl scout leader by day and swindler by night, would have worn something similar with a chunky knit cardigan. Yeah, I got bored of her very quickly.

Leaving my purple hair free to swish along my lower back, I leave the Elites building just as Carter storms past the pool. Owen has returned, lounging with Sebby on recliners, shirtless in board shorts. Sunglasses shield their eyes from a perfectly warm Autumn day. Probably one of the last we'll have this year. Myles surfaces from the shimmering water, every muscle of his torso flexing as he pushes himself free of the pool. Whole gang's here.

"Wanna explain this to me?" Carter booms, slamming a brown file into my left tit. Ow.

"Is it a manual on the quickest way to give someone breast cancer?" I glower, taking the file and rubbing myself as Myles appears at Carter's back. Dripping wet, dangerously moist. Peering inside the file, my eyes flick back to Carter. "There's nothing in here, dickwad."

"Exactly," Carter growls, taking the final step closer to get in my face. "That's the background check I had pulled on you along with the other applicants. None of my contacts could find a single thing."

Despite myself, I snigger. Any validation I needed was just freely given, knowing not even Carter's top connections could break through the webbed layers I put in place to keep myself off the radar. Tension radiates from his bunched shoulders, anger seeping from the fists at his side. Had the present company not been within sight, I'm sure those hands would have me pinned against the building.

"You're in my home, eating my food, meddling with my affairs, so I'm only going to ask you once. Who the fuck are you?" It's on the tip of my tongue to whisper 'your worst nightmare,' but another response leaves my lips. One which will undoubtedly rile him more.

"Aren't you property of Hudson and Sons? Making everything around us, his," I jerk my head to Myles. Amber eyes seek me out through the darkness of Carter's persona. Flecked with brown, caged behind a glaze of misery as much as he is. I heard plenty during his counseling session, and knowledge is power.

"Get the fuck out of my sight," Carter moves in a flash, punching the wall beside my head. I don't even flinch. Holding his green glare for a moment longer, until I'm sure the vein in his temple will burst, I smile sweetly and scoot myself free.

"Gladly," I mutter beneath my breath, already entering the manor. The Elites are busy steam cleaning the lounge and moving the furniture back to their original positions, before being used as a waiting room. I make it all the way to the entrance lobby when Myles finally catches up to me. I nearly thought I'd be venturing out alone.

"Hey, wait up," he calls. Concealing my smile, I turn and tilt my head in question. This close, and seemingly alone, I allow myself to admire the damp expanse of his torso. His entire body is inked from jawline to waistband, a mixture of skulls, roses and all-seeing eyes. Entirely colorless, they blend into each other with the help of swirling smoke, weaving amongst the symbols. Over his heart, a giant cross has been shaded to perfection, the jewels encased within glimmering with white highlights. Beneath his chin, the wide wingspan of a dove follows the length of his jawline.

"I'd like to, if you don't have plans, possibly spend some time with you, outside of the manor. Away from...people and..." A hand runs through his blond hair. I roll my eyes. The way his shorts are dripping onto the marble, his stalling only increases the slip hazard he's creating around his Air Jordans.

"Well, since I've aged about forty years since you started that sentence, I'll just speed things up. Let's get out of here." Grabbing the handle of the front door, Myles continues to stutter.

"Wait, really? Okay well, um, I'll just change my clothes-"

"No time," I announce, trotting down the porch's stone steps. "It's now or never, Beasty. I'm going either way." Stopping in front of the orange Ferrari, I whistle low. A feline of metal, the body bends to the will of the road. Utterly smooth, perfectly aerodynamic. I watch myself approach the polished sheen of a fresh paint job, the heady scent of unbroken leather leaks from cracked windows. Like a burst of pure sunlight against the tarmac, it demands attention. Craves to be driven.

"Ami," Myles unknowingly latches on to the nickname Charley calls me by, "Carter is precious about his cars. Give me five minutes, I'll have the limo brought around." There's an edge of panic in his voice, which spurs me on further. Entices me to step closer. "Come on, it's brand new. I can't let you hotwire it already." A gentle tug on my arm does nothing to deter me.

"Who said anything about hotwiring?" Although that was my plan B. Producing the keys I pickpocketed from Carter by the pool, I unlock the doors and hop into the driver's seat. A groan of indecision sounds behind me, and as I lower myself behind the wheel, a pair of hands shove me along into the passenger side. The only other seat in the low sports car.

Taking the keys from my grip, Myles slams his door closed and is tearing down the driveway as a bellow penetrates the air. Loud enough to be heard over the roar of the engine, Carter's outline appears in the rearview mirror. I expect his reflection to shrink, but as his arms begin to pump and we're forced to slow at the iron gates, my heart hammers.

Holy shit, he's taking chase.

Myles spots him too, a flash of panic crossing his features. The gates smoothly but slowly open, Carter gaining on us. Muttering beneath his breath that he's so dead, Myles slams his foot on the accelerator and peels out of the driveaway, the gates grinding along either side of the Ferrari. Sparks fly, a guttural scream leaving Carter as he just slams his hands on the trunk before we're gone.

Racing down the narrow path, towards the highway and beyond. The wheels absorb every bump along the way, the suspension deliciously agile. I smooth my hands over the seat beneath me, growing damp between my legs at the rush of robbing another rich bastard of his prized possession. All that's left is to convince my anxious companion to enjoy it too.

"Loosen up Myles," I place my hand on his thigh and squeeze. His swim shorts, the only item of clothing he is wearing, are still soaked through and becoming molded to the seat. His thigh tenses beneath my touch. Lowering the window all the way, my other arm flies outward to the rush of wind we create, whooping and laughter leaving my lips until Myles finally cracks a smile too.

***

Sunset is impending by the time we reach Myles' destination of choice. I didn't ask where we're going, preferring to live by the spontaneity of it all. When I had woken this morning, sprawled across Myles' sculpted body, I was seriously questioning my life choices up to this point. Searching for the objective which sees me from one day into the next. But now, everything seems different. *He* is different from the arrogant asshole I believed him to be, and dare I say we have more similarities than I knew of yesterday.

I hear the water first. A gentle lap blown to me on a light breeze infused with a salty tang. Rounding the front of the Ferrari, Myles heads back to check out the trunk. A soft 'aha' lets me know he found something. We've parked on a large dirt patch, bordering the grassy bank dipping below. At the end of a lantern-lit path curving through the woodlands ahead, an understated boat house sits at the edge of an expansive lake.

"Carter usually ties his visits into the city with a trip to the dry cleaners," Myles tells me, appearing at my side. A powdered blue shirt stretches across his chest, his hair wild and curled about his shoulders from the forceful blow-dry our speeding provided. Dark jeans sculpt his legs, framing the same Air Jordans he's been wearing since leaving the manor. Offering his arm, I accept it with more ease than I should. Myles will start to think I've turned all gooey inside if I don't insult him soon.

"Your hairline is receding," I blurt out. Myles softly chuckles with the confidence of someone who thoroughly checks every hair follicle in the mirror each morning. Leading me down the path, a man steps out of the boat house, a jacket draped over his shoulders in the same tweed as his hat. Aged fingers push the key into the lock before spotting us. His white mustache twitches over a small and surprised smile.

"Mr. Hudson!" he exclaims, offering out that same hand, smudged with oil. Myles takes it without hesitation, greeting the old man as Percy. "It's been too long, my boy. Staying out of trouble I hope," he bobs his eyebrows towards me. I stiffen with the thought of being brought here, duped into playing into Myles 'different girl each night of the week routine'.

"Always," Myles nods, a similar mischievous smile playing about his lips. "We were going to head out, if that's okay with you?" Percy inclines his head, dropping the keys into Myles' hand.

"Lock up when you're done. You know where to leave the key." Bidding us a good night, Percy walks in the direction of the only other vehicle nearby. A large, beat-up truck tucked back in the tree line.

"How many girls have you brought here?" I ask, hating the envious edge to my tone. Neither of us are innocent, I know that. But I was stupid enough to let myself for one second believe I might be special in Myles' eyes. Permitting us entry into the boathouse, I make it two steps within the door before Myles is upon me. Shoving my back against the wood, his hands gripping my forearms quickly shift to a downward caress to my hands. His breath fans my lips, the shift of his chest against mine causing my nipples to harden. Between us, Myles raises my hands, kissing the back of each one in turn.

"This place is my sanctuary, where I go when I need to escape from the life which suffocates me. It's where I come to be alone. Once we're out on the water, you'll understand why."

"What's changed now for you to share your solitude with me?" I swallow the quiet, breathiness of my voice. Myles drops his head to my ear, his stubble grazing my cheek.

"I figured two lost souls like us...we could be alone together." I don't need to see Myles' unique amber eyes to visualize them. Enquiring and tentative. My skin dances with pulsing electricity which could so easily be misunderstood for more than simply lust coursing through my veins. When Myles is away from the manor, the money and the men, when I've spent all afternoon replaying his words of misery in my mind, it's easy to believe we're just a man and a woman. Engrained with need. Craving a release.

Moving away, taking the warmth with him, Myles switches on a light before preparing a rowing boat. While he enters a silent world of safety checking, I hunt for more feminine touches. Three rolled blankets, a mini fridge containing chocolate strawberries and a bottle of champagne. Either Percy stays stocked for a honeymoon experience, or Myles called ahead. I eye him suspiciously, recalling the toilet break I took at a gas station halfway here. Well, to leave them would be a waste now.

Conveniently, a wicker basket on top of the counter is ready with drinking glasses, expensive chocolate truffles and a pack of supersized condoms. Percy really thought of everything, but I won't be rocking Myles' boat this evening. All sympathy and understanding aside, I refuse to be another possession he owns.

"Ready when you are," Myles announces. Equipped with my arms full of goodies, the basket in the crook of my elbow, I'm soon sprawled comfortably in the base of the boat amongst the blankets. Untethering us from the wooden dock, I have a perfect view of Myles' biceps bulging with each powerful stroke of the oars. A lantern swings gently from the mast at his back, keeping the light with us for when needed.

Falling into a comfortable silence, I stare upwards. All around, a golden sky descends into vibrant oranges and red, beams of sunlight scattering through the clouds as it nears the horizon. Dots of eager stars try to pierce the earth's atmosphere. I could lie here like this forever. A rare sensation of contentment overtakes me, between the rhythmic sway of the boat, the beauty of our surroundings. I'd like to convince myself this feeling has nothing to do with the man watching over me like a stoic guardian. I should be worrying about how calm I feel, his soothing presence washing over me like a balm, I'm tired. So freaking tired of fighting, of constantly being aware, of being stubborn. For one single night, I'm going to allow myself to switch off.

"Why do you stay?" I ask after a while. The steady drag of the boat moving towards the center of the lake has eased, Myles releasing the oars to their holders either side of him. He doesn't need context to my question, not when he himself admitted to feeling suffocated often.

"I've never had a reason to leave." I call bullshit, but don't say anything else. I'm not in the market for saving rich boys from their woeful lives. Myles shifts from his wooden plank seat to join me in the shell of the boat, wriggling his huge frame beneath a plaid blanket. "The version of Carter you see now isn't who he always was. It's who he's become in order to help me."

"Because he's being paid," I grunt bitterly. Why that nugget of information has affected me so, I have no idea. But it's allowed me to put aside the distaste I felt for Myles' privileged life, and channel it elsewhere. Risky territory for the Adonis now snuggling into my side, threading his fingers through mine.

"It's not as black and white as it seems," Myles sighs deeply. "My father gave all of the boys roles in our main company, and went on to invest in their side businesses, encouraging them to make their own fortunes. He's a fair man, always believing in the lesson of self-procuring rather than being given. It's why it was so important to him that I completed rehab and approached our board of directors as a reformed man, rather than the 'spoiled prince' expecting handouts."

I catch the hint of a hooded smirk, referencing the term I called him this morning in his bedroom. So much has happened since then, so many truths becoming unraveled. Had I known all of this yesterday, would I have been so eager to jump out of his arms? Would I have been alone in the garden at all, presenting myself as an easy target?

"I should...thank you for what you did last night," I wonder out loud. Myles chuckles.

"You probably should, yeah. But I have a feeling you're not going to." The boat rocks gently, an easy lapping of water isolating us from the world beyond. "You'll be surprised to know we aren't as innocent as the media likes to think. Carter has a few skeletons in his closet and a side he keeps hidden deep behind his barricade of control. You should give him a chance."

"A chance for what?!" I push upright and spear Myles with a narrowed look. He doesn't answer, shifting a meaty arm beneath his head to focus on the sky all of a sudden. The sun has dipped behind the horizon of trees, drawing the impending darkness closer. Whispers of unforeseen promises linger, as if tonight not only has the potential to change my opinion of Myles, but to question many of the rules I live by. I'm a traitor to myself at this point, and becoming increasingly unsure of how far I'll go to prove it.

"What would it take for you to trust me?" his voice sails around with the fluidity of rolling waves, his aura too calm for me to deny.

"A PI who isn't afraid to give me the answers I'm looking for," I snorted and turned my head away so Myles couldn't hear me. It wouldn't do him any use to know of my past, regardless of how many 'skeletons' he's had to bury on Carter's behalf. With my back turned on him now, I hear Myles sigh which causes the boat to rock slightly.

"Okay, how about this - give me something real. One truth about you and I'll drop the subject." Myles draws me back down into the crook of his arm. I mold into his side, pressing against the firmness of his cotton shirt. When was the last time I was fucked by someone I actually desired, as opposed to someone I was in turn fucking over? Myles takes my silent insight as hesitation. Brushing the hair back from my forehead, he places a gentle kiss there and I swallow. Fuck, this is rapidly spiraling to a place I'm not prepared to go. "There's no prying ears out here, Amethyst."

"When I was a kid, every Christmas and birthday my parents would ask what I wanted. And every time, I gave the exact same answer." I grin against Myles' bicep. "*An adventure.* I never cared for dolls or toys, or whatever the other kids at school had. From a very young age, I collected memories like treasures. Craved the thrill of traveling without a map, finding the best pancakes in some tiny off-road diner, exploring the forest and happening upon a waterfall. Every moment was precious because you know you could never find it again if you tried."

"Your parents sound like incredibly special people," Myles muses. My smile fades, my voice dipping.

"They were." For a long while after, no words are exchanged and I'm thankful for it. I didn't want Myles' sympathy, just as I hadn't wanted to offer him so much of me so easily. Now the pandora's box of my memories has been opened, I delve through images appearing behind my closed eyelids, lulled by the steady breathing of my companion and the gentle rock of the boat. Had my parents still been around, they most likely would be encouraging me to give into Myles. I'd probably be in agreement. By the time he speaks again, a blanket of navy blue has coated our view, pricked by glimmering stars.

"Can I make an observation?"

"You can try," I snort. Myles moves so suddenly, I drop into the empty gap his body had created before hands grip my sides. Tossing me upright, I'm dumped in his lap, legs straddling his waist. Amber eyes, highlighted by the lantern, peer into mine with mirth crinkling their corners.

"Screw it, let's raise the stakes. I'm going to make an observation, try and read you in the way you decipher everyone else within moment's of meeting them." I raise a brow. Carter must have told him about the interviews. How I defended his best interest. My cheeks flame. "And if I get it right, you're going to reward me with a kiss." Myles beams. If he were a puppy, his tongue would be out like Pig's when I'm scratching her belly.

"I didn't take you for a gambling man," I smirk.

"I reckon, with you, it's the only way I'm going to stand a chance." Cold, dark feelings are chased away by his boyish appeal, the fingers at my waist drawing small circles over the black tank top. "Do we have a deal?" I incline my head, chewing on the inside of my lip. Myles studies me a moment further, delving deeper into my purple eyes than I expected. Then, he inhales.

"It's not the luxurious life, or even the money you despise – it's the person who uses that wealth in the wrong ways or for personal gain. Am I right?"

A cocky, lopsided grin captures Myles' mouth as I sit in disbelief. He can't have figured me out that quickly. I didn't let him anywhere near close enough. Before I allow myself to consider what else he's seen, I lean forward to place my lips against his, only to be met with the palm of his hand.

"Not so fast," Myles chuckles. My mouth remains plastered to his hand, stunned he would deny the one thing he's been after this whole time. Well, maybe not the only thing. "I want my reward to be presented in the purest form." Removing myself from his personal space, I cock my head. "Lose the contact lenses." The air whooshes out of me on my next breath.

"I...can't," I frown, although it's more that I won't. Myles is asking for more than a brief connection of our mouths, he's asking for a piece of me.

"This once, I think you can," Myles implores. Serenity fills his expression, but it's not enough. "I want to look into your eyes as I kiss you and know I've had something special. Something no one else has." I snort.

"I've kissed many, many, many-"

"I mean your trust," Myles hastily interrupts. "I want to know if you trust me enough to let me see you as you are. No more hiding."

"You want my trust," I shimmy an inch closer. Myles' breath fans my face, his nod slow and sure. Toying with the collar of his shirt, I smile. "Then you'll need to work harder." Closing the distance, my mouth connects with his and this time, Myles doesn't deny me. He admits defeat, for now, but it's hard to believe either of us are currently losing. Teasing his lips with a gentle press, a soft touch, his hand slips to my nape and pulls me closer, taking the reward he earned. Fuck, he tastes better than expected.

Desire surges through my veins. His touch coaxes me to forget, to live for the moment. We mold together, our rushed kiss verging on desperation. My back arches, my chest pressing against his. A battle of wills take place, crushing of lips and eager tongues. Working me with a multitude of experience, I relinquish control. Very briefly.

His tongue delves into my mouth, drawing out mine to intertwine. To dance, to savor. Hands wonder, hips rolls. The intoxicating scent of passion invades my senses. A fire ignites in my core, aided by the hardening of Myles' crotch against my center. It would be so easy to have him. Take him to the hilt and leave my screams to mingle with the night. The very thought causes a shiver to roll the length of my back, a whimper to be lost to his possessive groan.

Cupping my cheek, Myles lies back when I finally catch myself following too eagerly. Pushing against his chest, I remain sitting upright, panting. My lips are swollen, tingling. Our eyes capture each other with a new height of intensity as the air shimmers with an invisible, yet undeniable energy. Somewhere within the pit of my soul, I manage to find an ounce of rationality.

"Be that as it may," I breathe in a voice foreign to my own ears. Filled with deceit and yearning. "I made a decision long ago to prevent greedy, rich men like yourself from getting everything they wanted. Even if, in some twisted turn of events, that happens to be me."

I expected Myles to shove me aside, speedily return us to shore and leave me stranded. Or to at least give up his hopeless pursuit. Sitting upright with all the grace of a feline, his breath fans my face, his amber eyes exploring mine once more.

"You're not an object I wish to possess. You're a rare and stunning jewel, just like your chosen name. To own you," he threads his fingers through a strand of my hair, "would be a crime." If there was a way to sucker punch me without warning, Myles just found it. My mouth opens, my mind reeling for the response.

"Then what is it you want, Myles Hudson?" I shudder again, and not from the lowering chill of Autumn.

"I want my name to always be a breathy whisper on your lips." Myles skates his lips over my mouth, following the line of my cheek. "I want the honor of being your first thought when you wake in the morning." He kisses my jaw, bringing his mouth to my ear. "I want to be the one you confide in, the one you finally trust with your secrets. With your body. I don't want you to belong to me, but I'll do whatever it takes to be yours."

Words fail me. Thoughts evade in a rush of adrenaline. Could it be so simple? Can I bend to this man's will so easily, after all this time? When his mouth makes its leisurely way back to mine, my body is languid. Lost to possibility, drowning in a sea of amber and desire. Arms band around my back, holding me upright when I'm sure I'd otherwise melt into a puddle. Sharing the same breath, the same thought, we close the miniature gap between us as a blaring sound penetrates the air.

Jolting, lights attack the forest. Flashing viciously in a warning cry, igniting the silhouettes of gangly teens, crowbars in hand. Being so far out on the lake, Myles and I can only watch in stunned silence, still tightly held in our embrace.

Glass shatters from Carter's Ferrari, the alarm raging as cans of spray paint assault its exterior. Around four kids batter the metal, whooping and laughing until they eventually get it moving. Pushed over the edge of the grassy bank, the Ferrari picks up speed, zipping like a bolt of orange light directly into the lake with a tremendous splash. We witness the wave of water encasing the shell, impressively dragging it beneath the surface in only a few minutes.

"Well," Myles says after the kids have run off cheering. "At least in one sense tonight, I'm completely fucked."

Chapter 16

Hooves hit the driveway with a repetitive clip-clop which rouse those in the manor. I couldn't have timed the main door flying open any better, as I tug on the reins and slow Nessa to a halt. She's a stunning mare of pure white, gray patches spotted over her rump. Her hair flows as freely as the lack of fucks I generally give. I'll have to make time to ride her properly soon, a full gallop through the woodlands surrounding the estate. Myles stops at my side on a stallion of jet black, both horses jerking their heads with impatience.

"What in the holy hell-" Carter screams, bashing the door against the inner wall.

"Shhh!" I scowl at him, skidding to the ground with grace. Soothing Nessa, I stroke her nose gently. "You'll scare the horses." After it took us all night to hitch a ride from someone who didn't look like an ax murderer, it was almost too easy convincing Myles to sneak onto his own estate and borrow a pair of horses from his stables. I do like to enter in style. A raging blur of stomping appears in my peripheral as I turn to hand Carter the reins.

"By the way, you have a hole in the back corner of the external wall, you might want to get that seen to." Moving to pass him, a hand latches onto the leaf-embedded ponytail at the back of my head.

"Where the fuck is my car?" Carter growls low into my ear, malice thickening his tone. I twist just enough for my stare to collide with his poisonous green eyes. Myles steps into my back on instinct, prying Carter's fingers free of my hair. Spoil sport. Released from his grip with a frustrated huff, I make it all the way to the door before realizing Myles has hung back.

"It was just a bit of fun-"

"Fun which will see you destroying the repubitable name you've made for yourself," Carter half-mutters, turning away from Myles with his phone pressed to his ear. Feet pad through the hallway, the Elites in silky pajamas rushing to aid Carter's request with the horses without giving me a second glance. As the men fall into step with each other, I slip behind the archway of the living area, keeping out of sight.

"Go get yourself cleaned up. We have a shareholder's meeting at midday and you're hosting the grand opening of a new club in the city this evening. The details are all on the calendar, if you care to look for once. Your plaything will stay behind." Oh man, Carter is furious. A smile creeps across my face and I give myself a mental hi-five. The sudden weight of exhaustion hits me as all adrenaline ebbs away, my feet heavy as I drag them up the stairs. Last night's jeans and tank stick to me uncomfortably, calling for a shower before I become one with the mattress. None of which, however, takes precedence over peeking in Owen's room to see Pig nestled in his arms, flat out on her back and snoring to high heaven. Traitorous little bitch.

***

Rolling my fingers against the mug in hand, my nails create a clicking effect on the ceramic. Over and over, as I watch the Elites in maid's outfits clean up from lunch. The guys had left before Charley forced me to rise from the dead, only to realize I'd gotten a meager four-hours of sleep. There can't be a single moment today where I am without coffee.

Click-click-click-click.

Across the kitchen and in her everyday sweater and jeans, Charley is helping unload the dishwasher, all small smiles and inside jokes. I hate to admit it, but she suits being here. Being amongst other girls, building the family she never really had. She's proved to me time and time again she'd have been a great sister, and with each flash of happiness glinting within her brown eyes, the more I realize I'm going to have to let her go.

Click-click-click-click.

The Elite closest, the skinniest of the four with a ponytail of honey brown, grimaces at me. "Have you got something to say, or do you just like to annoy everyone around you?" Her upper lip curls. I consider each question and opt for the first.

"It's occurred to me I don't know any of your names. It seems I'm going to be sticking around for a while, so maybe we should all get to know each other better." Pushing to my feet, taking the mug with me, I offer out my hand. "I'm Amethyst, a stripper from Wisconsin." All lies but it's the identity I live by for now. When my next target requires a more professional occupation, I'll slip into a character better suited.

"Kristina," the Elite tentatively slips her hand into mine as if I might snap her wrist without a moment's notice. I don't, giving her a polite shake instead. "This is Kayla," Kristina nudges the black-haired woman wiping the counter beside her. As Kayla stretches forward, a gap in her frilly tank top and skirt reveals the tattoo of a yellow duckling on her hip. "Over there is Lou," the blonde aiding Charley gives a quick wave, "and Joy is outside, hanging the clothes." Through the fully glass sliding doors, Joy pegs a pair of boxers onto the line, her vibrant red hair shining in the midday sun. Yeah, we've sort of already met.

"It's nice to meet you all properly," I put on a smile which is solely for Charley's benefit. She's followed me around for years, being pushed to the edge of her comfort zone – it's time I repaid the favor for her. Watching the four of them work hard at work to organize and buffer every surface in the kitchen, something Carter said during the interviews pops into mind. "Shouldn't at least one of you have a day off? I mean...the guys aren't even here."

"Until we're back up to five girls," Kayla huffs, rolling her shoulders, "Carter has us all working to pick up the slack. It's a big manor to be kept in order." She signals across the kitchen to a space beside the refrigerator. I would describe this as where the infamous calendar lives, if anyone could call the mindfuck of color and writing that. The entire expanse of the wall up to the archway is covered in a self-adhesive white board. Every single day for the month has an entry, including the Elites tasks, Myles' meetings, days marked as 'Owen Out,' and parties. So many parties, award ceremonies, galas. Their social life takes up as much space as their business. It's no wonder Myles feels suffocated – I can sense the tightening grip around my own throat from just looking at it.

"Technically, it's my day off," Lou breaks through my bewilderment. Scraping a plate of food into a dog bowl, she places it by the back door. A flurry of nails against the marble comes running through the manor, Pig skidding into the glass in her excited haste to eat. Lou smirks, stroking Pig's head. "But we've all been invited to the club opening, as long as the chores are done in time, so here I am."

"Sure Cinderella, that sounds completely reasonable," I mumble and roll my eyes. "Well, give me a cloth and some spray. Might as well get this over with quicker so you can all go to the ball." Everyone in the room stills, the staleness in the air causing me to turn and raise a brow. Did they think I wasn't up to a bit of hard work? They didn't get the chance to meet Sammy, the badass, non-binary grafter who helped build a conservatory for stray cats. They also gave any small fortune made to troubled teens in Brooklyn. I miss those days.

"Are you coming?" Charley queries. "To the club opening, I mean." Her voice is unsure, as if she doesn't know which answers she'd prefer me to give. In one aspect, she probably wants a night to have fun with her new friends, and Lord knows – drama follows wherever I go. But on the other hand, I'm not ready to relinquish all concerns over Charley's wellbeing just yet. She may trust these Elites, but I certainly do not trust Carter and the lengths he'd go to in the name of getting rid of me. Until Charley has signed a contract and is prancing around in a little maid's outfit, she's a variable I can't take the chance with.

"Sure, why not? I'm in the mood for a spot of dancing." Without saying much else, I'm handed a microfiber cloth and some antibacterial spray with the orders of cleaning door handles. I do pride myself on a decent knob polish. A radio is turned up in the kitchen, everyone falling into a joyful mood as I make my way through the lower level of the manor. Heading directly for the office, it takes me three whole tries to guess what Carter changed the security code to. The only date circled on the calendar in red - probably to help Owen and Sebby not to forget.

Once sealed inside, I work on keeping my promising to Lily – the interviewee who's about to lose her home. Bypassing Carter's security system and taking the extra time to set up a ghost server to prevent my actions from being tracked, I access my own personal accounts. Off-shore, in various names and completely hidden if anyone should try to find them. These are my contingencies if I should find myself in a bind in which I need to vanish quickly. Creating new personas, acquiring false documentation of a high quality and setting myself up in a different part of the country involves serious money to change hands.

Luckily, I've conned enough people to be able to comfortably help those who deserve it. Like Lily – now the proud owner of her three-bed condo, a second family minivan and enough in her savings to cover the hospital expenses after I stumbled across her medical files. Three months pregnant and type-two diabetic. No wonder she was desperate enough to seek out the job role here with the health benefits clearly mentioned. A few months and she'd be on paid maternity, much to Carter's annoyance. Maybe I should have let her apply, but this way is in Lily's best interest.

Hearing talking outside the door, I quickly sign out of the encrypted server, shut down the iMac and duck out without being seen. The Elites have moved into the rest of the manor, sounds of vacuums and general chatter sounds through the rooms nearby. Re-entering the kitchen, cloth and spray bottle in hand, I find the area deserted. Other than Pig, still chowing down her food by skidding the bowl across the ground, it's just me. Completely alone with the mammoth wall planner on my left.

"Well, you could do with a fresh start if I ever saw one," I muse to myself, and then get to spraying. Gloopy rivets of colored marker stream south, caught by my cloth before bleeding onto the wall itself. Wiping the remainder of the pen away, flicking post-it notes over the floor, I smile at the cleared schedule and exhale. "Much better."

"Amethyst!" a voice calls through the central hall. Sharing a look with Pig, I shrug. Either these girls have access to the security cams or they're psychic. But as I round the corner, I see neither is true. Lou is standing by the front door, looking at me expectantly. Over the threshold, a suited man in a flat cap I recognize as the limo driver is standing, a singular purple rose in hand. I approach with caution, a shuffling puppy around my ankles.

"Mr. Hudson requests you join him for an important meeting. He asked me to give you this." After I've accepted the rose, he returns to his limo and sits in the driver's seat facing forward. Lou lingers for a moment, eyeing the note attached to the stem, which I now realize holds petals in the exact same shade as my hair. I couldn't have color matched it better myself. Turning, I retreat to the BDSM room for some privacy before peering inside the folded paper in privacy.

I have a 40-minute window to sneak away, and a PI
session being held in your name. Let's get some answers.

My heart judders. He heard me on the boat. Not only that, Myles has arranged an appointment on my behalf. The limo horn honks from outside and I'm spurred into action without time to think. Sure, I've tried to hire a private investigator myself but we're not talking about tracking down a long lost relative. We're talking big money, men who deem themselves as untouchable gods and those who fear making a move against them. There's only so far a PI could probe before either being bought off or they suddenly go missing. Perhaps Myles can open doors my fake name is unable to.

Placing the rose on the bedside table, I quickly change. Forty minutes is all Myles can offer me, and it could possibly be the most important forty minutes of my life.

Chapter 17

Craig, as I've discovered the limo driver answers to, speeds away from the sidewalk the moment I've shut the rear door. I rock back on the sturdy Doc Martin soles, peering up at the looming skyscrapers lining either side of the street. Myles summoned me to the city, but I was expecting a backstreet office building hidden from view. Like the others I've used, and probably where I was going wrong. The wall of glass before me couldn't be further from that sense of familiarity, the door being pulled open by a smiling assistant.

"Miss Amethyst?" I narrow my eyes at her suspiciously, announcing my name so publicly for those passing between us. Her dark hair is pulled back into a too-tight bun, her smart attire polar opposite to my baggy rock band tee and torn jeans. Yeah, I went full incognito, although there seems to be no need. Her smile doesn't falter as I lift my chin and stride passed.

The lobby opens into a huge circular space, fitted with a plush waiting area opposite the reception desk. More beaming assistants sit behind, all too happy to see me. All of the furniture is white and gleaming beneath the biggest golden chandelier suspended in mid-air. Spiraling floors of offices wind upwards, creating 'Steele's Law Firm' as displayed across the entire back wall in gold letters taller than me. The door at my back is opened again, and in swoops Myles. The women nearby stand, drifting closer as if pulled by invisible ties. When his arm rounds my back and he places a kiss on my forehead, I hear the collective sigh of swooning. So it wasn't me they were so happy to see, but the company I apparently keep.

"I love your outfit," Myles mutters into my ear. I frown at the black t-shirt that touches the rips on my thighs, pointing at the death metal logo of skeletons raising their middle fingers.

"This is yours, isn't it?" I query. The t-shirt was in the dresser back in the BDSM room, but the longer its scent envelopes me, the more certain I am. Myles' smile stretches even wider.

"Indeed. Seeing you in my clothing draws out the primal side of me to take you in it." Any response I could have had is cut short by the assistant who is on door duty, appearing in front of us.

"Mr Hudson – Ms Steele is ready for your prenup meeting."

"Our what-wait-what?"

"Thank you, Samantha," Myles nods with a heavy dose of familiarity. Allowing Myles to guide me into a waiting elevator, I wait for the doors to close before stepping out of his hold.

"So, since apparently I'm marrying you now - how many of those women ogling out there have you slept with?" I resist folding my arms, gripping the railing.

"Are you jealous?" Myles cocks his head, his blond hair crinkling over the collar of his white shirt. Top bottom popped, sleeves rolled up, his golden skin fights to break free of the cotton confines. I shake my head, mimicking his smile.

"Who wets your cock is of no concern to me. I don't like being paraded around under false pretenses."

"What you mean is," Myles steps into my personal space, "you don't like people thinking you'd be another notch on my bedpost." Dipping his mouth close to mine, Myles reaches behind me to halt the elevator mid-journey. The entire vessel is glass, drawing the attention from those in offices across the other side of the balcony. I can't pay them too much notice, when Myles' presence consumes the air. Authority seeps from him, a quiet confidence I've seen evading him at the manor. This isn't Myles, the man who is ordered around by his best friend. This is the business mogul and cover model the rest of the world sees. Drawing the backs of his fingers down my arm, I conceal a shiver.

"To answer your question, Ms Steele was my lawyer during the rape trials. While she was in court defending me, I was ironically screwing my way through her entire staff body. Kind of like a score card I just had to complete. The press had already decided I was guilty - I didn't see the point of going celibate by then."

"That was dangerous. Anyone could have claimed you forced them and seen you committed to jail instead of a rehab facility," I raise a brow. His fingers find my hand, interlinking them with mine and in one swift move, my hand is pinned above me against the glass.

"Is that concern I hear?" Myles smirks, pressing his lips against my jaw before guiding my arm to lay over his nape. "I was stupid back then. The spoiled, gluttonous heir you believe me to be. But that's not who I am anymore." Lowering himself, my hand falls naturally into his hair.

"What the fuck are you doing?" I ask as Myles settles on his knees, his mouth inches from my center. I'm not against being licked out with an audience, but where Myles is concerned, there's a point of no return. A barrier I can't let him breach, because one taste wouldn't be enough. He's too experienced to not rock my fucking world and turn me into one of those sappy girls downstairs. Yearning from a distance isn't my style.

Yet my hand remains in his hair. I toy with a curl as his breath fans my thigh through the jeans gaping hole. Stroking the exposed patch, I can all to easily imagine his fingers slipping beneath the fabric and discovering I didn't bother with underwear. Except he doesn't. Sitting back on his heels, Myles blinks those stunning amber eyes up at me, wide and transparent.

"I, Myles Hudson, pledge myself to you. I will not screw, indulge or flirt with anyone except you, Fiery." My hand drifts from Myles' hair to his shoulder, anchoring myself for stability. On the outside, I force a skeptical expression. Inside is a completely different story.

"And if I don't want you?" Myles produces the cockiest, lopsided smile, pushing himself to his feet.

"Oh you want me. As soon as you stop lying to yourself, I'll be ready." Cupping my cheek, he restarts the elevator without taking his eyes from me. The doors ping open while we're still searching each other's gazes for answers.

"Um, should I come back?" a voice slices between us. Pulling away, I rush to hide how breathless I am, greeting the woman on the balcony. "Felicia Steele," she shakes my hand. "Please, this way to my office." Keeping my back to Myles, I leave all thoughts of his proclamation behind in the elevator. Now's not the time to question if my first impression of him was wrong, not when I have a promise to keep first. But my mind can't let it go so easily. Following Felicia into her office, I stop in the doorway, the most pointless thought giving me pause.

"Wait, during the rape trials, weren't you like seventeen?" Myles only chuckles, crowding me onto the office and closing the door. I take a high-backed leather seat before an impressive desk, assessing the décor. Whereas the rest of the building is open and airy, Felicia has opted for deep mahogany's, rich woods and leather. Heavy blinds block out the sunlight, reinforcing the need for two tall lamps with stained glass shades. All that's missing is a pair of antlers mounted beside the mounted portrait of a greyhound in a suit with a top hat and monocle.

"Myles tells me you need some assistance in acquiring some answers." Felicia sits across the desk. She's an interesting character, her face soft within a curtain of blonde hair and eyes which are neither blue nor green. Within her blouse, she is equally as muscled as endowed by good genes, leaving me at a loss of where to look. I lift her name plaque, reading the title beneath her gold imprinted name. *Senior Partner.* So much for bringing me to a private investigator. "I take client confidentiality extremely seriously," Felicia adds, sensing my hesitation to disclose anything to her.

"Felicia has an extensive amount of influence over politicians and such, with many reliable sources she can turn to. She has run searches for me several times without Carter knowing," Myles adds. I snort, placing the plaque down to swivel an incredulous look his way.

"I hardly think the information I'm searching for is akin to you avoiding the tight hold of your master. Nothing I have planned regarding what I find out here will be legal. Quite frankly, I'd rather you weren't involved." Turning to face me only, Myles takes my hand in his, gently stroking circles with his thumb.

"Do you remember me groveling on my knees in the elevator?"

"I should hope so. It was three minutes ago." His amber eyes glint with mirth before his face drops into a stern, serious expression which leaves me longing for the smile to return.

"That means this has become my vendetta too. Those greedy, rich men you mentioned, wanting to rid them of their prized possessions? It's revenge you're looking for, and perhaps when I help you get it, you'll have a reason to trust me."

"Anything you say here stays between the three of us," Felicia pitches in. Panic claws at the inside of my throat, a moment of rare vulnerability shining through the walls I have carefully constructed. Something that happens too easily around Myles.

A throat is cleared. Myles' grip on my hand tightens. They're boxing me in, narrowing the cage of expectation. Fight or flight kicks in as I whip my hand back and prepare to run. Flee, jump out of the window. It doesn't matter how. I can't be here, can't trust these strangers with the information I've kept only to myself all these years.

"Amethyst," Myles commands my attention. His amber eyes, the shade of churning honey, swallow me whole as I struggle to remember to breathe. "If you could do this on your own, you would have already. Let me help you." His chair skids as he nudges closer but refrains from touching me again. "And if Felicia or I screw you over, I've already warned her you have the ability to destroy everything we've ever achieved."

"I'm under a strict NDA for anything related to Myles," Felicia nods, not showing a trace of fear about Myles' announcement. I wonder if he knows that for a fact or if he's..... "And even without such, he pays me enough to take his secrets to the grave. I will regard yours with the same discretion." I settled back in the seat. Well, no one can say I didn't give them the chance to back out. Centering myself, I will a wash of numbness to fall over me. Forcing my senses to become deadened, and detaching the memories flittering to mind from reality. It's the only way I'm able to bring my true self to the surface without causing lasting damage to my intricate persona.

"Fourteen years ago in Chicago, an entire block of townhouses were offered settlements to sell their properties. All took the deal, except one." I exhale, choosing to stare at the portrait. I should have one made for Pig, painted as a still life with a crown upon her head. Myles clears his throat and I bring my gaze back to the gaping hole of denim at my knees.

Deep breaths. This isn't for me. It's for the scared girl I left behind and the life which was stolen for someone else's gain.

"Around the same time, the housing officer at Crest Financial Holdings received a huge bank transfer from an anonymous source and the last remaining property was repossessed."

"I'm so sorry that happened to you Ami...but surely-"

"Oliver Reynell is his name," I interrupted Myles and whatever simple placate he was about to give. No one understands the weight of what I've been through, what it's like to walk away from your last remaining relative and tackle this cruel world alone. "I need to know who paid Reynell to file the foreclosure documentation."

"Sounds simple enough." Felicia shrugs, jotting down some notes in her notebook. I grunt, for my life is anything but simple.

"If you do manage to find a name, cross reference it with Bio Medical Supplies and LiteSource." I tap my finger on the table when she pauses, making sure she doesn't miss a single detail.

"The energy company?" Myles asks the question floating in the air, sharing a frown with the woman listening intently across the desk. I nod stiffly, slipping my hands to the edge of the leather cushion and tugging at the side-stitching.

"On the same day the bank representatives came, so did the Bio-Med to reclaim their equipment. When they didn't manage to gain entry, the power was cut." A flash of light behind my eyes goes black as I remember scrambling around in the dark, starting heart compressions on an already lifeless body.

"I don't understand-" Myles mutters on the edge of my subconscious. The next words tumble out of me on a labored breath.

"My mom was being kept alive by a ventilator." I vaguely catch the too-close amber eyes widening, but I'm drawn back into the memory I don't want to relive. Grunted counting as I performed CPR, silent prayers for her to hold on until the power returned. Panic set in within minutes, cramping my fingers and I knew I couldn't continue.

Instead, I hunted for the back-up generator. I found it beneath the porch steps by torch light, and just as I glanced upon the jagged slashes ripping the exterior to shreds, the front door was smashed inwards. I had a single moment to make the decision which would alter the course of my life, and I ran. Tormented by fear and shock, I left, and never even returned to reclaim my mother's body.

"All three companies participated in an orchestrated attack that day. Someone targeted us. Someone with the power, money and influence to do so. I need to know who was pulling the strings, and I need to make them suffer." Through half-hooded eyes, I see Myles reach for me. My body is shifted, drawn into his lap while his face buries into the crook of my neck. I don't fight him, no longer able to push him away. Neither us or our present company speaks, letting the weight of my truth settle. I spent years cocooned in my self-loathing; only given reprieve by the person I was portraying at the time. Now it's second nature to hide, to pretend.

At some point, I melt into Myles. His breathing becomes echoed by my own, our psyche's falling into a rhythm where words aren't needed. Fiddling with the end of his blond hair, vibrating emanates from Myles' pocket. He ignores it at first, but on the second ring I pull it out from beneath my ass and hand it to him.

"Hudson," he grunts without looking.

"Is Amethyst with you?!" the responding, panicked shout comes through the handset and I straighten. Taking the phone, I slip from Myles' lap and pace to the back of the room.

"Sebby? It's me - what's wrong?" Heavy panting sounds on the other end, as if he's running from the shouting I can hear in the distance.

"You're in the city, right? I need you." Something clicks within me, and suddenly I couldn't care less where I currently am. Sebby called for me. *Needs* me. The past will have to wait, at least for one more evening. Acquiring Sebby's location, I tell him I'm on my way and toss the phone back to Myles. I'm halfway out the door when his voice finds me.

"Wait!" I glance back, finding both him and Felicia standing. "The conspiracy you've spoken of – what was the point? Why was it so important to force you out?"

"Look up the address I gave. I have to go." Darting for the elevator, my finger is jamming against the button as I picture Myles doing just that. Bringing up the location of my childhood home, discovering it is now a two-story casino stretching the length of the block. His bile-fueled reaction to the establishment's chosen name will be the same as mine and everything I think of it. Above the grand entrance in fluorescent lights with a pulsing heartbeat line underneath. *'Life Support.'* As I slump inside the elevator, only the railing keeping me upright, a roar bellows through the glass structure. Oh, there it is.

Chapter 18

Rasping my knuckles on the seedy motel door, I grimace at the overweight reception clerk who followed me up to the fourth level. Apparently, responding to his advances with a 'get fucked' seemed more like an invitation than a threat. Cleaning his ear with a little finger, the other hand dips beneath the stained vest barely containing his gut to swirl within his belly button. I throw up in my mouth as the door swings wide open, a hand at my wrist tugging me inside.

"Bucket. I need a bucket," I cover my mouth, feeling the overwhelming shade of green creeping over my face. Sebby locks me inside, although I'm not sure if I feel any safer. Limp curtains hang over grimy windows, casting the room in a dull orange which isn't helped or hindered by the bleak naked bulb above. The bedsheets are crumpled, clothes draped across the soiled carpet and as I turn to Sebby in just his boxers, I feel nauseous all over again.

"Dude seriously, what the fuck? I know I loathe extravagance but this," I signal around the cramped room, "this is where self-respect comes to die amongst the mites."

"It's not easy being associated with Myles," Sebby scowls. I'm so used to his calm, withdrawn nature, the strength of his emotion takes me by surprise. "We're followed by paparazzi everywhere, always on the exposé channels. Whether with him or not, these are the lengths I must go to for some privacy." Sebby angrily shoves his hair back from his forehead, his gray eyes glancing to another closed door. I didn't hear it until now, too distracted by the contents of my stomach threatening to rise. Telltale thundering of a shower seeps beneath a two-inch gap at the base of the bathroom door. Sebby isn't alone.

"Okay first off, breathe Seb." Gripping his shoulders, I mock the type of repetitive pants a labor-class would demonstrate, until he copies. Hee-hee-hoo. Hee-hee-hoo. "Now – what the fuck am I doing in this shithole?"

"After Myles went to the bathroom during our shareholder meeting and didn't return, Carter went looking for him. Owen had some business to attend to and I...sought out a gay bar across the more discrete side of the city." Sebby clears his throat, allowing his black hair to fall forward into his eyes again. "I met someone and we came here."

"Well, that makes complete sense," I nod, looking at the dirty room once more. I get why he called me and not one of the others. "Just so I understand properly - in this cliché scenario of yours, are you role playing Jeffery Dahmer or the victim? I know a guy who can have a barrel of acid here in two hours."

"I seriously hope you're joking," Panic bursts from Sebby's eyes. I don't respond. The shower shuts off and I shrug, mouthing *it's now or never.* Dragging me across the room, Sebby points to a pair of discarded pants, keeping his voice low. "I was looking for another condom to...well you know, and I found this." Nudging the pants with his foot, an ID catches the dim light.

Mitchell Huggan. Vlogger/Reporter for Inside Entertainment.

"Oh shit, it's a snake in the grass issue," I gasp. We are definitely the Jeffery Dahmer's here. Sebby pulls on a shirt, hastily fastening the buttons over his tattoos. At some point, I'll find a reasonable moment to admire the various caricatures I've spotted, but this doesn't seem like it.

"I'm not sure yet. That's why I need you to do that decipher voodoo thing you do. There's always the chance he actually...likes me, right?" I watch him tug on his slacks, noting the complete lack of hope in his face. All I'm getting is fear. Fear at being deceived maybe, or the fear this guy might be risking his own career to hang with Sebby in secret and force my closet-ed friend into the decision he's been avoiding. To tell Myles he loves him, or accept he might fall for someone else.

The toilet flushes, sending Sebby into full panic mode. Hands flapping and flustered whispers for me to hurry up. Inspecting the lanyard closer, I make swift judgments about this mystery man. First off, Sebby has excellent taste. Secondly, I would kill to have his natural eyebrows, but any further thoughts are halted by the bathroom door flying open. A mirror image of the photograph in my hand steps out from a wall of billowing steam, his tanned skin a natural contour to the valley of abs dipping into the towel he's holding over his junk.

"Oh er..." Mitchell pauses, those defined eyebrows shouting up-wards. "I didn't realize you wanted to include someone else, Seb. I kinda thought it'd just be the two of us."

"It is, I do – Ami was just dropping something off," Sebby flashes a look at me to go along with his lie. Dropping the ID back on the crumpled pants, I nod in quick succession.

"Yeah, that's right. I just came to give Seb this." Grabbing his face in my hands, I plant my lips on his mouth and kiss the fuck out of that gorgeous gay man. Freezing beneath my hold, I'm left to do all the work – typical. My lips shift over his delightfully soft ones, one hand drifting south to give his crotch a squeeze.

"Trust me," I whisper between his gasp and slipping my tongue into his mouth. On a lost sigh, Sebby obeys. His hands press against my back, closing the distance between us and returns my kiss with equal vigor.

"You bitch!" Mitchell screams. I push away from Sebby and duck, anticipating the loud crack of Mitchell's slap. Sebby inhales sharply, holding his cheek as Mitchell flies around the room in a flurry to retrieve his clothes and exits in a fantastically dramatic whirlwind. A huge smile grows across my face.

"Well that was fun." I shrug. Beneath his flop of black hair, Sebby has the shocked look of a deer caught in headlights. Refusing to release his reddening cheek, I reach for his suit jacket and drape it over his shoulders. "I still say we could have justified killing him for being a lying cheat."

"So...he was using me for his job?"

"What? No." I roll my eyes. Sebby really is clueless when it comes to this. "Mitchell genuinely liked you, or he wouldn't have been sneaking around on his spouse to be here." I understand not everyone has the knack for reading people like me, but it took three seconds to glance from the tiredness circling Mitchell's eyes to the indent of his missing wedding ring. Surely at some point, Sebby could have noticed the same, although I'm guessing the dick was just too good.

"His partner could be aware of the lengths he'll go to for a story," Sebby tries to twist the truth again. Dropping on the edge of the bed, his head hangs low. I lower beneath his knees, preferring to crouch than touch any of the furniture.

"Believe what you want Seb, but that reaction was real. And I highly doubt he'll expose himself as well as you. Now the real question is – what are you going to do about it? Chase him down and beg for forgiveness, or admit this was never really about Mitchell." We share a knowing look.

"Fuck, what time is it? I need to be at the club opening," Sebby distracts himself by looking all around and then settles back on me. More specifically, the baggy band t-shirt and torn jeans parting at my knees. "And you need a change of clothes."

***

Given the type of establishment I now associate with Sebby, as the limo nears the 'club', I gape in awe. Not some seedy bar with a spunky, pink-haired bartender like I was imagining. But an impressive building with several levels, all fitted with black-out glass. Aptly named 'Elysium', beneath the swirly sign displaying its name, the grand entrance is guarded by imposing bronze statues of a Greek goddess. The limo pulls to a stop beside the red carpet, an entourage of press patiently waiting behind ropes and a wall of security guards either side. Not the attacking kind, but the type who are paid big bucks to get the best images for magazines. The type who understand a little flattery aids them far better than harassment.

"Would you mind?" Sebby looks across the bench and offers me his hand. I glance at it for a second, making no move to take it.

"If you're sure it's what you want…" I bite my inner cheek. "But the truth will come out sooner or later, and it would be best doing so by your own admission. You should be unapologetically yourself. Who cares what the rest of the world thinks?"

"Ironic considering the false identities you've adopted." Sebby quips back. Touché. Taking his hand, our fingers are interlocked by the time he pops the door and helps me to my feet. Standing tall in a pair of stunning red heels, I'm almost the same height as a dashing Sebby. His smile is full of boyish charm, putting on a good show as we take our slow walk towards the open doors.

"Sebastian Lloyd! Who's your date this evening?" a woman with a microphone calls out. Sebby is all too happy to guide me over, laying on years of perfected charisma while I smile innocently. Cameras flash from all directions, catching every angle of the attire Sebby picked out for us both prior to coming here.

From the back, my dress appears classy. Sophisticated, covering every inch of skin from neck to wrists and down to my ankles. The velvet material hugs my body, a hidden corset within accentuating my curves and doing wonders for my ass. Around the front though, the dress opens from my nape to my breasts, highlighted with a low sweetheart neckline. Over my right hip, the velvet gathers into a large, floppy bow where the leg slit reaches dangerously high. All black, all risqué. Apart from the sleek ponytail of my violet hair, the red heels and matching lipstick are the only pop of color. I have to say, Sebby has impeccable taste.

Thanking us for our time, the reporter moves onto the next round of guests to arrive as we make our way inside. Catapulted into a world of sheer indulgence, all of my senses are brought to life. The rolling perfume of suede and eucalyptus trees positioned by a waterfall at the back of the room interweave like destined lovers. Music plays softly, the wave of a violin which complements the waterfall instead of combating it. Chandeliers hang from high ceilings, casting a warm glow over the marble floors below. The walls are adorned with intricate murals and art pieces, adding an artistic flair. Plush seating arrangements have been scattered throughout, deeming this as a more civilized meeting area.

The bar of Elysium, however, is a masterpiece in itself. Spanning the length of the room, showcasing the most premium of spirits and rare wines, those working behind the black and gold counter craft cocktails of all colors. In the same black shirts and slacks, bartenders await at empty booths to take orders. Taking a step in that direction, I crash into a wall of black and white which wasn't there a moment before. A hand automatically finds my waist, amber eyes consuming me in their feverish depths.

"You're so fucking beautiful," Myles rasps as if it pains him. As if he's been stalking me since the moment I stepped through the door and couldn't resist telling me. His blond hair is pulled back into a bun, his face freshly shaven to reveal the strength of his jawline. On this occasion, he wears his suit with pride, top button fastened above a black tie. I toy with the satin length of it, before remembering myself and dropping my arm back to my side.

"You don't fix up too bad yourself," I settle on, needing to reassert boundaries. The last time I saw this man, I was telling him about a past life I've never told anyone. Not even Charley. That possibly makes him my closest ally, despite barely knowing him.

"Is everything okay? The emergency..." Myles trails off as his gaze dips to mine and Sebby's hands, still tightly clasped. The man in question tenses, his fingers attempting to retreat but I hold him firm. This was his choice; he's not allowed to back out now.

"All good here. Sebby needed help picking out his shoes, and in turn took me shopping." My lips remain upturned, my eyes watching keenly for Myles' reaction and boy, there's a lot to see. Jealousy, confusion. Clenched jaw, a brief narrowing of eyes before Myles finds a forced smile to present.

"I'm glad someone was able to spoil you," he states in a tone which contradicts his words. Luckily, someone calls his name and Myles excuses himself, putting me back on my mission to reach the bar. I need a drink more than ever, my gut a swirling mess of I-don't-fuck-ing-know-what. Sliding onto a stool with more grace than the high-slit in my skirt should allow, I finally release Sebby to signal to the bartender. Two strawberry daiquiri coming up.

"It won't work, you know. Using me to make Myles jealous." Sebby mutters as the bartender sets up before us. As he turns to fetch the strawberries and ice, I take the rum bottle and tip it over my parted lips until Sebby scrambles to put it back in place.

"Perhaps I was doing the opposite," I shrug, licking my lips. "Allowing *you* to use *me* to make him jealous. Trust me, if one of us ends up in Myles' bed tonight, it sure as shit isn't going to be me." Leaning on my elbows, I make small talk with the bartender, letting him woo me with his vigorous thrusting of the shaker. Sebby spins my stool, forcing me to look into his sullen grey eyes.

"There's no distracting Myles when he has a new fascination. He won't stop until he's had you. I'm just...around for when he's bored, horny and lacking options." Pity douses the exciting prospect I might just enjoy tonight. In the background, an announcer speaks into a microphone, saying something about the grand opening but I'm too focused on the man before me. Attractive, loyal, guarded, withdrawn.

Raising my hands to cup Sebby's cheeks, he bristles as if I'm about to kiss him again. He'd be lucky.

"You're worth more than being someone's plaything, Sebby," I push his hair aside to stare into his grey eyes. "But I get it. We all put ourselves second when it comes to those we love." And just like that, the weight of the day falls on my shoulders. The memories, the emotions I keep suppressed. I haven't let myself mourn since the day I hid behind a tree to witness my mother's burial. Out of everyone who came, I only recognized my aunt. Police patrolled the graveyard, hunting for the missing girl who seemingly racked up thousands of dollars in debt and left her mother to die alone. I kept the knowledge of what really happened that day to myself, not trusting anyone else to extract my revenge. Until now.

"I'm sorry," Sebby whispers, drawing me back to this moment. I'm still cupping his face, idling stroking his cheek bones. "Wherever you just went – I'm sorry for it all." The pity is reversed and I despise the bitter taste of it on my tongue. Although I know Sebby doesn't mean to condescend me. Somehow in this lost and twisted world of power, we've found some common ground. A reason to stick together against those closing in on us.

Sitting back on my stool, I blow out a steady breath and see our drinks are ready. Complete with pink and orange umbrellas. Suddenly, I know I'm going to need something far stronger.

"Do you mind?" I ask the two men on my other side and take their whiskey glasses without waiting for an answer. Handing one to Sebby, I link arms with him and plaster on that smile I've learned to wear like a shield. "Come on. Let's get all shades of fucked up."

Chapter 19

"Uh huh," I absentmindedly agreed to whatever the woman beside me is saying. Raising the coke bottle to my lips, I yearn for something stronger whilst taking a long sip. The entire time, my eyes are glued to Amethyst in the crowd below. Strobe lights bounce off her purple hair as she moves, dancing like nobody's watching. But I am.

There hasn't been a moment since I entered Elysium that she has been out of my sight. Especially after I stood on the stage and relayed the speech Carter wrote for me, whilst she was cupping Sebby's face. Touching him. Drinking with him. When they left hand in hand for the stairwell to the nightclub floor, I ditched the microphone and took after them.

"Sounds riveting," I reply again when my current company pauses her idle chatter long enough to indicate I should answer. From the balcony, I have an open view of the dance floor below. Bodies jump and dance shoulder to shoulder, the speakers dotted around the lower level immersing them in a DJ remix of 90's anthems.

I'd give anything to throw my reputation in the gutter and rush down there to join her. But if it's not the tabloids or my father's expectations breathing down my neck, it's Carter. Sprawled across a suede sofa, his eyes are closed as he smokes a joint. My best friend, who gave up his own life to save mine. I can't fail Carter because he's never let me fall.

"Can I cut in?" Owen comes to my rescue, shooing the woman away to sneakily hand me a shot of vodka.

"You're a lifesaver. But also, you're fucking late." Tossing back the shot, I savor the burn and return the glass to Owen before Carter sees. Dressed casual as fuck, Owen smirks and leans over the railing in his white t-shirt and dark jeans.

"What can I say? Business is booming right now. How's our girl doing?" I grunt. Our girl? Owen has barely taken an interest in her except to steal her puppy, but then again – the Sebby and Amethyst hand-holding thing blindsided me so what do I know? Leaving his question unanswered, I change the subject.

"Do you ever wish you'd just let me rot in jail? Moved on with your lives and let me find my own way?"

"Jesus Christ, one shot and we're back here again. This is why you're not allowed to drink in public." Putting the Coke back in my hand, Owen turns to face the balcony instead. The security guards at the base of the stairs have free selection on the women they allow up here, a mini dance party forming itself in the back corner in a bid to get our attention. Aside from those behind the private bar, we're the only other men and as Sebby appears in the VIP section, our mini tribe is seemingly complete.

"The party's back here Myles," Owen tries to nudge me. "We can tag team, just like the old days." Not a chance. My heart has picked up a beat in my chest with the sight of Sebby, and not from the rise of jealousy I'm struggling to squash. If he's up here, there's no one down there watching over Amethyst.

Shoving Owen and Sebby aside, I fly down the stairs two at a time. Carter, shouting after me, is drowned out by the speakers as I barge past the security guards and weave through the dance floor. She's easy to find, considering the only margin of space between the dancers is the one Amethyst creates. Approaching her back, I freeze, unsure of what I was going to do at this point. So, I skid to a stop and simply watch.

She's magnetic. Drawing the attention of everyone nearby without even trying. Soaking in the beat of the heavy bass, Amethyst moves to the undercurrent rhythm, at odds with those jumping and fist pumping all around. Turning in a leisurely circle, I brace myself for her to see me, but her eyes are closed. Swaying arms, swirling fingers flick through the air, beckoning me to join.

I step into the roll of her hips, hovering on the edge of touching her. Of pulling her to me and holding her tight, just in the hopes she'll not push me away. I want everything she is. Everything she has. Passion, freedom, confidence. Amethyst holds the key to releasing me from my binds, because if anyone could break down Carter's walls, it'd be her.

"What the fuck is this, Grandpa?" Amethyst blurts out. I'd been so captivated by her body, I hadn't realized she'd opened her eyes. Taking the Coke bottle still held in my hand, Ami gives it to a stranger nearby.

Then, from her cleavage, she produces a corked test tube of bright blue liquid. Tugging the cork out with her teeth and spitting it across the crowd, she tries to tip the liquid into my mouth but I dodge aside.

"I can't indulge in any form of addiction in public. The paparazzi-"

"Yeah, yeah. Gilded cage, tight leash. I get it." Ami rolls her purple eyes and downs it herself. Her throat bobs, her cleavage bared. Any other woman would be using this moment as an invitation, but not Amethyst. She's teasing me. Forcing me to work for her, for the first time. In our story, she's the cat and I'm the mouse glutton for punishment and constant rejection. But any snippet of emotion from her, negative or otherwise, is worth it.

"Come with me," Amethyst grabs my hand and tugs. I'm at a loss to fight, the connection between our hands causing a zap of electricity to my libido. Navigating through the crowd, we disappear beneath the balcony where I know Carter will be watching. A shudder rolls the length of my spine, as if the shackles have just been snapped. Temporarily, but it's enough. I'll follow Ami wherever she is willing to take me.

Exiting the dance floor, we slip through a gap between the bar and opposite wall, entering a long hallway. It twists and turns, illuminated by flashing LED lights which run the length of the ceiling. At the very end, the hall opens into an oval of closed bathroom doors and a horde of people waiting. As one door opens, Amethyst rushes forward to jump the queue, dragging me with her. Protested shouts are shut out as she slams and locks the door, spinning her wide eyes on me.

Wearing a devilish smile to match the wild height of her hair from ruffling her hands through it, I marvel at her beneath the brightened light of the bathroom. Stunning, enticing, and - as she briefly stumbles on her heel, I realize - completely wasted.

"I'm going to make an exception," Amethyst smiles wide, so proud of her own announcement. Lifting one finger, she drags it down the front of my shirt and flicks my tie. "One. Single. Ex...cep...tion." I still her hand from hooking within my waistband, bringing Amethyst's slurring back up to my face. A look of hurt passes between her brows but I don't back down, stepping away from her alluring body.

"Whatever you're thinking, it's a bad idea. We can discuss your intentions tomorrow, when you're sober."

"Wow. I've never been so turned-off by a sentence before." She clicks her tongue, strolling around the large room. Each bathroom is private, and as opulent as the rest of Elysium. White countertops swirled with gold, huge mirrors and enough space for a gaggle of women to gossip and apply make-up – or whatever women do together in bathrooms. Amethyst swirls leisurely, continuing to dance to the song in her head. "And here I was thinking you'd want to prove you're a better kisser than Sebby." I straighten.

"Excuse me?" My voice sounds rough. I catch the hint of Ami's smile before she spins around again, giving me a moment to collect myself. She's challenging me, just as she has from the very beginning. Tugging down my jacket cuffs, I roll my shoulders. "Answer me one question. What's changed?" Ami stops, rolling her head towards me in a sigh.

"It's been a heavy day. As it stands, you've made me vulnerable. I usually deal with that shit via alcohol and orgasms. But if you're not up for the job-" Amethyst makes a move towards the door. I growl, catching her around the waist and dumping her on the countertop.

"Oh I'll give you an orgasm, Fiery. But you're not having my dick until you're sober." Spreading her thighs, the slit in her skirt shifts aside perfectly. My fingers trail a slow path towards her cunt, finding her completely bare. *Fuck.* The decision is taken from me then, and it's no longer a want, but a visceral need. I can't leave until Ami falls apart for me. Breaks in such a way, only I can piece her back together.

Gripping her nape, our mouths crash together, igniting the flames of our desire. Finally, Amethyst responds with the vigor I knew she had. With the battle of dominance I knew we'd awaken. Pushing against me, her lips kiss hard, her lipstick smears. As my tongue slips into her mouth, I slide two fingers into her soaking wet pussy. We both groan. She was so ready for this. The dancing, the teasing – it's all been part of the foreplay. Tugging my hair free of the bun, her nails scrape my scalp, her hips grinding to the rhythm of my fingers.

Shifting my mouth to her jaw, her neck and collar bone, I trail hungry kisses. The need to taste every inch of her skin has me throbbing hard in my suit slacks. Amethyst tugs her dress down for her breasts to be freed and pushes my head to her nipple. I gladly obey. Using a hand on Amethyst's throat, I ease her back to lie on the counter and take her nipple prisoner. My teeth mark, my tongue soothes. Both hands work either her breast or her pussy, my thumb applying pleasure to her clit. If there's one thing I know, one thing I'm good at, it's satisfying women.

Ami's mewls fill the bathroom, her back arched from the counter as I move onto her other nipple. Testing her tolerance between pain and pleasure, she gives no signal to having a threshold. *She will be the death of me.* Instead, Ami welcomes my nipping, moaning louder as I add a third finger into her incredibly tight pussy. Pushing on my head once more, I allow her to guide me south, sinking my teeth into her inner thigh.

"Fuck! Yes," she hisses. In the morning, she'll probably curse me for it, but for now I take my sweet time, ensuring the teeth marks will remain. Sucking hard, I leave a hickey in the center, my own form of branding. I wonder what Amethyst will make of calling me a beast now. My fingers, which haven't slowed, pull back as I stand. If I thought she was beautiful before, now she's a goddess. Flushed with pleasure, writhe with passion. Ami whines for me, her hands outstretched. I memorize the moment for when I'll have my cock in my hand later.

"Stop stalling and make me come," her voice turns demanding. I smirk, slowly shrugging out of my jacket. Using the white shirt cuff to wipe the lipstick from my face, I enjoy her squirming too much, slowly rolling up my sleeves. Ami has given me an opportunity tonight, one I'll make sure she doesn't forget within her drunken haze. Dragging off my tie, I grip her ankles and tug her down the counter. The skirt of her dress rides up, granting me open access. Then, I descend on her.

One leg over my shoulder, I spear Amethyst's pussy with my tongue. She's *delicious*. I can't get enough. Dragging my tongue to her clit, my fingers are back inside her, pumping her into a frenzy. Sucking her into a state of insanity. Each scream is music to my ears, spurring me on.

"Fucking...Fuck me,' she cries out. I smirk against her, drowning in her heady scent and the taste of her arousal. It would be too easy. I'm rock hard and aching to slam home inside her, but I won't. Not tonight. For the one woman who sees me as more than a sex-crazed billionaire, she deserves more.

"I'm not doing anything you'll hate me for in the morning," I mutter, my words lost to the slickened thrusting of my fingers. She claws at my hair again, tugging me close enough to suffocate me with her cunt. What a pleasant way to die. Curling my fingers inside, I suck her clit hard, before flicking my tongue rapidly and repeating the process. Again and again, until she stiffens and prepares to break for me.

"Oh shit...shit...oh, s-" Ami screams. I go even harder, giving her everything I can. My bicep shudders with the tension of my finger fucking, her pussy clamping around me. "Oh Sebby!" the next scream comes. My brows hit my hairline, my mouth going slack. Through the throes of her climax, Ami doesn't realize I've slowed, using her own hand to ferociously rub her clit. I stand, still pumping my fingers inside of her, although my own desire has truly been doused. Pulling back, I wash my hands and face in the basin, redressing and making it to the door while she's still squirming in the aftermath of her pleasure.

Amethyst is a self-serving woman. Someone who doesn't rely on others to get what she wants. After what I heard of her past today, I understand. Although it doesn't crush the misery blossoming in my chest. Amethyst may be the only one I want, but I was stupid to think I could be anything more than a convenience to her.

Chapter 20

"Wakey, wakey!" someone shouts, alongside a round of incessant banging. Groaning, I shove my head beneath the pillow, clamping it over my ears. The cover is ripped from my body, leaving me completely naked and exposed to my assaulter. Not that I care. The banging continues, similar to a wooden spoon on a pan, before the pillow is also torn from my head and tossed over my ass. "Get the fuck up, you've got a job to do."

"I was kinda planning to have a hangover today Carter, if you would kindly leave me the hell alone."

"I don't think so," the smug fucker chuckles, banging the pan beside my head. My skull tightens and cracks down the center. Through the fissure, a migraine strong enough to pulsate in my ears breaks through. Something frilly is chucked beside my face, brushing my cheek. Cracking an eye, I scoff at the maid's outfit laid out. Above, Carter looms like the oppressive bastard of my nightmares. "Consider this your penalty."

"For what?!" I push myself upright too fast and instantly regret it.

"This is for whatever you did to Myles last night," Carter nudges the outfit with his wooden spoon. Dropping the pan on the ground, the burst of sound causes me to wince and plays into Carter's plan perfectly. Slapping something across my forehead, I yelp at the assault, struggling against his hand holding it there and his mouth leaning into my ear. "And this, this is for fucking with my calendar." Leaving as quickly as I woke, he's gone and I flop forward.

"What the fuck?" I try to crinkle my forehead, but it's stuck flat by whatever is still attached to me. On aching legs, I maneuver into the bathroom, braving a look at myself in the mirror. No. No way. Through the slits of my heavy eyes, I inspect the wax sheet firmly stuck over my eyebrows.

A small voice in my head whispers that I probably deserve this. I may have drunk enough last night to put a sailor to shame, but I remember Myles. I remember him between my legs, remembering the yearning I felt. How I continually told myself it was the alcohol which made my body feel so good. And how, in a sudden burst of realization I wanted him with a feverish intensity, I screamed Sebby's name instead.

Teasing the edges of the wax strip, I cry out in pain. Each tiny tug is like a thousand needles piercing my brain, a chasm of pain about to explode from the dam. A few eyelashes and a clump of my hair are also stuck beneath. Bracing myself on the basin, I inhale deeply. There's only one thing for it, and I decide it is well deserved. Gripping the edge of the sheet, I hear Charley calling for me in the main bedroom as I tear it off in one, swift tug.

Wandering into the kitchen a short while later, my heels click loudly against the unforgiving floor. The underskirt of the maid's outfit tickles the bruise on my thigh, causing me to be hyperaware of it at all times. Actually, bruise is too gentle a word for the raised welt of vibrant blue and purples. All four men are sitting on the bar stools, lost in their reading. Carter holds an ostentatiously large newspaper, Owen is scrolling the newsfeed on a tablet, Sebby's on his cellphone and Myles in the center reading a book. Guarded on either side, protected from the heathen entering their presence.

"Good morning fellas," I force a smile. Charley is directly behind, sourcing a glass and a bottle of apple cider vinegar for me. She knows my hangover cure. Popping a Tylenol, I down a shot of vinegar, much to everyone's clear disgust. Well, all except Carter, who refuses to look up and note the perfect job Charley did in recreating my eyebrows. I'll need her to bring over her brow stamps and pencils every day until my natural ones grow back. Sebby slips from his stool first, rounding to my side and leaning on the counter with his back to his friends.

"I can't believe you actually put it on," he flicks the edge of the maid's skirt. I keep Myles out of my eyeline, not wanting to see his reaction to mine and Sebby's familiarity. I wonder if Myles told him about the name-screaming situation, but I doubt Sebby would approach me so brazenly if he had.

"Carter removed all the other clothes before waking me up," I shrug. The other Elites file in, also in knee-high stockings, frilly black-and-white outfits with criss-cross lace detail in the bodice. My chest fills out the white fabric cups more than the rest, as well as the flare of my hips causing the skirt to stick out further. That's what a life of cheesecake for breakfast and giving no fucks gets you.

"Now we're all present," Carter folds his paper and addresses the entire room with the old man persona he's perfected. "Since the calendar was mysteriously wiped clean, I'll inform you all on the events of today. We have two candidates from the interviews arriving shortly for their audition day, and clearly Charley is here also," Carter's lips tighten into a firm line.

"There's a business function at my head office this evening which you will all be catering and serving at. Work out amongst yourselves the details, for sixty-five guests. We need vegan and gluten free alternatives for seven of them. When the applicants arrive, show them the ropes. As always, your collective feedback," he points a finger to the four standing off to one side, "will determine if they make it to the final stage."

I crack a smile. Trying to withhold the bubble of laughter breaking free of my lips. Carter's green gaze swings to me for the first time, brimming with hatred.

"What's so funny?"

"Oh, nothing," I attempt to lie but the laughter pours more freely now. Ahh, screw it. "It's just the whole big bad gangster routine when I've just realized, you're no more than a glorified PA." Gripping my side, I fall into hysterics, turning to leave the room. Hands clamp down on my shoulders, spinning and shoving me into the closest wall. The vein in Carter's temple throbs, his jaw tight enough for the strong line to tease my imagination.

"Not so fast. I have a special task for you Amethyst. We have clients flying over from England for this function as we speak and they're made requests for the menu. You're on tart duty." My laughter fizzles out and I tilt my head, narrowing my eyes. "I believe it's British slang for a whore."

"Yes, I got the reference, thanks." I shove against Carter's chest. So this is my punishment. Losing my eyebrows and spending the day tottering about in heels, my cheeks coated in flour and playing out every man's homemaker fantasy. Peering over his shoulder, I note Myles has his nose back in his book.

I'm in the doghouse, and had I not felt like I owed it to Myles to grovel some, I'd leave. As it stands, I've let my own issues stand between us, even after he's extended his help and not expected anything in return. For that reason, I'll take Carter's taunting. Whatever it takes to repay the debt I now feel I owe Myles, whilst keeping him at arm's length and getting a grip on what the hell I'm doing with my life.

Moving back into the main kitchen, I switch on the oven and steal Owen's tablet from his hands. This bitch doesn't know the first thing about baking, but there's never been a skill I haven't excelled at. Switching on the radio, I crank the music up and tune out the gawking eyes all around. Let's make some of the best tarts this kitchen has ever seen.

***

"Something smells good," Owen enters the room, inhaling deeply. Pig awakens from where she's been lounging by the back door and rushes to greet him. The boys have returned from wherever they've been all day, suits crumpled and heading in different directions. Myles doesn't look my way as he walks towards the stairs, although Sebby gives a sympathetic wave.

"You bet your ass it does," I wipe my forehead with the back of my hand. While the Elites spent the day demonstrating Carter's standards to the newbies, Charley included, I've busted out one-hundred-and-forty-four summer fruit tarts. Owen reaches for one of the small pastry cups and I swiftly smack him around the head with an oven glove. I haven't been slaving away all day for nothing. When Amethyst puts her mind to something, she does it right. A trait I might mix up for the next persona because trust me, that shit is exhausting.

"Carter said something about seeing you in the office," Owen mumbles, more focused on picking up Pig and scratching her belly. He wanders away, lost to her kisses while I grapple for the last shred of my patience. Somehow, someway, I'm going to find a valid reason to add Carter to my kill list.

Taking my sweet time to arrange the tarts in containers for transporting, I'm out of ways to stall and resign to dragging my bare feet across the marble flooring. Screw cooking and wearing heels all day when no one is around to care. Entering the office keycode he has yet to change, I walk straight into Carter's office.

"How the hell-" Carter shoots up from behind the desk, his phone pressed to his ear. "Gina, I'll call you back."

"Gina? Lady friend of yours?" I smirk. I can't imagine it's a fun job but someone must be pulling the stick out of Carter's ass every now and then.

"My mother," he scrunches his nose slightly and purses his lips. Yikes – that's a touchy subject. Pushing my hip against the sideboard, I roll my hand in a 'get-the-fuck-on-with-it' gesture. Straightening his suit, Carter rounds the room to close the door and pulls a chair out for me. "Sit down. It's time we had a real discussion about your time here. Namely, how much longer you're staying."

"Sounds like a question for your boss. I didn't want to come in the first place." I drop down, crossing my legs. I wince at the contact pressing against the bruise, but keep my face casual. Unlike Carter, whose green gaze is drawn to where the maid's skirt rides up and gives a hint of the hot, pink thong he provided. A calculated move or general uniform code – I'm yet to decide.

"Myles is my *friend*, and he isn't saying much of anything right now. I suppose I should thank you, because whatever you did last night has finally stopped him from obsessing over you." Carter lowers into his huge leather chair, resting his elbows on the desk. He doesn't even try to hide his smirk. Inspecting my nails, I slowly lick the length of my top lip.

"Be that as it may...now I'm here, I think I'll stick around a while longer." His smirk drops, slips across the desk between us and takes residence on my face instead. Another one of Amethyst's best traits - unaltered stubbornness.

"For what possible reason?" Carter gapes, pushing his dark brown hair back into place.

"A few actually. To see Charley through this ridiculous hiring process, to give Sebby someone close by who actually understands him. Mostly because I know it will piss you off so much, you'll be hate-fucking your hand each night picturing my face." Outrage contorts his harshly beautiful face, a series of cursing on his lips when his phone vibrates. Taking it from his pocket, he's halfway through aggressively tapping out a message when a clatter and scream sounds from the kitchen. I merely sit there, watching the car crash of emotion take charge of Carter. For someone so controlled and calculated, he sure needs to work on masking his emotions. It's almost too easy to enjoy.

"I swear you radiate fucking chaos wherever you go," he points at me harshly, pocketing his phone and storming around the room, "and for your information – I understand Sebby better than anyone." Taking advantage of his suit jacket flapping wildly, I pick Carter's pocket when he passes and shrink into the seat. Carter's shouting trails through the manor, allowing me to pinpoint his location while I flick through his unlocked phone. Pulling up his messages with Craig, the limo driver, I note tonight's event is at 7pm. The Elites are to take the food via the limo while the boys drive separately. Or rather – that was the plan.

Shooting Craig a quick amendment, I delete the message for Carter and place the phone on his side of the desk. Then I'm rushing up to Sebby's room to change, considering there's no clothes in mine. He doesn't ask questions, keeping watch on the limo pulling up outside. The Elites do the hard work for me, loading the trunk with a whole day's worth of catering prep before heading off to get themselves ready for the function. Opting for board shorts and a baggy t-shirt, I halt in front of the mirror and frown.

"Nah – too Avril," I sigh.

"Avril?" Sebby asks, eyes widening as I find a large pair of scissors in a drawer filled with random shit.

"Yeah, the skatergirl I was back in my early twenties. You know the best way to attract a pedophile? Look like jailbait."

"Why were you attracting..." Sebby begins, but becomes too invested in me cutting the shorts high on my thighs and the t-shirt into a crop top. Tying it in a knot at the back with an elastic band – thank you drawer of random shit – I'm feeling much more Amethyst by the time he ushers me from the room. Apparently altering his limited Gucci collection was a trigger. The trunk beyond the entrance is slammed closed as I reach the stairs, ducking low and waiting for everyone to vacate the vicinity. Once clear, I slink down the stairs, grab the sneakers one of the interviewees left by the door and jump into the back of the limo.

"Good to go?" I ask Craig, patiently waiting in the driver's seat.

"Are you sure Mr. Carter wants me to take you here?" Craig frowns through the open divider, pointing at his navigation screen. Mr. Carter huh? I'll come back to that thought. Nodding, I shift, eager not to sit around in the driveway for too long. Craig picks up his phone, tapping on the side. "Maybe I should speak to him to confirm."

"No need Craig, Amethyst is only doing as asked. I'll accompany her myself," Myles announces, dropping into the seat beside me and slamming the door closed. Sitting up straight, Craig begins to drive immediately, closing the divider between us.

"What are you doing here?" I ask, my eyes roaming over Myles' casual jeans and t-shirt.

"I've spent the entire day pretending I wasn't thinking of you, when you're all I've been thinking about. And I've come to a decision."

"Oh yeah?" I raise one brow. We pass through the iron gates, leaving the manor behind and suddenly, I'm overly self-conscious about our destination. Myles takes my hand in his, placing them between his widely spread legs.

"I don't care who you are, or whoever you want to be. I don't care who you desire, or who you sleep with, as long as I'm on that list too. Wherever you are turns into an adventure. And adventure is what my life is sorely lacking." We fall into a comfortable silence, our minds working overtime to bridge the gaps words can't comprehend.

For someone who has spent her life making snap conclusions of others, I misjudged Myles. In my defense, he's the only exception of a cliché as old as time. Those with money hold all the power, and with power comes misjudged influence and terrible decision making. But Myles is as much a victim to his fortune as I am to those pulling the strings of my past. Money and power are our oppressors, yet maybe, just maybe we could provide a slither of salvation for each other. For a brief period of time at least.

The journey passes too quickly, since the side of the freeway traveling away from the city is practically deserted. Entering a rundown town, the limo judders over potholes, but that's not what draws the local's attention. It's the fact a freaking limo is gracing their streets, maneuvering between boarded up stores and an area dedicated to pitched tents for the homeless. Craig pulls into an alleyway around the back of a food kitchen, his eyes darting as we jump out.

"I don't know about this boss," he mutters, popping the trunk. Curious folk linger at the end of the alley, prying shadows with growling stomachs.

"Once we're unpacked, just get yourself out of here. And do not tell Carter where we are," Myles orders. "I have plans with Ami." Blinking a few times in surprise, the back door of the kitchen opens.

"Melissa! You're back!" a plump woman with frizzy orange hair and a warm smile opens her arms for me. I have to bend almost in half to receive her hug. "Love what you're done with the hair." I greet her with similar compliments, asking if she can spare some men to help unload. They respond quickly, a production line forming as the food is rushed into the kitchen. The soup-kitchen owner gushes about how many more people they'll be able to feed this evening and a rare blossom of warmth spreads through my chest.

It's been too long since I've been back here. It's where I found Charley, and even though I swore to never let her return, there's many more who still need help. A way out, a better future. I'm not in the business of taking on any more proteges, but I can at least know they won't go hungry tonight.

"Just how many personalities do you have?" Myles winds an arm around my middle to pull me a step back and mutters into my ear. I nudge him with a roll of my eyes.

"They're *personas*. I'm a con-woman, not schizophrenic. And I've lost count – some only last for an hour or a day, some can last years. Whatever serves me best at the time." Shrugging, we watch Craig slam the trunk and dive into the driver's seat as if he might catch poverty. Myles chuckles at my back, attempting to leave after the limo has skidded away. "Shall we get going then?"

"You think it's that easy?" I question, remaining by the back door with my arms folded. "Anyone can simply donate to the poor. Get your ass inside and get a hair net." And I track him every step of the way as he does just that.

Chapter 21

We burst into the hotel lobby arm in arm, my smile wide enough to make my cheeks ache. Announcing himself at the reception desk, I pick a piece of lettuce from Myles' hair. I don't think I've ever laughed so hard as watching Myles be man-handled by a group of women with more drive than teeth. They weren't shy, and he gently declined each of their advances whilst still appearing like a smooth-talking bachelor.

We stayed far longer than expected, and I also fell victim to watching him like all of the horny women were. He was quite something. His muscled frame crouched to help a young girl color with crayons. His full lips moving as he read a few resumés and gave feedback, offering to speak to his contacts on their behalf. I had to fan myself at the joy he found in helping others, my mind reeling with the need to have him. There's no need to deny Myles anymore. Dragging him away at closing was difficult, but the lust filling my gaze somehow managed it. We promptly took a taxi to the city, tipping the driver his yearly salary.

"Your guest has already arrived, Mr. Hudson," the receptionist bats her eyelashes at Myles, handing him a keycard. I withhold my questions, entering the elevator and walking to room 225 with him. The hotel is the lower end of extravagant, all white walls and wide hallways, rounded archways and navy-blue carpet with cream detailing. Pushing the keycard into the door's handle, a green light permits us entry.

Candles glimmer through the dark room, a scattered line of rose petals leading to a huge bed. I don't take much note of the other furniture in the suite, my eyes drawn directly to the reclined figure by a standing bucket of champagne on ice.

"Myles?" a voice calls out and I freeze. Confusion and dread crash through my gut like a tidal wave that renders me speechless. "What...is she doing here?" Sebby sits upright. Myles nudges me inside, closing the door. His smile is still as casual as ever, his arm forcing me to stumble further inside.

"It's okay," Myles soothes. Is it? Because I'm not sure what the fuck this is. "I know you two have become close, and I won't stand in the way of the relationship you're building. I may be possessive of those I care for, but I'm not the jealous type." My widened eyes catch Sebby's. He moves a pillow to cover his boxers, the caricature tattoos on his body catching the candlelight. Over his chest, a Gypsy witch smiles out from her head scarf, while Marilyn Monroe holds her skirt down on his thigh. Oblivious to the warning signals Sebby is mentally sending, Myles' continues.

"I thought, instead of sneaking around, you two should explore your connection. And if you'd like...assistance, I'll be right here." Pulling the t-shirt over his head, Myles unbuttons his jeans in preparation and sits in an armchair angled to watch. By his knees, a low table has been prepared with a range of sex toys and restraints. My mouth goes dry. I look from Myles, to Sebby and back again.

"Um, actually," I begin but Sebby clears his throat and shakes his head. Apparently, we're still playing coy. Okay – plan B. "Sorry to disappoint, but I'm out of action today. For the next 3-4 days, if you catch my drift," I hold my lower abdomen as if I don't have an implant and been without a period for the past few years. "But I am intrigued as to what you would do with this." Picking up a set of glass anal beads, I inspect them by candlelight. Myles's eyes zero in on me licking the end bead, his cock jumping behind his boxers. Walking a few steps backward, I hand the anal beads to Sebby and encourage him to nudge the pillow aside. Each movement is tracked, the shift in dynamics taking a moment to settle.

"What? You've never thought of Sebby that way? He's a stunningly gorgeous man." I run a hand through Sebby's hair. Grey eyes blink up at me, eager yet vulnerable.

"Um...I mean, we have...in the past," Myles replies.

"Really?" A devilish smile across my face as the bait is taken. I wink at Sebby before strolling back towards Myles. "Show me." No one in the room moves. Even the candles flicker with uncertainty. The men lock eyes, their chests rising and falling heavily. Rounding the chair, extracting myself from the silent conversation the pair are having, I lean across the back of Myles' shoulders.

"Myles?"

"Mmmhmm," he hums softly.

"You're in my seat." Pushing against his back, he stands so I can jump over the back of the chair, crossing my legs beneath me. Still, hesitation stalls their movements and I twist my lips. "Okay, new tactic. The only voice permitted in this room from now on is mine. Sebby, sit on the edge of the bed." He slides over, obeying immediately. Seems a stern nudge is all he needed.

"Myles, kiss him. Stroke his hair, give me tongues and a show. Make me ache to join in next time." A smile hitches my mouth up at the corner as amber eyes swing to me, desire glazing over their brown-speckled depths. Oh, it's so on.

Chapter 22

"Undress each other," Amethyst says from her chair across the room. I shoot her a side glance, still unsure of what exactly is going on. One minute Myles was trying to set me up with Amethyst, the next she was demanding to be in charge. She nods encouragingly and I turn back to Myles, my fingers shaking as they reach the top buttons of his shirt. He's nowhere near as nervous as I am, but he has not been harboring a crush on me for the past fourteen years. Along the way, I've become convinced I'm in love with him, but can I truly love a man who will never love me back?

My thoughts are spiraling as Myles slips my shirt off, his hands guided by confidence. Stroking my chest, he leaves a hot trail from my neck to sternum. I grow hard instantly. I should be more composed, bolder. Especially given our history, the familiarity with which we know each other's bodies, but I can't get Amethyst's presence out of my head.

"Unzip his trousers, Sebby," she says. My hands pause, mid-shrugging Myles's shirt from his shoulders.

"No. This is stupid, and weird. I'll just leave and let you have what you really want." Moving to stand, Myles stops me, his palms flat against my chest.

"Who says that's not you?" he tilts his head, blocking my view of Amethyst.

"I'm not sloppy seconds. You'll just be imagining I'm her," I sigh. Story of my life. The back-up plan.

"You're right," Myles agrees and my world shatters. A broken breath escapes my parted lips, the crack in my heart I'd been trying to hold together bursting wide open. Pushing me onto my back, Myles lowers onto the bed beside me, his head propped up by his elbow. "You're worth so much more than being a place holder. Which is why I would never consider you as such. You're special to me Seb, more than I've let you know. Our relationship is different, something others wouldn't understand. But I understand, and there is no one else I'm thinking of when I do this."

Cupping my cheek, he drags me in for a kiss which heightens all of my senses at once. A forceful stroke of his tongue, a crash of lips revealing the truth of his passion. His stubbled jaw scrapes mine as he rolls on top of me, pinning my wrists beside my head. I feel his hardness through the slacks separating us, as I'm sure he can feel mine.

Breaking apart, I lay frozen beneath his solid chest, lost in his candle-lit amber eyes.

"I'd like Amethyst to be a part of this, but if you're uncomfortable, she'll leave. No questions asked. It's been too long since we've allowed ourselves to indulge in each other like this. You're the only one I want tonight." This time, I do brave a look towards that chair across the room. It's empty, and my heart sinks. Did I force her to leave? My shyness often gets the better of me, or I might have told Myles how I felt years ago.

A shadowed movement catches my attention as the bed dips behind my head. Lassoing a collar around Myles' neck, Amethyst pushes the attached leash into my restrained hand.

"He's all yours," she whispers in my ear and begins to retreat. I gasp at the sudden loss, realizing Amethyst isn't an intrusion, but a much-needed help. In her actions, there's a silent promise to not use Myles' infatuation to take him away from me, but to help.

"Stay," I quickly state. Myles smiles down at me, a menacing grin which alludes to the fun we're about to have. Releasing my hands, he sits back, tugging on the leash I hold.

"You were unzipping his slacks," Amethyst reminds me. Not having enough patience to admire his sculpted chest, I eagerly dive for the button and zipper in question. Fuck, Myles is so hard, he's pulsing with need. His huge dick tents the thin material beneath my fingers. I rub it once, twice—

"Don't play with your food, Sebby." I shoot an annoyed look at Amethyst where she's settled on the edge of the bed, hiding a coy smile. Slowly pulling the zipper down, I want to take my time. To prolong how Myles is looking at me as if I'm the center of his universe. Unfortunately, Amethyst doesn't have the same idea in mind.

"Myles, get Sebby naked," she demands, her tone deep and breath shallow. I watch as Myles skillfully removes the rest of my clothes, then kicks off his pants, before we both turn to Amethyst in our naked glory. She's lazily touching herself through her clothes, her eyes half closed.

"Kiss." One word. That's all she says but it's all we needed to hear. Myles' strong hands grip my hips, tugging me up from the bed to stand with him, our bodies flush together as his mouth attacks mine like he's starving. I can feel his cock against mine as he licks and sucks my bottom lip. I want to wrap myself against him, feel him all over, or better yet bend over and let him fuck me as thoroughly as he always does. I want his dick inside me, now.

I pull him closer, my hand wrapping around the length of the leash to keep him joined to me. I fuck his mouth with my tongue, all passion and pent-up emotions. I tell him with my kisses how frustrated I've been. How he's been hurting me over and over, how furious I've been every time I've seen him with a woman. Then I slow and tell him that I love him. I nip his bottom lip, then soothe it with my tongue before touching my forehead to his, needing to catch a breath.

Myles strokes my cheek with his thumb. Did he understand? Does he know how I feel, how this might just be the best and worst moment of my life? Because as much as I've dreamt about it, I want to be dominated by Myles while he says he loves me too. Not because he's trying to please the woman he's growing attached to.

I turn away, needing to distance myself before tears start escaping my eyes. Crawling onto the bed, I brace myself on all fours, ready to get this over with. A brief drop of ecstasy in the ocean of longing I'm forced to contain on a daily basis. It always feels so right during, but I've come to expect that heavy weight of regret in Myles' deep exhale afterwards.

"No," Amethyst states sternly. My head snaps in her direction. The fuck? Is this all just a ruse to tease me? "Myles, you're the bottom today. Sebby, get the lube." My jaw slackens but we both do as she says. Fuck, he really must love her if he obeys all of her demands without question. I find the lube on the table and when I return, Amethyst is waving around the glass anal beads I watched her lick earlier.

"I expect Myles will need loosening up," she winks. I half want to hug and thank her, but the other half of me is ready to strangle that spunky attitude right out of this room. I'm not used to an audience. Or being a top. Coating the anal beads with lube, I drag my nails down the back of Myles' thighs to excite and relax him some. Then, I toy with the end bead around the entrance of his ass and dip it inside.

"*Fuck*," Myles tenses, as do I. Stuck in an impasse, I pause, looking to Amethyst for assistance. She blows out an impatient breath. Shedding her cut crop-top and booty shorts, she crawls across the bed, sitting before Myles.

"Here, focus on me," she tells him, stroking and kissing his face. I expect a wave of jealousy to consume me, a sense of worthlessness to clutch me in its unyielding grip. Instead, as Myles relaxes, allowing the beads to glide in a notch further, I realize this will take a team effort. The amount of times I've dreamed of taking Myles this way, I can handle an extra pair of hands, so to speak. At least she's wearing my boxers as Myles drops his head, inhaling her through them. His groans grow louder, his ass working in time with my gentle thrusts. My cock strains with need, eager to replace the beads, but not until he's ready.

Caressing his blond hair, Amethyst praises Myles softly. A new side I've yet to see from her as she winks, spurring me to go deeper. Harder. I work Myles into a frenzy, a mess of unhindered reactions. I've never heard these types of sounds from him in all the times we've been together. Each one empowers my thrusts, daring me to be bolder. The anal beads are fully inserted, stretching him in preparation of what's to come. Essentially – me, if we don't do this thing soon. Reaching between his legs, I fondle his bags, palm his thick and veiny shaft.

"Yes Sebby, just like that," Myles groans against Amethyst's thigh. As his head shifts, I spot an angry bite mark marring her skin. I caused him to do that. I pushed him to sink his teeth into her flesh with the height of pleasure coursing through his body. Amethyst mouths to me, ask if he's ready and I slowly nod.

"Myles," she commands Myles' attention, her hand guiding his head upwards. He's weak with submission for us both. "Sebby needs to be wet," she kicks out and knocks the lube to the ground. "Spit on his cock." My eyes bulge.

Obeying her every demand, Myles turns back on himself, his mouth taking my dick all the way back into his throat. I almost come for him then and there, utterly caught off guard. Swirling his tongue around my girth, he holds me hostage. In a state of limbo where I both want to live forever and pulse with the need to be inside him. It'll be my first time on top, and the weeping bead of pre-cum he moans at is evidence of that.

Licking me clean, Myles spits over my purple head, working my shaft with his hand. Then, he returns to face Amethyst who has a kiss waiting. Her chest is just as flushed, her desire just as heightened as anyone else's. I don't need any more confirmation that seeing Myles and I together is just as arousing for her. Dominating the warm mouth which so recently contained my cock, Amethyst doesn't even open her purple eyes to click her fingers at me, pointing towards Myles' ass. I smile to myself, unsure how I got into this situation but knowing there's nowhere else I'd rather be.

Guiding myself to Myles' entrance, I circle my soft head around his rim. Teasing, stalling. Dipping inside this time, Myles doesn't tense.

Not even as the sharp hiss leaves his mouth, his body is languid. Surrendered to me, encouraging my slow pumps. I refuse to rush, not wanting to hurt him. Myles is as much as a Switch as I am, but typically it's me in the all-fours position. Not this time. He waits patiently and after an eternity of desire, accepts every throbbing inch. Gripping his hips, I look to the ceiling, savoring his tightness on my own groan.

"How's it feel, Sebby?" Amethyst asks. I can only give her a strangled moan in reply. Easing my hips back, I take him hard this time. My vision blurs, my balls tight enough to burst. I wish I could last for him. To last long enough for the night to be imprinted inside of our minds until I ensure Amethyst orchestrates it again. On my third thrust, it's evident I won't be able to do that, so I decide to go hell for leather instead.

Pounding into Myles' ass, I lower my gaze, the room coming back into focus. Amethyst has shimmied down, her arm pumping in time with my momentum. She works Myles' cock, the pair of us pleasuring in time with the slap of skin on skin. We work together so easily, one might think we'd pre-discussed an action plan. As it stands, Amethyst seems to get me. To understand the connection Myles and I share, and she looks upon it as the beautiful union I keep hidden from the world. Tears spring behind my eyes as I squeeze them closed.

Myles screams my name as I grunt his, my hand stretching down the length of his back. Grabbing a fistful of blond hair, I force him to arch for me. To break for me. Tremors flutter through his ass, preempting the tightening which erupts within. Myles grips my cock so hard, stars appear before my eyes and I tumble over the edge too. My balls clench as my own release fills him, prolonged by wave after wave of ecstasy he squeezes from me. Our joined orgasms last for an eternity, yet nowhere near long enough.

Leaning over Myles' back, we pant together. Gasping for air, my heated skin prickles with electricity. The thrum of energy which has destroyed the barriers we hid behind. Coming to my senses, I peer around, noting Amethyst is nowhere to be seen. The bathroom door clicks closed, leaving Myles and I to flop onto the bed together.

Unaided at last, seeing each other for the first time. Amethyst is a crutch I quickly came to rely on, but now as Myles' glimmering amber eyes devour mine, I'm at a loss for words. Fighting the urge to wrap my arms around myself, or make an excuse to dress and leave, I force myself to exhale deeply. There's nowhere else I need to be than right here. Butterflies expand within my chest when his hand brushes aside my black hair, revealing all of me to his probing stare.

"Can I tell you something?" he breathes. I nod, biting on my bottom lip to resist from doing it to him. Myles smirks knowingly. "Every time we do this, I feel you pull away immediately after. It's why I don't initiate sex more often. I believe it to be a defense mechanism, but know this Sebastian." I shudder at my full name rolling from his tongue like the dirtiest of sins.

"Everything that just happened here is out of the love I hold for you, not Amethyst." Popping my lip free, I'm at a loss. A total disadvantage because nothing could begin to describe how I feel for him. How I yearn for him, care for him, love him despite everyone else's reservations. Since we were kids, Myles has been it for me. The crush doodled in hearts, the depiction of who I'd spend the rest of my life with. Myles may not be as head over heels as I am, but he loves me. In his own, unique way. Smiling mischievously, his thumb brushes along my wettened bottom lip, our solid erections pulsing against one another.

"And I'm nowhere near done with you yet."

Chapter 23

Buzzing rouses me. A heavy limb weighs down my waist, a leg draped over mine. Last night was incredible to witness, the coming together of two adrift souls. Sebby has no idea how much Myles cares for him, but I saw. I saw how easily Myles submitted, how he put aside the billionaire act and was just...himself. Dare I say, I liked what I saw. At some point, exhaustion took over and the panting, sated bodies were too much of an invitation to decline.

That insistent buzzing comes again. Lifting my head from our snuggle puddle, I glare at Myles' phone vibrating on the coffee table. Probably Carter demanding to know where the three of us are. I ignore it, but when the relentless calling persists, I drag myself from the mattress and peer at the screen.

Felicia Steele.

My heart jumps in my chest, all remnants of sleep disappearing. Answering the call, I dip into the bathroom.

"Hello?"

"Oh, um," Felicia stutters. "I'm looking to speak with Myles Hudson."

"It's me, Amethyst. Did you find any information on...that information I gave you?" I ask frantically. Surely she's calling for a reason, unless it's completely unrelated to me.

"Yes actually, I have a lead. But Myles specifically asked me only to refer to him about this."

"Well, fuck Myles. Not literally, although I have no doubts you already have. This is my life we're talking about. I'll pay you myself, just tell me what you found out." I'm rambling, but I can't bring myself to stop. Felicia potentially has the answers I've been hunting for. The break I need. "Did you find Reynell?"

"Well, yes I did. I have the coordinates of where he's hiding. A house within the New Orleans bayou, but I really need to speak with Myles-" The door opens and in walks the man in question.

"Is that my phone?" he asks. I hand it over, patting him on the back and running into the main room. I slept in my underwear, and whilst fishing out my clothes, I hear Myles murmuring on the phone. He steps into my way as I'm rushing towards the main door, dressed and ready to track down the man who ruined my life.

"Woah, slow down. Where are you going?" I meet his amber eyes, resisting the 'well, duh' which is at the tip of my tongue.

"New Orleans. Possibly onto my next persona. I'm thinking Jenni, the born hunter and renowned alligator wrangler." I can see her already. Black hair, firm muscles, camo outfits. Captain of the floating vessel she lives on. Although, her biggest downfall would be a distinct dislike of blonds and I'm nothing if not committed.

"No." Myles states the word as if knowing my mind has begun spiraling. Clamping his hands on my shoulders, he pushes me back towards the armchair until I'm eyeline with the morning glory poking over his Calvin Kleins. "I have the exact location; you're not trekking the bayou alone. I'll call a private jet and take you. No new persona needed. I'm growing rather fond of this one." My eyes narrow of their own accord as I raise my gaze to his retreating back.

"Surely you have a busy schedule that doesn't include flying me across the country. What's your motive?" Myles turns to me, jeans half tugged up.

"I just gave you my motive." Returning to dressing, I drop back in the seat. *He's growing fond of me.* Well shit.

"What's going on?" Sebby stirs from the bed, his black hair a mess. Myles sits beside him to pull on his Air Jordans.

"Nothing, Sebby. Go back to sleep. I'll have breakfast and a masseuse sent up later. Just...avoid going back to face Carter's wrath a while longer." Myles leans over to kiss Sebby goodbye and I kinda melt inside. Sebby is just as surprised, his eyes seeking mine out just before Myles pulls me upright and mouths 'thank you'. Waving the best I can, I'm ushered from the room with my heart in my throat. I'm going to find Reynell. I'm going to get answers, and then I'm going to make him pay.

The next few hours are a whirlwind of connections and influence. Gripping the armrests either side of a leather seat, Myles' private jet soars into the sky in the quickest take-off I've ever experienced. It was merely minutes ago we were welcomed aboard and handed bags of clothing and necessities for us both. As soon as we level out, I pop my belt, taking the bag and head for the bathroom. Except it's not a bathroom – but a full bedroom with a dresser and TV mounted over a double bed. Oh, how the other half live.

Dropping the bag on the bed and opening it wide, boxes of sanitary towels, tampons, a fresh menstrual cup and a pack of Panadol sit on top. A smile bites into my cheeks. At least I'm fully set incase my period does happen to make an appearance, but then I'll have to explain to Myles why I'm supposedly having two a month. Or rather – why am I explaining anything to Myles? When did I feel the need to justify myself? Movement shuffles behind, a tentative yet gorgeous man lingering.

"Should we talk about last night?" he offers, leaning his shoulder on the door jam.

"Other than the fact it was hot as fuck?" I shrug off, hunting through the clothes. The exact outfit Jenni would have approved of comes to hand. Camouflage cargo pants, olive green tank top, military style jacket and heavy black boots. All brand new with tags and in my size. Opening the door which I'm now certain really is a bathroom, my mouth drops open. There's a freaking shower in here and everything!

"Does it change anything between us?" Myles continues to follow me. I catch sight of myself in the mirror, barely recognizing the excited twinge to my cheeks. My eyebrows are smudged, in desperate need of re-drawing and the fact Myles didn't say anything makes me swoon a little harder. Fuck's sake Amethyst, pull yourself together.

"Well Myles, there isn't really anything between us," I withhold adding a 'yet' to not give him false hope. In that same mirror, I watch him glance at me with the look of a wounded puppy on the verge of whining. "But if you're asking if it could happen again, that'd be a hell yes from me." I nod to myself. I wasn't even involved and I was turned on to a fever pitch. Satisfied with my answer, I begin to strip from Sebby's cut clothing and shove them in a trash can. Something tells me he won't want them back. Hands grip my waist, spinning me against the cool glass of the shower door.

"That's not what I was asking." Myles groans at the sight of my breasts and seizes my mouth. I surrender, lacking the willpower to resist anymore. Myles has wormed into my psyche with the same casual effort as his tongue pushes into my mouth. Taking, claiming.

Arching my body inside the hard planes of his chest, I'm at a loss to fight. Hands smooth over my back, holding me close yet tenderly. Everywhere our skin connects, every brush of his lips and swirl of his tongue, sends shockwaves through my being. He awakens me from within, toying with pretty fantasies and a longing I didn't know I was concealing.

Fingers find my hair, trace the line of my jaw, cup my face. He's everywhere, consuming me as I drown in the intoxicating sensations he provides. Breathlessly, Myles pulls himself back enough for our eyes to lock in a silent connection. Tension radiates through the air, the unknown spurring me to dive off this cliff with him and see where I end up.

"I want you so much, it fucking pains me. Like a knife in my chest only you can remove. My every waking thought is of how I can win you over, because fuck knows in my dreams I have you trapped in my arms and refuse to let go." Stealing another rushed kiss from my swollen lips, his forehead rests on mine. "What will it take for you to make me yours?"

"I don't have the answers for you," I whisper back, only now hearing how hollow my words are. How broken my soul must be if I can't trust the one man offering me anything my heart desires. "But if anyone has a chance, I reckon it might be you." Myles' chest suddenly swells at my declaration, that hope I was trying to save him from swirling between us. Well, I've started something now – I might as well see it through.

"I don't want to keep pushing you away, Myles. But my revenge must come first. It's all I've been working towards for years. Maybe afterwards when I'm looking for a new purpose, you might be there to help me find it?" A responding smile is the only answer I receive as the shower door is opened inward and Myles crowds me inside, jeans and all.

I stop tracking how long Myles attends to my body. Kissing me with the passion of a lover, washing me with the care of something more. Every inch of my skin is tenderly stroked with a layer of foam and washed away by him maneuvering the shower head. Special attention is taken between my legs, his fingers lingering on the edge of foreplay but never crossing the precipice. At some point, his clothing is removed, allowing us to slip against one another. Continuously caressing, touching, stroking. Scents of jasmine fill the cubicle, my nerve endings alive with energy.

Replacing the shower head, Myles' skilled hands move to my hair, massaging and lathering. By the time I stumble into the bedroom and drop onto the bed, I can't resist the call of a nap. I'm too relaxed, too content with my surroundings, and as Myles snuggles in behind, no amount of whispered warnings in my head could keep me from falling asleep.

***

"This revenge plan of yours," Myles pipes up from across the room as he dresses, "how far is it going to go? What will be enough to sate you?" Sitting upright against the headboard, I catch a note of something in his tone, possibly just curiosity but enough to give me pause. Catching my side-eye, Myles turns away. "I just...can't bear the thought of you in dangerous situations." I suppose it's an innocent enough question, but he won't like the answer.

"When all those responsible - or failing that, all those connected to those responsible - have met the same fate my mother suffered," I nod to myself, reaching for my clothes. "Then I will be able to walk away with my head held high. Her life has to be worth something because currently, it's like she never even existed at all." Busying himself in the cabin, Myles exhales, resting his hands on the dresser.

"Ami, there's something I need to tell you-"

"This is your captain speaking. Due to approaching marshland, we will be forced to land early and acquire more suitable transportation. Please take your seats for our descent."

Pressing his lips together tightly, Myles pushes his sandy blond hair back from his face. "I'll give you some privacy to get dressed," he forces a smile and leaves the room. The weight on his shoulders seems to remain though. Tugging on the clothes, the plane begins to incline before I've managed to shove my feet in the boots. Rushing to the leather seat opposite Myles, he ties my laces while I buckle myself in. There isn't much to be done with my hair since I fell asleep with it still wet, so I toss the crinkled strands up in a high, messy bun.

The jet bounces and slows to a halt, the humming engine grumbling its final protest before surrendering to silence—no airport in sight, but a single tarmac in the middle of nowhere. I press my face against the window and try as I might, all I can see is an untouched, wild, landscape of varying colors from the surrounding marshlands. Tall grass covers the entire area, growing wilder along the water, swaying gently, turning from green at the base to that burnt orange at the tips, as if lightly toasted by the sun.

Peering closer at the water, which seems to sparkle as the midday sun dances over the surface, I notice the bent, gnarled trees that line the edge. Their branches hang low, decked with trailing moss which brush over the shining bodies of something I don't want to name as they slither into the water.

The cabin crew who have kept out of sight appear, releasing the door to guide us down the stairs. I blink away the invasive glare of sun, a wave of cloying heat and humidity making my tank top stick to my skin almost immediately. As the plane settles, silence bleeds into a symphony of buzzing insects and birds, calling out to each other across the bayou. I struggle to take a deep breath in the heavy air, my nose wrinkling from the overwhelming scents of damp earth, salt water and hints of sweetness from the surrounding flora fight for dominance. Blocking out the pervasive sun, I step into the slightly springy ground as Myles reaches for my hand, taking charge as if he knows exactly where to go.

An airboat is waiting, a bearded man in the driver's seat. Dark glasses cover his eyes, a fisherman style hat upon his head. Saluting to us, Myles eases me into the front bench as if I might crumple otherwise. How quickly he's forgotten I used to throw myself around a pole at the Thirsty Kirsty and land full splits. The huge propeller at the back of the watercraft whirls and we're thrust forward, navigating the bayou by the driver's memorized map. Deciding he must have been briefed prior to our arrival, I scoot to the edge of the boat, feeling the spray of water misting over my cheeks.

Suddenly, it hits me. I'm on my way to talk to a lead. An actual lead to avenge my mother. Over the years, being stonewalled became second nature. I knew the PI's I hired would come back with nothing, if they came back to me at all. Their disappearances wouldn't deter me, but I've grown complacent over the years. Until Myles presented me with the opportunity for real answers.

Braving a look over my shoulder, I find him watching me. Amber eyes, rigid jaw. I smile. God help me, I smile – coming to rely on his presence. As we slow by a dock, the hint of a roof can be seen through overgrown grass akin to a jungle. My sigh of relief, as a light breeze soothes my heated skin, turns into a wheeze as bubbles come from the surface surrounding the boat, and the previously serene waters, dotted with water lilies, ripple from the huge body of an alligator splashing nearby. I jump upright, chasing after Myles and instinctively hearing the grass crunch beneath my boots as we breach the land.

"Whatever you do," Myles wraps an arm around my middle, "stay close." The driver hangs back, tying his boat to a wooden post by the dock. Syncing our footsteps, we near the house, spying planks of wood nailed over the windows. A pathway presents itself from the foliage, crushed rocks amongst large slabs. The trees hanging around the edge of the house sway in the breeze, rustling a warning I can't decipher. The hair on the back of my neck gets the memo though, standing tall. What the fuck would Reynell, a housing officer from Chicago, be doing hiding all the way out here?

Breaching the porch steps, the aged wood groans in protest. I swallow past the dryness of my throat, squeezing Myles' hand. Reassurance, that's all I need. A moment of reassurance as I lift my closed fist, about to rasp on the rickety old door. A gurgled scream pierces the air from around the back of the house, sending birds in a rushed flurry to freedom. Dropping Myles' hand, I race to the edge of the porch, jumping over the railing.

"Amethyst! Wait!" Myles calls but my feet won't be stopped. Bushes rustle against my legs, my arms pumping as I follow the screams, skidding to a halt in a patch of flattened grass. There, at my feet, is Oliver Reynell. I've seen his picture enough to recognize his face, even contorted with horror and sprayed with blood. Protruding from his neck, a feathered arrow shifts with the ragged pants he struggles to take, a note wrapped around its intricate stem. A series of interlinking circles have been etched into the carbon shaft, like bubbles fleeing the point of contact. Myles rushes to my side as I unravel the paper, its typed message spilling ice-cold dread into my veins.

Stop digging, Amethyst. Or you'll be next.

"Holy fuck," Myles gasps. Peering back at Reynell, the arrow is imbedded in his neck too deeply to remove. He's a goner either way.

"I'm doing you a favor. Whether you deserve it is another question." I tell him, crouching. Yanking the arrow free, Myles falls into a fit of cursing and trying to tug me away, but I refuse to go. Not until I watch the life drain from Reynell's brown eyes, unlike I was able to do with my mother. She died alone in the dark, leaving her death to play out in my nightmares for years later. Reynell gurgles, blood spewing from his mouth. Sticky crimson pools around my boots, his last breath taken while I loom over him. I hope that bribe was worth it, asshole.

"Ami, we have to go." Myles drags the jacket free from my arms and uses it as a shield over my head. Somewhere between the jacket flapping above my eyes and the rustling in the trees, I come to my senses.

"Fuck that. I'm not running scared." Jumping over Reynell's body, my boots thunder through the long grass, my arms pump. No ducking, no creeping. I tear towards the rundown house, refusing to leave without the secrets it holds. Reynell was a pawn, and I need to know who decided he was so easily disposable. Who decided my life was so easily destroyable. A hand grips my ankle as I throw myself through a gap in the window, but as I kick wildly, Myles grunts and releases me.

"Amethyst," he hisses, appearing at the back door. I've already committed to flopping in a heap on the ground. Crawling on hands and knees, I pop up like a meerkat amongst a mess all over the floor. In fact, the entire room is trashed. Skidding across papers and shattered ornaments, my palm sticks to a wax seal on the back of a brown envelope. I shake it free, disregarding the decorative shield and dragon imprint, whilst dodging the broken shards around my knees. Arms scoop beneath mine, smoothly lifting me onto my feet.

"The boat leaves in three minutes, with or without you." Beyond Myles, flames dance within a large stone fireplace, the chopped wood tumbling into the room and threatening to take us all down.

"Got it," I agree. Let's face it, I don't want to be stranded and it's three minutes more than he was offering before storming the house.

I leave the main area, figuring whoever ransacked the house already found what they were looking for. My last remaining hopes of some answers may be stuffed in a mattress or under a tile in the bathroom. Fuck knows, I'm clutching at straws, but those are the first places I look. When I come up empty, I spend the rest of my two and a half minutes rifling through drawers. Reynell decided hiding out mainly consisted of black tank tops and lounge pants, but there's nothing to suggest he received the huge bribe I know he did.

"Bet the asshole gambled it away," I grumble. My mood turns sour thinking of the casino named to mock me – Life Support. Is that where Reynell camped out, lost his fortune and was then headhunted for owing a debt? I can only guess now. Mood ruined, I slump back towards the main area, almost announcing the hunt is over when I see Myles by the fireplace. With a flick of the wrist, he tosses a large brown envelope into the fire and prods it with a poker. Tossing it down, the metal rings out against the stone floor as I step fully around the corner.

"Time to go," Myles nods, reaching for my hand. I give it to him, looking over my shoulder as he tugs me along. Between the flames, the red wax scal I got my hand stuck on earlier glints before being consumed completely. My eyes narrow as we breach the porch, causing me to miss the arrow flying past my face. Catching my cheek, a slice of heat blossoms there and my world is upended. Thrown over Myles' shoulder, he breaks into a run.

"Jesus Christ Ami, what have you got me into?" he mutters and I doubt he is only talking about the crazed archer. The wind whistles as more arrows shoot by, piercing the air around Myles' agile body. Avoiding a straight path, I bounce against Myles' ass, the grass dragging on his boots. I hear the propeller of the airboat whirl and gasp. This is my last chance.

Pushing upright on Myles' lower back, I hunt the marsh. Trees rustle, leaves sway. A mess of the seasons, dying greens and burnt oranges at war with each other. The humidity still burns my nose, but not as much as the frustration flaring my nostrils. Myles doesn't put me down as he drops into the boat and orders us to go. That's when I see it. The figure which steps out from behind a tree. Too slender to be noticed by the others, too curvy to be a man. My hand shoots out, a shout lost to the loudness of the propeller.

It takes time to reign myself back in, to lessen the racing of my heart. In fact, I'm back in the jet before I have fully contemplated everything I've seen. Myles adjusts my belt tight before settling down in the opposite seat to do his own, and then we're airborne.

"Hopefully we're done with the adventurous escapades," he grunts. There's an edge to his tone, no longer eager to help my quest. What's changed, I wonder.

"Did you find anything?" I ask. Amber eyes swing upwards, his shoulders firm. "In the house. Find anything worth noting?" Squaring his jaw, Myles shakes his head and slumps back against the leather. I watch with keen interest as his eyes flutter closed, the heavy rise and fall of his chest easing. Unlike on the way here, he doesn't try to crowd me into the shower, reassure me with sweet words, kiss me like I'm the only woman on his mind. Instead, he feigns sleep and pretends I don't exist.

Okay Myles, keep your secrets. I'll find them out another way.

Chapter 24

"So, back up. Let me make sure I've got this right," Sebby pinches the bridge of his nose. I signal for another margarita from the cute bartender, wondering in what time zone it would be five o'clock. Oh well, it doesn't matter either way. "You saw Myles burn the envelope. He rushed you out of the house, tossed you over his shoulder and then you were chased out of the swamp by Ninja Merida?" Watching the lean, tattooed man refill the glass in my hand, it's my turn to sigh.

"Never said she had orange hair, and there was a shot before I was tossed over said shoulder." I point to the scratch on my cheek. Not much of a war wound but the weight of guilt in Myles' eyes every time he looked at it makes me think I could milk his shame until it fully fades.

"But after Myles dragged you outside, correct?" Sebby continues to badger me for details.

"What are you getting at?" I quirk a brow over the rim of my glass. Twisting the bar stool, his hands land on the denim at my thighs.

"If someone wanted to kill you, why would they wait until after you left the house? Why not sneak up to the window and open fire at you both?" My eyes narrow.

"Huh." I touch two fingers to the scratch, needing the feel of the burn as my mind reels. "I was more concerned with the way Myles has been avoiding me since we landed last night."

Avoiding is putting it gently. Myles has been like a ghost, putting me in a separate car to return to his home. Locking himself in his bedroom, refusing to come out whilst I was in the manor. Whatever he's hiding, he knows I'd be able to see through him easily enough. My only option was to drag Sebby to a cocktail bar whilst devising my next move. Let Myles feel a false sense of comfort and then *bam*, I'm going to creep out of nowhere, steal his secrets, then his money. He's just another con and I was stupid to let myself get too into character.

I'm going to need a stronger drink.

"Tequila shots," I raise two fingers. Sebby releases my legs, leaning on the bar.

"Ami, why am I really here? Because you clearly don't want to talk about New Orleans."

"I'm brewing," I point to my temple, "and when my plan falls into place, I'll need you to be the distraction." Sebby starts to protest as I shove a shot glass into his hand. We clink, drink and return to him moaning while I think. If I was Myles, where would I hide something of significance? Would Carter be aware? Most likely, Carter is a much easier nut to crack. Mostly since he's an emotionless douchebag and I have no reservations crushing him into dust.

"So, I'm torn between Carter's office, their bedrooms, the hidden corridors throughout the manor-"

"The hidden what?" Sebby sits upright. I wave him off.

"Where should I start digging?" I take the olive from my cocktail glass, tugging it free from the stick with my teeth. Pushing his black hair back, Sebby interlinks his fingers on the bar.

"You're not thinking outside the box enough. Myles has a central office in the city, he's supposed to visit every Friday to sign forms and save face. Then there's his dad's mansion; we all store paperwork relating to our businesses there. It gives his dad peace of mind, since he's the main investor for all of our ventures, to have open access to our files."

"What's your business of choice? I never see you working." I tilt my head to the side. Violet hair pools around my forearm, the silk cami on my body shifting beneath the large ceiling fans.

"I own a photography company. Everything is handled through my employees, and the photographers are mostly freelancers anyway. I only need to judge new applicants and look over their work once in a while. My name alone opens most doors for them so it's rare anyone really needs me," Sebby shrugs and sighs.

"Oh, for the love of pity," I raise my hand for the bartender once more. He slinks over with an easy smile, bottle of tequila in hand and eyes sternly on me. "Hi, can we get a refill and your phone number for my friend here? He's hopelessly in love with another and firmly in the closet, but a great listener and a monster in the sack. Trust me, I've seen it." The bartender raises his brows, finally looking at Sebby. It's about time; I've never known someone so insistent on ignoring the hottest guy in the room.

"I'm about to go on my break," the bartender hitches his shoulder suggestively.

"What the hell are you doing?!" Sebby whisper-shouts and tugs my arm from the bar, his brows fused together. "I don't know what's happening with Myles and I, I can't just...fornicate with someone else." My lids lower half-mast. *Fornicate*? Really?

"Get off your pity pony and on to this hardworking hottie. Nothing is going to happen between you and Myles until you're ready to come out and come clean about how you feel. Also, I can't scheme when you're all '*it's rare anyone really needs me,*" I mock his voice. "I need you, right here and now. So go, release those negative thoughts. I'll be elbow-deep in sheer genius by the time you return."

Shoving Sebby from his stool, I wonder how long I'll have to coordinate his sex life as I wave him goodbye. Then I'm back to plotting alone, writing possible ideas on the back of a coaster. I wonder if Myles would recognize me without these violet contacts and if I went brunette. I'd have to conceal my body beneath a nun's outfit, but it's absolutely doable.

My chest begins to ache, conflict warring within. I'd stupidly allowed myself to feel safe. To trust. Past experience has taught me better than to believe the lies so easily spoken. The smiles are too easily given. Happiness is an illusion, as deceptive as the make-up on my face.

Leaning my chin on my hand, I twist to look at the street outside. It's barely midday, yet there's a fair amount of traffic. A deep red Dodge Viper with a black strip down the middle pulls up alongside a café over the road, drawing my full attention. Not because it's glorious – which it is – but from the driver. Jaw cut from granite, tightly pressed lips, pushed-back chestnut brown hair and the cold green eyes I know glare out from beneath perfect eyebrows. Carter.

Exiting the car, I track his movements to the blonde waiting at an outside table. I hadn't seen her before, probably because she's donned a huge floppy hat and sunglasses, but there she is. *Felicia Steele.* Holding out his arms, Carter envelopes Felicia in a firm hug and my jaw drops open. Well, this is a revelation.

Jumping from my stool, I grab a hoodie from the back of a nearby chair without the owner realizing. It's wrenched onto my body, my hair tucked into the hood, by the time I've avoided the oncoming vehicles and lowered beside the Dodge Viper's driver door. Luckily, Carter didn't feel the need to raise his windows so I can listen to their conversation straight through the middle.

"Does he know?" Felicia asks. I brave a look to see they are still holding hands.

"I'm not sure," Carter responds. "He hasn't said much of anything since returning last night." Felicia draws him to the table she occupied, and I scoot around the trunk to listen in. Removing her huge hat, a fresh set of highlights mixes into the grey peppering her hairline.

"I hope you're right about this. You know what happened last time," she sighs, sliding Carter a folder of paper. He briefly glances at it, before tucking it into his side jacket pocket. I swear this asshole sleeps in a suit.

"It's a risk I'm willing to take."

"And the girl?" she asks tentatively. My ears prick up further.

"I'm taking care of it. If she knows what's good for her, she'll back off before my hand is forced." My brows furrow, my mind racing to put together a puzzle I don't have all the pieces to yet.

Felicia told Myles where to find Reynell's hideout, and probably gave Carter the heads up. The archer couldn't have been a coincidence;

they knew we'd be there and rushed to silence Reynell. Why...I'm not sure yet. But as Sebby pointed out – no shots were fired until we left the house, namely at me. Myles was never in danger because his best friend and self-proclaimed bodyguard orchestrated the whole thing.

"I need to get back to Myles before he does something stupid," Carter sighs heavily and pushes to stand. Ducking back from view and banging my head on the sport's car, I grimace at the license plate and realize it's new. Probably fresh out the dealership down the road.

Scrambling for a way to stall him, I spot a shard of broken glass on the roadside. The rest of the beer bottle trails towards a bar a few buildings down. I grab it, uncaring of my own hand as I make quick work of slashing Carter's wheels. His unnaturally long hug goodbye with Felicia gives plenty of time to create mischief and be back in my bar stool before Sebby appears, hair ruffled and cheeks flushed.

"That was quick," I raise my cocktail glass and wink. Sebby freezes.

"Do I want to know where you got that hoodie or why there's blood dripping from your hand?" He looks at me with a 'can't-take-you-any-where' frown. Spotting the red smear against the cocktail glass, my retort is interrupted by a screech of metal on pavement and Carter bellowing out of the window. "Is that...Carter?"

"Hmm, I'm not sure. Be a doll and call the limo; you can tell me all about your bartender romp on the way back to the manor," I smirk, hiding all real emotion underneath. Like what the fuck I'm going to do about the state of my life, how Myles has managed to carve an Adonis-shaped hole into it, and what it'll take for him to bare his secrets.

Chapter 25

High heels click on the marble floor beyond my bedroom. I've been waiting all morning for that sound. Straightening the white shirt buttoned to my breasts, a black bra underneath, I shoot out into the hallway and intercept the Elite at the top of the stairs, Myles' breakfast tray in hand. He refused to leave his room all of last night, and although I'm not against breaking the door down, this seemed classier. I didn't expect, however, the Elite to be Charley.

"Ami? What are you doing up so early, and...dressed like that?" Her dark eyes follow the length of my silhouette. It's ironic since we're wearing the same outfit. Fitted black pants, dangerously thin stilettos.

I opted for a French braid down the length of my back, as opposed to her high ponytail.

"What does it look like? I'm going to work." Reaching out for the tray, she holds it firm. "Let me handle this one. Myles needs a kick up the ass this morning and I've been practicing my roundhouse in heels."

"Please Ami, you said you'd support me in becoming an Elite. I'm so close to being chosen - all the other girls have recommended me the highest. Please don't ruin this for me." My mouth drops open before I can catch it. In all these years, I've protected Charley, kept her safe from her stepfather, took care of her needs, and she's obediently followed me wherever I went. The decision to become an Elite is the first time she's ever asked me for anything, yet I don't release the metal platter between us. I can't.

"I promise you will become an Elite. I'll see to it personally, but I'm going to need to take this tray. There's a plan-"

"There's always a plan!" Charley shouts, letting go to flap her arms around. I merely stare wide-eyed at her outburst. "Some scheme, a plot to get one over on people who don't even know you exist or why you hate them. I doubt you even know why half the time." Charley scowls at me with such venom, there's no way it's just appeared. She's been concealing this for a while, allowing it to build and fester. Maybe I would have noticed if I wasn't so caught up in revenge and Myles, and getting answers and Myles. Fuck, I'm in over my head. Not receiving the immediate answer she wanted, Charley scoffs.

"For once, you can't just let me do something on my own!" Storming down the stairs, she doesn't see the tears well in my eyes. See the pain her words have caused. All I've done is try to shield her. The weight of her words crash down on me, voices in my head screaming all I've achieved is suffocating her.

Pushing my emotions deep, deep down, I urge one foot to step in front of the other and near Myles' bedroom door. As much as the swirling in my gut wants to run after Charley and fix the first fight we've ever had, there's no time for it now. I'm on the verge of a major breakthrough.

Knocking twice, I stand patiently, steadying my breathing. A shuffle sounds on the other side of the door, and by the time it opens, my purple-painted lips are spread wide.

"Well good morning Sunshine," I beam, pushing my way inside the room. Myles stands aside, his movements robotic and stiff. Placing the tray on a table, my nose wrinkles at the stench held within the room. The bedsheets are a crumpled mess, last night's dinner tray on the floor. When I peer at the man himself, shrouded by the drawn curtains, he looks like he's both overslept and not slept at all. Blond hair all matted, his amber eyes dull and sunken, only a pair of boxers on his sculpted body.

"Okay, that's enough of that. It's Friday – and I'm coming to the office with you. Go shower, dress. I'll...fumigate in here."

"I'm not in the mood Ami," Myles sighs and drops onto the bed. I didn't think it was possible for him to be so dejected, but it turns out there's sides to everyone I've yet to see. Sitting beside him, I lay my hand on his knee.

"All of this because someone shot at us? It's part of everyday life in Brooklyn and they're not moping around. I lived with a Latina woman and her four kids for a short while. She'd get mugged and say 'for fuck's sake Milo, I'm telling your mom about this', and then invite them over for dinner. Same shit, different day for some." Twisting, Myles crushes me into a bone-cracking hug I wasn't prepared for.

"I never should have taken you into a situation where I couldn't protect you. I thought if I hid in here...at least I wouldn't be the one delivering you into danger." Shifting my head from beneath his huge bicep, I managed to find a small space to breathe, my mouth squished against his chest.

"I'm always going to be in some kind of danger," my words slur. "I'm not going to stop until I have someone to blame." Freeing me from his hold, I gulp in air to refill my lungs.

"I understand, but you saw that note. If you keep digging, they're going to come after you. I can't lose you now Amethyst." Myles tugs a loose strand of my braid behind my ear, a fragment of the man I know coming back to the surface. Turning my head away, I withhold the loving sentiment I was about to give. Jesus, our periods must all be synced or something.

"Either way, Myles," I take his hand in mine, just so he'll stop stroking my neck. "If I don't have someone to hold accountable for my mother's death, then I'll be forced to consider that the only responsible one is me. I got us into so much debt and trouble, and in the face of being caught...I left her to die alone. What kind of person does that make me?" Myles lowers onto his knees, peering up from between my legs.

"You were a scared child. Most adults would have done the same." Myles reaches up to cup my cheek, his thumb grazing the small cut still healing there. An emotion, I don't want to consider, pours from his beautiful eyes, reminding me why I'm up so early in the first place. Business, Amethyst, back to business.

"Hmm, well most adults don't stew in their own soup for two days when they have multibillion-dollar empires to run. It's a new day, so get the fuck ready. I feel like seeing your office." His responding smile is my undoing and thankfully, he's jumping into the shower and a suit before I do something stupid. Like push his face between my thighs and scream promises I won't be able to keep.

Myles doesn't touch his breakfast, but insists we stop by a Starbucks drive-thru on the way into the city. Carter, Sebby and Owen are all with us. Apparently, the wheels for Carter's new ride need to be specially ordered and have left him without a vehicle for the next week. Oops. Although, I do take great pleasure in knowing no amount of money could hurry the manufacturer and the constant tick pulsing in his jaw is here to stay.

"You'll have to tell me how you got Myles out of his funk so quickly," Owen murmurs by my ear, his arm dropping over my shoulders. "They usually last for weeks." Unlike the others, he's opted for jeans and a t-shirt, and on his lap is my treacherous puppy. I let Pig lick the back of my hand, indulging Owen while Myles is ordering coffee through the open window.

"I could tell you, but it would require a double ended dildo, ball gag and copious amounts of lube."

"You say that like it's not a given," he winks. I can't quite pinpoint Owen, but his cheekiness is hard to resist. Carter catches me laughing, his scowl deepening so I melt further into Owen's side. Pig stretches across the pair of us, coating my black trousers in small white hairs.

"Double shot americano for Carter," Myles hands over a travel cup. "And chocolate Frappuccino's with extra cream for everyone else," he grins, passing me the Venti plastic cup. Owen mutters under his breath it must have been one hell of a ribbed dildo as Myles settles into the seat on my other side. Lost to their own thoughts, the guys watch the world pass through blackened windows, but my curiosity is caught elsewhere.

On the adjacent bench, Carter sits next to Sebby, their legs pressed together. Where arms meet in the middle, they disappear from view beneath their thighs as they absent-mindedly sip their drinks and stare in opposite directions. *Are they holding hands?*

"Problem with your eyes?" Carter growls, not even looking my way. I hold my tongue, only to save embarrassing Sebby. Soon enough, the sunlight of morning is stolen by skyscrapers, the shadow of the city pressing down over the limo. I take a moment to remind myself about today's order of business – search Myles' offices for anything suspicious. Anything relating to Reynell, what he might have been burning or felt the need to cover up. Then there's investigating Felicia and Carter's connection. My mind begins to spin and before I know it, Myles is offering me his hand, leading me from the cab.

Rising hundreds of stories into the sky, the building is as sleek and modern as I knew it would be. Floor-to-ceiling windows span the glass exterior, which I'm sure provide amazing panoramic views for those on top. Reaching higher, stretching wider, there's no doubting Myles' skyscraper exudes more power and opulence than any of the others surrounding it. Like a sparkling gem amongst murky stones, and kept that way by the cleaner's elevated high up, continually washing the smears and their own lives away.

Bolstered by the high heels, I accept Myles' arm and reach out for Owen's. Pig's lead meets my hand instead.

"Not me, Pauper. I have business elsewhere," Owen salutes. Before he skips away, I slip the leash up my wrist and snatch the sunglasses postered on Owen's honey brown hair. Something tells me, I'm going to need them more than him. With my eyes shielded, I walk up to the reflective entrance and shun the image I see there. I look every bit like the billionaire arm-candy I resent; sunglasses, tight-fitting suit, puppy on one side and the stunning man who is swooning at me on the other. All in the name of vengeance, I tell myself, as the door is opened inward.

The glare in here is twice as bright as outside. Gold and white flooring, matching furniture around the largely spanned reception desk and overhead chandelier. In fact, a rush of déjà vu hits me.

"Do you have the same interior designer as the Steele Law firm?" I tilt my head, catching the extra rigidness to Carter's stride as he takes the lead. A series of high-speed elevators whisk important executives and guests to their desired floors in mere seconds. We don't stop by the reception, passing security and entering an elevator ourselves. Luxurious offices, boardrooms, and meeting spaces, all adorned with plush furnishings, state-of-the-art technology, and curated artwork whizz by until we're stepping out on the top level. My head suddenly goes light, my arm clinging onto Myles as I adjust.

"This way," Myles smiles. Any sign of this morning's pity party has disappeared, and instead, a flash of eagerness is barely contained in his glimmering amber eyes. A part of me reckons Myles has wanted to bring me here for a while, wanting to show me what he does, but has held off. Leading me through the top level, I understand his excitement, and a miniscule part of me joins in.

There are only four offices up here, two on either side of the entrance lobby. The rest of the floor holds a secret sanctuary, bespoke to privileged tastes. In an open plan restaurant, a chef is visible behind a tall counter as he preps his kitchen for the only table in the center of the glassed-off room. Beyond double doors, a rooftop garden terrace boasts of artificial green grass and outdoor furniture set up in a way I imagine men sit around to smoke cigars at. Not to mention the shimmering pool set within raised decking.

"Do you actually get any work done up here?" I ask no one in particular. Sebby appears to take Pig's lead from me, leading her outside while Carter disappears into an office next to the one Myles guides me towards.

"Work happens on the forty-eight floors below us. This is our oasis." Leaving the door open, Myles drops onto a sofa, crossing one ankle over the opposite knee. I prefer to stay standing, noting how these are the first and only offices in the entire building to have privacy. The windows above half walls hold thick blinds, and as far as I can see, a complete lack of prying cameras. I've stayed in apartments smaller than this entire office, the desk towards the back seemingly somewhat lonely and unused. Still, if Myles was to hide information he doesn't want Carter or anyone else to easily access, that desk or the iMac upon it could be my salvation.

"Although, speaking of work, there is a meeting I need to attend in about thirty minutes, and Carter will want to talk numbers beforehand. Do you think you'll be able to entertain yourself in the meantime?" I glance towards the personal restaurant and swimming pool, appearing as if they have my full attention.

"I'm sure I'll manage," I smile. Stretching out a hand, Myles beckons me over. I attempt to sit beside him, but he shifts me onto his lap instead.

"Are we okay? I know I haven't been around much. I was going through some things and..." he twirls the loose tendril of my hair. "I didn't want you to see me like that."

"Like what, Myles?" I cock my head.

"Weak, I suppose. You're always so strong, so determined." His fingers brush my shirt collar, dipping down to where the material opens at my cleavage. "I want to be like that for you too."

"I'm strong because I've had to be. I dread the moment my barriers crumble, and every day I spend with you brings that moment closer." Myles' brows raise, clearly in shock at my revelation. I wish I was lying. I've played men like instruments before, but the more time I spent in Myles' company, the harder it is to differentiate what is real and fake.

"When that time comes, know that you'll be wrapped within my arms, safe and protected. Nothing is going to hurt you as long as I'm around." Just when I think he's going to pull me in for a kiss, and as I convince myself to let him, Myles remains in place, studying me. Allowing me to see the truth of his words through his gaze. The room falls away, that light-headed feeling returning for a whole different reason.

He truly is stunning. The way his warm amber eyes blend so perfectly with his long, sun-kissed hair. The length of it is silky smooth, never appearing the disheveled mess it could easily be. Behind his looks, he smells fucking delectable all the time without the scent being overpowering. As if years of pricey products and expensive cologne have seeped into his skin. And the suit – as much as it pains me to realize – the suit is doing all kinds of fluttery things in my lady region. In another life, there wouldn't have been a moment's hesitation. I'd have had him here on this sofa and not cared who saw.

"Myles," Carter grunts at the door. "We have real business to discuss. Lock your whore outside so she can't cause any trouble while we're gone."

"I could jump off the side of the building screaming 'Carter makes women suicidal'?" I offer with a half shrug. Myles chuckles, kissing my forehead before rising.

"Shannon, manning the lobby desk, will aid any request you might have, and Gabriel in the kitchen can make you something if you're hungry. I'll be back as soon as I'm able." Myles leaves with Carter, who pauses long enough to remind me he has his eye on me, and then I'm alone. A quick glance shows Sebby isn't attending but instead, has remained on a swinging egg chair in the garden while he rubs Pig's belly. I can't deny she's an attention whore, and damn if she's mastered how to get it.

I remain on that sofa for far longer than necessary. Reading a random magazine from a nearby table which all of the boys are on the cover of, waiting for the elevator to take Myles and Carter downstairs. Then, I wait a little bit longer just in case. Risking another glance out of the door, I note Sebby has swayed himself and Pig into a nap, and no one else is looking my way. Time to slowly close the blinds and begin my search.

Loading Myles' iMac, I'm met with the expected password screen while I'm picking the locks on his drawers. It really makes no sense to leave a pot of paperclips on the desk for anyone to help themselves to. Breaking my way into the first, a notepad sits at the top of the drawer and inside the front cover – *Computer Password*. Too easy.

Managing both simultaneously, I open the deleted files on the computer while popping the bottom three drawers. Upending folders, I find page after page of investment logs, online banking reports, phone transcripts. A whole load of business I don't have the expertise to decrypt. When his computer files also prove useless, I move into more high-tech methods. Hacking the central server, downloading as much as I can onto a random flash drive I found in the drawer. I'll spend my time making sense of it later.

Tapping my thumb on the desk, I grow agitated, deciding I must have missed something. I drop to the floor, spreading out paperwork, hunting for that symbol. The decorative shield, surrounded by flourishes and a roaring dragon in the center, which has become imprinted on the inside of my brain. The more I dream of it, the clearer it becomes.

"The code to the safe is 8256," Myles' voice suddenly states from the doorway. "It's behind the Rembrandt." I look up to see him pointing at a portrait on the opposite wall. Slowly, I gather up all of the papers scattered on the floor and place them back in the bottom drawer. Mostly out of courtesy, but also to avoid his probing gaze.

"I figured once you're sated from going through all of my belongings, we could go for dinner. Or you could ask me to give you whatever it is you're looking for, and we could still catch the lunchtime rush." There's a hint of mirth to his tone, but I'm not laughing along. Fine, we'll play it this way.

"You burned that brown envelope. At Reynell's house, I see you – and when I asked if you found anything, you lied about it. Proceeded by locking yourself in your room. All highly suspicious behavior and I want to know why."

"Oh, I see." Myles nods, steps inside and softly closes the door. I stand, folding my arms. "I understand it's in your nature to look for the bad in people - I just thought we'd come to an impasse where you gave me a little more credit than that." Strolling towards me, there's confidence in his steps, and more so in the way Myles grips my waist and plants me on his desk. Attempting to push him away, his hands close over mine, holding them heavily on his chest.

"Your prints were all over that envelope, there was a dead man in the grass outside and an archer rearing back an arrow intended for you. I was merely burning any evidence which could be traced back." Myles catches his eyes and holds me captive. He stares at me for so long, not daring to blink and break the trance.

"You were...protecting me?" I whisper. That's it? All of this, all of my delusions and spiraling schemes, are just that? Versions I would prefer so the outcome is the same – my heart is secure and Myles is inevitably the bad guy I always thought he should be.

"Really shouldn't be much of a shock. I've been nothing but forthcoming with my intentions," Myles states. His knuckles brush my neck, stroke my cheek and I roll my eyes.

"To fuck me?"

"To love you. As soon as you're ready to let me." My breath catches. His touch is everywhere, taking ownership of the body I thought was mine. The way it reacts to him though, tells a different story,

"A few weeks ago, you didn't know I existed," I try to reason with us both. Myles is right there, at the edge of the cliff, ready to drag me back into his safe embrace.

"A few weeks ago, I didn't know what it meant to feel alive. To be looked at for more than the image Carter has worked hard to create. To have someone challenge and provoke me when all others bend over backwards to kiss my ass." His hand skates to my nape while I grunt.

"Not a visual image I needed."

"What I mean is, I'm a man who has everything. Could possess anything. Until the day I saw you; free and wild, and realized nothing that came before mattered. I want to spend every day waking up to you, unknowing what may happen or where we will end up. You're an adventure, and I'm on board for as long as you'll have me."

My heart yearns to believe him. My head pleads to give in. To believe I might be worthy of love. That I could have a shot at finding light and laughter amongst the darkness I've become comfortable in.

"Will you have me, Ami?" Myles repeats. He's so close now, his breathing fans my lips. And it's in that moment, a thought so visceral slams into me, it brings with it the weight of a wrecking ball.

It doesn't even matter if I'm wrong, if I open myself up to being betrayed. Because I have no reference to know what true happiness feels like. Myles describes me as a free, wild being, but he has no idea of the self-imposed barriers I've built. Of the cage I trap myself inside. I could give Myles the power to destroy me beyond repair, but at least I could say I loved. I could say I lived a portion of my life, and no matter how short, it was glorious.

"I'll let you tag along." I finally nod. Smiles take residence on both of our faces as he closes the final gap between us, coaxing me to melt in his kiss.

Chapter 26

We make it two whole floors down before Myles is jamming his finger on the stop button, and then dragging me free of the elevator. Quizzical eyes watch us rush past, Myles' hand in mine the entire way. Nearing a door at the end of the hallway, he throws the door wide and shouts at everyone to vacate immediately. I'm used to Carter shouting the orders, but seeing Myles in full-boss mode does something primal to me. It reminds me, no matter how laid back and softly spoken he is, Myles is an alpha through and through.

Employees scramble from the door with the same haste I'd expect for a fire alarm, leaving us to duck inside and lock the door. I instantly understand why he's brought me here. There are no windows, except for the exterior wall peering into an adjacent building. The room is similar to a small library, stacked with bookcases and none of the contents are anything I'd have the patience to read.

I barely glance at a spine about global market crashes when I'm spun around for his mouth to take mine hostage. A light brush at first, captivating in its gentleness. His lips command my full attention, as if nothing else exists but the casual caress, the warm press, the slip of his tongue. Parting my lips, Myles lingers on the safe side of tongue-fucking me, as if giving me the final chance to back out.

"Get on with it or I'll go find Sebby," I groan, cementing my decision. I once vowed Myles would never have me. Now I can't think of a single reason why I don't want him. Need him, right here and now before I explode with unspoken emotion. Grabbing my ass, Myles hikes me up his body, pressing my back into the bookcase. Our kiss deepens, heating me to my core. With my legs wrapped around his waist, Myles skillfully holds me up with one arm and brushes the knuckles of his free hand over the apex of my thighs. I'm already wet, soaking through the material of my thong underneath.

"I wanted our first time to be special," Myles breaks away to mutter, more to himself. I roll my hips in encouragement.

"That's a stupid idea," I grunt. Myles flashes me a warning glare. He's rock-hard against my thigh, past the point of being reigned back in. "The first time is a rushed nutting sesh, that's all. Just a release of base needs – the second time is when it gets special." He misses my air quotes behind his back. Sex is sex, there's nothing romantic about it. The orgasms don't last, the passion quickly fades and as for my interest...it's never held this long before.

Drawing me in for another heated kiss, Myles dips his fingers beneath my waistband, seeking out my clit. As soon as his fingers flick over the sensitive bud, arousal floods my body. Fuck, I didn't realise it had been so long – but this is something uniquely Myles. Dropping my head back, his mouth finds my neck, and I'm suddenly aware of how hot I am. Pushing enough distance between us, I drag my shirt over my head without needing to undo the buttons and move to do the same to his.

"You know, for all the taunting you've given me, I think there's enough time for a little payback," he smirks. My hands drop against his chest, sucking in a breath. Perhaps I'm seeing through lust-tinted glasses, but holy hell. *He gets hotter every time I see him.* Firm, smooth pecs give way to a valley of deeply ingrained abs, the V above his slacks causing me to salivate. I stutter some sort of compliment, which is lost as his fingers push inside me. A solid, slow thrust which has a direct correlation to the curling of my toes. I sigh at the relief bucking my hips to do it again.

"Who's in a rush now?" Myles tilts his head, his tousled hair dripping over his shoulder.

"Just fuck me already," I moan as his fingers curl inside of me. A long groan is torn from the pit of his chest.

"I thought you'd never ask." Leaning forward to pin my upper half against the shelves, Myles peels my trousers beneath my ass, leaving them at the tops of my thighs. He finds me again instantly, no longer taunting. Two fingers push back inside as his hand begins to move. Pumping faster and faster. My moans are stifled by Myles' mouth, his tongue twisting with mine. He drives me higher up the shelves, my back arching and squirming against his assault. I tilt my hips forward, meeting him for each thrust.

On a shared, strangled groan, I'm suddenly moving. Spun mid-air, losing sense of gravity until my back is gently lowered onto a table.

Stretching my arms wide, I send everything nearby crashing to the floor.

"Remember what you promised," Myles says, unbuttoning his slacks. I raise a brow as his solid erection thumps against my pussy deliciously. I gasp at the dull contact, at the sheer heaviness of it. The smile taking residence on Myles' face isn't like the others. This one is full. Dangerous. Carnal. "This is for base needs. Next time will be special."

I begin to protest I made no such promise, but he's beyond listening. With the trousers still caging my legs, Myles lifts my ankles and holds them together at his shoulder. My body is bent into a 'L' shape, my ass hanging off the edge of the wood. His blunt head pushed against my entrance, rubbing against my wetness before he stills. I squirm, about to get violent when Myles' face softens.

"I can't do it like this," his brows pinch.

"Why the hell not?!" my voice is erratic, my pussy weeping to be destroyed. The fingers at my ankles smooth over the soft patch of foot between the heel's straps.

"I've envisioned this moment over and over, and I made a decision." When he doesn't continue, I shimmy myself down the table in an effort to penetrate myself. I don't need all of him, just his cock. It's been far too long since I fucked for pleasure. "I'm not going to start until I can see you. The real you. Remove the contacts, Ami."

Swallowing, my heart thumps for a whole different reason. A shiver rolls along the length of my back. Myles wants to stare into my eyes, my real eyes, as he fucks me. To gaze directly into the depths of my psyche without any barrier. The eyes are the key to the soul, and I've hid mine for so long, the contacts have become a crutch. Another layer to the mask. A whimper is drawn from my lips, writhe with need and uncertainty as my hands slowly rise. I've already come this far in changing my mind about Myles. If there's anyone I should give the benefit of the doubt, it's the man who wants to fuck me senseless for pleasure. Not money or material gain.

"Don't look," I tell him, my cheeks heating. If there's one way to turn a man off, it would be fingering my own eyeballs. Removing the contacts, I flick them to the floor, figuring I can get Shannon the receptionist to fetch me some more. Smoothing down my hair, I prepare myself for what's next to come. "Okay...ta da?"

Opening his eyes, Myles doesn't react. Doesn't say anything, and that further fuels the tension thrumming through my body. I dare not blink, fighting the urge to turn away.

"Well...what do you see?" I chew on my lip, dreading the answer. Myles tightens his grip on my thighs and as he maintains my gaze, his cock eases inside of me. Slowly stretching, steadily pushing.

"My redemption," he responds. The air rushes from my lungs, leaving me panting. My body shifts as he fully sheathes himself, my hips raising as I force myself to accept every hard inch. Just as I brace for him to retreat, he remains there, rocking back and forth until I adjust.

"Don't," I grit my teeth. Myles smiles like the freaking Joker, lavishing in the way he's got me all pent-up. Reaching for my cheek, I slap his hand away. "Don't go easy, or I'll make you a bottom again." This gets the reaction I wanted. The gleam in his amber eyes retracts, plaguing his gaze with darkness.

Finally, he takes me. Fully, brutally. Savage thrusts that rock the table, heavy slaps of skin meeting skin which draw screams from my throat. I grip the edges, my nail embedded in the wood in an effort to hold on. Myles's girth, his solid length, his powerful thighs. He holds a heady combination meant for fucking, designed to pleasure.

Suddenly, it's my own urges I'm worried about. He could screw me into oblivion, and I wouldn't need to come back.

Lowering my legs into the crook of his elbow, Myles twists me, gaining deeper access to my soaking cunt. Nestled deep inside, he rocks my hips, and I'm not responsible for the mewling sound I make. He's too deep, filling me to the hilt. I can't believe I managed to hold back from him this long and now I know what I was missing, I'm wondering who exactly I was trying to punish.

"I could have you like this forever," Myles rolls his groin flush against me. "At my mercy, coated with lust. Just when I thought you couldn't get more beautiful."

"Stop talking," I plead, covering my face with my hands. He's there in an instant, his weight leaning over my hip to grab my wrists and pin them either side of my head. There's no hiding where Myles is concerned. No character I can portray which he won't seek to break.

All he wants is you, the real you, a voice fleets through my mind. I can't take his gaze anymore, can't risk revealing anything I've spent years hiding. Shifting my legs, I turn myself onto my front, his hold on my wrists causing them to criss-cross. My feet, aided by the high heels, find the floor, giving me the perfect height advantage. Those damn trousers around my thighs continue to keep my legs tightly bound, but I can't deny how incredible Myles feels, adjusting his stance and jerking back in from behind.

It only takes two formidable thrusts to cause my undoing. A fierce orgasm slams into me, consuming my body with tremors of electricity. It continues to roll from the flush on my cheeks to the tingling in my legs, and Myles doesn't give any reprieve. He plows into me like a man possessed, a beast who's insatiable.

"Fuck Fiery," he moans by my ear, although I'm not sure how I heard it. My cries echo around the empty library, somehow filling the vast space around us to feel claustrophobic. His hands shift to my ass, spreading me wide against his assault. Fingers toy with my pussy as his cock slams in fast, drags out slow, and I can't contain the continuous climax. It pulses around him, squeezing him to the point of no-entry, but Myles manages. There's no denying him now.

Riding the waves on prolonged mewls, a heavy weight follows, the length of Myles' body pressing along my back a soothing comfort to the thick cock nestled inside me. This probably isn't the activity intended for the table creaking beneath our weight, rocking on its slender legs. I stretch for the far end, looking to anchor myself. To steady the flutters worming from my cunt to my chest, expanding faster than Myles can thrust into me. Not that he doesn't give it a good go. Crying out, I beg for him to finish me. To ruin me.

"There's no version of this where I don't get to watch you fall apart," Myles pulls out so suddenly, I gasp. Dragging the trousers down the length of my legs, he makes quick work of tugging the heels free and discarding them all. I remain still, frantically grappling for my perfected self-control. A sharp smack on my ass reverberates around the room, the sting blossoming with warmth.

Stripping himself, Myles whips me around, fully pressed against his sculpted body. He doesn't attempt to kiss me, maintaining eye contact as he lowers us to the floor, lifting my waist to sit me atop of him. I'm left with nowhere to hide, my hands splayed across his chest.

"Ride me," he orders when I stall too long. Gripping the erection jerking insistently against my ass, I guide him to my entrance and sink down with excruciating slowness.

"What did you say about payback?" I tilt my head cockily, as if I could deny either of us now. Violet hair strokes his abs, which Myles quickly wraps around his hand and tugs downward, hard. Leaning forward as if to kiss me, Myles diverts at the last moment, freeing my breasts of the lace bra. It's been driving my pebbled nipples crazy, and Myles provides an instant balm.

Cool breath fans my nipples before he takes one into his mouth. Tongue flicking, sucking gently before biting hard, he draws me towards another impending orgasm and then pulls back. Tethered in limbo, seated on the precipice. I can't draw a full breath, lifting my ass and slamming back down, rolling my hips and repeating. I need him closer, deeper. Anything to drive me over the edge of this cliff and drown in the stars bursting behind my eyes.

"Myles, please," I beg. Fucking *beg*, like I never have before. I just need to make noise. Say anything to get the words out of my head.

"What do you want Fiery?" Myles chuckles, moving onto my other nipple. He doesn't stay there long, returning to my face. But he doesn't kiss me, merely watches. Or rather - stares. Every contorted movement of my features, every plea of my eyes. Memorizing each strangled sound I can't contain. Myles absorbs it all. He's relishing this.

"I want you-" I don't get to finish my sentence. I can't pretend I had an ending in mind – probably similar to wanting him to go to hell, but it doesn't matter now. Grabbing my waist, Myles holds me an inch over his body and slams up into me. Driving his cock to the hilt, he holds me in place. Fucks me into nothingness. A void where nothing but the building and burning within my core exists. Riding the waves he takes me on, I slam my hands onto his chest to be released from his hold. What's about to happen to me will rewrite every climax I've had before, and I'll be damned if I'm not a part of it.

Following Myles' quickened rhythm, I fall into meeting him halfway. Bouncing my ass in time, taking him thrust-for-thrust. Where Myles ends and I begin becomes irrelevant. All that matters is what's about to happen. We move in unison, becoming one beneath the bright lighting. Lost to a world of possibilities and passion. Myles regards me with such interest, such allure, I can't look away. His blond hair blends around us like a curtain, those endless amber eyes devouring my entire being.

"Come for me Amethyst."

And I do. I break for Myles as if his words control me. Shattering around his cock, never to be fully put back together again. The room fades away as I float from my body, the sounds leaving my throat foreign to my own ears. A few more hard thrusts and Myles swells, cursing and praising beside my ear. Hands find mine, our fingers becoming interlinked. Our panting is silenced by a hungry, desperate kiss, wanting to prolong the moment. Drag out the way our tongues skate over each other's, how our lips crash and nibble.

Rushed nut sesh, my ass. This was something more. So much more.

Chapter 27

We arrive at the manor just before sunset. Swamped in my jacket and nothing underneath, Amethyst presses into my side, her hair still damp. Nothing could sway her to leave the rooftop pool, especially when she discovered the outcropped base was transparent and visible by multiple levels below. A lesser man would have been furious that she swam naked back and forth until business closing, but not me. Let the world see how incredible she is, when I know she's staying in my bed from now on. It's not been pre-discussed, but I've decided. We've come so far, there won't be any slamming on the breaks.

"Go dress," I encourage her with a warm smile as we enter the front doors. Those purple eyes are blinking up at me again, her contacts back in place. I'm not complaining. Knowing I've had the privilege to see what no one else has fills me with a sense of profound satisfaction. What's underneath, fuck, I can't even begin to fathom.

"I want the entire household to have dinner together within the hour," I speak loudly enough so the Elites will overhear. They're never far enough away not to eavesdrop. Kissing Amethyst on the forehead, she obeys my instruction almost too easily, and I make sure to repeat it to the guys. Owen is last in, having returned in time to catch a ride home.

"Do I get a kiss too?" he jests, bumping my shoulder. Both Sebby and Carter look back from further within the lobby, genuinely curious.

"I don't think I can afford you," I raise a brow back at Owen. He smirks so wide, his dimples pop out.

"Damn straight." Leaving me to my own devices, I make a beeline for the downstairs office. Usually, Carter is the only one who uses it, but Ami was only too happy to trade me the door code for a slice of toffee cheesecake. Permitting myself entry, I drop down behind the computer, glad Carter uses the same passwords as he does on the work computers. Locating the file with my own name on it, I'm deep diving into contracts when the door swings open.

"Myles," Carter stops mid-step. "What...are you doing here?"

"I live here Carter," I reply sarcastically.

"I mean, what are you doing here in my-" he catches himself, "the office?" Tugging on the cuffs of his shirt, he tries to relax. Rolling his shoulders, stretching his neck. It doesn't work, the rigidness too deeply embedded.

"I just need to check something before dinner." Returning to the screen, I scan signed contracts I'm only seeing for the first time. It's my fault. I've never taken an interest before, but something changed within me today. Staring into Ami's eyes, in the throes of great sex, I realized how much of a hypocrite I've been. She's the con woman playing a role, but I'm the billionaire who's been hiding behind a charade.

"Anything I can help you with?" Carter asks, nervously edging around the room to peer at the screen. I minimize the window before he can see what I'm doing.

"I'll manage," I spin in the leather chair, facing him straight on. "It's time I took back control of my life, I reckon. I've become too complacent letting you sort everything, but that's not realistic. At some point, I need to stand on my own. Unless, there's something you're hiding from me?" I challenge him. Carter doesn't react, and that's as much a guilty omission if I ever saw one. My best friend, the boy I grew up with, somehow became this hardened shell of a man. All precise hair lines, daily clean-cut shaves, hollow green eyes and aggressively pressed suits. And I was too complacent to stop it. I encouraged it, in fact, with my own laziness.

"Not at all," Carter nods, backing away. "Enjoy your snooping." I watch him all the way to the door, curious as to what he's referencing. Although, I make no move to ask.

Only when the door clicks closed, do I resume my search. Committing clauses and fine prints to memory, plunging into the structured way my life is controlled. I start taking notes at some point, noting the time is nearing dinner. I push up, hastily clicking and closing windows, eager to leave when a folder catches my eye. I'm sure it wasn't on the home screen before – I wouldn't have missed 'AMETHYST' in all caps.

Hovering the cursor over the file, it opens of its own accord. The contents cover the screen, a cursor untouched by me moving images around. I scowl, imagining Carter on a laptop upstairs as he orchestrates this. A feeble attempt to disguise my intentions.

Regardless, I lower into the seat and absorb what I'm seeing. Photographs of Ami as a child, both alone and with her parents. Newspaper articles declaring her as a missing child. Snapshots of police reports under false names, describing robberies and a gallery heist. ID cards from various job roles, bank statements, loan applications. It would seem Carter finally found her backstory, and I'm not interested.

There's a reason I told Felicia not to pass on Ami's birth name when she discovered it, but I misjudged their relationship. I thought the client privilege I pay millions for meant something to her. At the bottom of my list, I scrawl *'fire Felicia'*, and then make my way to the door.

I meant what I said to Ami earlier – how I yearn to be free. Until today, I thought that came in the form of relinquishing control to Carter, unburdening myself of big decisions, but it's the exact opposite. Freedom is having the choice to change the direction of my life, and that starts now.

I find everyone except Amethyst seated at the dining table. The best friends I consider to be brothers, the Elites who have served me well, Charley with a hopeful gleam in her eye and in Ami's seat, Pig pants heavily while Owen scratches behind her hind leg. A fine spread of roast turkey and all the trimmings is laid across the table, like a rehearsal thanksgiving ahead of next month. I smile at all the faces turned my way, taking the seat at the head of the table.

"Good evening everyone," I nod, the paper still folded against my palm. "I'm glad we all have this chance to talk before Amethyst arrives."

"Is everything okay?" Sebby frowns, his foot seeking out mine beneath the table for reassurance.

"Better than okay. I feel..." I search for the right word. "Liberated." Smiling widely, Joy takes the initiative to raise her wine glass, declaring a toast.

"To being liberated." Saluting our glasses, we all drink, exchange grins and pass around bowls of food to serve ourselves. All except Carter. He doesn't move, preferring to glare at me from the other end of the table with suspicion.

"And on the subject of liberating, I've decided it's time for a change. I've reviewed the Elite contracts and after we have enjoyed this last meal together, I'd like you to pack your things and leave. You're all fired."

"Myles!" Carter bellows, shrouding the shock in the room with a slam of his fist on the table.

"Wh-what?!" Kayla begins to cry quicker than I thought possible. "What did we do wrong, Mr. Hudson?"

"Where are we supposed to go?!" Lou raises her voice. Kristina is quick to wrap her arms around her friend, whispering into her ear. Lifting my knife and fork, I cut into my turkey, keeping my voice level.

"I'll put you all in five-star hotels for the weekend, and send you off with three months' worth of pay in your pockets. I would like to personally thank you for your wonderful service, but you're no longer needed." Keeping my eyes downcast, I begin to eat as chairs screech and heels stomp away. It's pretty shitty of me to not even stand as they leave, but it's been a long time coming. Bringing Amethyst here was a mistake because the second she entered the manor, I saw my life through her eyes. It was a bleak revelation I can't feel ashamed of any longer. When I glance up, I notice there's still one woman at the table. Charley.

"I love Amethyst like a sister," she breathes as our gazes meet. "But she will hurt you. It's only a matter of time before she moves on. She can never stop running." Sliding her chair back, Charley walks away slowly and gracefully, leaving me with Carter's enraged glare.

"Who do you envision cleaning the house? Cooking our meals, handling everyday chores? I can hardly see Owen pinning his own thongs out to dry." Owen scoffs at Carter's words, fully invested in eating his meal and ignoring everything happening around him.

"We will hire butlers and maids," I half shrug." Regular maids who aren't hired under the pretense of-" I pull out my paper now to make sure I get the wording exactly right, "sexually relieving Mr. Hudson when and how he sees fit, without complaint or dispute." Bile rises in my throat at those words. The contract went on to a silencing agreement of anything which happens under this roof. Returning to look at Carter, we become locked in a battle of wills. A standoff of dominance which makes Sebby squirm.

I only went in search of the contracts to see what the agreed termination period is. I wanted free of all ties, able to give myself wholly and fully to Amethyst – whether she accepts my heart or tramples all over it. Turns out, the clause states I don't need to give one. I can pick up and drop these women at my leisure, and they're not allowed to deny me. To reject me. Waves of nausea roll through my stomach, putting me off my food. I've spent my entire adult life trying to shake the reputation of a sex-crazed rapist, and those living in my own home were effectively silenced. Prevented from having a choice.

How many times did they want to say no? How many instances have I taken from them what wouldn't have been freely given. It all comes down to money, and I know the shame will slowly consume me. I let this happen. Today shouldn't have been the first time I saw these contracts, or witnessed the digital signature I scribbled without reading the fine print.

"You can stop with the judgmental looks now," Carter growls. His jaw is pulsing, his mouth barely moving as he grits through his teeth. "I didn't plan on being your caregiver. On advancing your career as well as my own, having the upkeep of this manor, multiple businesses, your safety, or having every aspect of multiple lives on my shoulders. Your father asked all this of me, and I didn't hesitate in saying yes."

A hand touches my thigh beneath the table. I sit back in my chair, dropping my arms to lock Sebby's finger with mine. He, like the others in this room, have been a stoic presence. My salvation in a world seeking to destroy me. I'd have drowned if it weren't for them, because fuck knows I've done nothing to pull myself to the surface. Sighing, my anger dissipates and turns inward.

"I understand this is all my fault, and I take full responsibility. For too long, I've been complacent, taken the easy route. It's time I woke up and relieved you of the burdens I've created. This manor is in my name. I will handle the hiring and firing from now on, and any fallout which comes as a result."

Squeezing Sebby's hand, we share a small smile. This is a new beginning for us all. For better or worse, I'm present now and I can see so much clearer.

"Myles," Carter huffs, bracing his elbows either side of his empty plate. "She needs to leave. I'm happy you've come to this conclusion, and I'll support you. But not with her. Find someone else. Anyone else. I'll help you." My back straightens and I instantly release Sebby's hand, although it remains on my tensed thigh.

"Amethyst isn't going anywhere. In fact, I'm preparing to tell her I love her." Owen stops eating now, peering up at me in disbelief. Sebby's hand shrinks away, his warmth retreating like the lowering of his grey eyes. He visibly withdraws, but it's Carter who demands my attention.

"How can you possibly think you love her when you don't even know her? You may love the idea of '*Amethyst*', but that's not who she really is." Shaking his head to himself, Carter downs his glass of wine. "It's all fake." I see red. I've never fought with Carter, but he's wrong about this. Amethyst may present a character to others, keeping everyone at a safe distance, but I saw her today. She's unknowingly let me break her walls, it's only a matter of time before they crumble for me completely.

"Despite your stunt to reveal her past to me," I spit, shoving myself to stand. A flicker of confusion crossed Carter's face.

"Stunt?"

"I've heard quite enough." A stern voice announces, a fifth man in a suit entering the room. Blond hair on the verge of silver, straight nose, a knowing tilt of his chin. I gape at the future image of myself, his pale brown eyes cold with contempt.

"Dad? What are you doing here?" Carter moves to my father's side, pushing his hands into his pockets.

"The front door was unmanned. Where are your maids?"

"Don't ask," Owen chuckles, taking that moment to excuse himself from the room. Asshole. He's always been wary in my father's presence.

"Carter called, and he was right to. This obsessive behavior of yours has to stop," my dad sighs. Adjusting the Rolex on his wrist, he tucks his hands in his suit pockets. The pair of them look like two peas of the same pod. The same calculated, uncaring bastards controlling my life.

"I'm not obsessing. I've met someone incredible. I can see myself spending my life with her." I fight my case, pleading with my father to see sense. When I envisioned him meeting Amethyst for the first time, it was under better circumstances. Turns out, he's already decided how he feels about her.

"I know all about the stray you've brought home. Caught her robbing your own jewelry store and thought – there's some wife material. If it was company you were lacking, you'd have been better off looking in the local animal shelter." Narrowing my eyes at Carter, the anger from earlier rises with a vengeance. Sebby tries to leave but I catch his wrist. I need someone in my corner for this.

"You don't understand. Sebby will back me up. If you'd just meet her, you'd see-" Waving a hand through the air, my father silences any further protests. He excudes power. Radiates dominance. It's no wonder I sought a release from his iron grip when I was younger, although he raised Carter like his own and Carter feel the tightening of the noose. He relished it.

"It won't seem like it right now," my father puffs out his chest, "but this is for your own good. Again."

"What do you-" I'm interrupted by the widening of Sebby's eyes over my shoulder. I look back in time to see three burly men in white coats as they seize me. Grappling with my arms, they tug them tightly behind my back and slam my chest down into the dinner table. A sharp sting bursts at my neck, sending me over the edge.

I roar with so many unspoken emotions, writhing to get them off me. To pry myself free long enough to run up the stairs, throw Amethyst over my shoulder and leave with her. Fuck the money, screw the luxuries. If these are the conditions of my life, I don't want it. I want a future crafted by my own design. Ultimately, I just want her.

Chapter 28

I wake with a start, unsure of what caused it. Drool pools over the sheets, my hair stuck to my cheek. Damn, a day of sex and swimming really took it out of me. Wiping my mouth with the back of my hand, a crash sounds from downstairs. My awareness picks up, my feet already moving. I'd only gotten as far as showering and pulling on underwear before the bed's sweet calls lulled me to lie down. Peering into the hallway, a series of whispered shouts catch my ear from the base of the stairs.

"I'd get down there if I was you," Owen announces. I spin to find him leaning against his bedroom door, Pig nestled in his arms. Blue eyes track the length of my body, lingering on my tattoos with a cocked eyebrow. Creeping towards the railing, I see two men akin to hairy monsters in white jackets, dragging a seemingly unconscious Myles to the front doors. Another is there to hold the door open, and I'm spurred into reacting. Flying down the staircase, Carter whips around the banister to catch me by the waist. Almost as if he was waiting there on purpose.

"What the fuck?! Get off me!" I scream, elbowing Carter's back. "Where are you taking him?!" My throat scratches from the high pitch, my stomach twisting in all kinds of knots. I watch through panicked eyes as Myles is stuffed into a Rolls Royce, the door slammed closed. The finality of the bang causes a gasp to be torn from my throat, one I don't have time to contemplate. I only know it happened and whatever I'm feeling will have to wait until I know Myles is safe. A man steps into my eyeline, blocking the entrance from view.

"It's even worse than I thought," he clicks his tongue. I stop fighting Carter for a moment, frowning. He's somewhat familiar, but I can't quite put my finger on why. "You were never going to be the benefi-ciary of my son's fortune." *This is Myles' father.* Questions – I have so many questions, and none of them are heard as he chuckles and stares down at me like a common whore.

Nodding his head of slickened black hair to Carter, Myles' father tugs on his jacket lapels, and that's when I see it. The glint of a gold ring on his middle finger. It's ostentatious in size, but that's not what causes me to fall still in shock. The flash of a shield, the shape and size. All a perfect match to the wax seal on that envelope. *Myles lied to me.* Because of that thought, I pause long enough for him to retreat to a matching white Rolls Royce, taking the back seat behind his driver.

"Get off!" I shove Carter and fall aside when he releases me imme-diately. I run to the door, watching the two cars drive side by side to the iron gates. They peel open, my heart slamming against the walls of my ribcage. I can't deny the fissure working its way through my chest, dread mixed with betrayal tainting my thoughts.

The vehicle containing Myles' father turns left, while the one with Myles indicates right. His head of sandy blond hair rolls about on the back seat as they turn and disappear from view. Fuck. I need to do something.

Turning to head back inside, probably to find clothes while concocting a plan, I bump into Carter's chest. He shoves me hard, and as I stumble over the threshold, my world tilts. Hitting the stone outside hard, the air is knocked from my lungs. Pain bursts along my back, my torso clenching as I wheeze. Briefly, I spot Owen at the top of the staircase, holding Pig and giving me a mocking wave until Carter steps in the way. His face is sterner than I've seen before, taut brows pulled over his malicious green eyes.

"If I so much as see your face again, I have a body in the freezer, a metal stake with your prints on it and two witnesses who will testify they saw you kill a man." He glances over his shoulder at Owen and Sebby. My gut drops into the base of my ass. "My lawyers will ensure you never see the light of day again."

"Myles told me that situation was taken care of," I scrunch up my face, leaning up on my elbows. Or was that all a lie too? Carter shoves my ankle with his shoe, ensuring all of me is outside of the threshold.

"It is, but I wasn't going to let decent blackmail go to waste. I don't owe you shit." Slamming the door, it's bolted before Carter's silhouette retreats through the frosted glass. I stall from getting up, unsure of where to go or what to do. Multiple options flash through my mind, the first being to break in and take my dog back. Half of the manor is made of glass anyway. But then again, as much as I want to punch Owen in the face right now, he does take good care of her. Just as Charley will be looked after here. The only one with a grievance is me, and it was just drugged and escorted away.

Myles. What have they done to you? Then again, his father holds the next clue to unlocking my past. For once, I'm truly torn between my head and heart. What I should do and what I want. Myles owes me an explanation for sure, but that's not what I'm thinking as I ease myself upright and start walking. There's only so long I can put my past first. Only a certain amount of times I can deny myself a future.

A guard in the booth reopens the gates for me, his eyes dragging over the length of my body as I stride out in just my underwear. A sexy, lacy set too, in black lace with hot pink bows. Pausing on the graveled road, I look one way, then the other. Then I turn right and begin to walk.

The sun is against me, lowering to meet the horizon by the time I breach the woodland which hides the manor from civilization. A long highway road stretches before me, miles of hiking drawing into the night ahead. I don't even know where Myles has been taken, or why, but each step feels like one in the right direction. That's as good enough a gauge as I'm going to get.

I couldn't have been walking more than ten minutes, when the low hum of motorcycles sounds behind me. Increasing in volume, they near, the headlights flashing over my ass in this thong. I don't bother looking back, preferring to ignore and be ignored, if it's possible. One passes, then the next and so on until five bikers appear in a line, their helmeted heads peering backwards. At first, I thought it was to get a look at my face, but soon a quad bike takes up the rear, pulling over with a hasty stop in the dirt bank alongside the road. I stop to admire the pink paintwork and vinyl love hearts and gummy bear on the back. The owner tugs her helmet off, producing a head of fuchsia hair in the same color.

"Oh honey, I've been there," she smiles at my underwear set. Shrugging out of her leather jacket, she holds it out for me. "Hop on, we'll see that you get where you need to go – after giving you some clothes and a stiff drink."

"Sold," I choke out as soon as a drink is mentioned. Taking the jacket, I pull it on and zip up the front. She offers me her helmet but I decline, and not just because of the strangled sounds which come from those looking on. "I'm Amethyst, by the way." Holding her shoulders, I swing my leg over the back seat of her quad bike.

"Candy," she winks, pulling the helmet over her face, muffling her voice. "Let's go have some fun."

It turns out, that stiff drink Candy offered, came from her very own bar. Not a mini bar or a counter in a basement, but a freaking biker club which converts into a nightclub after 10pm. Apparently, she lives above with all five of the hunky bikers who escorted us back.

Knocking back a tankard of glittery clear liquid which tastes too much like berries for my own good, I slump into the high-back leather armchair. A bunch of guys with cigars previously occupied them, but Candy had no qualms about kicking them to the bar stools. Her boots are crossed on the low table between us, a Viking goblet in hand.

"Then he said," I point my tankard in her direction, "I don't owe you shit, and slammed the door in my face." Glittery liquid spills onto the high-waisted PVC trousers Candy gave me, rolling across my thighs in pebbled beads. "They stole my dog." I pout, hoping Charley takes care of Pig in my absence. I'll return for them both when I've got my shit sorted...eventually. Candy nods, absorbing the half-story I gave her. As far as she knows, I'm simply a brokenhearted, jilted lover who's at war with my boyfriend's best friend. I was hazy on the details.

"Well, we can find your billionaire, no problem. Ace is our in-house tech genius." As if summoned by her words, a man who easily rivals

Myles in size appears. Huge muscles stacked on top of biceps, on top of shoulders, on top of traps. His white vest does nothing to hide any of his bronzed skin, a compliment to his honey hair and large puppy dog brown eyes which are fixated on Candy's face.

"Ace babe, can you track down where Myles Hudson has been taken to? We're playing matchmakers tonight." Her pink lips stretch wide as he lowers to kiss her, slowly and deeply enough to make me look anywhere else. The moment feels too private for me to gape and yearn at. Across the bar, a pair of identical blonds joke and laugh with each other whilst serving the sea of woman trying to catch their attention. Ace leaves with Candy's goblet, handing it to a gorgeous male with dreadlocks down the length of his back.

"Now we wait," Candy stomps her feet on the table. "Feel like having some fun?"

"Always." Standing, I wobble as the alcohol rushes to my head. Candy slips her arm into mine, pulling me along in the biker boots a size too large. The grunge-styled look is at odds with a flowy blue top, the shoulder straps draped loosely across the tops of my arms. My hair is scrunched from falling asleep with it damp earlier this afternoon, and Candy insisted on my eyeliner. A true biker rockstar appearance to match her charisma.

Leaving the bar, we stride across the parking lot, weaving between all types of vehicles. There's even a bicycle with a basket taking up a whole space. Candy leads me to a building, encased with metal walls and a sliding garage door which she avoids. We enter through a side door, passing an orange pick-up truck. There's a scuffle as another joins us, a man in a suit. I've had my fill of suits by now, but I have to say his is exquisite. Sharply pressed, not a single spec of lint or a crease in sight.

"Who's that?" I whisper as Candy releases me. She peers over my shoulder, her smile widening.

"Oh, just ignore him. I do. He's here to regulate my fun."

"Ahh - you have a Carter too," I nod in understanding.

"What's that supposed to mean?" he steps forward on a low growl. I shift to put him in my eyeline, but it's Candy who skips over to place a soothing hand over his tie.

"Just that you're a controlling, overprotective, micromanaging ball ache who struggles with the concept of freedom."

"Fair enough. I look forward to taking you upstairs later and micromanaging each spank I deliver to your ass." He spanks her now for the fun of it and my eyes widen.

"Oh," my cheeks flame. "No, my Carter is never, *ever* going there with me." Even just referring to him as my Carter makes me want to gag. "Anyways. What are we doing here?" I change the subject. Candy laughs knowingly, handing me a thickly coiled rope.

"Are you any good with knots?" she asks. I look from her to him and back. I'm not sure what freaky shit she had planned, but as Candy opens a large wooden box on the floor, strangely similar to a coffin, I realize it's about to get a whole lot weirder. There's a naked man inside, bound and gagged. I tilt my head curiously, a warning alarm blaring in my mind. I'm supposed to be helping Myles, not...doing whatever this is.

"Um..." I pause. I've done my fair share of shady shit, and it might be because of that, I don't want to be implicated in whatever is happening here. For all I know, this gang will all point the finger at me and there's only so many times I can disappear or talk my way out of jail. I posed as my own attorney once and announced the woman they'd arrested had skipped the country. Amazing what some prosthetics can do. "You know, maybe I should get back to Ace and help him search."

"Are you doubting my man's abilities?" Candy abruptly straightens, her face devoid of all emotion except for the slight downward tilt of her mouth. There's a crazed emptiness to her chocolate brown eyes. Almost as if she's looking through me, and that's when I decide this woman could gut me, leave me at the roadside and not lose a second's sleep over it. Suddenly, she bursts out laughing, her tightened posture loosening again.

"I'm kidding. Don't worry about this piece of shit," she kicks the coffin. "He was my father's driver, before I knew he was my father. The mob boss, not the driver. Anyways, it's a long story. Fact is, he drove me off a cliff once." The man in the coffin screamed from behind a gag, shaking his head. "Trust me, he deserves it. Don't you, Nigel?" I watch Candy bend low to scrunch up his face, and take the opportunity to look back to the suit now leaning against the truck.

"Do as she says," he shrugs. "It's easier that way." It would seem whether I like it or not, I'm in this situation for the long haul. Tying the rope around his ankles, which feels as heavy as lead now, I pass it through the middle of his shins and create a knot I'm sure won't unravel. Or at least, I hope won't. Candy claps her hands in glee, taking the rest of the rope from my hands. Pulling up a step ladder, she makes quick work of hooking it up to a pre-made pully system. The blond twins from the bar appear at the side door, one with a pink baseball bat in hand.

"Oohh goody, a human pinata. I knew you'd choose my idea," the one holding the bat approaches, his green eyes filled with a crazed glint akin to Candy's.

"Nah ah. Don't be rude Jest. Guests first." Candy jumps down to take the bat and hand it to me. I dare not refuse at this point, not when the men all work together to heave the rope and string their captive upside down from the ceiling. I get an eyeful of his tiny dick and balls flopping downwards, his groin already battered and bruised. Securing him in place, all eyes fall on me. Curious, encouraging, probing.

"Don't be shy. You get first hit, but we'll be the ones finishing him off," Candy winks. I look at the bat, turning it to read the inscription. '*The Candy Crusher*'. Well, I don't want to appear rude. Rearing the bat back, I swing hard and hit the naked stranger in his gut. A strangled cry is muffled by the gag in his mouth, a tingle of exhilaration seeping through my arms.

Holy shit, that was awesome. I swing again, hit again. His skin inflames with each contact and somewhere along the way, I stop hitting out of enjoyment. The blows delivered via my hands come as a necessity, a visceral need to rid myself of the torment I've allowed to settle deep in my soul. I let Myles worm his way in, I let myself care for Sebby, I let Charley go. And then there's me. I allowed myself to become too attached, too comfortable.

"Okie dokie, I think that's enough," Candy pries the bat from my hands. I'm panting, drawn to an abrupt halt. Those watching me are all smiling, seemingly impressed by something I can't fathom. Taking the other side of the man strung between us, Candy strikes his back. It's only then I realize the screams have stopped, her captive hanging unconscious. Taking a few steps back, I bump into the pickup and make my way towards the door. A hand flashes out from the suit, his dark eyes holding me prisoner.

"Don't feel embarrassed," he urges me. I shrug him off. "There are troubles many of us must carry without the rest of the world knowing. Ones which aren't easily understood and there's rarely a remedy. Candy has a knack for finding people similar to herself, otherwise she wouldn't have brought you here. Should you ever need a safe place to go, you're always welcome to return." I swallow thickly, lowering my head. I was wrong. He's not like Carter at all.

Stumbling out into the night air, I gasp to fill my lungs. To break the constriction they've been under. One day too soon, I'm going to start questioning why I can hurt people and not feel guilt. How I can kill without giving it a second thought, and what that means for the people I actually decide I love. Am I even worthy of receiving such emotion?

"Hey!" a voice shouts over the parking lot, Ace waving me over from the porch. I run to him, eager for the information he holds in his hands. Passing me a set of papers, I see a copy of the waiver Carter has signed to commit Myles back to rehab. The cosigner, Charlton Hudson, and the witness – Felicia Steele. I grip the pages hard enough to crumple. In the top corner is an address.

"I need to go," I breathe, halfway down the steps before Ace stops me.

"Hold up," he bars my way with his arm. "I've already called a cab to take you to the bus station. There's a timetable and the connections you need printed on the back," he flips the papers to point out. Nodding my thanks, he doesn't shift his arm. "Here, take this. And don't worry about paying it back," a wad of cash is stuffed into my hand.

"Why would you do all of this for me?" I frown, trying to give it straight back. Ace retreats, putting a few feet between us. Spotting an approaching set of headlights, he signals to the cabbie and sighs.

"I know something about impulsive women, and the love they refuse to acknowledge. Do me a favor, when you find Myles, just tell him how you feel. It's not weakness or a character flaw. It's human nature. The only person you're kidding is yourself." His voice remains gruff, as if I'm testing his patience until he opens the cab's rear door. I wait long enough to catch his attention.

"I don't like being in debt to people."

"Fine. I'll take repayment in the form of being told my wife isn't in that garage committing an illegal act right now." His large, brown eyes hold mine for a moment too long.

"You know what, I think I'm okay with this debt," I shrug and slide into the cab as Ace curses and storms away.

Once hidden in the safety of darkness, I release a smile. If Candy can manage to enthrall five men, I reckon I can handle one, and somewhere along the way with that thought train, I realize I'm no longer mad at Myles for lying to me. I'm going to kick his ass and make him grovel, but I'm not mad because deep down, I know Myles. He's not the asshole everyone believes him to be. At least...I'm fairly sure he's not.

Chapter 29

"**G**ood afternoon. Welcome to Serenity Heights Recovery Centre." A woman shoots up from behind the desk as soon as I enter. The automatic doors slide closed on the manicured gardens beyond, shutting me inside the finest rehab lobby I could have imagined. Soft furnishings fill a waiting area, huge canvas' of abstract art cover the walls. Approaching the semi-circle counter, my eyes snag on a self-serve coffee machine on the far end.

"How may I assist you today?" The receptionist continues. Her hair is pulled back so tight, there isn't a single wrinkle on her middle-aged face. Neutral make-up and a standard black blouse allow her bright, red lips to pop from their stretched smile.

"Are you here…to visit a family member?" she starts making guesses when I don't announce myself. I rest my boobs on the counter, the low plunge halter neck I bought doing nothing to keep me contained. The strap of my handbag does a better job, crossing over my cleavage. What can I say - I put Ace's money to good use.

"Actually, I came here looking for some help, but now I've seen you," I bite my bottom lip. "You look like a squirter."

"Excuse me?!" she balks, her face whitening beneath the make-up.

"I bet you squirt all the time. Just so you know, I swallow and mama sure is thirsty." I cringe internally, kissing goodbye to the portion of my soul which just withered and died as she calls for assistance. Reaching out to brush my fingertips over her breast, a gigantic male nurse tackles me to the ground.

I'm man-handled through a set of doors only accessible by keycard, along a hallway to a grand staircase. I knew from the information Ace provided and presumed from the asshole Carter is, this wouldn't be a standard luxury facility. Those committed here are some of the worst cases and members of the most affluent families. In short – they need a quick and quiet fix without the chance of easy escapes. Putting on a show, I gyrate against the nurse's leg as he forces me to keep moving and shoves me into an office.

"Sorry to barge in, Sir. We have an extreme case," the male nurse eyes me as if I'm infectious. I brush off his touch with the same notion.

"It's fine, Carl. Thank you," an aged man nods from behind a walnut desk. Dr. Edwin Winters, as his pinned name badge indicates. His grey hair has been oiled back, his face riddled with long-term scarring and an off-set nose. He finishes scrawling his signature on some papers and puts them in his top drawer, giving me his full attention. "How may I help you, Ms..."

"Lloyd," I fill in, taking Sebby's last name. I worked out my persona on the way over here – Sasha Lloyd is to be Sebby's cousin. Our mothers were twins, providing me with the same black hair and pewter grey eyes as him. I push a strand of the wig back over my bare shoulder, batting my lashes over colored contacts. "I have decided after years of prostitution and stripping, it's time to face facts. I love being railed and degraded by strangers because," I suck in a loud breath, "I am addicted to sex."

"I see," Dr. Winters signals for me to take the seat opposite. I prefer to stand, wandering around his office. At first, I thought my perverse mind was deceiving me, but the more I move, I'm convinced. This room is filled with genitals, everywhere. Uvula shaped trinket dishes and cushions, the angled shaft of a lamp, girthy table legs with veins engraved, curtains printed with ball-outlines.

"Your office is one, giant orgy. Do you enjoy taunting your patients?" I run my fingers over a vase shaped as a woman's naked body. Mostly for show, but also with curiosity.

"The intention is not to taunt, but to test control. There are temptations everywhere in the outside world. If my patients can't handle my office, they aren't ready to be discharged." Oh, he's one of those God above men type people. Good to know, playing up to his ego will serve me well. Finally taking a seat, my leather mini skirt rides all the way up to my red thong when I cross my legs. Dr Winters doesn't seem impressed.

"I'm sorry to disappoint Ms. Lloyd, but we will not be able to accommodate you. Regardless of how you find us, this facility is top of the range. A place where our clientele can receive the finest care.

Only for the wealthy and mostly famous. We don't take walk-ins off the street."

"Are you implying I can't afford to be rehabilitated here?" I press a hand to my chest. I think you'll find my cousin is the owner of Solstice Photography and co-owner of various, multimillion dollar businesses." Yeah, I did my research. The seven-hour drive left plenty of time for some light reading. "Not to mention, I can fund my own stay. How about I pay two months upfront?" Tugging a fake AMEX from my cleavage, Dr Winters seems to suddenly have a change of heart. A small smile lights his aged face, his gnarled finger pushing against the intercom system on his desk.

"Elizabeth, prepare suite 101. We have a new guest." His expression takes on a few edges which makes me feel slimy, but I thank him regardless and make my way to the door. Carl is there to open it for me, and pry the dildo candle from my hand as I snag it on my way out. His hands are bigger than my face, tugging me down the hall to a second pair of locked doors. I watch his keycard be extended and then snap back to his waist on a retractable cord. Mentally logging every security system and camera along the way, I'm escorted to room 101 where a copycat of the receptionist stands.

"We'll require you to fill in a few forms, given you're admitting yourself to our care," she smiles her red lips. I look beyond her black blouse and trousers, to the room I've been provided. A suite indeed – fitted with a kingsize bed, corner library, reflection zone in front of a large window overlooking the pool and gardens. A personal bathroom can be seen through another open door within, boasting a jacuzzi bathtub.

As far as accommodations go, I don't know why I didn't book myself in here for a permanent stay earlier. I've resigned Charley, Pig and myself to some shitholes for the sake of staying under the radar, but this would have been a much more pleasant option. Taking the papers from Elizabeth's hands, I'm one foot inside the door before being tugged to a stop by Carl and his face-hands.

"We'll need to confiscate your personal property," he reaches for my bag. Tugging myself free, I scowl and look to Elizabeth for back-up.

"Until I've signed these forms," I lift them aggressively, "my property still belongs to me." Then I lean in, whispering beside her ear. "I need certain lady products, if you catch my drift." Elizabeth nods, soothing Carl with a courteous smile.

"We will retrieve your bag and clothing when you've been fully processed, and should you need any feminine care products from now on, just let an orderly know." I thank her generously, waiting for Carl to ease the tension in his shoulders and stalk away. That's the second time I've successfully used my shark-week card this month.

"Once you're settled, wander downstairs to our rec room. There is a bulletin board in there of daily activities you may enjoy until your care plan has been drawn up. You'll be expected to attend daily counseling sessions and at least three group-therapy talks per week. It also goes without saying - sex is strictly prohibited, no guests in bedrooms and doors are to always remain open when in the company of other patients. I hope you enjoy your stay here," Elizabeth smiles and leaves me to push the door closed.

Setting my bag on the dresser, I hide the contents I wish to keep before turning my attention to the papers. The background information is easy enough to make up and I fill in Sebby's card details from memory to cover my fee. Creating an autograph-worthy signature, I sign the dotted line and sigh.

Well, Sasha Lloyd, you've successfully entered yourself into sex-rehab and you didn't have to screw the receptionist to get in. Con phase one – check. Now I just need to locate Myles.

***

Entering the rec room, I take a moment to adjust to the glaring sunlight streaming through the all-glass ceiling and outer walls. Warmth floods the white t-shirt and grey sweatpants I'm wearing, standard issue thanks to the fully stocked wardrobe in my suite. Canvas shoes with soft insoles scuff against the tiled floor as I move further within.

Shielding my eyes with my hand, I find a cluster of tables pushed against one side. In the space where they were, several women in matching attire kneel on the floor over the biggest jigsaw puzzle I've ever seen. A sea of penguins cover the part they've managed to piece together, the mix of black and white making it nearly impossible to decipher which bit goes where. Avoiding them, I head outside to where a tall blonde is playing cards alone on the patio. There's a few more women scattered around the grounds, doing lengths in the swimming pool or playing in the tennis court.

"Um...where are the dudes?" I ask the card player, not bothering to introduce myself.

"Oh hi, I'm Jo. A pleasure to meet you," she drawls, rolling her blue eyes. Despite wearing the same as me, she somehow carries herself with a regal manner. Basically, her back is extraordinarily straight and she smells like money.

"Yeah, yeah. Sasha – where are the hunky men?"

"You're in the female building," she pauses long enough to raise a brow at me. Rearranging the cards in her hand, I drop into the empty seat across from her.

"I'm in the what-e-what?" I stammer, envisioning my perfect plan shredding before my eyes.

"The men's building is across the lake," she points without looking. Exactly like she said, beneath a glorious landscape of mountain ranges, there's a mirror-image of this damn building across a shimmering body of water. *Fuck.* "It's a sex addiction clinic. They're not going to have mixed living quarters. Watch out for Ruby though," Jo leans forward to whisper, "she's a raging lesbian."

I follow her eyeline to a sun-kissed woman sitting on a bench amongst the grass. She's hunched over a stack of notebooks, seemingly writing in five at once, a huge pair of headphones over her ears. As if sensing my gaze, she suddenly lifts her head, spearing me with wide eyes through huge-rimmed glasses. I spin around, dealing myself into Jo's game.

"So...we never get to see the men?" I try to sound nonchalant. I think we're playing an OCD version of snap, stacking cards by number and color.

"Well, only in the group therapy talks, under supervision," Jo shrugs. "There's occasionally an afternoon tea party mixer. We have to prove we're under control around the opposite sex before we can be discharged."

"Did someone say sex?!" Ruby jolts upright like a meerkat. How the hell did she hear that through her headphones?

"No Ruby, go back to your writing," Jo sighs.

"Word porn! My fingers are ejaculating fictional cum all over these pages like I'm fondling the ink into submission!" She licks the tip of her pen and returns it to the page, moaning as she . "Come for me, my sweet, naughty cursive. Yeah, you like that don't you?" I don't know whether to watch in fascination or ask for an orderly to bring a chastity belt. Jo continues, her tone bored and unamused.

"She's the daughter of a senator who loves writing stories of lesbian fae with vaginas for mouths."

"They have pussy lips for lips. It's fucking genius and hot!" Ruby shouts, followed by the tumbling of books. Oh god, she's coming closer. "Imagine if my tongue piercing was a clit," she takes the seat beside me and rolls her tongue in an impressive notion. "We could pleasure each other every time we made out. Mouth fucking just got a whole new meaning." Leaning far, far back, I speak for Jo's ears only.

"Are you sure she's in the right facility? Maybe a psych ward would be better suited."

"I'm not crazy?!" Ruby's light brown eyes widen as she climbs across the length of my body like a crazed koala. I shake my head, mumbling of course not. "I'm horny, and eccentric but mostly horny as hell. We could help each other out right? You could be my late-night love bug and I'll be your daylight dominatrix. It would be beautiful." Lifting a hand, Ruby shifts my black wig to peer at my neck. Then, she growls like a freaking bloodthirsty vampire and I'm sure she's about to bite me.

"Anyways," I shoot to my feet. "I've got...something to do, somewhere else. I'll see you guys..." I walk away before finishing that sentence, "hopefully never again." Sprinting inside, I crash into Carl. He grumbles, correcting his white jacket before shoving an envelope into my hand.

"Here, your care plan. Don't lose it. I'm not printing you another one." Retreating, I watch Carl take a side door which also requires a keycard to access. The clanging beyond would suggest it's a kitchen before the smell of freshly baked bread reaches me. My stomach growls on instinct. Retreating to a shadowed table near the back of the rec room, I pull out my care plan, finding a copy of the leisure classes and an enclosed map. *Idiots*.

I was right, the kitchen is next door between this rec room and a restaurant. Directly above, mixed in with the personal suites, are various spa and beauty rooms, hydration and aromatherapy chambers and such. The sauna and steam rooms seem to be beneath me in an inground pool grotto. At the other end of the building, the counseling and therapy rooms backing onto a parking lot, providing easy access for our male visitors.

That only leaves my care plan. I scan the document, only picking out what I need to know and my heart sinks. I have to survive four days here until my first group therapy session, and even then, there's no guarantee Myles will be in attendance.

"Attention ladies," Elizabeth walks into the room with a clipboard in hand. "There are still slots open for massages and pedicures. Do we have any takers?" Everyone ignores her in favor of finishing their jigsaw or heading out to the pool, so I tentatively raise my hand. "Oh Sasha, what a fantastic way to begin your stay with us. Come have some pampering before dinner."

You know what – maybe these next four days won't be so bad after all.

Chapter 30

AKA 'Sasha'

My foot taps against the chair leg impatiently. Unfolding my arms, I huff and fold them again. How long is this going to take to get started? I was forty-five minutes early, but in my defense, there was only so many kinks Helga, the butch masseuse, could press out of my back. I'm as limber as a gymnast and if I touch anything, I might break one of my perfectly manicured nails.

The therapy room begins to fill from behind, women taking the seats in a circle around me, leaving every other one free. Two seats over, Jo lowers herself down as Ruby bounds into the room like a rabbit on crack. The last to enter is the only one of us to not wear sweatpants, and it turns out – she's not one of us after all. A tall, full figured woman with a flashy lanyard strides by to open the rear doors as, fina-fucking-lly, a minivan pulls up outside. My foot stills.

What if he isn't in here? What if Myles isn't in any of the buses and I'm stuck in this rehab for the foreseeable future? The pampering is delightful, the food is phenomenal, but there's an emptiness within which no amount of pillow chocolates can fill. Clenching my hands into fists, my palms feel sticky.

Holy shit, am I nervous? Although there was no need to be, since the second man to exit the vehicle is a glorious giant of muscle and sandy blond hair. Myles' chest pushes against the white t-shirt, wearing the same as me, his eyes downcast and shoulders sagged in defeat. Butter-flies burst inside my stomach, flipping my organs over themselves as the truth punches me in the gut. I've missed him.

Taking the seat directly opposite me, Myles thankfully doesn't pay any attention beyond the floor by his feet. I jump up and round the refreshments table. Now I know he's here, I can put the wheels of my masterplan into motion. Untucking the Ziplock bag of cocaine from my waistband and using my body as a shield from onlookers, I tip the contents into the provided drinking jug, giving it a quick stir. I put Ace's money to really, really good use.

I'd brought enough crack in my handbag to taint the main water supply, but when Myles and a room of raging addicts is packaged so neatly for me, I'm not going to argue. All I needed was the right kind of distraction. Tugging my t-shirt back in place, I rejoin the group as the therapist locks the back door and pockets her keycard.

"Let's get started, shall we? It's lovely to see a full house today," she smiles at me. Taking her unoccupied seat, she opens her white jacket and reveals a huge bust concealed within a black dress. What a distraction for those struggling to look away, myself included. "For those who are new or have decided to grace us with their presence today, I'm Mila." Crossing her legs, Mila loosely shakes her heel and raises a brow cockily. Damn, I don't want to like her. I'm about to traumatize her into early retirement.

"How about we start with a roll call? Tell us your name and what brings you here today." Nodding a head of chocolate brown hair to her left, we're introduced to Julian, Adaline, Sam and then there's Ruby, having turned the chair backwards to grind her hips over the wood.

"Mmm, yeah – I'm Ruby, or Madam, depending on the situation. My father committed me here and I don't think there's a plan for any real rehabilitation. I just need...some fucking...friction," she bears down, dragging her crotch against the seat.

"Thanks Ruby," Mila drawls. Her tone would suggest she's no stranger to such antics. "Myles, you're up next." I sit a little straighter, my throat dry. He's yet to look up, to assess the room around him. I wonder if he'll even notice me within the wig and changed eye color. Inhaling deeply, Myles' shoulders lift and fall, his dejected voice barely audible.

"Pass."

I feel his resentment in the pit of my soul. The only reason he's here is due to a betrayal. Myles and Carter know as well as I do, he's not an addict. A liar perhaps, although I'm surprisingly giving him the benefit of the doubt. Seems we've both come far. Jo introduces herself next, announcing her soon-to-be ex-husband couldn't handle her affair with the pool boy. I half-listen to the rest, until it's finally my turn. My moment.

"Hey all, I'm Sasha," my voice rings out. Myles' head snaps upright. I watch the confusion pass through his features, the silence weighing heavily within my ears. "I've played many roles in my life, most of them revolving around using my body to get what I want. I'm no stranger to sexual blackmail or a stripper pole but," I wet my lips, "I recently got this billionaire boyfriend. Turns out he thinks there's more to me, and I'm here to prove I'm worth his devotion. Even if it turns out he's a dirty liar and I end up destroying him, it's about time I listened to my heart."

"Well, thank you for your honesty," Mila interrupts, hurrying the rest of the introductions along. Myles holds my stare, hardly blinking through his disbelief. Keeping my nerve, I will the erratic beat of my heart to slow. I've never put myself out there so bluntly, revealing my true cards so openly. Let's hope Myles is worth it, or I won't ever be doing so again.

"So, for today's session, I was thinking we could role play a scenario," Mila begins, causing Ruby to moan out loud.

"Fuck yes. Let's do nurse and patient. No, teacher and student. No! fireman and burn victim!"

"I'm not participating in any of the above," Adaline interjects, holding up a hand.

"It's okay, no one is," Mila reassures us all. "What I meant was, how about we try a simple conversation? Would anyone feel comfortable with a light touch on the arm, maybe a friendly hug to demonstrate not every interaction has to be a sexual one?"

"I'll do it," Myles shoots out of his seat, staring at me expectantly. Pushing down Sasha's nerves and bringing Amethyst to the surface, I stand. Two strides put me in front of Myles as he meets me in the middle, my hip popped and lips pursed.

"Hi," he mutters, possibly regretting his urge to have this conversation in front of an audience.

"Hello," I tilt a brow. "How are you finding your stay?"

"Miserable. I don't belong here," Myles' amber eyes flood with desolation. The spark is missing, his frown too easily accessible. I yearn to make him smile, hear his laugh, but I have business to take care of first.

"I know," I whisper, clearing my throat. "But perhaps you've pissed off the wrong person," I shrug. This gains a reaction.

"Perhaps I was just trying to be happy."

"Then maybe you shouldn't lie about burning envelopes and the crest which your father wears on his signet ring," I prod Myles' chest.

"Um, maybe a touch which isn't so hostile," Mila advises.

"It wasn't his crest. Similar yes, but not the same. Besides, don't be a hypocrite," Myles scoffs. "I deserve better than that."

"How the hell am I a hypocrite?" I slam my hand on his chest this time. Now that's hostility.

"You're hiding so many secrets, I doubt you know what's real anymore." Myles growls, his brows tightly pinched. "Tell me you would have done anything different if it were your family? You lie for a living. I did it once and have been at war with myself ever since." We fall into silence, a battle of wills ensuing as Ruby leans over to Sam.

"I think they know each other," she whispers loud enough for the whole room to hear. Flaring my nostrils, Myles is first to bow out and look sympathetic.

"I was going to tell you when I had more information." Reaching up, he brushes against the t-shirt's neckline and I'm a goner. So simple, yet desire pools in my core. The sight of him, the smell, the feel. Sasha returns with a vengeance and she's a needy bitch. Leaning into his touch, I close my eyes. How can he feel this good? His touch ignites a spark, trailing his fingers along my jaw, cheek, to my hair line with extra care not to dislodge the wig. Even now, still protecting me and the secrets he knows I hold.

"I think this is a good time for a break," Mila jumps up and walks between the two of us. I stagger backwards, immediately replacing the walls Myles had brought down too easily. It turns out our little display has everyone in the room gasping. *Perfect.* Whilst Mila pours cups and hands them out, I slip through the crowd to lean up by Myles' ear.

"Don't drink the water." Slinking away, I return to my chair to watch the carnage unfold. Myles watches me closely, a strange emotion tainting his features. What is that? I tilt my head at him, curious about the stubborn rigidness of his back. How his hands ball into fists and mouth sets in a firm line.

"No more secrets," Myles mouths and walks straight over to the refreshments table. Mila passes him a styrofoam cup and as he catches my eye, I shake my head. He drinks the entire cup in one gulp, crunching and tossing it in the trash can. Now?! He picks now to be a stubborn ass?! Then Mila helps herself and I lean my forehead on my palm. Sure, picking her pocket will be much simpler, but I didn't bank on dragging Myles out of here whilst hanging out of his ass. My plan rests on a quick, unnoticed escape and then a vigorous run.

Sparing him a glance, he's crunching another cup and accepting a third. Oh holy hell, it's over. Well, if you can't beat them – join them. Striding to his side, I take the jug and down the last quarter of the water directly from the spout. Accepting another few days of being spoiled while hatching a new scheme, I make my way back to the seat and lower myself slowly. As I'm the only one aware of the drugs taking root in everyone's systems, it seems to hit me first. Or maybe it's the anticipation which allows my blood stream to accept it quicker.

Mila is talking, her words lost to the ringing in my ears. Her hand moves back and forth, swimming through the air like a bejeweled fish. That sure is a nice wedding ring, I wonder how much it's worth. Indicating towards Myles, her fingers shift my way, bringing everyone's attention this way. All except Ruby's – her hand is dipping beneath her waistband, a rambling of what might be Spanish escaping her mouth. How does she talk so fast?

Wiping my nose on the back of my hand, it tingles. Continually dripping without sign of stopping. Is it hot in here, or is it just me? I tug on the neckline of my t-shirt, puffing out my cheeks. Why is everyone looking at me still? Maybe my face is as red as it feels. I struggle to swallow, panting in small heaves.

"Look at something else!" I stand and throw my chair towards the refreshments table. Heads whip around, cooling me with the absence of their stare. But it's then I realize – it wasn't the heat of everyone looking at me, just Myles. His stare remains. Quizzical, knowing. My skin grows too tight, too heated. Needing to rid myself of the warmth, I start to strip. Sweatpants, t-shirt, and as my hands fly to my bra, Myles is suddenly there. Barreling through me before I noticed he moved. Slamming my back against the wall, his chest crushes me. His cologne infects me. I inhale him as if he's the sweetest nectar of life, burying my face in his neck.

"God, how do you always smell this good?"

"Why is the room spinning?" he asks back, his body pressing against me harder. His crotch growing stiffer. Pressing his dick against my lower stomach, I shove my hand between us to close my grip around him. We both groan.

"No, no! Stop that!" Mila is shouting. I force my face out of Myles' neck to tell her to get fucked, but it's not us she's referring to. I gape as I find Ruby's face between Jo's legs amongst the various other pairings. Adaline is entertaining two men at once, a mess of tongues and groping.

Sam rounds the back of Mila, his hands shaking as he only just refrains from grabbing her ass. His limit snaps, clutching her, caressing her, thrusting her back against his strained dick. Gray sweatpants are a terrible choice for a sex clinic. Mila's protests are swallowed on a moan, her legs giving out. Sam goes with her, falling into a puddle of lust on the floor. I see my chance.

"Myles, I need...something," I breathe as he kisses my neck. Fuck, his lips are tantalizing against my skin.

"I'll give you everything. The world is yours." Bracing my hands on his chest, I almost cave. My strength waivers, as does my grip on reality.

"Soon. Let me just-" I shimmy sideways. Myles follows, his hands on my waist. His lips on my cheek, my jaw, my collar bone. He makes holding onto my plan impossible. When his mouth takes mine hostage, I can't resist.

Tongues collide, passions crash. Days of pent-up frustration, of this growing need slam into us both and my world spins. I tumble downwards, only saved from a concussion by Myles' strong arms banded around my upper back. He slows my descent, places me down with too much care. Three words pop into my mind as quickly as I cast them aside, rejecting the notion. Deepening the connection between our lips and tongue, a moan is torn from the man pressing onto the length of me.

"I can't have you like this," he whimpers, touching a hand to my wig, purposely avoiding eye contact. "I need the real you." Twisting my head, I swallow dryly against the sudden rise of emotion which clogs my throat. Myles is one of the only people on this earth who can claim to have seen the 'real' me, never mind ask for it. He sought me out in the dark, probed behind my exterior, accepted my flaws. Catching sight of Mila's white jacket discarded nearby, I remember what it is I want.

"Not here, let's go somewhere private," I vaguely hold onto my train of thought. I need to get Myles out, I need to take him far away.

Wherever that may be, he stays with me from now on. Dragging myself out of the cage he's created with his body, I stretch. My fingers toy with the hem of the jacket before working it an inch closer. Diving my hand into the pocket, I grab the keycard and conceal it between Myles and I as the door bursts open.

"What the fuck is going on in here?!" Carl bellows. More men appear at his back.

"Myles, we need to run. Don't let go of my hand," I hiss. Instantly met with his blazing amber gaze, I see the adrenaline pulsing behind his dilated irises. Whipping me upright, held by his arm around my waist, Myles' legs fly with the power of a tank to the back door. I grip the keycard tight enough to cut into my palm, slamming it against the pad with a beep. A green light gives us access to outside. To sweet freedom. The roar of nurse Carl right behind, does not.

"Hey, what are you doing?" the minivan driver calls from where he's leaning against the door, smoking a cigarette.

Dodging aside, Myles runs like a man possessed. Like an addict fueled by the rush of pure cocaine saturating his system. He'll crash soon enough so I struggle to be released and run at his side, arms pumping, heart racing. A self-created wind blasts against the barrier of my underwear, a string of laughter pulled from my lips. This is what it means to be alive, and the wide smile on Myles' face shows he's ready for it. Ready to embrace it, and everything that comes with loving me.

Reaching the edge of the car park, a long stretch of road spans before us, one lone limo speeding this way. It turns sharply, narrowly avoiding a ditch as the driver's window peels down.

"Get in!" Sebby shouts, Charley leaning forward for her brown hair to catch the sunlight streaming through. Elation, greater than any high the drugs could provide, soars from my head to my feet, fueling the long leaps of my running like a graceful ostrich. I'm practically floating, only touching the ground when absolutely necessary, all the while my hand in Myles'. As promised.

Ignoring the shouts from behind, Myles skids to a stop to yank the rear door open and shoves me inside, his body flying in a moment later. We're skidding away before the door is fully closed, hysterical laughter filling the cab. I laugh until I cry, toppling onto the carpeted floor with Myles joining me a second later. Sobs rack my body, tears spilling from my eyes. Hastily ridding myself of the contact lenses, I drag the wig free.

"Hey, it's okay. We're free," Myles soothes me, cupping my face. A faint whirring sounds as the divider between us and the front seats rises.

"What's happening here?" I whisper regardless, scared of my own voice. "Between us? I don't...like being vulnerable, and that's all you make me feel." Shivering, Myles twists me, pressing my body against his. Amber eyes consume my soul, devour my thoughts.

"I've felt that way since the moment I watched you rob my jewelry store. Then I got to know you, your spontaneous nature, your quick wit, and feisty attitude. I suddenly saw my life through your eyes, and I didn't like what I saw." Briefly pressing his lips on mine, they become tainted with the salty moisture from my tears. "You expose the weaker parts of me," he kisses me again, soft and slow. "And it's fucking terrifying, but I'm not backing down."

Draping one leg over Myles' hip, I press myself against his hard length. Still solid and eager. My eyes reveal the nature of my intention, their hooded lust difficult to contain. The drugs causing my skin to tingle have nothing to do with how I brush Myles' blond hair back from the hard planes of his face. That's all me. Lingering by his ear, I long to touch him for eternity. Contained in this bubble where the rest of the world doesn't exist, where mourning and pain can't touch us.

Taking my hand in his, Myles cups his own cheek, shifting my thumb to stroke his stubble.

"Do you know what fuels a sex addict?" he breathes. I hang on his every word, needing the husky deep tone to fuel my next heartbeat. "The speed. The chase. The exhilaration."

"Is that so?" I respond vaguely. Myles nods against my touch.

"That's how the counselors here describe it, and I'm inclined to agree." Rolling onto his back, he takes me with him. My chest leans into his, my neck straining to hold my head high enough to maintain his gaze.

"After a while, sex becomes boring. It's all in the hype, the new, the daring. An impulse to do unspeakable, implausible things in the name of feeling a rush of excitement. Just like the first time, over and over again." Licking my lips, Myles tracks the motion with his thumb. "Being with you – everything is like the first time. And taking you right here and now, well that certainly feels exhilarating, doesn't it?" It feels like many things and I'm at a loss of how to put my scrambled brain into one, coherent thought. Only one answer seems acceptable, and it causes Myles to beam a pant-melting smile I will never tire of seeing.

"Then stop talking and do it."

Chapter 31

No more words are exchanged. Tugging at my sweatpants, Amethyst shifts herself downward. I attempt to stop her, too impatient to waste time, but my arms don't respond. Limbs weighed down, a rush of dizziness catches me off guard. I don't know what was in that water, but I'm powerless to stop Ami and as her lips glide over the head of my cock, I no longer care to. She takes me, wholly and deeply. I remain frozen, forced to encourage her with the groans escaping me and filling the limo. We hit a bump, forcing her to take me deeper into her throat.

Holy fuck.

Amethyst refuses to rush, dragging her mouth up my shaft with excruciating slowness. From halfway up, she sucks hard, causing spots to dance over my vision. Then she releases me with a pop and does it again. Her personal hobby seems to be teasing me. Finding use of my arms, I bury my fingers into her hair, the violet strands cascading over my knuckles. I never want to see her change persona again. This is my Ami and I'll be damned if she doesn't know this is the only way she needs to be.

I lose track of time, lost to the sensations she draws from my dick. The limo speeds onwards, my feet against the rear seats holding us both in place. Taking me completely, Amethyst moans deep within her throat, the reverberations driving me closer to blowing my load. Not a chance. Tightening my grip on her hair, I drag her off me, needing a moment to compose myself. I don't get that chance, as Ami's tight cunt closes around my shaft, slamming down to the hilt.

Reaching for her, my hands find her back as my clouded vision clears. Sitting in reverse cowgirl, Ami braces her hands on my thighs, working her body to give me a private show. Her skin is flawless, devoid of tattoos unlike her front. Her waist dips above the most stunning, curvaceous ass I will never tire of. Just watching her makes me throb, the tip of my cock weeping inside of her before she's really begun to move.

Unhooking her bra, I flatten my hands against her back before dragging my nails south. She arches for me. So responsive, so fucking perfect. She works me effortlessly, her heat driving me into a frenzy. I haven't been able to stop thinking about her, stop replaying our library session over and over since I woke up in rehab. Amethyst is my obsession, my personal brand of craving. If I'm an addict, she's my drug of choice. Her wetness speaks to me, sheathing my cock entirely.

Caressing her ass, my fingers travel to her pussy. Either I'm still under some unknown influence, or she has the softest lips possible. I reach around, finding her clit and circling it through her own wetness. With the other hand, my thumb dips through her crack to locate her puckered hole, teasing the outside before pressing inside. She doesn't tense, but rather pushes back against me until I'm fully seated inside. Splaying the rest of my fingers across her cheeks, I use Amethyst's ass like a grip, encouraging her bouncing. I feel myself in her other channel, withdrawing and entering along the length of my thumb, as my hands pleasure her into a similar state of desire.

"Fuck, Amethyst. You're incredible. I lo-" Ami whips back, stuffing her discarded panties into my mouth before I can finish that sentence, and proceeds to fuck me harder. Her skin slaps against my hips, challenging the volume of our combined moans. I notice her back tense before she falls apart, clenching my dick so tight, I'm worrying about blood circulation. Amethyst screams my name, splitting a crevice through my heart which won't be knitted back together. She's mine. At this moment, for the foreseeable future, Amethyst belongs to me and I won't believe anything she says otherwise.

Reaching for her chest, I tug Ami back. Her back to my chest, I spread her thighs wide, jerking upwards from beneath. Her tits fill my hands, bouncing keenly against my thrusts. I seek out her nipples, rubbing and twisting. Spitting the panties aside, my mouth finds her neck, biting and sucking. She will be marked, utterly fucked and unable to replace me.

Needing to be deeper, buried further in her cunt, I push us upright onto the nearest seat. At this angle, Amethyst is speared in my lap, aided by my hands on her shoulders. Brandishing myself inside her, I pummel her g-spot, my balls beginning to tighten as my hands close around her neck. She forces them tighter. Dropping her fingers to her clit, I feel the desperation of her rubbing to push herself over the edge and manage to hold off just long enough. Amethyst bucks, cries and surrenders to me.

"That's it, Fiery," I praise, my dick exploding like a rocket. Swelling, pulsating, a euphoric groan I can't contain roars in my ears. Ami falls against me, squirming and panting. We lie together in complete bliss, coming down from multiple highs. My dick remains hard, nestled within as if he never wants to leave. Regardless, I ease Ami forward to tug off my t-shirt and offer to clean her up. She takes the shirt, moving over to the opposite bench. I've only just tucked myself away when the divider opens a few inches and Charley tosses a drawstring bag into the back.

"Rule one of saving Amethyst's ass, always bring clothes," Charley adds, leaving the divider slightly open.

"How did you even find us?" Ami asks her friend, although it's Sebby who answers.

"Serenity Heights took two-hundred-thousand-dollars from my account, and Charley felt the need to warn me after Carter hurt you, you'd probably do something stupid."

"He did what?!" I still so suddenly, some leftover cum leaks into my sweats. Amethyst waves away my concern, pulling on a pale-yellow mini dress which doesn't require a bra.

"Don't worry yourself with finer details. It's all taken care of," she taps her forehead. I'm not so easily convinced.

"You can hash it out with him when we get back to the manor," Sebby drawls. He's heard me and Carter argue more times than we've been amicable, but this won't be like those other times. This time, words won't even be exchanged, but I have more pressing issues to deal with first.

"We're not going back," I announce. Sebby's grey eyes swing to me via the rearview mirror, Charley's face the picture of concern and Ami, well Ami remains indifferent. "Not yet at least. There are some questions which need answering."

I'm fairly certain Amethyst didn't realize she called me her boyfriend in the group therapy session, but I heard it loud and clear. More than that, I just felt the strength of our connection, and there's no use holding back now. I need to do right by her.

"Seb, take us to my father's house."

Chapter 32

Sebby pulls up a street over from my childhood mansion. He's not the best of drivers and as soon as the roads became narrow, he's struggled to keep the limo straight. Yet, he still came to save Ami and I. Exiting the vehicle in just my sweatpants and canvas shoes, I hold out a hand for my woman. My fiery sunrise amongst a perpetual dawn, finally casting light in my life. Approaching Sebby and Charley, I thank them both as Sebby's pocket vibrates.

"That'll be Carter asking why you've been reported missing. I better get Charley back and explain." Pulling him in for a hug, Sebby lingers against my body.

"Be safe. I'll have my father's car bring us home soon." *Home*. The manor has never felt like such, but once Carter and I have settled our differences, I believe it will now. Ami falls into my side, keeping pace along an outer stone wall. Electric barbed wire coils over the top to keep intruders out.

"Can we settle something, while there's a moment of peace," Ami states without room for being denied. "Regardless of whatever this means-" she holds up our joined hands, "I want you to continue sleeping with Sebby."

"Seriously?" I frown. There's no denying the warmth which spreads through my chest at her words. Sebby means more to me than anyone knows, especially him. I've never been able to provide stability or comfort, so I kept him at arm's length to save his feelings. However, when those lonely nights come where I just can't deny either of us anymore, it's pure magic.

"If it makes you feel better about it, I'm more than happy to participate, but for the love of fuck, tell the poor guy you love him." I stop still, tugging her a step back to do the same.

"Why would you suggest that?" I ask tentatively. Again, not denying it, but to hear those words so raw and spoken allowed, I dare to think thoughts I've previously pushed away.

"Look, I've been patient, but you guys are the most stubborn men I know. Sebby is gay. Completely, irrevocably, beautifully gay and he only has eyes for you. Unless you've already forgotten, I've seen how you are together. Put him out of his misery and tell him he's the only man you want. It just so happens, there's also a wo-man currently holding his attention." I snort at the insinuation Amethyst is a fleeting distraction in my life. Rolling her stunning, crystal blue eyes, I smile. She's known of mine and Sebby's relationship all along, and is still standing here holding my hand.

"How are you so amazing?"

"Practice," Ami shrugs. I pull her into my arms, drowning in her kiss. Now she's not pushing me away, I can't stop. I refuse to even try. I want her branded on my lips and snuggly pressed against my chest at all times. Hang on, if she's aware Sebby is gay, then that means...

"So, you and Sebby never-"

"Nah-uh."

"And when you screamed his name at the club, you were just-"

"Uh huh." Ami's smile is purely evil. She's been teasing me all along.

"Such a little minx." Smacking her ass, I pull her along before I give into the hardening of my cock again. I'd take her right now against the wall if we didn't have other reasons for nearing the electronic gate up ahead.

Bracing myself, I round the telecom system and jam my finger against the button. Barely a minute passes, my face staring into the camera, before the gate slides open and permits our entry. The flutters of happiness Amethyst ignites within, dissolves and fizzles out as the cold shadow of the mansion chills my skin. When I think about the amount of people who'd swap places with me in a heartbeat, only to realize oppression is writhe wherever you go. Those with money, rule all. Those with power, abuse it.

The front door is swung open by Leonard, a butler older than the antique handles, his arm out-stretched for our jackets before noticing we have none. My father is two steps behind, tsking at the sight of my bare chest. His scowl hitches even further at Ami and my hackles rise.

"We need to talk," I state coldly. Lowering his hazel gaze to our interlocked fingers, my father nods.

"It seems we do. I just got off the phone with Carter. I had a feeling I'd be seeing you today." Falling into stride, I keep my eyes fixed on the back of his head. I see this lobby enough in my nightmares to relive it in real life. From the hanging art installation above a grand staircase to the antique grandfather clock which chimes hourly, and my stepmother's minor feminine touches presented in potted plants and a Persian rug. She desperately wanted to redecorate, but refuses to admit she's just as much of a shiny fixture as the ornate molding along the walls, ceilings and doorways. Under my father's roof and rule, we don't get to have preferences.

I shift uncomfortably, sensing the leash tightening around my throat. The last time I was here, I was being dragged out by cops and swiftly committed to rehab. Between the trials and a prolonged depressive low, I realized how expendable I was. How easily silenced and cast aside I could be. It's taken too long to pull myself back from the verge of worthlessness, to become the man I'm comfortable seeing in the mirror. I don't need any more memories to fuel a setback.

Walking directly to his office, a chamber consisting of two floors, bay windows in a semi-circle peering over the acres of land beyond, and expensive artwork, my father tries to close the door in Ami's face.

"The kitchen is down the hall. Try not to break anything."

"Not a chance," I force my foot against the door, dragging Ami inside. "Amethyst is my girlfriend, and you will treat her with respect as such." Her grip on me tightens, wide eyes peering up at my set jaw.

"Myles, you don't have girlfriends. You have brief obsessions, and this too will pass. I will not have her privy to our conversation." Entering into his stare-off, I pull Ami closer against my body, wrapping a protective arm around her back.

"The conversation we need to have involves her, or has Carter not informed you we were shot at in New Orleans?"

"What were you doing in New Orleans?" his graying brows rise. I press my lips together, refusing to give another inch until he backs down. My father sighs, sitting before a striking stone fireplace without pushing the issue further. The wood logs lay untouched, only for show. Dragging nearby armchairs away, I position them so Ami and I can see his face. There's no getting away from the questions I'm about to ask. Although, opening my mouth, it's not me who asks them.

"Where did you get your signet ring?" Amethyst jerks her chin towards my father's crossed hands. He immediately retreats them from sight, straightening his back.

"I know who you are," he replies, eyes narrowing. The air shifts, discomfort prickling my skin. "Leave my son out of your suicide mission."

"Trust me, I tried. He's like a leech," Ami twists her lips until I give her a narrowed look. Raising one brow, she shrugs. "A very attractive leech."

Coming to an impasse where no one wants to volunteer information first, I push to my feet, dragging a hand through my hair. If I know one way to soften my father's cruel exterior, it's to prepare him a cigar. I've seen my stepmother do it a hundred times, then witnessed Carter adopt the same trick on the many meetings they've had at the manor. Ones I haven't been invited to, as they talk business, pleasure, and discuss my future as if I'm still a reckless teen.

I gave up long ago caring for my father's opinions. Around the same time I gave into the media's portrayal of me, deciding I would be the deviant they created. I frequented clubs, bars, and parties. Treated sex like a remedy, a way to rid myself of my thoughts. But after every single time, the weight of guilt doubled and soon enough, I caved. Withdrawing from society completely. Only interested in the Elites now and then. Only vaguely aware I was still living at all.

Still, my father looks at me with such disappointment, I want to claw out of my own skin to get rid of the disdain. It wouldn't have made a difference. When all else is said and done, I'm not Carter. I'm not the perfect son.

Clipping the end of the cigar, I light it, puffing a few times for the cherry to blossom fully. Then I abandon the residue left on his desk and present it to him.

"Amethyst and I are trying to find who killed her mother. We followed a lead and discovered an envelope with a shield and dragon wax seal. I know it wasn't yours, since you have a Pegasus, but the pattern was too much of a coincidence to ignore." Dropping back into the armchair, I lean forward, elbows braced on my knees.

"Did you read what was inside?"

"No, I burned it. I feared what the implication of finding it would mean, given our crest is so similar. I know how important reputation is to you," I attempt to sound sincere. To carefully pick my words in a way my father would prefer.

"I'm not a part of this," he grunts, adjusting his tie. Suddenly, I feel icy trepidation entering my system. Somehow, I think there's more to this than just a wax seal.

"But you know who is," I pressed. The man opposite doesn't respond. Puffing on his cigar, I glance over the wrinkles lining his mouth. The silver in his hair he's given up dyeing. Even his suit doesn't seem as sharp as it once was, and the amount of time we've lost hits me. Full of disappointment or not, he's my father. The only one I have.

"Dad," I breathe, bringing his stoic gaze back to me, "Amethyst isn't a fleeting fixation. She's it for me." Perhaps this conversation would have been better in private, but it's nothing I haven't already shown her with my actions. Ami is free to trample all over my heart, run for the hills and never look back. It won't change how I feel. How I finally understand what love is and can be. Whether she's in my life for weeks or years, I'll hold onto this feeling for eternity. "And someone hurt her. You of all people know the lengths you went to for mom."

My father's throat bobs. His lips purse tighter around the cigar. He doted on my mother as much as I did as a boy. She was beautiful, smart, always laughing. The life of every party, until the light dimmed in her eyes. Watching her crumble was worse than accepting her death, I'd already lost her by then.

"Myles, trust me," my father's teeth are gritted. "Leave this alone. You're not the only one who messed up in high school." My breathing swallows. Glancing back to Amethyst, she nods reassuringly. She knows we're not backing down from the path we've started walking together. No matter the outcome, Ami will see I'm here for her when it matters. I'm all she needs.

"I'm perusing this, Dad, with or without your help." Finally, after an age of staring into the bleak fireplace, he passes me the cigar. "Whose ring sealed the envelope, and why did you look so worried when you thought I'd read it?" Hazel eyes hold mine with such emotion, I barely recognize them as my own kin. The cool, collected man I've grown estranged from, now looking at me with such emotion. Such...fear.

"Not here. Meet me in the pool house shortly." Rising from his chair, my father pauses by an aged, oak cabinet to lift the lid. Lifting a black bundle, he drops it in my lap as he passes and makes his way to the door.

Unfurling the material, a college sweatshirt emblem beams back. Yellow and brown quadrants create the shape of a shield in the center. Flourishes border the outside, opening out to underline the name stitched in arching ochre. Hamilton University. The symbol on his signet ring is derived from this school logo. I twist back to ask my father if this has something to do with his secrets, but he's already gone.

Gripping the sweatshirt, I lead Amethyst to the rear of the mansion and down stone steps leading beneath an overhanging balcony. She's yet to say anything, and her silence is more ambiguous than a balm. I wish I knew what she was thinking, although her warm palm against mine is enough reassurance she's not about to take her answers and run. Night has fallen during our time in the office, a sudden chill being brought in with the start of winter. I pause long enough to tug the sweatshirt over Ami's head, uncaring of the goosebumps lining my own chest and arms.

The pool house is a large building at the end of a path winding east of the property. Under the same roof, a gym, sauna and indoor squash courts provide year-round access, whereas the outdoor amenities are only open May through October. The door is left unlocked until the house staff perform their final checks, locking up before turning in. Guiding Ami inside, the chlorine hits us immediately, the air a thick balm against my chilled skin. I locate the light switch to the main hall, illuminating the crystal-clear pool in the center of the room.

"Woah, woah, hold up," Ami stops, holding her hands up. I raise a brow in confusion. "This is a full-blown competition pool."

"Um, yeah?" I frown.

"With diving boards and bleachers and everything," Ami walks around a corner, temporarily disappearing from view. "And full-size locker rooms!" I chuckle under my breath.

"That's the first thing you're going to say?" I follow. I find her stretching her arms wide, trying to judge the size of the shower space. "What about...wow, your dad is a cold bastard. Or, huh, no wonder you needed a distraction after your mom killed herself." Dropping her arms, Ami gives me a rare look, devoid of all sass and attitude.

"Pointing out the obvious seemed like a waste of time. I make snap observations, not judgements." Drawing my bottom lip into my mouth, I turn away, taking a moment to myself. How the fuck did I happen to stumble upon someone so perfect? I hate to think about that first day - had we driven away just a moment earlier, how different my life would be now. I would never have known what it's like to be challenged, recognized and understood all at the same time. Swallowing hard, I seek to fill the silence.

"My parents hosted swimming events and were renowned for their garden parties. Given we are one of the founding families, many of the summer competitions from their high school were held here, as well as auctions and all kinds of functions back when I was a child."

"Not now?" Ami's hand settles on my back, softly guiding me to a wooden bench.

"If they do, I'm not invited. There would be concerns the disgraced sex-addicted son would try to rape all of the guests," I try to laugh off, but it's really not funny. It's tragic. "My mom lived for the organizing. She was already three parties ahead before we'd finished the current one." Once sat, Ami kicks my ankles wider before climbing over my lap. Her blue eyes consume me entirely, not offering any apologies or fake words. I love her all the more for that. She's simply here.

"How long do you think we'll have to wait?" her fingers toy with the ends of my hair. Seated over my thighs, the heat seeping from her pussy blooms directly over my dick. My hands immediately sink beneath her dress, kneading the soft curves of her ass.

"Depends on what you had in mind," I half groaned at the wicked smile hitching up her mouth.

"A distraction," she raises one shoulder. I now regret covering her chest with the baggy sweatshirt, but there's no time to worry about it as Amethyst lunges at me. My back hits the wood, her mouth hot and demanding on mine. Dragging her nails up my chest, her hand wraps around my throat. I smile against her lips. Our tongues collide, desperate to have me tainting her sweet taste. My heart soars.

The tighter Ami's grip grows on my neck, the harder I fist her ass until I can't bear it anymore. Grinding her against my erection, I spank her sharply. The sound ricochets through the connecting hallway, echoing across the pool. My father could be here any moment, and that only heightens my need. Let him see what Ami does to me. How enamored I am.

"Fuck, Firey," I moan, shifting my face. Kissing along her cheek and jaw, I bury my mouth into the base of her neck. The curves of her body respond, rolling along the length of me as if no clothes are barring our senses. I can't have her close enough. Will never be far enough inside of her, but I'm sure as hell going to try.

"Hey Myles, who's S.M?" Ami vaguely asks beside my ear. Feeling her still, I force the haze of my lust aside to ease back from her neck.

"Hmmm?" Shifting her hand upwards, she gently twists my head to the initials carved into the side of the lockers. I spy them upside down at first, but upon remembering what awaits them, I jolt upright.

"Oh shit, I forgot about those. It's been a while," I stammer. Keeping her nestled in my lap, I fight against my head and my dick for control. "My father and his buddies weren't always the emotionless assholes they are now. During their college days, they were as tight as their sons are now." Wide blue eyes swing back to my face.

"You mean…" Extracting herself from the tangle of my limbs, the cold sets back in from Ami's absence like a bucket of ice. I hastily follow, repositioning my shaft into my waistband. The collection of etchings haven't aged with the rest of the lockers, the once blue sheen now a peeling green. Beside each set of initials, awful depictions of stick animals have been scratched into the metal. The Pegasus we know of beside the C.H for my father, a horse, what I imagine is supposed to be a gryphon and centaur, and finally the dragon. Its spiked tail curves around S.M. Well, shit.

Ami closes the rest of the distance to brush her fingers over each symbol. These men, these powerful moguls who are somehow connected to her past.

"P.L is for Lloyd, as in Sebby's dad?" she asks. I nod.

"Not that I'd bring up the conversation. His father abused him so often, Sebby would stay here when school was out. He'd sneak me out during the nights to hold him through his nightmares." I clear my throat, swiftly changing the subject. "G.G is Owen's, although he's never met him. Owen's mom was the maid at his father's mansion, it was a big scandal. They put money in a trust fund for when Owen came of age, but she was cast aside. Provided the basics and nothing more, and she didn't have the lawyers to fight it."

"That's awful." Ami breathes. Perhaps it's refreshing to know we weren't all raised with platinum spoons in our mouths or why my connection to Sebby is so special. Moving her fingers to the centaur, Ami continues her exploration. "What about S.C?"

"Silas Carter," I fill in. I know Ami's follow-up question before she whirls her disbelief on me. "Yeah, Carter is his last name and no, I won't tell you his first. It's a sore subject."

"All the more reason for you to give it to me! I could goad him to no end!" Ami tries to plead with her big, beautiful eyes. I smirk and shake my head.

"I'll give you the world, but this is one aspect you'll have to let go. I'm sworn to secrecy." Pretending to lock my lips, she pouts hers. The urge to swoop her into my arms and kiss it away raises, but I refrain.

"You don't owe him the loyalty you give, you know. He committed you back to rehab, cut you out of your own life."

"I know it's difficult to understand, but all Carter does is for my benefit. Believe me, he thinks he's doing the right thing. We'll just have to show him you are what's right for me." This time I pull her into my arms, dragging her back to my front, my chin resting on her shoulder. We both stare at the last remaining set of initials, a dozen unanswered questions floating around in the air. "I don't know who S.M is," I twist my lips.

"Myles?" my father's voice calls from the pool room. Kissing Amethyst on the head, I mutter into her ear that I won't be leaving until I have that information she needs, when a bellow spills through the hallway. I jerk upright. The sound comes again, a continuous gurgled shout by the rasped voice I know too well. My feet are moving, arms pumping as I skid into the pool room just as my father's body hits the water. Red blossoms from this chest, tainting the water around the two arrows speared into his chest. I hesitate, rendered still by shock as a flash of purple hits the back of my head on the way passed.

"Myles! Save him!" Ami shouts, her voice filling the domed ceiling. She doesn't falter, running out of the open door after the assailant and tearing my heart out to take with her. Diving into the pool, I numbly drag my father's body to the edge, heaving him onto the tiled side. The sweatpants try to drag me down, my arms shaking with the weight of dread as I pull myself free of the crimson water.

I already know before my wet fingers slide against his neck there's no pulse, but I uselessly wipe my hands on my pants to try again anyway. The arrow heads are so far in his sternum, all that protrudes are the carbon shafts with circular detailing. The same ones which killed Oliver Reynell. I should scream, holler, cry, do *something*. But as I stare upon the face I've come to resent, nothing comes. The state of shock envelopes me, distant memories fleeting by, unspoken sentiments causing my jaw to ache. Hollowness burns within my chest, my hands laying uselessly by my side.

Eventually, I look around for something. Anything which might help, despite knowing it's pointless. It's too late. Further along the tiled floor, a note lies in the place my father fell. I scramble closer, peering at the words without disturbing the scene.

I warned you.

Chapter 33

Two days.

Two days since the archer asshole got away. I chased her all the way to the wall, where she vaulted herself over the top and caught her black bodysuit on the barbed wire. The police are yet to make a match to the patch left behind.

Two days since Carter and Owen dragged their best friend from the floor beside the swimming pool, long after the body of his father had been removed. Sebby waited in the limo, cradling Myles' head when he numbly toppled into his lap. It took all three of them to convince him to get out at the other end, their hands all over Myles' back as they climbed the stairs to his room.

Two days since I've seen him. I only know this due to the amount of trays stacking up, filled with barely picked at food Charley insists on bringing, and by the rise and fall of daylight beyond the balcony to the BDSM room. The one I've claimed for myself, where I await the inevitable. Storm Carter is due any minute, tearing through the door to rip me from the life I've started to become comfortable in. It's my own stupid fault - I know better than to get attached. And now, thanks to my lack of judgment, I've made Myles an orphan too.

Right on time, the door swings open. I'm physically prepared, my limbs far beyond restless. Too used to packing up and moving on without warning. But it's different now. There's not enough time in the world which would prepare me to walk away from Myles. From Sebby, or the small alcove of happiness we've carved into an unforgiving world. What lies ahead is anyone's guess, but there won't be light. No laughter, no relief in conning the rich. Through the guilt eating me alive, it became all too apparent the only person I've ever truly conned is myself. Conned out of a life, out of love.

A heavy weight drops onto the bed. A deep sigh reverberates throughout the spacious room.

"Go to him." The voice startles me, because it's the last one I'd expected. Owen leans his elbows on his knees, the arch of his back against the window bearing an untold amount of weight. I slowly rise to a sitting position.

"He-" my voice croaks, raw and unused. "He won't want me around. I...caused the death of his father." And in that one statement, the truth of my choices threatens to swallow me whole. It's selfish to stay, to remind Myles of what I caused everytime he looks at me. But to leave of my own accord...that seems unfathomable in itself. Owen spares me a side glance, his blue eyes, which rival my own, peering out from beneath the sweep of his chestnut hair.

"Then why is he waiting for you? Why does he call for you each time glimpses of sleep find him in the dark. He's suffering, and you lazing about in here is only making it worse."

"Lazing about?" My brows clash together, nostrils flaring. "Does this look like I've been *lazing about*?!" I throw the covers aside to switch on a bedside lamp, revealing the tear-stricken marks caked down my face. The sunken proof to my blue eyes that I am also suffering. It may be Myles' father who died, but these past few days are the first I've ever taken to stop. To grieve, cry, burn and *feel*.

Owen doesn't react. Instead, he casts a glance to the windows where the sun is setting on another day in a fantastic wash of oranges and pinks.

"A few tears aren't enough," he shakes his head slowly. Rage bubbles within me, the urge to slap him up the side of his shaggy hair is fierce. But I clench my fist, clinging to the emotion, if only to suppress the others churning inside. "Anyone can cry. You need to do something no other woman has. Prove to Myles you're here for more than the money, the fame, or whatever your angle is. Fight for him, mourn *with* him."

I shudder. Owen knows. He understands I haven't been solely hiding from Myles, but distancing myself from a world which has hurt me too. Robbed me of the chance to say goodbye to my mother. To repair the lasting damage, to let my soul heal. Yet Owen has come to plead on his friend's behalf. Myles' pain is new, the surface barely scratched - and I'm the most experienced to aid his recovery.

"I didn't think you cared whether I stayed," I mutter, not bringing myself to spring out of the bed just yet. Another minute, another way to stall.

"I don't," Owen shrugs, bringing his gaze back my way. "But I care about Myles - enough that I can't stand staying in this house to see how Carter treats him. To witness how constricted he has allowed himself to become. He's a sliver of the man he could be, and only when you threw yourself in to our limo did he have something worth fighting for. I've seen glimpses, but as usual, life gets in the way. It's time to prove if you're up to the challenge." I snort.

"The challenge of boosting Myles' self esteem or knocking Carter off his pedestal?" I swear the hint of a smirk hitches in the shadowed corner of Owen's mouth.

"Both. You've already done wonders with Sebby." My own smile grows. Nudging forward, I bump Owen's shoulder, settling into a comfortable silence in his presence. This is the longest we've spoken, or been in each other's company without Pig nuzzling into the middle.

Slender shoulders shift with the deepened breathing rocking through his chest. Ink coats Owen's arms, masking the biceps I hadn't taken the time to notice before. Raising his head to the two-way mirror, his eyes drift from one thought to the next, unfocused and stoic. His jaw is strong, the perfect accent for a large adam's apple which bobs as he swallows. A fine specimen of a man, a genuine example of a friend. Yet there's something I just can't ignore.

"You knew what Carter was doing to Myles, how he was caging him. You could have spoken up, done something about it at any point." I try to keep the accusation from my tone, but it's near impossible. Especially when Owen sought me out, telling me how I am supposed to aid Myles when he's done nothing.

Raising from the bed in a sudden, jerked movement, Owen strides for the door, not pausing as his words fill the room.

"I have my own issues to deal with. We can't all live to serve Myles, you know." He exits the open door, leaving me to stew a moment longer. Pursing my lips, I jump from the bed myself and stumble on pins and needles for the bathroom. It's time I faced Myles, addressed the shame I've been battling, and I'm going to need a shower before I do.

***

The rasp of my knuckles on wood are merely a courtesy, as I push my way inside regardless. The door codes have been disabled for the time being; Myles posing no threat of going sex-mad and attacking someone while he's grieving. It's a travesty, because had he felt inclined to fuck his pain away in such a manner, both Sebby and I would have happily volunteered as tribute. Instead, I'm greeted first by Myles' outline sitting on the balcony, and his personal pitbull scowling from the chair just inside the french-style doors.

"Leave," Carter growls, more animal-like than man. When I don't scamper away, as the remaining Elites might have, his knuckles whiten from the grip on his armchair. Owen is nowhere to be seen, his advice alone spurring me to walk further into the room and lean against the dresser.

"This is Myles' bedroom - if he wants me to leave, he can tell me so himself." Pausing to check my nails, I wait out Carter's reply. I know it's coming and figured I'd let him get it out of his system. Call it my last kindness where he's concerned.

"I know your type," Carter huffs, easing back in his chair.

"Doubtful," I roll my eyes.

"You must have been waiting for him to crash to his lowest point, break him down to the point where you can take advantage. Bleed him dry. I wouldn't be surprised if you orchestrated the entire archer bullshit yourself." A snarl twitches Carter's upper lip, his eyes like emerald spears. Unlike with Owen, this time I keep a solid grip on my anger. Whilst standing beneath the scolding shower spray, I'd replaced the unbreakable mask which had been my shield for years. I couldn't remember at which point I'd let it slip. Looking over my nails at Carter, my voice remains smooth, icy yet calm.

"You want to talk about breaking Myles and taking advantage? There's enough mirrors around here Carter, go look in one. Better yet, watch back your precious footage. You might not like what you see." I toss a glance to the red flashing light in the corner of the room. Carter is out of his chair in half a second, his finger directed at my face.

"You have no fucking idea-"

"Enough." Myles states the one word, his voice clipped yet loud enough to hear through the glass. Locked in a staring contest, my head tilts to the side, a smirk taking residence on my face.

"Don't get comfortable," Carter mutters, intentionally barging my shoulder on the way past. I wait to hear the click of the door behind him before gathering up the cover from Myles' gigantic bed and slipping out onto the balcony. The frigid air hits my heated skin, briefly stealing the breath from my lungs, but my mind is too distracted to care. Too focused on the stiff posture of Myles' back, his legs dangling through the balcony bars to swing absentmindedly beneath. His very own prison. Lowering myself whilst wrapping the cover around our backs, Myles makes no move to tuck himself beneath it.

"I'm..." I pause, unable to find a way not to sound pathetic. "I'm sorry it took me so long." A cloud appears before my face, quickly dissipating before the next forms. Winter has hit, and as I touch the tips of my fingers to Myles' arm, I can tell he's been outside far longer than he should have.

"Myles, you're freezing. Let's go inside," I plead, lightly tugging. No response. Okay, I suppose we're doing this the hard way. Shifting and contorting myself, I force my gangly leg between his torso and the bars, my wide hips and plump ass squished as I plop myself onto his lap.

Dragging the cover around his broad shoulders, I tuck it behind me, straddling Myles' hips best I can like a human cocoon. If he refuses to accept logic, I'll shield him with the warmth of my body.

Blond hair tickles my cheeks, the stubble of two difficult days scraping my jaw. I push myself into his personal space, burying my face into his neck. Anything to avoid the dulled stare which slices straight through me. I caused this. I knew trouble followed wherever I went, knew staying around this long would only bring hardship. Normally I'm gone before I fall victim to my own past and never care who gets hurt in the process, but I hadn't expected to fall for him.

My lips soon turn cold, but it doesn't stop me from peppering kisses against his skin. Myles can hate me, as long as he doesn't toss me aside. My heart is only just peeling back the protective layers, prying open to beat wholly once more. Pushing my hands beneath Myles' t-shirt, I glide soft touches and light scratches over his chilled back.

"You can ignore me all you like," I whisper into his ear before nibbling the lobe, "but I'm not going anywhere." Dragging my lips across his cheek, I place a kiss on the corner of his mouth. "I should walk away." I kiss the other side. "I should have never come in the first place." My hands shift around to his front, both coming to settle on his chest. "It takes a huge feat to feel like I've found a place I belong. Somewhere which feels like home. And this right here," my index finger taps over Myles' heart, "this is home to me."

Braving a look up to his amber eyes, glistening by moonlight, I find Myles is no longer looking through me, but directly at me. Inside of me as if I've become the two-way mirror he's lived his life behind. His tears spill over like the bursting of a dam, streaming down his cheeks. Free flowing along the path my kisses trailed. Withdrawing my hands, I attempt to wipe them away but Myles grabs my wrists first. Sliding his fingers upwards into mine, he holds them intertwined between us, his forehead leaning against my own.

"For most, life is an uphill climb. A struggle to reach the peak," Myles murmurs so quietly, it's a strain to hear him. "I've been sitting on top of the mountain my whole life, and it's the loneliest place to be. The air is too thin, the world is always watching. And no matter how many times I jump, trying to plummet to the bottom, there are people there to catch me and drag me back to the top." The grip on my hands tightens, as if the next words to leave his lips are to be the ones which pain him the most. "My father was never one of those."

This isn't news to me. I tilt my head, refusing to let Myles' gaze divert from mine. Not now, never again.

"Then why are you so sad?" I ask bluntly. Myles inhales, steeling himself. I know what it's like to conceal the truth of emotion, and the difficulty it is to finally bring it to the surface.

"Because Carter is. Carter has never, *never* let me fall. At a cost to his own future, he's been by my side, orchestrating my existence. I know you believe him to be suffocating, but I wouldn't be here if he hadn't intervened. My father would have sent me to a sex clinic, a psych ward, wherever I could be out of sight and mind. Carter vouched for me, has kept me sated and content all this time."

"I don't really understand," I admit, preferring not to listen to Carter being praised. He's a control freak. That's all there is to it - right?

"To placate my father, and fill a hole in Carter's own life, he took over my position in the household. Shouldered my duties, attended family dinners, became a business partner and named the Hudson protege by multiple magazines. My father was so damn proud, for once. So you see, it's not me who's lost someone. After everything

Carter has been burdened with, I've cost him the only parent he really knew."

A fresh wave of tears leak from speckled orbs of amber. The anguish he can't contain pulls at the veins around Myles' eyes. Such sorrow, and when he tries to hide his face, I let him. Sobs rack through his hands, his shoulders jerk violently with movement. My heart cracks. With Carter having posted himself in the chair directly behind for two days, I imagine this is the first time Myles has surrendered himself to this guilt. The exact same one I was feeling, but my grief had been misplaced. I'd ached for Myles' loss, while he mourned for Carter's.

After a few minutes, I pry those hands away, greeting Myles with a small, loving smile. "Make love to me," I state huskily. It's a release we both need. A reminder of mortality. A reason to live. Wiping his own face clean, Myles cups my cheeks with wet hands. His kiss is demanding, imploring me to whisk him away from here. Perhaps back to the top of that mountain, only this time - he won't be alone.

"Should I call for Sebby?" Myles pulls back to ask and my chest expands. The casualness with which he asks has a 'yes' on the tip of my tongue. Whatever the three of us have is unique, special. A bond between three lost souls who find their home in each other. Regardless...

"Not tonight." I find myself saying. Sebby can see my body, tag-team pleasuring Myles with me anytime, but that's not what is about to happen. Even as Myles' thumb scores my lips, an unfamiliar burn flares from my throat to chest, the stoic mask I've mastered slipping all too easily once more. It's Myles. His infinite amber eyes which are prying me open effortlessly, searing away the shadows I've learnt to hide behind. No, Sebby doesn't need to see any of this. Myles seems to see straight through me, his slow-growing smile mimicking my own. Tonight is about healing, about fresh beginnings and newfound understanding.

"Tonight is for us."

Chapter 34

Sitting in the back row, I people-watch as Myles greets funeral guests in his back garden. You can't see a trace of the guilt etched into his face, his smile understanding and head bowing in thanks for each apology he receives. Whether he feels like he deserves to be or not, Myles is legally head of the Hudson legacy now. 'The man of the hour' according to the weeping widow clinging to his arm and the magazine clutched in my hand. Anything to avoid awkward introductions when people get too close.

Over the past few weeks, I've stayed with Myles in his bedroom, absorbing his grief as if it were my own. I may not have felt an attachment to Charlton Hudson, but Myles' mourning continued to bring mine to the surface. I've never given myself grace or the time to stop running and simply *feel*. Between frenzied fucking, passionate love making and extensive talks, I've grieved for my own mother, seeking comfort from one another. Sebby was with us most of the time, learning the dynamics of what could be a beautiful open relationship. I wish we could have stayed lost in our own fantasy. In a place where Carter's judgement and the outside world didn't exist. I much preferred it to this.

An arch has been erected at the far end of a white carpet, fifty chairs split evenly either side. Those waiting for the ceremony to start are lingering, not committing to a seat before seeing who else will be beside them. It's all about image with these people. The star of the show, however, is Charlton. He's a vision beneath the streams of sunlight, his face perfectly powdered and a crisp, white shirt concealing how hard the morticians had to work to stitch him together.

"How are you holding up?" Sebby asks, leaning his forearms across my shoulders.

"I'm wearing Prada and surrounded by rich snobs. How do you think I feel?" Nudging the fur shawl higher up my shoulders, I purse my lips. I wouldn't have been here at all if Myles hadn't asked. It's strange enough I had just met his father, never mind looking at his open casket amongst a procession of flower wreaths. At one point, I was sure I counted more florists than photographers, but now it's more of an even split. Apparently, Charlton's wife isn't one to miss an opportunity.

"Come with me, I've got something far more entertaining to watch." Holding out a hand, Sebby lifts me to my feet in a pair of black Jimmy Choo's. Despite the occasion, he's in a delightful mood. The police stopped by this morning with a final report – which detailed absolutely nothing and was of no help. The only good it did, was to give Myles the clarity of watching Sebby interact on his behalf, and the moment Sebby had closed the door behind the cops, Myles pounced on him. Love was professed, promises were made and I gave those two beautiful men the time to indulge in each other before the ceremony started.

Leading me through throngs of people, we enter a gazebo where tables are being set for a formal sit-down dinner after the ceremony. The rich don't do finger buffets at wakes either. I'm learning so much today. Protected from the midday sun, Sebby positions us by a pillar. Invisible to those who don't care to look our way, but with a clear view through the open front.

"What am I-"

"Shhh, it'll come," Sebby reassures me. His hand toys with the inside of my arm, in a move which I've come to know isn't in any way sexual. Sebby requires security, always seeking out human touch and comfort. Thanks to Myles revealing the truth about Sebby's father, I now know why.

Exiting the rear of the mansion, Felicia appears. Movement shifts at the other end of the balcony, Carter stepping out of the shadows. He moves with such grace, his suit cutting through the light breeze as if melded to his body. There's more gel in his hair than usual, slicking the brown lengths back in a similar fashion to how I saw Charlton's. Stopping before Felicia, she falls against his body, taking a hug he wasn't offering. Winding his arms around her, Carter's face buried in her neck.

"What's the deal with those two? Are they an item?" I tilt my head, curious about the bitter taste that question left in the back of my mouth. Probably because Carter deserves many things, and love isn't one of them.

"Oh buckle in sister, this is a juicy story." I narrow my eyes at Sebby, pursing my lips.

"You know enough though you're out in the world now, you can still talk normally right?" Another revelation in the past two weeks. It turns out all Sebby needed was the confidence that Myles would accept him, and he orchestrated an entire feature expose with Mitchell from Inside Entertainment straight away. Sebby hides a grin, his cheeks pinkening.

"Sorry, I saw that on TV. Sounded better when it wasn't me saying it. Anyway, Felicia and Carter dated for a few years after Myles' trial was over. She would frequent the manor often, helped set up the Elite system and draw up contracts. They mastered the plan together so they could live their lives and not have to worry about Myles relapsing." I snort. Imagine relapsing face first into pussy.

"So, what happened? They still seem to dote on each other." As I speak, an older man steps into view. Dark hair, an even darker presence. His suit and size rivals Carter's, six foot three and more muscled than I'd expect a man of his age. Setting his jaw, he turns away, holding his arm out for Felicia and she quickly takes it.

"She married his dad."

"No!" I shout, slamming a hand over my mouth. The caterers and serving staff nearby all still at my outburst, so I twist into Sebby's jacket and laugh. Laugh until I cry while he pretends to console me. No wonder Carter can't accept Myles wanting to keep me around. Dropping my voice to a whisper, I lean into Sebby's ear. "Okay, who's next?"

"Um, actually," Sebby stiffens. Looking over my shoulder, I see a couple approaching us. The man, graying with a walking stick, bears a gold signet ring on his little finger. The horse.

"Sebastian," he grumbles. "There's no use asking who your lovely date is. The news channels are writhe with your recent outburst." I deduce within seconds there's no use asking about the origin of his ring. The disapproving scowl at where Sebby's arm is wrapped around mine is a firm no. I'll have to find the answers I'm looking for elsewhere.

"This is...um..." Sebby stammers. Even with his father's back straight and how he's pretending the walking stick is just for show, he doesn't reach much above my five-foot-eight. His hands are weathered, as are the grey eyes which appear almost ethereal. So then, why does Sebby's grip try to stop me from moving away. Maybe this old man was worth fearing in his prime, but it's time to break the hold he has on Sebby for good.

"Amethyst Boudreaux," I kiss his mother's cheeks and offer his father my hand. "It's lovely to meet you both. I'm Sebby's business partner."

"What business? Carter mentioned nothing of a new venture," his father grunts. I tuck away that tidbit of information. It's always good to know Carter keeps tabs on more than just Myles.

"Oh, it's still very fresh. I manage the ass which has been receiving Sebby's business on a regular basis. Lube supervision and douching regimes are a full time job." I snort to myself at the double entendre of referring to Myles' butthole and the man himself.

"Oh good heavens!" Sebby's mother turns as pink as her cocktail dress. That will teach her for not wearing black to a funeral.

"Weird, huh? It's almost as if our poor Sebastian has been resigned to feeling insecure by years of soul-destroying beatings and degrading punishments." Taking his arm, Sebby and I stride away without looking back at his father, huffing and puffing about appropriate discipline. Sebby's tension dissipates, his shoulder leaning heavily against mine causing me to wobble along in the heels.

"Needless to say, that was amazing," he breathes when we're free from earshot. I lean into his shoulder, glad I could have helped a miniscule amount, although it won't last. Sebby will have to fight his own demons eventually.

"Would you consider yourself to be in my debt now?" I peer up, a twinkle in my eye. Sebby's face falls.

"Oh shit. I would consider myself to have just been played. What is it you're after?"

"Carter's real name," I put on my best pout and fluttering lashes. It's not Amethyst's strong trait, but I reckon it would work if not being used on a gay man.

"No way," Sebby bursts out laughing. "It's not worth my life. Some secrets are destined to go to the grave." A woman gasps nearby and without realizing how far we've walked, I find us standing before Charlton's casket. Oops.

A funeral director announces the ceremony is about to begin and I'm suddenly wrapped in a pair of strong arms. Myles drags me into a seat in the front row and I groan, questioning my life choices. Sebby takes his other side and the two of us slide our hands into Myles'. A team. A unit. Something I can't fathom feels so strong after such a short amount of time.

"I know you'd rather be anywhere else," Myles murmurs into my ear, "but the fact you're not means more than you will ever know."

"I'm here for the free food," I shrug. We share a knowing smirk as the director begins to speak, welcoming us all. The empty seat to my right is hastily taken, a heavy thigh slamming against mine by the man-spreader.

"Sorry I'm late," Owen chuckles. I spear him with a glare.

"Let me guess – you had business to attend to?" I drawl. A term Owen uses often and I'm now sure is a euphemism for sex. He rolls his blue eyes.

"No. I had to take pictures of a beautiful girl." Tugging on a diamond leash, Pig trots around his feet, tongue hanging out with pride. She's in full black, a cute dress banded around her rolls which fans out into a tule tutu. The fascinator between her ears is just adorable, as is her attachment to Owen's leg. Rubbing her face against him, his smile doesn't lessen at the slobber or white hairs marring his suit. He's not wearing it properly anyway – missing a tie, top button popped, and sleeves rolled up to display his brightly colored tattoos of gnarled branches amongst flowers in full bloom. If anyone could look hot at a funeral, Owen manages it with ease.

Luckily for me, the ceremony doesn't drag on half as long as expected. Turns out, no one felt the need to give a speech, preferring to make their peace in private. Between stroking Pig and consoling Myles, we collectively bid goodbye to Charlton. My thoughts keep trying to pull me back to the funeral I witnessed from behind a tree, the goodbye I never got to give. Yet in the mist of sorrow, I have hope. I have leads, one which apparently seemed valuable to kill over. I'm on the right track. The guests stand, creating a line down the center aisle to bid their goodbyes. Here in the front row, we all remain seated.

"I should have been a better son," Myles states, only loud enough for us to hear. I tighten my grip on his hand, looking across to the adjacent row. Between the queue, I catch Carter's eye from where he sits among his father, Felicia and Charlton's widow, sobbing on his shoulder. He glares at me and I give him my middle finger, licking the length of it. Myles, oblivious to it all, sighs. "I'm...struggling to remember why it shouldn't be me in that coffin instead. At least I'd have died for the one I love." His amber eyes seek out mine as I'm licking the tip of my middle finger, quickly retracting it.

"Myles," I breathe, at a loss for words. I know how he feels about me; I've known it for a few weeks now. Yet the vulnerability in his gaze has nothing on what I'm harboring inside. He wants verbal confirmation, although I've been giving it to him via my actions this entire time. "I-" my gaze snags on Charley hovering near the back of the service. "I'll catch you guys in the gazebo. I need to handle something first." Leaping up like my ass is on fire, Pig barks at my ankles. Yeah, I know girl, it was a pussy move but I need to clear my head. Correct multiple wrongs here today.

"Hey," I force a smile as I approach. Charley reciprocates. We haven't had the chance to speak since I've been staying in Myles' room twenty-four-seven. "Look, I owe you an apology-" Charley jumps into my arms, almost knocking us both flying. The Elites are already seated, watching on with curiosity. Sebby filled me in on Myles wanting to fire them, and how Carter has now provided them with a month's notice. I can't feel guilty, not when they are all worth so much more than being cleaners and fuck toys. The only reservations I still hold are what this means for Charley. Her heart was set on having a home, feeling needed.

"It's okay Ami," Charley's breath fans my neck. "The girls and I found a wonderful house to share in Seattle, right beside the university of law. I have a few steps to go before then, but Myles also paid me the three month's advance. I'm going to school." Her face is the image of excitement.

Brushing her chocolate brown hair back behind her ears, I match her smile. A true chance at life is all Charley ever wanted, and something I haven't been able to give her. She's like a sister to me, but also a crutch when I needed to feel worthy. To need someone to care for.

It's going to hurt like hell, but it'd be even more selfish for me to ask her to stay.

"I'll call when I need bailing out of jail," I smirk. Charley laughs harder than she should, given the present tear-stricken company, and we share one last hug. Turns out it's a day for goodbyes all round. Nothing I'm not used to and it's what's best for her future. Then why does my heart feel like it's about to collapse? Opening my eyes, I know exactly why – because he's standing beside his father's casket, head hung low.

"Excuse me ladies," Sebby interrupts. I scoff. He doesn't think I'm a lady. Slinking his arm around my waist, I quickly whisper for Charley to take the duffle bag of jewels and cash from beneath the bathtub with her as Sebby tugs me down a stone path, deeper into the garden. Breaching a set of steps, I cast a glance over the weaving columns of a rose garden before entering it. Even with the upcoming frost, they bloom in all shades of red to white. One last fuck-you before being driven into wilting.

"Wait here," Sebby orders, running back up the steps and reappearing a few minutes later with Myles on his arm. I duck my head, sensing exactly what is happening before the pair stop before me. Sebby gives a stern stare. "You helped Myles and I open up to each other. Now it's your turn." Then, he sits on a nearby stone bench and locks his fingers around his knees.

"Are you going to stay right there and watch?" I ask. Sebby nods. Shaking my head, I bring my attention back to Myles, and still at what I find there. The bravado has slipped, a day of grieving finally catching up with him. Not for his father, but for the chance to prove he's the son worth being proud of. Stepping into Myles' eyeline, he watches me blankly. Resigned to the three words I can't say.

"Okay fine, you wanted validation for why I need you alive...well, here it is." My hands open, but no words follow. For a woman who's navigated through life playing various roles, relying on her quick wit and smooth humor, thoughts now fail me. I guess I should just say the first thing that comes to mind.

"There's not much I fear in life, but I fear you, Myles," I wet my lips. Hesitating, Myles uses one finger to lift my chin, forcing me to speak while drowning in his amber eyes. "I fear what you could do, the power you hold and the ways in which you could destroy me if I allow you to. I'm afraid to let you see what's underneath this," I hold up my violet hair, "in case you don't like what you find." The irony hits me as I remember spying on Myles' therapy session and him saying the exact same thing. "I've spent my whole life running, hiding, and searching. I've avoided intimacy or becoming attached. And when it comes to you, I'm just scared."

"I used to be scared too," Myles nods, "but I'm not anymore."

"Why?" I sniff, the rise of tears causing me to look away. Sebby clicks his fingers, forcing me to look straight back. Stepping forward, Myles' chest blocks out our surroundings, his fingers playing with that same strand of hair.

"Because I know you, Amethyst. I know your spirit, your soul and your heart. The characters you play don't change any of that, because their purpose is all stemmed from the same concept. You care more than you like to admit, and you love too hard to let go."

"It sounds like you already have the answers you're looking for," I hedge, glad we've come to a mutual decision.

"You have to say it," Myles smirks and I groan. I guess not. It's stupid really, three little words. A singular sentiment which then means I need to live up to it. Once the words are spoken, there's no taking them back. Opening my mouth, Myles holds up a hand. "Wait – eyes." A groan escapes me. In a haste to get this moment over with, I turn and remove the lenses, flicking them in Sebby's direction. Hands cup my cheeks, bringing my face back to Myles' peering gaze. He smiles, filled with adoration I struggle to accept.

"I've never told you this, but your natural eyes are the most beautiful jewels I've ever seen. Crystalized blue, purer than any aquamarine diamond found. When I picture your eyes in my mind, I find tranquility. An endless sea where peace reigns and love thrives. I know how you feel about me, but I'm going to make you say it. Just this once, on the day of my father's funeral."

"Oh, guilt trip me, why don't you. For fuck's sake, I love you! Okay?!" I blush at the volume of my voice. Pressing his lips together, Myles fights a smile. Perhaps a laugh. All I know is he's immensely humored right now. Well here goes nothing. "I love you more than I thought physically possible. It's like you steal the oxygen from the room when you enter, forcing my heart into overdrive. I can't think straight when you're around, can't keep up with who I'm supposed to be so somewhere along the way, my act slipped and that's it now. This is me?! I hope you're happy!"

Everything I said was intended to sound more like a round of insults, but Myles' gaze softens regardless, sensing the sincerity in my words. My blue eyes are wide, cheeks flushed, and I can't seem to stop my hands from waving around.

"I've never been happier," Myles finally claims my mouth, putting an end to this cringey nonsense. I part my lips on demand, wanting his taste. His rich cologne, his eager touch. Too many emotions are congesting the air, it seems only fitting we disperse them. Curling my fingers around Myles' belt buckle, I walk him two steps backwards before he pulls away.

"We can't," he whimpers, looking up to where the tip of the gazebo can just be seen on the hill above. Carter has taken control of a microphone, not-so-nicely telling the guests to take their seats for a sit-down meal. One the three of us will not be attending. I continue walking backwards, slowly lowering my ass into Sebby's lap.

"You can do whatever you like. You're the crazed, sex-obsessed son and considering all the photographers on standby to witness your relapse, you selfishly haven't tried to rape anyone yet."

Running a finger across Sebby's shaven jaw, he plays along, placing a kiss on my neck. We've seen each other naked and done enough together now for the impulse not to be uncomfortable. In fact, as the amber highlights in Myles' eyes sparkle with mischief, Sebby eases my shawl from my shoulders, his fingers toying with the straps of my dress. I bite my bottom lip, playing up to how the cold pebbles my nipples.

"So Myles, what do you want?"

Chapter 35

Stumbling along, my heels scrape against the stone path, Myles' grip on my wrist bound to bruise. Turns out, Sebby and I are better at teasing than I thought. He drags us both through the gardens until the sheen of a roof becomes visible. The greenhouse is bigger than apartments I've stayed in, entirely built from glass on a raised brick platform. Masked with tall hedges, I figure Myles was looking for privacy but as he all but throws me inside, the humidity is a blessing to the goosebumps lining my skin.

The door is slid closed while Sebby sheds his jacket, laying it upon the floor. Holding my hand while I click off my heels, we share a humble smile. One filled with understanding and affection of a simple nature. We long to provide Myles with the life and love he deserves, and will work together to do that. Besides, having a best friend in the bedroom – or greenhouse currently – is a gift I hadn't considered acquiring before. Lowering onto my knees, I wait patiently as Sebby makes the first move.

The two of them come together as if pulled by gravity. As if another moment without their mouths melding together would be the last one they have. Tongues loll, hands caress. Their kiss is slow, languid in its beauty. I bite my own lip, aroused by their show as much as I'm warmed by the love they share.

When I can't resist joining any longer, I kneel upwards and reach for Myles' belt again. He doesn't deny me, his dick throbbing with need. Prying it free of his boxer shorts, I take him deep into my mouth. Sucking hard, drawing back with a slowness which has him groaning, bucking his hips forward. A bead of salt graces my tongue, his plump head weeping for the swift end it's not going to get. Gripping the base of his shaft, I pump and work Myles as Sebby shifts in closer. At this point, his sexual orientation is on hold.

Squeezing Sebby's cock through his slacks, he grinds against my hand, needing the friction. Two sets of hands reach for me, Myles cupping my jaw and pushing my hair back as Sebby grips my ponytail, forcing me to take all of Myles. I choke but he doesn't relent, pumping my head back and forth, using me as an instrument for Myles' pleasure.

Reaching a fever pitch, Myles pulls back from me with a pop. I'm briefly released, two more bodies and another jacket joining me on the floor. I shift before the boys get any ideas of taking control.

"On your back Sebby," I point. He smirks, obeying. Leaning across his body, deftly opening his belt buckle with one hand, I reach for Myles' nape and kiss him, hard and fast. Then my mouth is by his ear, telling him how this is going to play out. Catching sight of his smile, Myles shifts, kneeling between Sebby's legs. Liberating his dick, the man I love bends over to take an impressively thick cock into his mouth while I tug down his slacks to the knees. I wasn't lying about the douching routine, now these situations seem to arise more often than not lately. Spitting over Myles' ass, I work my fingers around his puckered hole before sinking inside. Preparing him, pleasuring him. Myles never thought when we started this venture, he'd become my bottom.

"Fuck Myles," Sebby moans. The greenhouse doesn't miss a sound, amplifying each moan around its glass walls and pointed ceiling. The shrubs conceal us from the outside, our own private jungle of desire. Pushing back against me, I spank Myles' ass with my free hand. He jolts, causing Sebby to gasp in a ripple effect.

"Don't rush me," I demand, smiling all the while. Twisting my fingers, I wait until Myles is whimpering with need until finally giving him the brief reprieve he needs. "He's ready for you Sebby. Swap places with me." Leaving Myles on all fours, we do just that. His hands grip my dress instantly, tearing the material up to my sternum before I've even laid down before him. My panties are torn next, a carnal blaze held within Myles' amber eyes. He's in the mood for revenge and I'm all too happy to wrap my legs around his head and let him have it.

Without a trace of affection, Myles spears me with multiple fingers, his lips wrapping around my clit. My back arches upwards. The sensations drawn from me are all encompassing, all consuming. I can hardly inhale through the deviousness of his tongue, worshiping my clit like his last meal. His arm pumps, his digits gliding into my wetness. I feel the moment Sebby enters him, his hand slamming against my pussy hard. Holding it there, Myles' shoulders tense against my thighs, a prolonged groan rumbling through him and into me. Through hooded eyes, I roll my head against his to see Sebby watching himself intently. How his dick eases into Myles' ass, how fucking incredible it must look. Raising his gaze to mine, I nod my head.

"Fuck him, Sebby. Make him scream. Make him suffer." Myles' head bobs up, his face stained with pleasure. Stroking a hand through his blond locks, I smile. "You wanted our love baby, now take it like a good boy."

Myles' argument is lost to the slap of skin on skin, the pounding of Sebby taking charge. Polar opposite to the shy, closeted man I first met, he takes control of Myles, dominating his body and owning his every moan. Myles drops his head again, stifling the sounds against me. I'm not complaining, the added vibrations pulsating around my pussy and directly into my core where his fingers roll within me. The building within my core grows, wavering on the edge of an orgasm which could shatter me if I had a little bit more. Something...bigger.

Cursing, I remove myself from Myles' hold and roll onto my stomach. Shimmying back, my dress rolls to my breasts, the jacket crumpled beneath me. Myles doesn't need instruction, grabbing my hips and yanking me the rest of the way back for his dick to drive against the curve of my ass. My legs slot perfectly between the pair of them, my chest pressed to the floor. Using his cock to seek out my soaking wet pussy, Myles guides himself inside, filling me completely. I shift my ass higher, taking him greedily as Sebby's thrusts now benefit us all. A ricochet effect, pumping Myles into me on collective moans.

Increasing our pace, we move as one. Components of the same machine, one goal in mind. A connection between my head and my heart clicks into place, spurring me on to break for both Myles and Sebby. Shuddering against the ground, I fist my own hair, at a loss of rational thought. These men have broken my façade, crept beneath my walls and settled there. Whether from perpetual or platonic love,

my list of ride-or-dies has gained two more members. I clench Myles'
so tightly, blocking his re-entry, he has to splay my ass open to thrust
himself back inside. I cry out, the sensitive aftershocks of my cunt still
pulsating.

"You're fucking perfect," Myles leans over me to whisper. I shudder
at his praise. "Let me taste how perfect you are." Pulling himself back,
I army crawl myself free. Myles mutters to Sebby and by the time I've
righted myself, I find they've switched positions. Myles on his back
smiling up at Sebby as he straddles him. Using my cum smeared over
his shaft and balls, Myles pumps his dick a few times and I swear I almost climax again. He's so confident, so bold. So stunningly gorgeous,
no one would ever know of the insecurities he faces. Easing into Sebby,
their union is solidified by matching moans.

"Come sit on my face Fiery." Myles doesn't have to ask me twice.
The man's tongue skills surpass any I've experienced before. Remov-
ing the remains of my dress, I crawl over to him before remembering,
I'm one curvaceous bitch.

"You know I'll suffocate you," I tentatively lift a leg over his shoulders.

"Then I'll die a happy man," Myles grips my thighs and thrusts me
downwards, mumbling about not needing to plan a second funeral.
His words are muffled, lost to my pleasure as his tongue spears me.
Opposite me, Sebby rides Myles, his rhythm too enticing not to copy.
Grinding my hips, I hope Myles meant what he said because he's about
to die eating me out. Put that on a gravestone.

Our pants are heavy, our bodies prickled with sweat. The leaves
seem to close in on us, preparing for what's to come. Namely, me.
Reaching out, I brace myself on Sebby's shoulders. Grey eyes bore into
mine, his open face strained. Holding onto me with one hand and

fisting his cock with the other, neither of us can hold back a moment longer.

"Together?" Sebby asks.

"Together."

"Hmm-mm-mm," Myles agrees. As a trio, we splinter, losing the grasp on our bodies to float elsewhere. My limbs are not my own, only Myles' fingers digging into my thighs allowing me to hold onto reality. Sebby's cum explodes over both Myles and me, soaking us in the evidence of our union. Thrown into the release of inhibitions, I drift further than I've let myself before.

I never envisioned this being the life I settled down with, and that's all part of the allure. Instead of a standard relationship where I would inevitably grow bored, I have Myles, and we have Sebby. A partner, a lover, a best friend. Is it weird to say a brother figure considering our affiliation with the man currently groaning beneath us? Either way, we're making our own rules here. No one can tell us what's right or wrong, how we should behave or love.

Swaying sideways, I seek out the cool floor on my heated skin. Myles gasps for air, his face red and cheeks puffing.

"Told you I'd suffocate you," I pant between bouts of laughter. Myles rolls his head my way, his eyes wild.

"It was fucking glorious." Sebby joins my side soon after, the three of us staring at the ceiling on a come down. A high I'm experiencing more and more lately, and I'm not scared anymore. Something deep within tells me my trust has been put in the right place. In the trials we're due to face, I have a solid backing. Hell, I even told Myles I loved him today. There's no going back now. Nothing we can't face, nothing we can't overcome. And we'll do it together.

"You know," I breathe, smiling to myself. "I'm starting to think you are a sex addict after all." All three of us laugh, Myles sitting upright to clean myself off with a jacket.

"I'm addicted alright, to the pair of you," he throws the cum-ridden jacket our way. "I will never tire of this. Of us. You're both insatiable." Giving a cheeky wink, Myles is oblivious to how Sebby finds my hand amongst it all, giving a reassuring squeeze. This throuple situation could have easily become possessive and bitter, had it been with anyone else.

Leaning over to kiss Sebby's cheek, I clean up too, donning the clean jacket as my outfit. My cleavage is pronounced in the lacy bra, squeezing tighter as I fasten the jacket button beneath them. My legs and ass remain bare, my feet easing back into the heels. How do I always end up dressed like this?

"Hey, did Owen's father attend the funeral? The dinner should still be happening. We should talk to him," I come to my senses. Had I not been so focused on concealing my distaste for mourning, rich assholes, I'd have interrogated everyone in attendance by now.

"No, he didn't," Myles' nostril flare, his jaw clenched. Seems I've found a sore spot.

"Well, as far as we know. We've actually never met him," Sebby shrugs, buttoning up his shirt. The pair of them look as presentable as when we stumbled in here, a refreshing glow to their cheeks. If only it could stay that way a little bit longer. Feeling the weight beginning to settle, Myles sighs.

"I still need to witness my father's burial. Let's give ourselves one last day, then I promise," Myles drags me into him, circling my back with his arms. "I promise with all my heart and everything I am, we will find the answers we all deserve." Lying my face against his shirt, Sebby plasters himself against my back.

"Our parents are involved," he grunts, him and Myles resting their foreheads together. "This is all of our war now."

"And we're not going down without a fight," Myles finishes. There it is. A pledge created by our bond. A vow cemented by our love. Whoever is pulling the strings, puppeteering my downfall, had better start running. I have these two well-connected, beautiful men on my side now, and this con artist will stop at nothing to protect them.

Afterword

Hello beautiful reader! Thank you for picking up a copy of Wreckin'
Amethyst, I hope you're enjoying the wild ride as much as I am!
The next in this series, Unravelin' Amethyst is due to release around
November 23. Keep an eye out for my newsletter updates and follow
my socials (flip for more details!)
As you will have noticed, Amethyst lives in the same world as Candy
– another sassy female from my backlist. Candy's trilogy is complete,
and more information about here can be found below!

Crushin' Candy

Book One in the I Love Candy Series

By Maddison Cole

Download Now: www.books2read.com/crushincan
dy~

So damn sweet, I cause cavities.

S'up? I'm Candy. Excuse the name. Mom was a strip-per back in her prime and I was a client gone wrong. Now stuck behind the bar, she was eager for me to join the family business. No thanks.The only circles I run in are the ones my bubblegum bubbles make. Don't worry about my teeth though, sugar-free as always. I'm not a complete psycho. Oh, except for my pas-sive-aggressive, potty-mouthed, imaginary best friend who happens to be a gummy bear. That part is pretty nuts.

I was thoroughly enjoying myself, doing whatever the hell I wanted until a group of model-worthy bikers try to muscle in on my heist. They don't seem to realise those with barely any personal belongings tend to grow protective of what's theirs, and by taking one of my beloved possessions, they've signed their own death warrants.Fooling them with a sickly sweet smile, I'll slip past their defences and claim back what's rightfully mine, no matter the cost. Putting bullies back in their place when no one else can is my special-ity. No one screws over Candy Crystal twice.

P.S, yeah - stripper name game is on point.

Trigger Warning: This is book one of the I Love Candy series, featuring a feisty female lead. Candy is spontaneous, impulsive and reckless, which makes this book inappropriate for under 18's. She gives as good as she gets, causing chaos and leaves you wondering who is bullying who! Expect excessive amounts of steam, violence and cursing throughout. This series is a RH trilogy with a HEA...eventually.

Acknowledgements

Gosh – where do I begin? There are so many people who boost me on a daily basis. Especially with this whirlwind of a novel that took even me on a wild ride, I've relied on those close to me for their constant strength and love to keep me sane.

To my Keyboard Whores – Every single one of you is a beautiful, inspirational and incredibly hardworking woman I have the pleasure to write with and talk to on a daily basis. From valuable insights to smut-filled conversations, each day brings me so much joy! I'm forever grateful for the friendships we have formed.

Peas in a Taco – For all of your boosting, comforting, brainstorming and friendship, I will always be grateful for the book community bringing us together.

My Street Moles – For proofreading and content sharing, you guys are my lifeline. The support is unreal and I'm so grateful to have you all in my corner.

To Mr. Cole and the kiddie Cole's – Pursuing a career as an author was never going to be smooth sailing, and isn't one that brings instant gratification. I cannot thank you all enough for the support I receive at home, for the cups of tea after pulling an all-nighter, for the evenings of family games I've missed to make a deadline. You're all my motivation and my solace when the dark, imposter-ish thoughts creep in, and I could have never achieved any of this without you.

To my incredible readers – It's plain and simple; I'm nothing without the readers that support me! Thank you all for devouring my books, and also becoming my friends. I love getting to know you, seeing your gorgeous book shelves and building connections with so many talented and wonderful people!

Also By

If you're a new reader to Maddison – welcome to the Mole's Burrow!!
Maddison is a married mum of two, and a serial daydreamer. As a huge
fan of all romance tropes herself, it was time to pen the stories which
consume her mind most hours of the day.
As a child, Maddison was a jet setter and has lived all over the world,
only to return to the south east of England, where she is now happily
settled. With a double award in applied arts and art history, Maddison
is a creative with a dark passion for feisty females and spicy stories.
Join my Newsletter here or on my website:
www.authormaddisoncole.com
Facebook – **Author Maddison Cole**
www.facebook.com/Maddison.cole.314
Facebook readers group - **Cole's Reading Moles**
www.facebook.com/groups/colesreadingmoles
Instagram and TikTok - **@authormaddisoncole**

Other Works:

<u>I Love Candy</u>
<u>Dark Humor RH - Completed</u>

- Findin' Candy (novella)

- Crushin' Candy

- Smashin' Candy

- Friggin' Candy

All My Pretty Psychos
Paranormal RH with ghosts and demons - Completed

- Queen of Crazy

- Kings of Madness

- Hoax: The Untold Story (novella)

- Reign of Chaos

Bound by Fate
Fated Mates Shifter Romance

- Moon Bound

- Soul Bound (Due to live release Summer 2023)

- Mate Bound (TBC)

A Deadly Sin
MMA Fighter BSDM RH - Standalone

- A Night of Pleasure and Wrath

A Wonderlust Adventure
A Twisted Menage Retellling

- Descend into Madness

- Embrace the Mayhem (pre-order)

<u>The War at Waversea</u>
<u>Basketball College MFM Menage - Completed</u>

- Perfectly Powerless

- Handsomely Heartless

- Beautifully Boundless

<u>Co-Writes</u>

- Life Lessons with Emma Luna

<u>Pre-order:</u>

- Unravelin' Amethyst – Billionaire Badboys Book Two

- Embrace the Mayhem – Wonderlust Adventure Duet Book Two

- Chasin' Kelsii – Mafia Ties Book One

9 781916 521155